"I want some answers to what's been going on, and I want them now."

"Or . . . ?" Drew rested his elbows on the table and gave her a look that screamed *I dare you.*

"Or I call my supervisor." Never one to back down from a bluff, Annie rose to her feet and headed for the phone sitting on the nightstand.

Quick as lightning, he grabbed her upper arms from behind. Pulling her hard against his chest, he breathed into her ear. "Not a good idea, Annie."

"Let go of me."

He snaked his arms around her middle and clasped his hands under her breasts, lifting her off the floor. "It's too soon to tell your supervisor anything."

A jolt of electricity sizzled from her stomach to her toes and back again. She struggled, then remembered his superior strength and went limp in his arms. There was no way she could outmaneuver him in this position, even with her training.

"What's that supposed to mean?"

He loosened his hold, and she slid down his body. When her feet hit the carpet, he turned her in his arms. "It means that right now I don't know who to trust. Everyone is a suspect."

HEAVEN IN YOUR EYES

Judi McCoy

ZEBRA BOOKS
KENSINGTON PUBLISHING CORP.

http://www.kensingtonbooks.com

To Kate Duffy, editor extraordinaire.
Thank you for everything.

PROLOGUE

"Look out, comin' through." Tom McAllister raced by with a drink held high in each hand, unconcerned whether or not his wife had one of her own. "Sorry, Annie, I'll be back later. Gotta get to the action in the game room."

Annie watched her husband dodge past two women wearing enough diamonds between them to light up Broadway. And she didn't miss the smiles they threw each other as they admired his departing backside. All around her, men in tuxedos they owned, not rented, and women in designer originals laughed loudly or gossiped in huddled groups, while she stood in a corner, dressed in the Halston knock-off Tom had insisted she buy in order to "fit in."

Annie McAllister hated this kind of party, especially when the guests were the type of people her husband dealt with at his job: big-talking producers, brash radio personalities, self-absorbed recording artists and other celebrities who spoke mostly to hear the sound of their own voices. Tom was a born salesman, and over the three years they'd been married, he'd picked up all the nasty habits associated with the dubious profession.

Tom knew how to ''work'' a room. He knew how to sell more ad space than anyone at the radio station, while Annie doubted she could sell life preservers on the *Titanic*. He'd been a bit of a snob in college, a champagne and caviar kind of guy, while she'd been beer and pretzels. She never understood why he'd gone after her, but she suspected it was because she'd been the one girl he hadn't been able to charm. After her parents died, she'd been so overwhelmed with responsibility that she'd allowed Tom, a business major, to handle everything. Before she'd known it, they were married.

Annie wended her way onto the elegant penthouse balcony. It was New Year's eve, and she was alone. Tom was in another room of the upscale apartment, encouraging a group of coworkers who'd decided to ring in the new year by playing strip poker. Knowing her husband, he wouldn't be so crass as to join them, but he'd want to stay and watch. Whoopee. What a way to spend the night.

She raised her glass of club soda toward what she assumed was Times Square and gave a half-hearted toast.

Here's to tomorrow, the day I tell my husband I'm going to apply to the police academy—with or without his permission.

Annie had been a criminal justice major in college. Her job as a dispatcher for the Westfield, New Jersey, police department was as close to her chosen career—law enforcement—as Tom would let her get. The idea that he refused to understand how much that goal mattered was eating her up inside. She'd tried to get him to marriage counseling to discuss it, but he always had an excuse for not attending the sessions. They'd drifted apart over the years, even though she'd tried to be what he wanted. She had never failed at anything in her life, and it was important she keep their marriage together; but now that her younger sister Julie was happily married, Annie decided it was time she had the life *she* wanted.

She inched her gaze to the heavens and decided to pour her heart in another direction. Picking out the brightest star she could find, she set her glass on the balcony railing and clutched her hands to her chest.

Please, just this one time let Tom agree to do things my way. Oh, and while you're at it, see if maybe you can get him to work a little harder at our marriage. I've tried my best to love him, but it would be nice if you could make him a more caring husband, as if he really did love me in return.

Annie opened her eyes and focused on the star shining, she thought, a bit more intensely than when she'd first started her prayer. She really did love her husband, but she was so darned tired of always being the one to compromise. The one to say, "Okay, we'll do it your way."

Tomorrow was going to be her independence day. If Thomas Robert McAllister loved her, he would understand.

CHAPTER ONE

Tom woke with a muffled snort. Jerked from the snooze he'd apparently been taking at his desk, he slammed his feet to the floor and ran a hand over his jaw. Rotating his shoulders, he winced as he looked around the bustling radio station newsroom. Why hadn't someone gotten him up?

Still groggy, he scanned the office a second time. Rubbing his eyes, he blinked back his surprise. How the hell long had he been asleep, anyway? People were talking on phones, standing at the water cooler, or working at their desks, and he didn't recognize a single one of them.

He set his palms flat on his desk and gave his head a shake, then took inventory of his desktop. Yep, this was his personal space, all right. There sat his leather-bound blotter and daily calendar, the gold-filled pen and pencil set he'd received last year for being named top salesman, and the Krugerrand encased in Lucite he'd won the year before that.

Swinging his chair around, he tapped at his PC keyboard, but the monitor remained a forbidding black screen. Great, not only had he fallen asleep at the switch, but personnel had gone and hired a raft of new employees, and now his computer was acting up. At this rate, he'd never make his monthly quota.

Though he was in sales, he and the other advertising executives worked in the same bull pen with the news staff, copy writers and other desk jockeys. But it was fine, because he was on the road most of the time, schmoozing with the customers. Technically, he was only required to go to the office to log in with the station manager and do weekly reports.

Tom stood and took a third, more careful survey of the room. It was the start of a new year, and he'd been on vacation since the week after Christmas, so maybe all these unfamiliar faces were the result of a company reorganization. Squaring his shoulders, he stepped from behind his desk, ready to make nice with the new drones. Then he looked down.

Damn if he wasn't wearing a tuxedo. Except his red silk tie was hanging around his neck like a dead snake, his crimson cummerbund was twisted, he had a torn jacket sleeve and there were rusty brown spots all over the front of his shirt. He couldn't remember wearing a tux since the New Year's Eve party he and Annie had gone to a few nights ago . . . or was it yesterday?

He raised his gaze from the tawdry outfit, thinking he'd better go home and change before someone noticed. Then he realized he had no idea why he would have bothered coming to work dressed like this in the first place.

What the hell was going on?

Smoothing back his hair, he cleared his throat, then shot his best welcoming grin at the attractive blonde seated at the next desk. She didn't look up, so he walked over and tapped on the top of her monitor. Still getting no reaction, he said, "Excuse me, I'm Tom McAllister. You must be new around here."

The blonde continued to work the keyboard.

Oo-kay, he thought, *time to find a friend.* He meandered through the maze of desks, puzzled when he couldn't locate one recognizable face. And none of the desktops had name-plates, either, so he couldn't even pretend he knew any of these people. Bizarre, totally bizarre.

Irritated, he decided to head down the corridor and find the station manager. Mitch Howell would know what was going on.

Tom stopped in front of his boss's door, or at least where he thought Mitch's door was supposed to be. Strangely, there was no nameplate on the dark wood, even though he remembered quite clearly the name Mitchell Howell, Station Manager, printed in script on a handsome brass plate mounted at eye level.

Looking back down the hall, he counted, one, two, three doors on the left. Yep, this was Howell's office. He knocked, then walked inside, just like usual, and was surprised to see someone else at Mitch's desk.

This tears it, he thought. Never mind that the station had hired an entirely new office crew; no one had even shown him the courtesy of a memo apprising him of a new station manager. He might not spend much time at WROQ, but he sure as hell deserved a heads up when there was a change in management, especially if it was his new boss.

Ticked, Tom walked the ten feet it took to stand in front of the massive desk and the chubby man wearing an old-fashioned white tuxedo with white satin lapels. Talk about a fashion statement. The old guy looked like a geriatric version of the Pillsbury Doughboy.

Tom cleared his throat. "Excuse me."

The guy continued writing in a large book, his partially bald head bent in concentration.

Tom knocked on the desktop. " 'Scuse me, buddy, I—"

The man snapped up his arm and made a sharp talk-to-the-hand gesture. Tom held his tongue. Without a doubt, this had to be the weirdest experience he'd had at the station since he'd begun working here five years ago.

He folded his arms and tapped his foot just to let the guy know he didn't appreciate being kept waiting, but his black patent loafer didn't make a sound. Heaving a sigh, just in case that might get him noticed, Tom waited, but there wasn't a flicker of recognition. The man just kept scribbling with his feathery quill pen. Guess the old guy had never heard of a computer.

Finally, the doughboy raised his head, steepled his fingers under his chin and looked Tom straight in the eyes. "Thomas Robert McAllister?"

"That's me," Tom answered. Okay, so the man knew his name. Big deal. "Who are you? Oh, yeah, and where's Mitch Howell?"

The man closed the book and folded his hands on top of the cover. "You may call me Milton. Mr. Howell isn't here right now. From this moment on, you report to me."

Funny, thought Tom, how the name seemed to suit the moon-faced little guy. He held out his hand. "Nice to meet you, Milton."

The man narrowed his brilliant blue eyes, but showed no intention of accepting the friendly gesture. Miffed, Tom folded his arms across his chest again. "So, what happened to Mitch? Did he finally get kicked upstairs?"

"Actually, Mr. Howell has never been here. This place is merely a figment of your imagination. We thought it best to bring you back this way . . . just in case."

A figment of my imagination . . . ? Just in case . . . ? In case of what!

Tom furrowed his brow. Sleeping at his desk; the unknown coworkers and their frigid reception. . . . "This is a dream, right? I'm still on vacation, and I'm at home in bed. I'm worried about my job, so I've let my mind wander back to the office and what might happen if—"

Milton shook his head. "Afraid not."

Suddenly, Tom's throat clogged. An unfamiliar terror enveloped him, but instead of screaming out loud, he sucked in a chest full of false bravado.

This wasn't a dream. It was a nightmare.

"I don't like guessing games, so if you'll excuse me, I'll just go back to my desk and wait to wake up. If you don't mind."

He tried to walk away, but his feet wouldn't move. Hesitantly, he looked down and saw nothing but swirling white clouds. No tile or linoleum or plush gray carpet . . . just vast empty space. Goose bumps popped out on his arms as his stomach did a flip. Holy Jesus, he'd been kidnapped by aliens!

Milton's full lips turned up at the corners. "Aliens? Not exactly. Why don't you have a seat and we'll talk."

Well, shit, what was this guy, a mind reader?

"Hardly. I just have your number."

Tom fought the urge to walk around the desk, pick the pompous jerk up by his shiny white lapels and shake him. Instead, he tripped into salesman mode and gave his best let's-make-a-deal smile. "Look, there's obviously been some mistake. I don't know why I'm here, but I know a nightmare when I'm in one. So if you don't mind, I'd like to wake up now." He stuffed his hands in his jacket pockets and waited . . . and waited.

"Anytime you're ready, asshole."

Milton sat back, his gaze piercing. "I'd tone down that smart-mouthed attitude if I were you. It's one of the reasons you're here in the first place."

In a heartbeat, Tom found himself folded into a chair. He struggled to stand up, but his butt felt as though it had been Crazy Glued to the seat. Swallowing hard, he tugged at his decidedly tighter shirt collar.

Looking very much like a school principal, Milton rested his elbows on the desk. "Tell me the last thing you remember, before you found yourself here."

Tom ran a shaky hand over his jaw. As nightmares went, this one was a doozy. Almost as bad as the one he'd experienced after that New Year's Eve party a few days ago . . . or was it last year? Why couldn't he remember?

He raised his gaze, and Milton nodded. Inhaling, Tom gave in and did as he was told, but all that came to mind was that gathering at his boss's penthouse. "I . . . um . . . I was at a New Year's Eve party, I guess. I mean, I had to have been since that's where I was the last time I remember wearing this monkey suit."

"Good, very good. And then what?"

Tom brought his fingers to his temples, which had suddenly begun to throb.

"Don't force it. Eventually the memories will come."

Confused, he leaned back in the chair and closed his eyes. Mist swirled, then parted. Like a home video, he saw himself in Burton Tyler's magnificent apartment making his way through a crush of well-dressed guests.

"Better," murmured Milton. "And who's there with you at the party?"

"My wife . . . Annie . . . she's standing by my side." He could see Annie's straight wheat-colored hair brushing her shoulders, her face set with a grim smile. Jeez, why did she always look so miserable when they were with *his* friends?

"What did you do at the party?"

"Played strip poker," Tom said quickly. "And I drank. A lot. I was having a great time."

"Tell me, where was your wife while you were having this *great time?*" Milton asked, only he made it sound as if Tom were shooting squirrels in Central Park instead of celebrating.

"I don't know. Probably where she usually was, standing in a corner alone, sipping club soda and acting as if I forced her to come."

"And did you?"

He bristled at the doughboy's imperious tone. "Hell, no.

Annie's my wife. She came because she wanted to be with me.''

"Did she now?''

Not all the time, Tom admitted to himself. But he'd be darned if he'd tell this bossy butterball of a man the intimate details of his marriage. "Well, sure. What wife wouldn't want to accompany her husband to a company party where she could get all dressed up, meet bigwigs and guzzle champagne?''

"Annie, perhaps?''

Instead of answering, Tom grasped the arms of his chair in a white-knuckled grip. He thought of all the times he'd had to coerce his wife to come to affairs like the one his boss had thrown on New Year's Eve. No matter how he explained it, Annie just never seemed to understand what it took to succeed in the high profile world of entertainment.

"Really, Tom, it's time you were honest with yourself. And this is the last place you'd want to tell a lie.''

Tom heaved a sigh. "Well, okay, maybe she didn't *always* want to come. But she usually—''

Milton shook his head.

"Sometimes—''

"Annie *never* had a good time and you know it.''

Tom shot to his feet in a blast of frustration. "Who are you to tell me what my wife does and doesn't like to do? This is stupid. It's my dream and I want out. Now!'' Jerking his legs, he made to stride away, but found his shoes stuck to the floor. Stifling a groan, he held his hands to his head and took a few deep breaths.

"Sit down and think. Try to remember the rest of what happened on the night you were at that party.''

Tom glanced at his hands, now clenched into fists at his sides. Maybe this really was an alien abduction instead of a dream.

"You don't really believe that, do you?'' Milton's voice

sounded sympathetic, almost as if he knew what Tom was experiencing.

Resigned, Tom blew out a breath. "Okay, so if I sit and think, I'll get it?"

The doughboy nodded, and Tom sank back in his seat. Placing his elbows on the chair arms, he threw his head back. This time, when he closed his eyes, things appeared more clearly. He saw himself half-dressed with a drink in his hand, stumbling down a corridor, then crashing onto a bed and falling into a stupor. How many times had he done that in the last six months?

The scene grew dark, then brightened again, until he was in his car, fully dressed and driving through the Lincoln Tunnel toward home. When he reached the New Jersey side, it began to snow so hard he could barely see. What had possessed him to get behind the wheel on a night like this?

Without warning, headlights arced across his path. A wave of nausea bubbled to his throat. He jerked the steering wheel right, then left, then right again. His car hit a patch of ice and shot into a slide. He slammed on the brakes, but it didn't seem to matter. Horns screamed, tires squealed and he heard the deafening sounds of shattering glass and metal screeching against concrete.

His heart racing, Tom heaved a breath. Pain, he remembered excruciating pain . . . a cold, wet darkness, then a warm white light. After that, nothing.

Placing his palms on his cheeks, he made to wipe the sweat away, but his hands touched cool, dry air. The enormity of the vision hit him like a lightning bolt, and he jolted upright.

"I'm dead, aren't I?" Tom asked aloud, but it came out sounding more like a statement of fact than a question.

"Congratulations," Milton said. "You've just passed the first test."

* * *

"So, how's it going up there in U.S. Marshal territory? Arrest any escaped fugitives yet?"

Julie's voice sounded calm and collected, even though Annie could hear kids whooping and the television blaring in the background. She loved talking on the phone with her younger sister. Julie always managed to cheer her up or put problems in the proper perspective, and she usually gave good advice. It was Julie who had stayed beside her while Annie had worked through the grief of Tom's accident and helped her to reorder her life.

In time, Annie had come to realize there was nothing she could have done to prevent the tragedy that had occurred nearly six years before. Ever since Julie's husband Phil, a computer programmer, had been transferred to Dallas, Annie had felt more than a little alone.

"Hey, anybody home?" echoed Julie, bringing Annie to her senses. "I'm waiting for a full report."

"I got it." Annie knew her voice sounded silly, choked up on unshed tears and all, but Jules would understand. Her sister knew she'd waited a long time to get her first big break—a real assignment that didn't involve pushing papers or standing guard in a courtroom.

"Eee-hah!" Julie's Texas-sized scream was so loud Annie had to jerk the phone from her ear. "I knew they'd give you something important. They're too smart to let a woman who graduated third in her class at G-man academy languish at a desk for long."

Annie let out an exasperated sigh. "I graduated from the Federal Law Enforcement Training Center, Jules, not the G-man academy. You came to Georgia for the ceremony, remember?"

"I remember. I was so proud of you I wanted to pop."

Julie had been eight and a half months pregnant with her second baby at the time, so "pop" was pretty much the right description. "I also remember you screaming like a maniac when they called my name. I thought you'd gone into early labor, for gosh sakes.''

Julie giggled. ''Little Rory Kenyon didn't wait long, but there was no way I was going to miss my big sister's shining moment.''

Julie and Phil had been Annie's only guests at graduation. Without them, she wouldn't have had a soul with whom to share the happy event. Thank God for her extended family.

''So, what's the assignment?''

''Hm? Oh, it's really hush-hush. I'm part of a WITSEC team protecting a mob guy until he can testify at a major crime boss's trial.''

''Wow, you mean like a mafia type? What's the guy's name? Has it been in the papers? When will it happen? Where—''

''Stop with the questions. You know I can't reveal any of the juicy details. Like I've told you before, everything in the Witness Security Program is highly confidential. I could lose my job, never mind endanger the operation if word of my assignment leaked out. All I can say is this is a biggie.''

Julie's sigh came through the wire loud and clear. ''Yeah, you'd better not tell me. I might spill my guts to the *Dallas Morning News*, or maybe go on 'Good Morning Texas' and announce it to the entire state. Cut me a break, sis. Between Peanut's gymnastic lessons, Rory's day care and my pottery business, I don't have a spare minute to gossip about your career. I live vicariously through you, kiddo.''

''And you love it,'' Annie reminded her. ''Besides, you already have what I really want some day—a husband and kids who love you. You're the lucky one.''

''Stop. You're making me all teary-eyed,'' the younger woman said with a touch of sarcasm. ''You'll find it some day. Just hang in there. And while you're waiting, be the best officer on the force. Who knows, maybe you'll be the first female J. Edgar what's his name.''

"That's the FBI," Annie said, rolling her eyes. "How many times do I have to tell you the Marshals' Service is a completely different agency?"

"I know. I know. Your job opportunities beat the FBI all to hell. But it seems to me the only difference is you get to carry a bigger gun."

Annie tried not to giggle. "Make that a bigger badge. And more interesting duties. And—"

"Speaking of bigger guns, have you had a chance to date any of those square-jawed, nicely packaged deputies yet? Are they all as yummy as they look on TV and in the movies?"

"No. I've spent all my time getting my career in order and training for WITSEC. Besides, dating coworkers is frowned upon, which is fine, because I haven't felt a spark of attraction toward any of them."

"But marshals are allowed to get married and have families, aren't they?"

"Some do, but there's a whole group out there who are dedicated to the point of no return. If I ever married and the guy wasn't with the program, he'd have to be extremely patient and understanding. I don't want another relationship like the one I had with Tom."

"Tom was an idiot. And you let him get away with too much. You look fantastic with the added curves. And I like your hair its natural color, not that Palomino blond he kept insisting you dye it. You look like my sister now, not some plasticized Barbie doll living for Ken."

"Jeez, Jules, tell me how you really feel," Annie said sourly. "Was I that bad?"

The pause lasted way too long for Annie to not guess her sister's response. "Okay, okay, don't answer me. It's been six years. I don't have nightmares or the guilty sweats anymore, and I don't mind buying a bigger dress size, so I guess I'm finally over Tom and the way he died."

"Hallelujah! So, when do you start this thrilling new assignment?"

She bit at her lower lip. This was the part her sister was not going to like. "In three days."

"Three days?" Julie's voiced fairly shrieked across the wires. "Then you're not coming to Dallas for Thanksgiving?"

" 'Fraid not. But I might be able to get some time off at Christmas. It just depends on how long this thing goes."

"Well, shoot. The kids and Phil will miss you almost as much as I will. Can you call, or drop me a line to let me know how you're doing?"

"That shouldn't be a problem, but I'll have to check with my supervisor. I'll e-mail you after my briefing. How does that sound?"

"It sounds dismal, not being with your family during the holidays and not knowing when you'll get time off. But it's what you've wanted for so long, I guess I have to say okay."

They talked for a few more minutes, then hung up. Annie sat back at the computer desk in her apartment's small second bedroom and exhaled a breath. She really would miss having Thanksgiving with her family, but if she'd said so, it would have dampened Julie's own enjoyment of the upcoming holiday. Her sister had been seventeen when their parents were killed in a boating accident on Lake Hopatcong. This would be the first Thanksgiving in years they wouldn't spend together. One thing about Tom, he'd always understood her need to be close to her sister, probably because he'd been an only child and often remarked how much he'd wanted an older brother.

Tom. Even now, she wondered what would have happened if she'd commandeered his car keys that New Year's Eve so long ago, instead of taking the train to Westfield. It hadn't mattered that his boss and coworkers had promised they wouldn't let him get behind the wheel in his condition. He'd left before anyone was up and driven home in a snow storm.

And he'd ended up smashed against a bridge abutment for his foolishness. Poor Tom.

Annie decided to skip dinner in order to get to her regular Monday night basketball workout at the rec center, where she coached a group of teenage girls as part of the local Big Sister program. She needed to catch Jim Summers, the men's coach, before he left for the evening, and ask him to find room in his heart to let her girls share court time with his boys until this assignment was over. Jim never stuck around the center long enough to see how her girls were doing, but they had discussed the possibility of playing a coed game sometime after the first of the year to raise money for new backboards.

She knew Jim thought the boys would win in a walk, but Annie had planned to publicize the game as a "battle-of-the-sexes" thing anyway, and he had grudgingly agreed to the idea. Too bad she wouldn't be there to see his face when her girls whipped his boys' butts during practice.

She was scheduled for an early morning briefing, then she had to pack clothes to fit the city where she'd be staying. She didn't know who else had been put on the case, but she doubted there would be any other new marshals assigned. Annie was at the bottom of the totem pole in the WITSEC program, and she imagined the other deputies would be part of the old guard.

She walked to the window and watched the snow fall. If she was lucky, she'd be sent to a warmer state, southern California or Florida; either way, she would go willingly. It was her chance to prove to the powers that be she could do it; she had the right stuff.

Annie opened the rear door of the nondescript gray sedan, a standard agency issue vehicle. The trunk popped up and she walked to the back of the car to retrieve her luggage. After hauling out her suitcase and a large tote bag, she gazed at the farmhouse to her right. If she didn't know better, she'd think she'd been transported back in time to the turn of the century.

The house, a plain two-story behemoth in the center of ten acres at the end of a dirt road, sat literally in the middle of Nowhere, New Jersey. *So much for a warmer state,* she thought, cataloguing the stark scenery dotted with dirty, half-melted snow banks and barren patches of weedy lawn. Sitting the way it was, no one could approach the house without being seen, which was one of the reasons the saltbox-style building made a good safe house.

There were other reasons the government used this home, she was sure, but right now not one of them came to mind.

Bob Fielding dragged his duffel bag and briefcase out of the trunk and slammed the lid, then nodded toward the wide front porch. "Home sweet home, at least until after the first of the year. God, you gotta love this business."

Annie ran a hand through her short tousled hair and cleared her throat. "It's not exactly the Short Hills Hilton, is it?" she asked the man in command of the operation.

Bob hoisted the duffel over his shoulder. "Trust me, this is one of the better safe houses. There are a few in the inner city that would take the wave right out of that curly hair of yours. Let's just say Uncle Sam's budget doesn't allow much for frills."

She watched him walk to the stairs with authority. A tall man in his mid-fifties, well-versed in the ins and outs of his job, Bob had tried to warn her on the ride over of what to expect. Mob types didn't deserve luxuries, and the marshals assigned to protect them had to suffer the consequences as well.

Pete Butterworth, their driver, stuck his head out of the window and gave a sharp whistle. "Hey, Annie."

She trotted to the driver's side of the car and crossed her arms, feigning annoyance. "What lottery did you win, seeing as you don't have to stay here with the rest of us?"

Pete cracked a grin. "I'm on lookout duty in town, which won't be any more exciting than staying here, believe me. And the house isn't so bad on the inside. Smithers will be here with our pigeon later tonight, then the fun really starts." He gave a wave, rolled up the window and barreled down the drive, leaving Annie to wonder what Pete knew that she didn't.

Slinging her purse strap over her shoulder, she lifted a bag in each hand and made her way into the house. After closing the door, she rested her backside against the wall and took stock of her new home. Living area with fireplace to the right, dining room with bay window to the left, hall straight ahead, and in front of her a stairway that led to four bedrooms and two baths. Hers was the one in the back, next to a small bathroom with a shower. One of the perks of being a female deputy marshal, she supposed, was not having to share private space with three men.

She heard a racket from the rear of the house and meandered through the dining room and into a spacious kitchen. Bob had already started a pot of coffee and was now rooting in the large refrigerator's freezer section.

He turned and held up a package of steaks, his lean face wreathed in a smile. "How do strip steaks and baked potatoes for dinner sound to you?"

"Fine." Annie surveyed the fairly modern kitchen, noting Pete had been correct in his assessment. Sparkling white cabinets, marbled green countertops, a black-and-white tile floor and a cozy eating area under a large window made the room homey and inviting. "The inside of this place isn't half bad, is it?"

"If you say so. The service was here yesterday, stocked the fridge and freezer with all the necessities. A deputy will come every Monday and Thursday with fresh milk and produce. If you have any dietary cravings, just leave a note." He glanced at the chalkboard mounted on the inside of the rear door. "We aim to please."

"So," Annie said, taking in the U-shaped cooking area, "who mans the stove?"

"We take turns, divide it up whichever way we want. You a morning or an evening person?"

"Morning, mostly." She walked to the gas range situated on the far side of the kitchen across from the double sink. "What about you?"

"Me? I'm a night owl. I'll make a pot of coffee after dinner, take the night watch and meet you at breakfast, then hit the sheets. Steaks are my specialty, and I bake my potatoes in the oven, no foil. But I don't do vegetables."

"Well, I do," she said, opening the refrigerator and pulling out one of the bottom bins. The housekeeping service had left them a plastic bag of designer lettuce, three tomatoes, an onion and little else. Checking the freezer, she found two boxes each of spinach, string beans and corn. "I'll make my own if you don't want any."

"Why don't you take your stuff upstairs and unpack? I'll get the potatoes going. We should eat in about an hour, so you have time to get settled, walk around and get familiar with the place. Go over the floor plan again, and bring your questions to the dinner table. I'll try to answer them as best I can."

Darkness crept over the farmhouse well before they'd finished their meal. Bob loaded the dishwasher, saying it went with the cooking. They discussed chores and agreed each deputy would be on his or her own for a midday meal. Lou Smithers could do some of the more ordinary tasks like emptying the trash, carting dirty laundry down from upstairs and walking the drive for the morning paper. Bob had worked with Lou a time or two and assured her the easy-going deputy wouldn't mind taking care of the grunt work.

Annie had studied the layout of the house and grounds earlier. Sitting at the dining room table, she and Bob had already gone over the faded blueprint in greater detail and were discussing their schedule.

"Unless there's a conflict, we usually take the watch that fits our body clock. I can say from past experience that Smithers will want the three to eleven shift, and I'll take eleven to dawn. When you come down to make breakfast, we'll go over the day's lesson plan together. You'll be on lookout, and Lou will baby-sit. We just keep rotating until the job's finished."

"And what about our charge?" asked Annie. "Where does he fit in?"

Bob pushed away from the table with a disgusted sounding snort. "Hell, Viglioni can do whatever he damn well pleases twenty-four-seven, so long as he's in sight of one of us or locked in his room. Believe me, before this is over, you're going to resent the hell out of him."

Annie remembered her briefing on their *guest*. Dominic Viglioni was one tough wiseguy. He'd been a point guard and alleged hit man for one of the most notorious crime lords on the East Coast. When he'd been caught driving the getaway car during a sting operation, he'd sung like the proverbial bird, adding a lack of loyalty to his list of sins. The government deal he'd cut had been sweet, no time to serve and a new life for his full cooperation. He'd even managed to avoid incarceration, if you could call being locked up in the middle of nowhere until going to trial the same as avoiding a jail sentence.

"How well do you know the guy?" She only asked because Bob sounded so bitter, as if he had something personal against the man.

"I've never met him. I'm from the Chicago office, remember? But I've dealt with enough wiseguys to know the type. Smooth as silk on the outside, rough as burlap within. Men like Viglioni would rat out their own mothers to keep from doing time."

"But we have to interact with the guy. We're protecting him, for gosh sakes. That has to count for something."

"We just need to be civil, make sure he's fed and keep

him safe until the trial. Then it'll be up to the department to build him a new life.'' Bob gave her a quizzical stare. "This is your first job with WITSEC, McAllister. Please don't tell me you're going soft already.''

"I'm not,'' she assured him. "I just wondered how you dealt with a guy like that without treating him like something you scraped from the bottom of your shoe.''

"It's as boring as watching paint dry and a downright shitty assignment. Just wait and see for yourself.''

Gravel crunched as headlights streaked through the dining room window and bounced into the hall. Both deputies leapt to their feet and drew their weapons. Bob nodded for Annie to go to the front door while he slid to the window and stared into the darkness. Car doors slammed, and he sidled to the foyer, where Annie had taken a stand.

After peering through the peep hole, he tucked his gun away. "It's okay. Lou's here with Viglioni. You stay inside, just the same. I'll go out and help them with the car and luggage.''

Her heart racing, Annie did as she was told. She heard voices on the porch and sucked in a breath. Smoothing a damp hand over her plain navy slacks, she assumed the position as she'd been taught, just in case something went wrong.

The inside door swung open and three pieces of Louis Vuitton luggage shot across the foyer floor. "Take it easy, don't wrinkle the suit,'' she heard a man say.

The deep, dark voice laced with the cocky accent of a streetwise thug sent a shiver straight up her spine. *Fear,* she reminded herself. *You're frightened and that's to be expected.*

The door opened again and a tall, broad-shouldered figure sauntered into the house. Annie stiffened her back, prepared to dislike the man on sight.

Then she saw his face.

CHAPTER TWO

Annie opened and closed her mouth. Her fingers were wrapped so tight around her gun they'd turned white. A man she assumed was Lou Smithers walked into the foyer and nodded his shaggy head.

"You must be Anne McAllister. I see you've already met our guest."

Dominic Viglioni smiled, his laser white teeth cutting a rakish slash through his tan, whisker-darkened face. His chocolate-colored eyes crinkled as he smoothed back precision-cut, dark brown hair with a large hand. Looking Annie over from head to toe, he said, "The lady and I haven't been formally introduced. How about you do the honors?"

Deputy Smithers sighed. "Stuff a sock in it, Viglioni. There isn't anyone here to impress."

Annie lowered her weapon. Flustered to be taken aback by the sight of such a beautiful man, it took her two tries to get the Glock in its holster. Heat flamed in her cheeks and she knew she'd turned the color of a spring blooming poppy, at the very least a peony. She could only hope the dim foyer lighting would cover it up and neither man would notice. Besides, from the way the mobster was acting, she was fairly certain he was well aware of his effect on women. She was just one more ogler in the drooling crowd.

"Dominic Viglioni, Deputy Anne McAllister," said Lou. He gave the man a shove toward the staircase. "Now let's take the luggage upstairs and get you settled in. It's late and I'm beat."

"Hang on a second," Viglioni said, not budging an inch.

Annie wondered if the guy was as solid as he looked. Then again, any man vain enough to pay a thousand dollars for a suit would make sure it was tailored to enhance his physique. The charcoal gray pinstripe, white shirt and hundred-dollar tie only added to the picture of a well-put-together gentleman with money to burn and enough good taste to light the match.

He held out his hand. Without thinking, Annie raised hers, and he grasped it in his cool, dry palm. Lifting a brow, he brought her hand to his mouth and almost, but not quite, brushed it against his sensuously carved lips. "Dominic Viglioni at your service, Ms. McAllister. And may I say I look forward to us getting better acquainted."

Lou's snort echoed in the foyer. Viglioni dropped her hand when the agent gave him a sharper shove. "Forget it, Dom. The lady's a professional, and she's not going to be swayed by your macho charm. Say nighty-night and get your butt upstairs before Deputy Fielding and I carry you up."

Viglioni picked up two bags, Smithers grabbed the third of the matched set and a duffel, and together they climbed the stairs. But Annie didn't miss the wink the man, *the mobster,* she reminded herself, gave her before he turned his head.

She heaved a breath. Holy crap, would her heart ever stop beating like a kettle drum? *Get a grip, McAllister. You've seen plenty of good-looking men.* Tom had been handsome in a blond, Nordic sort of way; Julie's husband was no slouch either. But this guy was a cross between Pierce Brosnan and Antonio Banderas—dark and dangerous—with a dollop of Bruce Willis's naughty little boy thrown in just to muddy the waters. She set the back of her hand to her cheek and found it still warm to the touch.

The sound of feet shuffling on the porch snapped her to attention. Bob Fielding barged through the door, slammed it shut and threw the bolt. "So, where did they go? Upstairs?"

Annie nodded. "Smithers said he was tired."

Bob shrugged. "He probably is, but he'll be down as soon as he locks our guy in his room. It's only nine-thirty. Come on."

Annie followed him into the kitchen. When Bob started a pot of coffee, she put the kettle on for a cup of herbal tea. It was obvious she needed to be more aware of agency protocol. With their guest out of the way, this was the most logical time to discuss schedules and make plans. There would probably be a lot more of these late evening powwows so the three agents could talk without Viglioni listening in.

Sure enough, ten minutes later Smithers ambled into the kitchen, a frown etched into his bony face. "That guy is a trip and a half. Has to be one of the most arrogant bastards I've ever met." His gray eyes took in Annie, who was sipping at her tea. "Oh, hey, sorry about the lame greeting back there." He held out a hand. "I didn't want to break stride with Viglioni. I guess we need to get the formalities over with. I'm Lou Smithers."

"Anne McAllister." She shook his hand firmly. "It's nice to meet you."

Lou raised a dark brow and grinned, the gesture making his craggy face almost pleasant looking. "You might not be saying that in another week or so, right, Bob?"

The other agent handed Lou a cup of coffee. "You nailed it. She's going to know you almost as well as your wife does. Hell, I already do."

In tandem, the two men sat at the table. Lou pushed out a chair with his foot, and Annie gathered it was her invitation to join them. Bob unrolled the blueprint of the house and began to talk out loud.

"Viglioni will be in the back bedroom across from Annie. Lou, you and I are here and here." He tapped a forefinger onto the paper. "The guy can't make it down the front stairs without us hearing him, and the windows in the bedrooms are nailed shut. Annie's bathroom is at the end of the hall, but the window in there is so small only a three-year-old could crawl through. I think we're okay."

"I've worked this house before," said Lou, setting his cup down. "Unless the guy turns into a phantom and manages to slip by all three of us, we'll be all right."

Annie cupped her mug between her palms. She had a dozen questions, but she didn't want to sound stupid. Still, she needed to know a few things to get her mind straight. "Why would Mr. Viglioni want to escape? I mean, he's here because he needs to be protected until the trial. If he runs away, he'll be a target for anyone who doesn't want him to testify."

"True," said Bob, folding up the blueprint. "But these guys always have an angle, a better plan. Viglioni probably has a ton of money stashed in a Cayman bank account. And he's sure to have friends on the outside. More than likely there's a woman who's vowed to help him escape to some out-of-the-way place that doesn't have extradition. He thinks if he can slip by us and get out of the country, his ex-boss won't find him and gun him down."

"Besides, no one in the mob trusts the witness security program. They always think there's a better way," added Lou.

Annie committed their explanations to memory. It figured a guy like Viglioni would have a woman or two waiting in the wings. Men who looked like he did never wanted for female companionship, even if they were known felons.

"Okay, but if he gets away from us, he still runs the risk of being killed," she said, talking as much to herself as the other men.

"Guys like our guest think they're invincible. He sees how isolated we are out here, knows we're human and figures he's got a better than fifty-fifty chance of slipping away before the mob finds him. If he had a lick of common sense, he'd have stayed in jail for the duration." Bob took his cup to the sink, rinsed it out and set it in the drainer. "Did you check his luggage for a transmitter or phone?"

"Done," said Lou. "Now, if you'll excuse me, I really am beat. Did you and McAllister divvy up the workload?"

Bob nodded. "You're on three to eleven, as usual. We lucked out because Annie here is a morning person. She'll do dawn to three, then run surveillance. I know you don't mind grunt work, taking out the trash and hauling laundry, so I volunteered you for those jobs."

"Just like home," sighed Lou. He ran a hand over his face, then headed out of the room. "See you in the morning."

Annie figured that was her cue. After taking care of her teacup, she said good night to Bob and went to bed.

Annie woke well before dawn. Birds twittered in the distance and she strained to hear past the cheerful sound. They were so far from the main road the silence seemed deafening. No voices, sirens or horns, not even the rumble of a truck cut through the country air. At least the house had a television and a shelf full of board games. Between that, the books she'd packed and the few computer games loaded on her laptop, she hoped there would be enough to amuse her for a while.

After rising from the queen-sized bed, she tied the belt of her cotton robe tight and peeked into the dim hall. The other three doors were shut, Viglioni's, directly across from her own, double bolted from the outside. What a way to live, she thought, caged like an animal and dependent on strangers who monitored your every move. Then again, the man could be in prison right now, instead of in a safe house waiting to testify. He was one lucky bastard.

She took her morning shower, washed and blew dry her dark blond curls and applied a bit of mascara and blush, then returned to her room and dressed in a pair of gray wool slacks and a turquoise sweater. She'd been told the atmosphere on this type of assignment would be more casual than in an office. Living away from home was bad enough; they didn't need the constraints of suits and ties.

Unfortunately, she was still required to wear her gun, which put the Glock in plain sight. Sporting a weapon was the one part of the job it had taken her the longest to get used to. She wondered if she would ever learn to ignore the weight of the semiautomatic hanging at her hip and usually hidden by her jacket.

Annie headed down the stairs and into the kitchen, where she found Bob fiddling with the coffeemaker. Following the agency's guide for precaution, she tapped on the doorframe to announce her presence. "Having a problem?"

He glanced over his shoulder, then went back to business. "Nothing I can't handle. Damned thing leaked all over the counter. If it does the same with the next pot, I'm going to add a new one to the supply list."

Annie walked to the refrigerator. "Okay, you make the coffee while I start toast and scrambled eggs. Do you think Lou and our guest will want any?"

"Just toast for me, thanks, but I'd make enough eggs for the other two. Once they're at the table, you can take future breakfast orders. Our pigeon will probably want eggs Benedict or homemade waffles, but we're only expected to supply normal stuff. He'll eat it or starve, plain and simple."

"I like to cook," she said brightly. Living alone didn't give her much chance to show off her culinary skills, but she'd certainly have the chance to do it here, in a house with three captive men. "Give me the proper equipment and ingredients and I can make all of what you just said with my eyes closed."

Bob groaned. "I should have guessed. Not only are you a morning person, you're friggin' *Martha Stewart*. Next thing I know, you'll be wanting us to eat by candlelight and use cloth napkins. Christ, wait until Lou finds out about this."

It took a second for Annie to realize he was kidding. "Oh, I get it. You're not a morning person, so you can't stand anyone else being chipper before noon, right? That's okay. Julie, my sister, is unapproachable until her third cup of coffee, and even then it's touch and go."

"I'm not your sister. I'm your boss. And I say anyone this cheerful before dawn ought to be staked out in the sun over an ant hill. I hope Viglioni is a night owl. You'll be just what we need to set his teeth on edge."

Annie grabbed an apron from the pantry and wrapped it around her waist, then dug under the counter until she found a Teflon fry pan. After setting it on a medium heat, she beat eggs into a mixing bowl and added milk. Humming a tune from *Cats,* she grinned inwardly when she heard Bob's impatient sigh.

Thinking this job might not be so boring after all, she placed slices of bread in the toaster oven, went back to the eggs and poured them into the hot pan. The timer rang and she gave the eggs a stir, then took out the toasted bread, put four more slices inside the oven and began to butter the finished product.

"Holy Christmas, McAllister," Bob hissed. "You remind me of my ex-wife. Is there anything you can't do at this hour of the morning?"

By now, Annie was laughing out loud. "I wouldn't want to change a flat tire at this time of day, but I guess I could if I had to. And I really hate doing laundry any time."

Muffled footsteps sounded from the stairway. Seconds

later, a disgruntled-looking Lou and a smugly smiling Dominic Viglioni walked into the room from the short hall that curved around the rear of the staircase.

"What's up," asked Bob, his eyes narrowed in suspicion.

"Our choirboy here thought he was being smart. Tried to make a call on my cell phone," grumbled Lou, snatching a piece of toast off the plate Annie had set on the table.

"Hey, you can't blame a guy for tryin'," said the wiseguy, eyeing Annie as she crossed the kitchen with a platter of eggs.

Bob poured a cup of coffee and set it in front of Lou. "How the hell did that happen?"

Obviously embarrassed, the other deputy gave a growl. "I screwed up, okay? Went to take a leak and forgot I'd left the phone on my dresser. I'd already unlocked this asshole's door. He was supposed to be getting dressed and I—"

Though aware of their guest's blatant stare, Annie focused on her boss and waited for the explosion. Instead, Bob shook his head. "See that you're more careful in the future. And Dominic?"

Viglioni tore his gaze off of Annie. "Yeah?"

"Don't think that's going to happen again."

Amazed her supervisor hadn't blown his top, Annie surveyed the table. No one had bothered to pour either her or their prisoner a cup of coffee, so she took care of it herself.

"Thanks," said Viglioni when she placed a mug near his plate. "Breakfast looks great. You gonna cook like this for us every morning?"

Not sure just how friendly she was supposed to get with their guest, Annie slid her gaze to Deputy Fielding.

"That's the plan. You got any complaints?" Bob took a bite of his toast while Lou devoured his eggs in silence.

"Not me," said Viglioni, raising a forkful of food to his mouth. "This looks just like my momma use'ta make. And that's saying a lot." He winked in Annie's direction. "You married, Deputy McAllister?"

Annie felt heat flood her cheeks, but forced herself to pay it no mind. Something told her blushing for any reason was frowned upon while on duty. Having other marshals think she had no self-control would not be good for her career, even if it was a completely involuntary act.

"I was," she finally answered. "I'm a widow."

"Nice goin', jerk face." Lou pushed his empty plate away. "Sorry, Annie, the guy's a moron."

"Hey, I resent that." Viglioni sat back, his expression wounded. "I was only tryin' to make polite conversation."

As far as Annie was concerned, the entire scenario was surreal. She was in the kitchen of a strange house, wearing a gun and an apron, cooking for three hulking men as if they were one big happy family. The situation was definitely going to take some getting used to.

"It's all right," she said to no one in particular. "It was six years ago. Talking about it isn't painful anymore."

Tom McAllister gazed into the mirrorlike top of Milton's oversized rectangular desk. Just like watching a big screen TV, he thought. Who would have expected to find such a thing up here in heaven?

"You're not exactly in heaven, Tom," the angel reminded him. "I thought I'd already explained how this works."

Tom shrugged. It had taken a while, but he'd grown used to the pompous man's intrusive habit of reading his thoughts. He'd already figured out there were more important things for him to worry about.

"Yeah, yeah, yeah, so you told me. I've been in a holding pattern these past six years. Now I'm on the runway, waiting for takeoff. I got it."

Milton pursed his pudgy lips. "Not exactly. If you remember correctly, I merely used the airplane scenario as a meta-

phor. You're only going to take off—depart the airport—
if we get your flight plan approved.''

"Approved? By who?'' Tom peered into the desktop.
"What in the hell ... uh ... heck are we looking at,
anyway?''

The angel tapped him on the shoulder and pointed upward.
Tom followed his raised index finger, swallowing hard when
he realized what the cherub meant. "Oh. Him.''

"Yes ... Him,'' repeated Milton. "He has to sign off on
everything we do—the flight plan, the ETA, the takeoff and
landing. Do I make myself clear?''

It was clear, all right. Clear as mud. And from the sound
of it, they didn't have a snowball's chance in August of
getting the go-ahead for whatever nonsense the doughboy
had in mind. Not that Tom had any say in the matter.

Training his gaze on the desk, he squinted at the three
men and lone woman eating a meal at a kitchen table in a
house he didn't recognize. Two of the men, dressed in slacks
and white shirts, reminded him of policemen—or lawyers.
Lawyers with gavels up their butts, if he had to hazard a
guess. The third man, wearing a dark gray cashmere sweater,
seemed more polished and not quite as stuffy looking. In fact,
he was the only man at the table with a happy expression.

The woman stood and he let out a low whistle. Seated
with her back to him, she hadn't looked too interesting, but
now that she was on her feet, he had to admit she was
something else. The apron tied around her waist emphasized
her full figure perfectly. Though he wasn't usually attracted
to the Anna Nicole Smith type, there was something about
her. . . .

The woman turned, walked to the refrigerator and bent
to peer inside. Tom stifled a curse. He'd know that profile
anywhere—and that shapely behind. The woman was Annie.
And she had a holster with a gun in it strapped to her hip!
He scanned back to the table. They were *all* wearing guns.

Everyone, that was, except the smooth dude in the pricey sweater.

He rubbed a hand across his eyes, then turned to find Milton staring with a silly grin on his rotund face. "All right, I'll bite," said Tom, pretty sure he wasn't going to like the answer. "What the heck is my wife doing with those men? And why is she wearing a gun and that ridiculous June Cleaver apron?"

"So, you recognize your wife," stated Milton, his smile a bit too smug for Tom's liking. "I was afraid you wouldn't. She's changed so much over the last few years."

Tom stared into the desktop again and took a better look. "What the heck happened to her hair?"

"Oh, that," said Milton. "It's her natural color, and it has a lovely curl to it. Doesn't she look fabulous?"

Fabulous my fanny, Tom thought to himself. This woman didn't look anything like his Annie, not really, now that he'd had another glance. What the heck had she done to herself?

"Don't tell me that's her natural color. Her natural color is blond—very blond. And it used to be long and straight. How come it's so short?"

"I suppose you only remember her hair the way you liked to see it," snapped Milton. "That's so typical of you. You're the one who kept after her to dye it that abysmal color and wear it straight as straw. It was never Annie's choice."

He cringed. The doughboy made it sound as if he'd been some kind of evil Henry Higgins bending Eliza Dolittle to his nefarious will. He'd never made Annie do anything she didn't want to do. Ever.

"Oh, really," came the angel's smarmy reply. "So you're saying you never forced Annie to color her hair or demanded she go on a diet? Then I suppose it wasn't you who bought her that Weight Watchers membership for her birthday, or dragged her out of bed every Saturday and Sunday morning to go to your health club. And I guess it wasn't you who ordered her food whenever you went to a restaurant, either.

"My wife will have the broiled chicken breast, steamed rice and broccoli, dry, no butter or sauce," Milton deadpanned, his voice an exact echo of Tom's.

Tom stuffed his fists in the pockets of his tuxedo jacket. He was getting darned tired of sounding like a jerk with every memory Milton dredged up from his past. Still, when he concentrated, he could vaguely remember things being exactly the way the annoying little man described them. Jeez, had he really been that overbearing? That much of a chauvinist?

"I'm happy to see you're putting things into perspective." Milton smirked. "I'm sure you'll find a few more names to call yourself before we're through."

"Don't sound so happy about it. And whose side are you on, anyway? I thought you were my guardian angel?"

"Your angel?" Milton's cobalt-colored eyes grew wide. His full lips twitched, and he snorted. Holding his hands to his ample belly, he chuckled merrily, and much too indelicately for a heavenly being.

Tom rolled his eyes.

"So-so-sorry," he stuttered. "I thought you understood."

"Understood what?" Tom asked sullenly.

"I'm not your angel. *Your* angel gave up on you quite a while ago. I believe it was the third, or maybe the fourth time Annie begged you to go to a marriage counselor. Eloise washed her hands of you and said you were on your own, if I remember correctly."

"Annie and I didn't need counseling. We were doing just fine without some busybody shrink sticking their nose into our business."

"Your wife didn't think so. And she's the one I'm concerned about. She's the reason you weren't sent directly to— to that *other* place."

"The *other* place? What's that supposed to mean?"

"Don't take that tone with me, young man. I can still send you packing."

Tom's bossy attitude deflated faster than an untied balloon. "Okay, okay. No need to get so defensive."

Milton nodded, then peered into the desktop. His blissful-sounding sigh gave Tom the creeps.

"Isn't she beautiful? So much prettier than when she was being forced into the role you wanted her to play. I think she's finally reaching her full potential."

Instead of hiding the ridiculous thought, Tom laid it on the table. "If I didn't know it was impossible, I'd think you were in love with her yourself."

Milton's shoulders drooped, then lifted as the angel puffed out his chest. "I am . . . in a purely heavenly way. You see, I'm *Annie's* guiding angel."

Well, didn't that just figure. Not that it made any difference, Tom supposed. He'd already been told his own angel had dumped him. Had he really been that bad a person?

"Not bad. Just hopeless. You need to know that right after World War II, the Big Guy decreed guiding angels no longer had to work with the hopeless if they didn't choose to. That war had Him hopping mad, you see. Besides, we angels are overworked and underpaid, pretty much like it is on earth. If we feel our efforts are being wasted, we're allowed to turn in our charge's time card and tell Him the soul is on its own."

Tom frowned. "Don't you mean *guardian?* You're Annie's guardian angel?" *Something I don't have,* he wanted to add.

Milton shook his head. "A minor misconception that evolved throughout time. Angels are put on earth to *guide* the humans in their charge, help them make good decisions and keep them on track, until He decrees it's time for their souls to be called home."

Interesting. Okay, so he'd need a little time to digest that tidbit. Right now, it was more important that he figure out his own situation. "So my angel decided I was hopeless and bingo—just like that—I was on my own?"

"Believe me, Eloise didn't make her decision lightly. Knowing you were married to Annie, she discussed it with me at length several times before she made up her mind."

"So you were the one who advised her to . . . turn in my time card?"

"I did not. I asked her to continue working with you, for Annie's sake. The night we had our last discussion, I distinctly remember advising Eloise to give you another chance. Annie's plea touched my heart. She had asked for so little in her life up until then, you see. I felt it was time to step in."

"What night? And what plea? Now what the heck are you babbling about?"

Milton sighed. "Try to pay attention, Tom. I'm talking about the night of the New Year's Eve party. The night you . . . um . . . passed over."

The last thing Tom wanted to dwell on was Burton Tyler's stupid party and his own even stupider decision to drive home without all his mental and physical capacities functioning on full power. But the itch to know the entire story was more than he could stand.

"You're the one who's not being very clear here, buddy. If you could just spell it out for me in plain English—"

"It was the wish."

"The wish?"

"Annie's wish . . . on the balcony. Since Eloise had given up, I knew I had to do something. I had no idea you were scheduled to pass over that night, you not being mine and all, so I rushed to put Annie's wish in the *To Be Granted* box. Once an angel does that, the wish and the angel's intent to fulfill it can't be taken back."

Low, thought Tom. He was so low in the gutter he had to look up to see the bottom of a cockroach's feet. He wasn't here because he was a good soul, or even a redeemable one.

His own angel had dropped him like a rusty razorblade. He suspected he'd had one more step to go before he'd been sent to that *other* place, as Milton had so charmingly called it.

It hurt to know that the only reason he was here in this holding pattern was because of Annie and her wish. Whatever it had been.

"So, what exactly was it Annie wanted? If it isn't against regulations to tell me, I mean."

"I don't think so. In fact, you need to know what she wished for in order to help me fulfill it."

Here it comes, thought Tom, *the detailed plan.* But all Milton did was stare forlornly into the desktop. If the chubby cherub didn't already have eternal life, Tom would have happily throttled the answer out of him.

"I'm waiting," he said with a loud sigh.

"Hm ... Oh, sorry." Milton laid a hand on the "new" Annie, as if he could feel her through the mirrored glass or send her some kind of comforting vibe. A few more seconds passed before he finally said, "Annie's wish was about you, Tom. She asked that you try harder to make your marriage work, listen to her more, be a better husband and love her for herself, instead of the woman you wanted her to be. And, with your help, I have a plan that will make her wish come true."

CHAPTER THREE

"Hey, doll face. How's about making me another omelet? That last one was terrific, only lighten up on the chives, would ya? They give me gas."

Annie refused to turn around or even shrug her shoulders in acknowledgment. Dominic Viglioni had to be the rudest, most self-centered, egotistical man on the planet. She'd thought Tom was a fusspot, always cutting his sandwiches into four equal triangles or asking her to butter just one slice of his bread. This jerk had Tom beat all to hell.

And he smoked. Ugh. Ugh. Ick! The disgusting habit turned her off completely. The one time she'd kissed a smoker in college had only verified the truth of those old antismoking commercials. Locking lips with a smoker was akin to licking a dirty ashtray.

Then again, she wasn't supposed to be thinking about kissing the guy. She wasn't even supposed to like him. He was a mob informant—the lowest of the low. And from the sound of his past accomplishments, a truly unscrupulous man. So what if he had eyes the color of melted chocolate?

Who gave a fig about that Tom Sellack dimple sitting square in the center of his chin? And those quarterback-sized shoulders? No biggie. Men who looked like Dominic Viglioni were a dime a dozen . . . in *GQ* magazine maybe, or Hollywood.

"Yo, Annie. You hear what I just said?"

Annie stiffened her spine and went on a DNA search for her *polite* gene. Bob and Lou had told her to stay focused and tune out the wiseguy whenever possible, but it was tough. The man was about as easy to ignore as a thousand-pound gorilla. So what if he had what her sister Julie called presence—the kind of personality that took over a room? She wasn't impressed.

Besides, she'd been raised by the Golden Rule: Treat everyone you meet in life the way you would like to be treated. To her, the tenet sounded like the recipe for a perfect world. Dominic Viglioni might be a compelling man, but she was positive the world would be a better place if there were less men like him in it to begin with.

Pasting a smile on her face, she turned from the sink. "I heard you, Mr. Viglioni. Unfortunately, we're out of eggs. We're expecting a grocery delivery later today."

"What's with the Mr. Viglioni crap? I thought we agreed to call each other by our first names?"

"I don't know who you had that conversation with, but I distinctly remember telling you I was going to keep our relationship professional. Breakfast is over, and so is this discussion." Annie opened the dishwasher and started loading plates. The faster she finished, the sooner she could go to the living room and play solitaire on her laptop while she watched their pigeon pace, or fiddle with the television or pretend to be interested in a book.

Heaving an impatient-sounding sigh, Dominic fished in his pocket and dug out a gold Cartier lighter and equally expensive cigarette case. Holding the cancer stick to his lips, he caught her disapproving glare and winced.

"Oops, sorry. Guess it's time for another trip to the out-house." His smug expression reminded her of a sixth grade boy who'd just told a crude joke. Bending at the waist, he thrust out an arm. "After you."

"Hey, Lou," Annie called, accepting the inevitable. She went to the mudroom and slipped on her coat. "We'll be on the rear porch if you need us."

Deputy Smithers didn't answer, and she figured he was off on one of his regular rounds, scouting the perimeter. Not that it mattered. She'd escorted their guest by herself a few times before. All she had to remember was the law enforcement officer's code of survival: stand well away from your prisoner, never show your back, and *never* give him access to your gun.

Keeping the rules in the forefront of her brain, she held the door wide and nodded, indicating he should walk ahead of her. Dominic complied, but not before he gave her a wink. The creep.

Out in the cold, Annie settled her bottom against the porch railing, as far away from the mobster as she could get, yet close enough that if he decided to take off running, she could catch up and tackle him to the ground. She'd racked up a great mile and a half at FLETC, closer to the men's required eleven minutes than the fourteen needed by a female recruit. She'd finished above average in all the other fitness tests, too, a fact of which she was inordinately proud.

Viglioni lit his cigarette and assumed a casual pose on the opposite side of the porch. He knew the drill and, so far, didn't seem to have a problem with it. He took a drag and blew the smoke out slowly, letting it mingle with his frosty breath.

Annie shivered inside her new wool coat, a splurge she'd bought on sale at Neiman Marcus. Why was it she froze out here, while he always managed to stay toasty warm in nothing but a soft-as-sin-looking cashmere sweater. She could have asked for a transfer to a warmer state after graduation, maybe Florida or Texas, but noo-oo. She had to be close to her roots. And the graveyard where Tom and her parents were buried.

"You need a mink coat," Dominic said out loud, as if he'd read her mind.

"Excuse me?" Taken aback, Annie could barely string the two words together.

"Blackglama. Female pelts. Female pelts are the warmest and most luxurious. Of course, you'd want them to be hand matched and sewn."

"I'll be sure to order one," she said, her voice dripping sarcasm, "right after next payday."

His chuckle came out deep and rusty, as if he didn't laugh very often. "I'll buy you one. What are you—a twelve? Fourteen?"

Too surprised to be offended, she answered automatically, "Fourteen."

"Figures. My guess is you need it at the bust line."

Pulling the coat tighter around her midsection, Annie felt heat rise to her cheeks. Keeping her weight down had always been a problem, even though Tom had insisted she stay a single digit dress size. Anything bigger, he'd told her, and she'd be too plump to wear current fashions. In the past five years, she'd put on about twenty pounds, most of it muscle she'd needed to survive her rigorous training. Julie said her figure suited her five-foot, eight-inch frame, but that didn't keep old insecurities from rising to the fore, especially with comments from a man like Dominic Viglioni. It was rumored he'd romanced hundreds of women, all of them svelte, glamorous and a lot more interesting than a female U.S. Marshal.

"Never mind about my bust line. And forget about the coat. I couldn't accept a gift from you even if I wanted to. Which I don't."

The wiseguy kept on grinning. "Yeah, right. You and about a million other women."

"I do not want a mink coat. Nor do I want the diamond

bracelet you offered yesterday, or the Jaguar convertible you promised me the day before that. What do I have to say to make you understand? I'm not a normal—er—a regular—'' She raised her gaze skyward. ''I'm a federal marshal, Mr. Viglioni. It's against the rules for me to accept gifts from anyone. Especially men like you.''

''Men like me, huh?'' He took a sharp pull on the cigarette, his eyes as dark as his venom-laced voice. ''Thanks, doll face. I'll remember that one.''

''You know what I'm trying to say. You're a confessed felon and I'm—'' She leaned back against one of the posts supporting the overhang. ''Sorry, I didn't mean to be so insulting.''

''Sure. No problem.'' Time ticked by in long, uncomfortable seconds. He took another drag, held it in his lungs, then blew a series of smoke rings into the chilly air. ''So tell me a little bit about yourself. What makes a woman decide to go into such a tough profession?''

''I don't think that's any of your business.'' *And I wouldn't want to discuss it even if it was.*

''Hey, why not? We're alone in the effin' wilderness, no phones or restaurants, not even cable. What else have we got to do but get to know one another better?'' Flicking the cigarette onto the porch, he crushed it under the sole of his Italian leather shoe.

''We could play cards or a board game. There's a stack of games on the bookshelf in the living room,'' she offered, unwilling to let him know she agreed with his colorful assessment of their hideaway. She missed her team at the rec center and was beginning to feel claustrophobic herself. She'd even been thinking about asking Bob for the okay to go for an early morning run a few times a week just to work off her own nervous energy.

His expression turned surly. ''Board games are for kids. Do I look like a kid to you?''

Nu-uh. Not by a long shot, but she wasn't about to tell him so. "I just thought it might help to pass the time."

He stuffed his hands in his tailored navy slacks and turned to scan the scenery. The grounds around the farmhouse were barren for about a hundred yards, then a wilderness of trees ringed the back semicircle of the property. Beyond that stood the Abram S. Hewitt State Forest. The front of the property was flat and scrubby, as well. To the left of the house was a long driveway that lead to a dirt road, which in turn lead to the main artery into town.

At the near end of the drive sat a sturdy-looking two-car garage with a rectangular apron of concrete jutting out about thirty feet. Someone had attached a backboard and basketball hoop over the double door, the one concession to human inhabitants.

"Hey, Annie, you shoot hoops?"

She followed his gaze to the garage. It was spooky the way he'd just read her mind. "As a matter a fact, I do. But I don't think it's allowed."

Viglioni turned and shook his head. "Aw, come on. There's no entertainment for miles, and I need exercise. I'm used to workin' out regular like, if ya know what I mean. What could it hurt?"

The temptation to say yes was strong. Still, she had her orders, and they were explicit. The prisoner was to go no farther than the back porch, for short durations only. And never alone.

"Um . . . I'd have to ask Deputy Fielding. Maybe something could be arranged. I don't even know if we have a basketball."

"Really? You'd do that for me?"

Annie tamped back a grin. She didn't want to like the way his face lit with pleasure, or the fact that his eyes crinkled when he cut the flirtatious bravado and gave a true smile. "It never hurts to ask, Mr. Viglioni. Now let's go inside. It's freezing out here."

* * *

"No. Absolutely not. It's against regulations. I can't allow it." Bob Fielding paced the kitchen, a cup of black coffee in hand. Lou Smithers was upstairs securing their charge for the night. The dinner hour had come and gone. Annie had done her best to serve a delicious meal, hoping it would put her boss in a mellow mood. Unfortunately, that didn't seem the case.

"I was told during training I'd be allowed a little personal time to exercise if we could arrange it. Couldn't this be it?" Annie reasoned. "And what if I talked Lou into standing guard? What could go wrong if we had a watchdog?" She couldn't believe he was being so hard-headed about such a simple request.

Bob let out a snort. "You want Lou to stand guard in the freezing cold so you and our pigeon can play a little one-on-one? Don't make me laugh, McAllister. Lou doesn't even want to haul the trash to the curb when the temperature drops below forty. He's from the Miami office. He hates the cold. He only does it because it's his job."

Dunking her herbal tea bag in her mug, Annie gnawed on her lower lip. One thing she didn't relish was spending any more time holed up in this house with nothing to do. After she and Viglioni had their talk this morning, she'd used the day to think about his request. The more she thought, the more the idea made sense. A little one-on-one out in the fresh air would take the edge off, and Viglioni would shut up about needing exercise. She'd remembered to pack her sweats. If she layered a sweater and leggings over her thermal underwear, then added a sweatshirt, two pairs of socks and gloves, the frigid temperature might just be bearable.

There had to be some way to guarantee their wiseguy would have no chance to escape. . . . Suddenly, she smiled.

"I can see the wheels turning. Now what are you think-ing?" demanded Bob.

"How about something radical . . . like leg shackling him, or maybe chaining the two of us together at the ankle? You know, like they did to Tony Curtis and Sidney Poitier in that prison movie. Viglioni couldn't run if he had to drag a hundred fifty pounds of dead weight along behind him, could he?"

Bob stared at her as if she'd just asked to be crowned the next queen of England. "You're nuts, you know that?"

Annie straightened in her chair. "Lou could watch from the porch. That way he'd stay warmer. We could put a time limit on it—say, sixty minutes. If anything goes wrong, though I don't see what could, I swear I'll take the blame."

"It wouldn't matter, McAllister. I'm in charge here. If something out of the ordinary happened, say the guy escaped, it would be my head on the chopping block. I'm the only person responsible for this operation. Trust me."

"Look, why don't you think it over tonight? Meanwhile, I'll sleep on it and see if I can come up with something more clever. When they bring the next grocery order, I'll request the leg irons and the basketball, just in case you change your mind. We don't have to use them if you decide you're absolutely positively against the idea."

"I *am* absolutely positively against it," he deadpanned.

Annie raised a corner of her mouth. "I'll make beef stroganoff twice a week for the next month."

Fielding ran a hand over his face. "You're an evil woman, McAllister."

"And lasagna, with lots of cheese and ground sausage."

"Spicy Italian sausage?"

"Is there any other kind?" she teased.

"What about garlic bread? With real garlic, not that garlic salt and margarine spread crap?"

"Honest to God garlic, crushed and creamed into real butter, then grilled under the broiler until it's hot and bubbly." She held up three fingers and gave him a Girl Scout grin.

"Lou would have to say yes, too."

He ran his tongue over his lips and Annie figured the old saying the quickest way to a man's heart was through his stomach held true for Deputy Fielding. The guy was melting into a gooey puddle of agreement right before her eyes. He just needed one more persuasive shove to push him over the edge.

"Oh, and did I mention the homemade cheesecake with fresh strawberries and real whipped cream?"

"It's friggin' November. How are you going to make that happen?"

She thought about Art Donovan, the marshal who dropped off the grocery orders and filled their special requests. The man was chubby, balding and didn't wear a wedding ring. He also seemed overjoyed to be dealing with a woman. So overjoyed, in fact, he hadn't been able to take his eyes off her chest when he'd made the last delivery. At the time, Annie had been offended. Right now, Donovan's drooling was looking pretty darned good.

"Oh, I have my ways." She stood and stretched, letting the culinary bribes sink in. "Look, all I'm asking is that you give it some thought. I'll work out a plan in my head, sort of a dry run. If it doesn't sound doable—"

"You're sure you can get fresh strawberries to pile on that cheesecake?"

"Does the sun rise in the east?" she quipped in return.

"All right," said Bob, shaking his head. "I'll think about it. Now go on up to bed. I'll give you my answer in the morning."

Tom glanced up from his post at the desktop TV. The doughboy wasn't kidding when he said his idea was a radical one. "Let me see if I've got this plan of yours straight. I'm supposed to return to earth and enter the body of another human being, someone who can get close enough to Annie to push her in the direction needed to find happiness. And my only choice is one of those three exemplary subjects on the view screen.''

"That's it exactly,'' said Milton.

"Well, gee, let's just review the lucky contenders. Behind door number one we have Annie's sixteen-year-old paper boy—an oversexed, acne-prone, dope-smoking adolescent who's been peeking in her window at night to watch her undress . . .''

Milton stared down at Warren Beavers, six feet of gangly, testosterone-laden teenager. To say he had the IQ of a chimpanzee would be too kind. "Warren's body is young and malleable. If you're able to get it off drugs, you'd have a long life span; you could relive your teen years, go to college again, be or do anything you wanted.''

"Swell. I could go through the agony of drug withdrawal, the uncertainty of getting into a good college, the misery of trying to get laid, the difficulty of choosing the right career— all the good stuff that makes kids want to grow up fast— all over again.'' Tom ran a hand over his jaw. "Just what every man wants to hear at my age.''

Milton *tsk*ed. "You make adolescence sound like hell on earth. It isn't that difficult. Besides, you've already committed your share of mistakes. You know what works and what doesn't.''

"And I don't want to do it over again. My life may not have been one you approved of, but I worked hard to get where I was. I had a good job, money in the bank, a happy mar—''

"Tom.''

"Whatever. Let's get back to my choices, pathetic though they are.''

"All right.'' Milton sighed. "Take a look at panel number two—Esther Rabinowitz. She lives in Annie's building. If you picked Esther, you wouldn't have to do much more than find the right man for Annie. You'd be back up here in no time."

Tom studied the cranky-faced, gray-haired woman sitting in a wheel chair. She was leaning out a window with a rifle of some sort in her hand and looked mean enough to eat rattlesnake for breakfast. "What's she doing?"

"Oh, she's just keeping occupied," the doughboy muttered. Esther pulled the trigger, and the recoil slammed her backward in her seat. "Shooting at the rats that scavenge the alley behind the apartment building."

Tom shuddered. "Great, a senior psycho. What would I do, wing some homeless guy scrounging in the dumpsters and tell Annie to go out back and bag her man?"

"There's no need to be flippant. She is your first available. If you don't choose her, Mrs. Rabinowitz won't be with us past today."

Tom made a rude noise in the back of his throat as he peered into the desktop. "And choice number three is that— that criminal. A man so devoid of decency his only thought is to save his own hide. A mobster turned informant who if he does manage to survive long enough to testify, will probably disappear to another state."

"I agree that Dominic Viglioni is a long shot; but he's closest to her right now, and Annie's supposed to be on this job for a while. Besides, he'll need an agent to accompany him to his new life. That agent could be her."

Tom bit back a snort of laughter. Right about now, the *other* place was looking darned good.

"You don't mean that," snapped Milton. "No one in their right mind wants to go there, even for a visit."

"Okay, okay. I was just thinking." Tom rubbed at his chin. "So, I have to become one of these three people to get a second chance at heaven. Somehow, through them, I'm supposed to insinuate myself into Annie's life and help her find a husband. Do I have it right?"

Milton sniffed. "Not just a husband. The perfect husband. One who will make her truly happy."

"And after she's happily married, I'd get the chance to live out my life in one of those bodies, then get sent back up here. Only I'd go straight to the *good* place."

"Not automatically," Milton clarified. "There would still be rules to follow. The remainder of your life would have to be exemplary. You couldn't go out and commit mayhem, just because you helped Annie find happiness."

Mayhem? What the hell was mayhem anyway? Tom wondered, staring at the blue and white expanse of ceiling above him. "And if I say no way, no how, no thank you to this mind boggling offer? Then what?"

Milton puckered his lips. "Then it will be the *other* place for you."

"Hell?" Tom's eyes shot open wide. "I'm going to hell just because I was a failure as a husband? Jeez, I think there are a whole lot of men down there who deserve to be informed of that little news flash, don't you? Once word gets out that being a lousy spouse is a one-way ticket to eternal damnation, it's going to change the face of marriage around the world."

"Not that place," the angel said with a *tsk*. "The *other* place—where you were before you came here. And I guarantee you'll be in a holding pattern for a lot longer than six years." Milton bounced on the balls of his feet. "Trust me. One of those three humans is your best ticket for getting into heaven within a reasonable amount of time."

Tom wanted to scream. He wanted to stomp and shout and curse at the top of his lungs. Why hadn't someone informed him of the rules while he still had a heartbeat? The only tenet he'd ever learned was the one that said life wasn't fair. Whoever had coined that little gem had obviously never talked to a heavenly being.

Milton stared at him as if he were a first grader cheating on an exam. "Don't be childish. You knew very well what the rules were. I believe He sent the human race a raft of men and women who listed them quite clearly. You simply chose to ignore them, as do so many of your brethren. Next thing you'll be telling me is you didn't know there was life on other planets.''

''Aliens? There are aliens?'' At last, a topic Tom could handle. ''I knew it. I always believed they were out there. Chris Carter was right.''

The doughboy glared. ''We're wasting time. Mrs. Rabinowitz has just a few hours left. Warren Beavers a few days.''

Tom stared down at his choices. Slipping into any one of their skins was going to be about as comfortable as wearing a pair of wet jockey shorts in February. He'd disqualified Esther Rabinowitz from the get-go. Besides the fact she was a woman, he figured she was too old and too immobile to do much good at husband hunting. The Beavers kid wouldn't be such a bad choice if the punk had a brain left.

His gaze shifted to the end panel, the one with the mobster standing on the back porch holding a cigarette in his hand. It would take some getting used to, shaving that dangerously chiseled face every morning. Tom always thought he had a decent body, with the long, rangy muscles of a runner. This guy was close to six feet and built like a boxer, or maybe a football player. He'd never seen the man naked, but he'd bet the guy was male centerfold material. And it was clear he had enough money to buy just about anything he wanted.

''The wiseguy smokes. I never smoked. I can't stand the filthy habit,'' he said, just to impress a point. Deep down, he thought it might be nice to be wealthy and have women think he was a stud.

''So, help him to quit. He—you would certainly live longer if you did.''

Tom drummed his fingers on the desk. ''So when is this mob guy's time up?''

"I'm afraid I don't know."

"Can't you find out, ask his guardian angel or something?"

"His angel is involved in a crisis right now and can't be reached for consultation. I just know it will happen at this house."

"Well, isn't that dandy." Huffing out a breath, Tom began to pace. "And you're sure I could do anything I wanted with this new life, after I helped Annie, of course." He had to ask again; better safe than sorry.

"The path you choose would be up to you."

"How much would I recall of what we just discussed? Would I remember how I got down there or why I was sent? Would Annie or any of my old friends recognize me?"

"No one will know it's you. You'll have fragments, bits and pieces of your old life and the new one, floating in your mind, but only long enough to realize your mission. It might be confusing to you for a while, but gradually, those memories will fade and you'll grow comfortable in your new body . . . er . . . life."

"What happens to that Viglioni character? I'm not going to be like him, am I?"

"Not at all. You have to remember that his soul, the very essence of his existence, will be gone. Yours will take its place."

"So, once I take care of Annie, I'm free to do whatever I like, provided I follow the rules, lead a good life, yada-yada-yada."

"That's the plan."

Tom still wasn't convinced he liked the idea, but it was better than waiting around in that *other* place for a couple of centuries. He wasn't exactly enthralled with having to find his widow another husband—heck, what man would be? But he didn't think he'd deserved to die when he did. Though it was now apparent he hadn't been everything

Annie had wanted in a man, she had been everything he'd ever dreamed of in a woman.

"You're procrastinating again," scolded Milton. "And you're back to thinking drivel. If Annie had been everything you dreamed of in a woman, you wouldn't have tried so hard to change her. Now, who's it going to be?"

Sighing, Tom stared down at the desk and the three humans clearly defined there. Esther Rabinowitz, Warren Beavers and the mobster. Oh, hell, he thought. He might as well go for broke. "I choose that one," he said, pointing to a screen.

"Excellent. Let's just go get ready, shall we?"

CHAPTER FOUR

"I still don't like this idea of yours, McAllister. That beef stroganoff had better be friggin' fantastic." Bob Fielding inspected the ten-foot length of chain attached to a pair of leg irons that Deputy Donovan had dropped off shortly after dawn. "And I'm curious. How the heck do you expect to play ball with twenty pounds of jewelry hanging off your leg?"

"Very carefully?" Annie said, smiling. "Look, if it's too difficult, we'll stop. No harm done. Besides, if we make an effort, it'll be one less thing for Viglioni to gripe about."

Bob stared out the window into the backyard, as if surveying the territory. "Humor me. Tell me the plan one more time."

She put away the silverware, then wiped down the kitchen table as she talked. "It's simple. Viglioni and I get shackled together and hobble to the garage, while Lou sits all nice and cozy on the porch where he has a perfect view of the two of us. I lock my weapon in the trunk of Lou's car. That way, Viglioni isn't tempted and I can get to the gun if I need it. He and I play a little one-on-one. Lou tells us when our time is up, I retrieve my gun and we come inside, where we unhitch and take a shower. Our wiseguy will have worked off some of that obnoxious energy he seems to have so much of, thus making him too tired to complain.''

She rinsed the dishrag in the sink, hung it to dry and rested her bottom against the counter. ''I get some exercise and you get a month of gourmet meals.''

Fielding turned from the window. ''Okay, but be careful. And keep those car keys out of sight.''

''Will do.'' Annie bent and checked the laces on her sneakers, then pushed from the cabinets and headed into the mudroom. ''This is going to be great. You'll see.''

Deputy Smithers and the prisoner walked into the kitchen. Lou's mouth twisted in a frown, as if he'd swallowed a lemon for breakfast instead of an omelet, while Viglioni's expression was smug. Though dressed the same as Annie, in generic gray sweats and athletic shoes, he looked more like a man modeling for *Esquire* magazine than an athlete.

''I can't believe you actually want to do this, McAllister,'' Lou groused. ''You've complained about the cold every time you've gone outside. It must be all of twenty degrees this morning.''

Annie tugged her sweatshirt over her head, then ran her fingers through her curls. She hated the cold as much as he did, but she hated the inactivity more. Holding up the agent's coat, she helped him into it.

''I'm wearing layers, Lou. Lots and lots of layers. And think of the fun you're going to have, watching us freeze our butts off while you sit on the porch toasty warm. I even found an old blanket you can throw over your legs.'' She tossed it at him and he caught it with one hand. ''Now comes the fun part.''

She gathered the chain and leg irons from the counter, set her left foot onto a chair and snapped one of the shackles around her ankle. Holding up the other end, she offered it to Lou. "Here, I'll let you do the honors."

Dominic Viglioni sat down and stuck out his right leg. Deputy Smithers cuffed the leg iron in place. "This has to be considered cruel and unusual punishment," the wiseguy said with a raised brow. "I want to call my lawyer."

"Shut up," snapped Bob, "and be grateful Deputy McAllister is such a persuasive woman. If you blow this opportunity for a little freedom, I'm going to duct tape you to a chair for the rest of your time here. You got that?"

"I got it." Dominic glanced at Annie, his face a mask of confidence. "I promise I'll take it easy on you, doll face, just to show how grateful I am."

"Don't do me any favors." Annie picked up the basketball from the counter. "I'm doing this for myself as much as for you."

Lou ambled out the door, followed by Viglioni, with Annie bringing up the rear. He settled into a white plastic patio chair, drew his weapon and covered himself with the blanket. "The clock's running," he said, checking his watch. "You two have sixty minutes or until I turn into a block of ice before I call it quits."

Annie and the mobster walked to the garage, the chain clanking between them as it dragged across the frozen ground. When they stepped on the cement, she turned and shot the basketball into his belly, grinning when he doubled over with a grunt. She unlocked the trunk, then raised up her sweatshirt, pulled out her gun and set it inside. After pocketing the keys, she slammed the trunk and tried to ignore the awkward weight of the chain and the leg iron clamped around her ankle as she walked onto the playing area.

Dominic was already dribbling the ball, his big hands sure and supple around the leather. "You ready?"

Annie nodded and crouched in response.

Dominic faded left as he smacked the ball into the cement. Turning on one foot, he spun right and jumped toward her.

Taken by surprise, she reared back and landed flat on the concrete while the ball sailed over her head and dropped into the hoop.

"That's one," he said with a cocky grin. He waited until she stood, then tossed her the rebound. "But it's a freebie. You bein' a girl and all."

Annie could hear Lou's cackle from the back porch. She wasn't sure what hurt more, her fanny or her pride. She'd joined a coed basketball team in high school, and trained her girls' team at the rec center to play tough, but she and Tom had never done much in the way of competitive sports. She'd learned to play a man's game at Glynco or risk a hazing from the male trainees. Knowing she could hold her own empowered her and she grew bold.

"I don't need any freebies, Mr. Viglioni. You can have the point. And the game is twenty-one." Slow and steady, she bounced the ball against the concrete. Kicking the chain aside, she did a quick pivot, raised her arms overhead and lobbed the ball through the net. "Or until you cry uncle."

Viglioni put his hands on his hips and boomed out a laugh. Annie grabbed at the rebound and thrust the ball hard into his chest, but this time he was ready for her and caught it smoothly.

"Tie score." She assumed the position again, ready to block his shot. "I believe it's your side out."

Almost an hour later, bent at the waist, Annie rested her hands on her knees. Sweat matted the curls framing her face. Her lungs burned, her breath hitched in her chest and her bruised tailbone throbbed. Damn, how could she have let herself get so out of shape? The girls at the rec center gave her a good triweekly workout. She kept up with her morning run and did her sit-ups and push-ups, but they hadn't prepared her for anything this rough.

She swiped her arm across her forehead and focused on

the bouncing ball, or rather, the man crouched in front of her pounding the ball into the concrete. At least he looked as wrung out as she felt. Perspiration dotted the chiseled planes of his face, his breath bellowed in and out of his lungs, and his movements had slowed enough for her to notice.

"It's twenty a piece, doll. You ready to lose?"

"In your dreams, buster." She did a shuffle step from side to side, waggling her fingers in a come-and-get-me gesture.

Viglioni darted left, then right, pivoting as he dribbled into her. Annie followed with her shoulder and back, blocking his charge. With a grunt, he turned in the opposite direction. She kicked out her leg and the chain snaked away, giving her more room to maneuver. Slamming into him from the side, she reached for the ball and jerked it from his hands.

Dominic hung on, and she shoved with her hip and upper body, jamming her elbow into his ribs. The nasty street move took him by surprise, and he loosened his grip. Annie snatched the ball to her chest. Whirling on her toes, she shot forward into a layup and arced the ball from her hands. It circled twice before it dropped outside the hoop and hit the cement.

She cursed silently and dived onto the ball, but Viglioni landed on her back and slammed her to the concrete. Together, they skidded like a double-decker sled without runners, his arms wrapped around and under her from behind. Her knees and elbows burned with the force of the slide.

"It's my ball, you jerk. Let go," she wheezed.

"Not a chance." Dominic's breath rasped against her ear. "You blew the shot."

She clutched the basketball closer to her chest, but that only drew his arms tighter around her middle. Struggling for air, she wiggled her bottom and tried to roll out from under him. "But I got the rebound."

Using his superior strength, he flipped her onto her back and thrust his knees between her legs. Before she knew what had happened, the ball slid to the side and rolled onto the concrete, and he was looming over her.

"And I got you."

She blew at a curl dangling across her forehead. His move had been textbook self-defense, and she'd been a sucker to fall for it. "Get off me."

He trapped her in his chocolate brown stare. "Make me."

Annie shoved at shoulders as immoveable as a brick wall. Viglioni grinned, nestling his hips against the juncture of her thighs. She pushed again and he focused on her mouth.

"It's my shot," she muttered, grinding her back molars. The unmistakable length of his erection lay hard and probing against her belly. The cold air crackled with a jolt of sexual awareness. Embarrassed, Annie turned her head, refusing to get caught in his sardonic gaze. It had been years since she'd had this kind of effect on a man.

He moved his hands from the cement to her ribs. Resting his thumbs below her breasts, he inched his face lower, until his breath stirred the damp curls at her cheek. "Depends on whose viewpoint you're in. Right now, I'd say it was a technical foul."

Squirming, Annie tried to worm a leg between his knees. If she played her cards right, she could wipe that smirk off his face and do some damage at the same time.

The warmth of overheated bodies steamed the air, sending the scent of his expensive aftershave and her frustration billowing around them. He kept his legs together as he rose up onto his knees. "Don't even think about it, doll face," he growled.

Annie snapped up her head, ready to glare, and found him gazing intently. Besides the subtle odor of cologne, she smelled the elemental scent of an aroused male. She opened her mouth to tell him off and he took full advantage, lowering his lips to hers.

The taste of mint overpowered the smoky tang of cigarettes. Dominic's tongue stroked hers and Annie turned to stone. Then he eased the pressure, teasing at her lips, and she felt herself go marshmallow soft and hot all over. As if sensing her surrender, he settled into her chest.

Their bodies shifted, until he was cradled against her, yet he'd wrapped his arms around her back to cushion her from the cement. Taken in by the thoughtful gesture, her hands worked their way to his neck. Her fingers threaded through his thick silky hair. Crazy. She was crazy . . . and so was he.

He sucked the air from her lungs, and she thought she'd faint with the need to let him. Deepening the kiss, she hooked her calves around his thighs. She bit at his lower lip as she arched into him, trying to devour him from the outside in. The world faded, until his mouth became the center of her universe. Nothing mattered but the man in her arms. Consumed with heat, all she could do was feel.

Dominic slid his hands under her sweatshirt. Obviously flustered by the layers she wore, he groaned low in his throat as he plucked at her nipples, circling his thumbs up and over breasts hidden under an inch of cotton fiber. She quivered at the sensation, the jolt of electricity that arrowed straight to her womb.

Without warning, he pulled back. Annie blinked through a heady fog of desire. A gust of cold air chilled her back to reality. Her eyes focused, then locked onto his scowl.

"Damn, that wasn't supposed to happen," he muttered. He stared at her, his steely gaze almost a slap. "Jeez, McAllister, what the hell did we just do?"

"I—I—don't know." Still dazed, Annie shook her head. He removed his arms and jumped to his feet, and she hit the cement with a thud.

Standing over her, he offered his hand. She ignored it and fumbled to her feet. Oh, hell. Oh, crap. Was she insane? Inhaling a long, slow breath, she averted her eyes and smoothed the front of her sweatshirt, then ran her fingers through her damp curls. His pointed question echoed in her brain. What the heck *had* happened? Not only had her experiment flopped, but her career was in ruins. And it was all her fault.

Raising her gaze, she checked the back porch, certain Lou had seen everything. He'd probably run to get Bob . . . or he was laughing his head off.

But the porch was empty.

Swinging around, she squinted across the yard. Maybe she'd gotten lucky and Lou had slipped away to the bathroom, or decided to do a perimeter check. Prepared for a wise crack, or at the very least a leer from Dominic, she turned, surprised to find him scanning the trees, his body tense, his eyes narrowed in concentration.

"Get down!" He jerked around and shoved her to her knees.

Annie batted his hands away, but he pushed at her shoulders and gave a harder shove. "Just do it, McAllister."

She read the fear in his eyes, and a hint of something more. Operating on instinct, she rolled toward the car, rose to her knees and drew the keys from her pocket in one smooth move. Opening the trunk, she grabbed for the gun just as three shots rang out.

Whipping around, she spotted the bright red stain spreading across Dominic's left shoulder. With his eyes fixed on hers, his face paled. In slow motion, he took a few stumbling steps toward her and fell to his hands and knees at her feet.

Annie's heart did a triple stutter. Crouching, she shielded his body with her own and raised her gun to pan the grounds. *Where the hell was Lou?*

Her WITSEC training took over and she concentrated on her prisoner. He'd pitched forward and rolled to his back. Blood continued to soak his sweatshirt, broadening the stain until it covered his chest and stomach. He moaned and she tucked the gun in the waistband of her pants. Still in a squat, she put her hands in his armpits and dragged him backward into the shelter of the garage.

After laying him flat on the cement, she tugged off her sweatshirt, stuffed it up and under his and pressed down hard. Raising her head, she again scanned the farmhouse, then the yard. Where was Bob Fielding? What had happened to Lou?

Her instructions were to protect Dominic Viglioni at all costs. She studied his ashen face, felt the blood seep into her sweatshirt, and a rush of utter helplessness overwhelmed her.

His life was slipping away under her hands. His breathing turned shallow and she started to panic. "Don't die," she whispered. "Please, God, don't let him die."

Perched on the garage roof next to Milton, Tom observed Annie and the mobster pivot, slam and charge at each other like two angry street fighters. Equally matched and determined, they paced off and attacked full tilt time and time again, until he wondered if it was a game or a battle he was watching.

He'd never enjoyed physically violent sports, instead preferring contests of skill like tennis or golf. He'd taken his share of ribbing in college when he missed football and soccer games in order to shoot a bow and arrow or run track. But this contest of wills combined skill, strength and stamina, along with street smart slamming.

Instead of being repulsed, he was strangely fascinated by his wife's surprising strength and agility. Until this moment, he'd never found athletic women to be much of a turn-on. Seeing Annie complete impossible shots as she evaded Viglioni's larger body held him entranced.

"She's quite a woman, isn't she?" Milton said, almost to himself.

Tom shook his head, confused by his own reaction. "I guess I just never saw it until now."

Milton made a *humph* sound deep in his throat. "You didn't see it because you didn't want to."

"Lay off, would you?" Tom hissed. "I got the message loud and clear. I was a jerk. I didn't appreciate Annie and I blew it. I told you I was willing to make things right."

"Yes, well, that still remains to be seen." Milton shifted on the shingles. "I guess it's time I gave you the rest of the details." He winced as Annie absorbed a body check from the mobster. She spun to her right and dribbled the ball, then feinted left and broke away, charging to the net. The ball flew from her fingers and floated neatly through the hoop.

"Go, girl. You get him!" the angel shouted.

Tom raised a fist in triumph. "She's ahead, eighteen to seventeen."

"That she is." The doughboy set his pudgy white hands on his thighs. "Maybe we should discuss the rules again, one more time, just to be sure you understand them, of course."

Viglioni grabbed the rebound. Shouldering Annie aside, he forged past her and took a jump shot into the net, tying the score. A tremor of disgust rippled through Tom, as if he'd been the one who'd given her the punishing slam and earned the point.

"You already gave them to me a dozen times," he reminded Milton, cheering inside at the way Annie commandeered the rebound and navigated the ball into position. "My soul moves into Viglioni's body as soon as his moves out. I stay close to Annie and help her find the perfect life mate. A man who'll love her and appreciate her for the woman she's become."

His gaze ran over her long legs, her fuller breasts and confident carriage. She was toying with the mobster, dribbling the ball as she kept him behind her, dancing from side to side as she set up her next basket. She jumped. She shot. She scored! Damn but she looked fine.

"Yes, but there are a few important details I need for you to understand. For one thing, Annie can't know that you are you."

Tom whipped his head around. "What do you mean, she can't know I'm me?"

Milton *tsk*ed. "It would be cheating. Besides, if she thought Viglioni was—that you were—oh, you know what I mean. How would you react if someone told you they were a loved one come back from the dead, only they were inhabiting another person's body?"

"Like they were insane!" Tom huffed out an invisible breath. This whole idea was insane as far as he was concerned. "Okay, so I don't tell her he's me . . . or I'm him . . . or whatever. You're forgetting one little thing. She thinks I'm a killer, the slime of the earth. Why in the hell would a guy like me . . . him . . . suddenly show an interest in her private life and act like a friend?"

Milton shrugged. "You're a smart man. You figure it out."

Tom and the angel glared at each other across the roof peak, then remembered they were there for a reason and focused on the activity below. Steam billowed from Annie's rounded lips. Viglioni held her in his impudent gaze, then took off on an up-court charge. She threw herself in his path, blocked the shot and sent it slamming against the backboard. But he snagged the rebound and pivoted like a pro, dunking the ball into the hoop and tying the score again.

"Damn," muttered Tom. "Can't that jerk cut her a break?"

" 'Fraid not," Milton said, almost to himself. "He has too much integrity to compromise."

"What the heck is that supposed to mean?" Lifted by his thoughts, Tom levitated from the roof. If he didn't know better, he'd guess the doughboy was blushing. "Whose side are you on anyway?"

"I don't take sides . . . well, not exactly. Let's get back to the rules, shall we?"

Annie had the ball now, and she was being very careful, dribbling and pivoting in a graceful yet tactical dance. Seeing her in this new light, Tom was having a hard time paying attention to the angel at his side.

"Ah-hem. Heaven to Tom."

"Hm? Oh, yeah. Okay." He sighed. "Lay it on me. What else is there I need to know?"

Annie changed direction and slipped around her opponent. Driving forward, she lobbed the basket dead center of the net. "Yes!" Tom pumped his fist in the air. "That's the way."

Milton laid a hand on his shoulder. "You might be a bit confused at first. You need to remember that things aren't always as they seem."

"You already told me that," said Tom, his eyes fixed on the mobster. Viglioni looked big and dangerous, and he wondered how he would ever get used to living in the guy's skin.

"I said you would have the man's memories for a while, but that's not quite true. Eventually, there will be a meeting of both minds, a melding if you will—"

"Sort of like the Vulcan Mind Meld from *Star Trek?*" Tom prompted, inordinately proud of his snappy quip.

"This is serious," Milton lectured in return. "Besides the two minds becoming one, your body is also going to have his instincts and reactions—I think you humans call it *muscle memory.* Don't be surprised if you find your physical self doing things his way for a while, so be prepared to go with the flow. You simply need to remember that you're the one in charge. You have the free will to do whatever you want. It will all be up to you, once you realize—"

"Yeah, yeah, yeah." Tom's gaze stayed centered on the

pavement below. Annie was ahead by one point, but it was obvious from the evil gleam in Viglioni's eyes he wasn't about to let it stay that way. In possession of the ball, he kicked at the chain, pivoted left, faded back and charged right. Shoving Annie to the side, he slam-dunked the ball, then tried to snatch the rebound from her hands. The man was a cretin.

"Tom, it's important you remember what I'm saying."

"Hm? Remember what?" Tom wished he could jump off the roof and clobber the guy for treating Annie so shabbily.

Milton sighed. "That things aren't always what they seem."

Before Tom could answer, Annie made a daring in-your-face move. Pounding into a layup, she arced the ball ... and missed. Racing after her for the rebound, the mobster dived onto her back, and the two of them went sliding along the concrete like a hockey puck on ice.

"Hey!" Tom shouted, jumping to his feet. "That's a foul. Did you see what he did?"

He scooted to the overhang, ready to fly to the rescue, but Milton grabbed him by the back of his tuxedo jacket. "Not so fast. Wait a minute. It isn't time yet."

"What do you mean it isn't—" Tom did a double take as he concentrated on the scene below. "What the hell is he doing?"

Milton peered over the backboard. "Oh, dear. This wasn't supposed to happen quite so ... I mean ...'um ...''

Tom tottered in place. "That creep is putting the moves on my wife. Hey! Hey you!" He struggled against the dough-boy's surprisingly tight grip. "Let go of me!"

"Wait, just wait," cautioned Milton. "The timing needs to be perfect."

Tom stopped wriggling and stared down in shock. If he didn't know better, he'd think he'd been thrust into an episode of *Cops*. Viglioni jumped off of Annie as if he'd been jabbed with a cattle prod. Tom heard a rushing in his ears and couldn't understand what the jerk was saying, but the guy was definitely confused. He reached down to help Annie up, but she refused his hand and staggered to her feet, looking just as upset and disoriented.

A flurry of gunshots shattered the morning air.

Viglioni shuffled in place, then stumbled toward her. Annie moved in double time, disappearing, then reappearing with a gun in her hand just as the mobster landed at her feet. In the space of a few seconds, she'd scanned the area, hoisted Viglioni up by his underarms and pulled him from sight.

Tom hung over the backboard, practically upside down, to see what was going on. Hauling himself up, he glared at Milton. "What the hell just happened down there? Where are those other marshals? The ones who are supposed to be protecting her?"

Milton smiled. "I can't say. Now, are you ready?"

Ready? Tom shook like a withered leaf. The noise of blood pumping through his veins in a kind of *flub-dub-flub-dub* sound washed out every coherent word or thought.

The angel raised his hands as if preparing to conduct an orchestra, and Tom began to freefall. The cement rose to meet him, and he figured he was dying all over again. His chest and lungs burned. He felt numb and tingly all at the same time, as if his entire body had fallen asleep and was now trying to wake up.

A gust of air passed through him just as he floated into Dominic Viglioni's bleeding body.

"Goodbye, Tom. Remember what I told you. And good luck," he thought he heard Milton say. "You're going to need it."

CHAPTER FIVE

Annie knelt over Dominic's corpselike body and pressed down hard on the bullet wound. Her scrambled brain couldn't decide what to do next. If she ran for help, he would bleed to death. If they stayed where they were, whoever shot him could come back and kill them both. He was too heavy to carry, and there was no other safe place to drag him, even if she managed to stop the bleeding.

The area around the house and garage had turned eerily still. All she could hear was her own breathing, matching the cadence and rhythm of Dominic's. But his thready gasps for air seemed to rasp slower by the second. The time lapse between his heartbeats lengthened under her palms . . . two seconds . . . three . . . four. . . .

With tears streaming silently, she kept pressure on the wound, waiting for the next beat, fearing it would never come.

Suddenly, a ripple of air passed through her; his pulse stuttered beneath her hands. Her entire body shivered in response to the strange sensation, almost as if someone had walked across her soul. She gazed into Dominic's slack face and blinked at the subtle changes she found. A flush of healthy color washed into his cheeks. His respiration increased from barely there, to shaky and shallow, to labored but steady in the blink of an eye.

"Ow. Hey, not so hard," she heard him mutter as he moved beneath her.

Amazingly, the flow of blood lessened under her fingers. His heartbeat grew stronger as did his breathing. Hesitantly, she raised her hands and wiped at her cheeks.

His eyelids fluttered and stayed open. "Annie?"

She gave a weak smile, not quite believing her eyes. "Are you okay?"

He groaned and rolled his shoulder, raised his wounded arm. Sighing, he nodded. "I guess so, but my chest hurts like a sonofabitch. When I get my hands on that pompous little jerk, I'm going to—" He glanced at the garage ceiling, then turned his head from side to side, as if checking to be certain where he was. "What the hell happened?"

Pompous little jerk? Some pompous little jerk had done this to him? Sniffing back tears, Annie went on full alert. "You've been shot. Lie still. I'm going to find Lou."

"No!"

He tried to sit up, but she pushed him back down. "You took a hit to the shoulder. The bleeding—"

She raised her arms and gazed down at her thighs. Spatters of blood covered her sweats; the sleeves of her sweater were crimson to her elbows. The cloying coppery smell made her weak and she swayed in place.

Dominic swiped a hand over his face. "Are you all right?"

She nodded, sagging onto her heels. "I'm fine . . . a little dizzy, is all."

"Take a couple of deep breaths," he ordered. Leaning on his right arm, he focused on the yard. "Did you see anyone out there prowling around?"

"No, but it looked like you did, just before—did you recognize who shot you?"

He ignored her question and rolled to his side. Reaching under his shirt, he pulled out what used to be her sweatshirt. "Holy Christ." Tossing it to the side, he met her wide-eyed stare.

Annie gasped, too shocked to speak. The sweatshirt was now a pulpy mass of red cotton, so bloody it might have been used to bandage an amputee.

He quirked up one corner of his mouth. "Trust me. It looks a hell of a lot worse than it is."

She swallowed hard, trying not to gag. "We—we have to find Lou and Bob. I thought for sure they'd come running when they heard the shots."

Dominic rose to his hands and knees. Propping himself against the car bumper, he wobbled to a stand. "Stay here. Whoever did this is probably out there waiting to see what we do next."

"Was it—do you think it was someone sent by your ex-boss?"

He shuffled to the garage door and peered around a corner. "I don't know who it was." Holding out his hand, he waggled his fingers at her. "Give me your gun."

Annie jumped back, clutching protectively at the waistband of her sweats. "Are you crazy? I can't give you my weapon."

Glancing at her over his shoulder, he drew his eyebrows together. "Oh, yeah, that's right. I'm the guy you're supposed to be *protecting*."

His sarcasm zinged straight to her heart. Some marshal she'd turned out to be. It was her brilliant plan that had gotten them into this mess in the first place. But she'd done it for him. If he hadn't been on top of her, kissing her senseless, she might have spotted the gunman before he'd taken that shot.

Her charge had taken advantage when she was flat on her

back, which made him partly to blame. The creep. "I'm sorry I missed the guy with the gun. I was a little distracted, thanks to you."

He continued to scan the area, and Annie thought the blood loss had affected his powers of reasoning. She took the Glock out of her waistband and tucked her right hand under her arm, just in case he decided to wrestle the weapon away. "Do you see anyone—anything suspicious?"

No answer, just a concentrated stare.

"Dominic. I asked if you can see anything."

Tom jumped when he realized Annie was talking to the new him—Dominic Viglioni—mob informant and king of the rat finks. And he didn't even know what he was looking for. An inner sense told him someone was out there, but he hadn't a clue who it could be. A mob hit man was the most obvious answer, but something niggled in his head, bristling against that theory. Lou had disappeared. And the man in charge, that Fielding guy, had yet to make the scene. It was difficult to imagine a trained deputy marshal sleeping through the sound of gunfire.

Beside him, Annie raised her weapon. "We can't stay here. We have to do something." She took a step into the open. "I have to find out what happened to Lou and Bob. They need to know what went on, if they don't already."

Tom grabbed her by the back of her sweater and hauled her inside the garage. She made perfect sense. But it just didn't feel right. He rubbed at his aching shoulder and saw that his hand was wet with blood. God, you'd think Milton would have warned him this was going to be messy. He tugged the clammy shirt up and over his head with his good hand, eased it down his aching arm and tossed it on top of Annie's discarded sweatshirt.

Drawing his brows together, Tom opened to the idea itching at the back of his brain. "It's possible whoever shot me had an accomplice. They could have sneaked into the house and killed Lou and Fielding while his buddy was out here taking potshots at us. They might still be inside, waiting to see what we'll do.''

Annie hugged the garage wall, her gaze locked on the sodden pile of cotton. ''I never thought about that.''

''Well, think about it now, doll.'' *Doll?* Had he just uttered that crass sexist term to a woman? Milton had mentioned something about muscle memory, but since when had his mouth become a muscle?

Christ, now what was he supposed to do? Annie was holding her gun in a death grip. He could probably strong-arm it away from her and hope that muscle memory thing kicked in, but with his luck, he'd shoot himself someplace important. Still, he didn't think he'd be safe charging across that yard without protection.

''Look, how about if I make a run for the house and you cover me?'' *Cover me? Yeah, that sounded right.* ''If nobody takes a shot, you can follow.''

Annie shifted her gaze to the chain pooling around their feet. ''I don't think that will work. We have to go together or not at all.''

Tom realized what she meant and sighed. ''Good point. Okay, just promise you'll stay low and close.''

''Hey, I'm the marshal. I know the drill. Besides, it's my job, remember?''

Annie's words echoed in his head. Something was going on inside of him, subtle shifts in his thought process he didn't have the luxury of examining at the moment. But the odd litany of ideas felt right, so he decided to go with them. He only prayed she would follow orders . . . though he hadn't a clue why he was the one giving them.

''Okay, we go on three.'' He crouched. ''Ready? One . . . two . . . three!''

They sprang out of the garage at a sprint. But they didn't make it more than ten feet before the bullets started to fly. Annie fired in the direction of the shots, and Tom's brain skittered to a stop. His heart jumped into his throat, and he did a quick one-eighty. The chain jerked Annie off her feet and she stumbled to the ground.

"Shit!" He rolled over and covered her with his body, felt her tremble beneath him. "I'm sorry, I—I guess I wigged out for a second. Are you hit?"

"N-no."

"Good, then we're both fine. We're heading back to cover. Stay close."

Before Annie could protest, he hoisted her up. They zig-zagged to the garage with the sound of gunfire, hers and the gunman's, ringing around them.

"N-now what?" Annie asked, her voice shaking. She held her weapon at shoulder level, close to her chest. Leaning against the garage wall, she was gasping for breath.

Christ, it was dangerous out there. That little weasel of an angel was such a liar, giving him the impression he'd have another fifty years or so in this body. At this rate, he'd be lucky to get another fifty seconds. And what the hell did Annie think she was doing, taking a job as a U.S. Marshal? This profession wasn't fit for anyone in their right mind, let alone a woman.

He stuck his head around the side of the garage and a bullet zinged into the doorframe, so close the splinters hit the top of his head. Darting back, he felt a tug at his sleeve.

Annie's eyes were shining with excitement, even though her mouth was drawn into a worried frown. "I said, do you have any more bright ideas?"

A round of bullets hit the cement, scattering chips of concrete at their feet. Tom grabbed Annie and pulled her against him. "Do you still have the car keys?"

She fumbled in the pocket of her sweats, pulled out the keys and dangled them in the air.

Tom snatched them from her hand and shoved her to the driver's door. Opening it, he pushed her into the front seat ahead of him, climbed behind the wheel and started the engine.

"You can't—I can't let you—" she squealed in protest, shoving the Glock in his side.

Gunshots chewed up the wood at the back of the garage. "Go ahead and shoot if you have to, but we're outta here."

He slammed on the gas pedal and backed onto the lawn. They raced down the drive under a hail of bullets.

Annie watched the countryside speed by. Once they'd turned onto the main road, Dominic hadn't said two words. Instead, he'd slowed the car to the posted limit and headed for Route 94, the most major artery in the area.

"Where are we going?" she demanded.

His hands tightened on the wheel. 'Morristown.''

"Morristown? What's in Morristown?"

He slid his gaze to the rearview mirror and stared. "Holy shit," he muttered. Blinking, he alternated between watching the road and checking himself out every few seconds.

"This is a lousy time to worry about your good looks, don't you think?" She glanced at the sleeves of her once white sweater. Pulling down her sun visor, she frowned at the face staring back at her. Dried blood matted her hair and streaked across both cheeks. Her hands were still covered with the sticky stuff.

But Dominic looked worse. Besides his hands and undershirt, his sweats were soaked red all the way to his knees. If it were Halloween, they'd probably win first prize for the most gruesome twosome costumes. Dressed like this, they'd frighten Dracula himself.

He turned to her, his sigh filled with frustration. "I'm not worried about my—oh, hell, just sit tight and stay quiet. I need to think."

He had to think? Hah! She was the one on the run with an escaped felon. She was supposed to be giving the orders. She raised her gun and pointed it at his head. "We need to go to the Federal building in Newark and report what just happened.''

"Not on your life." His grip on the steering wheel was so tight she thought his fingers might snap. "That's the last place we want to go right now."

"Why not? I have to report to my superiors. Bob and Lou could be dead. Someone is probably on our tail, still looking to kill you."

"You got a hairpin or maybe a nail file on you?"

"A nail file? You are crazy."

"Do something useful. Check the glove box and see what Lou stored away for a rainy day."

Puzzled, Annie switched the Glock to her left hand and fumbled for the latch. She pulled out paper napkins, a few road maps, a first aid kit. "Hey, we might be able to use this. How does your shoulder feel?"

He shifted in his seat. "Sore but bearable. The bleeding's stopped. Why?"

"You still need to see a doctor. The bullet might be lodged somewhere important. At the very least, we should sterilize the wound."

"I'm pretty sure the bullet went straight through," he murmured, but it sounded as if he doubted his own words. "Keep looking for something narrow and sharp. An awl maybe, or a—"

Absorbed in her task, she set the gun on the floor. "Tire pressure gage? Screwdriver?" The pile in her lap grew until she pulled out a small, leather-bound case, unzipped it and held up a thin shaft of metal with a hook on the end. "Tools for a midget?"

He glanced at the kit and gave a killer smile. "Well, what do you know. Lou, you devil, you."

Annie kept quiet, but her mind was running on overdrive. Not only had she never been in this type of situation before, but what had happened hadn't ever been covered in training. Dominic Viglioni, a confessed informant and her prisoner, was acting as if he were the one in charge. Though he still talked like a thug, he was sounding less like a wiseguy and more *educated* by the minute. Something about the entire situation didn't ring true, but she had no idea what.

In her gut, Annie knew he'd taken off because he was trying to escape an ambush. But all of it might be an act or a setup, a way to help him out of his predicament. If he gained her trust and she agreed to help him, he could still kill her later and dump her body someplace it might never be found.

Dominic slowed and put on his blinker, then pulled the car onto a side road and took the lock pick from her hand. "Give me your foot."

She swiveled on the seat and rested her sneaker on the dashboard before she realized she was letting him give her orders again. Thirty seconds later, he'd undone her leg iron and set her free. Then he twisted himself sideways and worked at his own ankle cuff. The shackle snapped open and he nodded. "Be a good girl and throw all this hardware on the back floor."

"I don't remember seeing breaking and entering on your list of accomplishments," she said with a sniff. "And in case you've forgotten, I'm a woman, not a girl."

"How could I forget?"

His wicked grin brought back every intimate detail of the way she'd surrendered to him on the cement, their bodies molded against each other as they'd kissed like lovers. If he hadn't broken away when he did. . . . She turned her head, refusing to give him the satisfaction of seeing her blush.

He tossed the pick into the case. "It's just a little something I learned at—"

"Mobster school?" she shot back.

"Not exactly. Now buckle up and sit tight."

Deciding to give him another chance to be reasonable, Annie waited until he pulled back onto the main road to say, "Okay, so *now* we drive to Newark and the Federal building."

"The Feds are going to have to wait." He set the cruise control. "We're going to Morristown."

Tom thought he was having an out-of-body experience, almost like the one he'd had when he first arrived in that *other* place. His brain was functioning, but it was sending a raft of mixed signals. He opened his mouth, but had no idea where the words were coming from. For some yet-to-be-revealed reason, he had to get to the bus station in Morristown and open locker C–101. The pull to retrieve what was hidden inside itched at him like a fresh mosquito bite.

To top it all, he needed a cigarette in the worst way. Shit!

He caught a glimpse of Annie out of the corner of his eye. Something told him she was giving serious consideration to retrieving her weapon from the floor and forcing him to drive to Newark, which he knew in his gut would be a really bad move. So why hadn't she done it, instead of sitting calmly beside him and watching the scenery go by?

"No more smart-ass comments? You're not going to try to talk me out of Morristown?"

She nibbled on her lower lip, then reached between her legs, slowly raised her Glock and aimed it at his head. "I don't want to shoot you. It's my sworn duty to protect you. Just give me one good reason why I should let you drive us to Morristown."

Well, duh! It was about time she started acting like a federal marshal.

He focused on the road. "Go ahead and pull the trigger. It's what you were trained to do, isn't it?"

"Why are we going to Morristown?" Her hands were shaking, but her voice sounded tough as nails. "And where. Just tell me."

"The bus station. I need to get something out of a locker in the bus station."

"What?"

She'd asked the sixty-four-million-dollar question. "I'll tell you once we get there."

Tom steered the car onto a side street, turned off the ignition and tucked the keys under the visor. They had to ditch the sedan and find another way to travel. But first he had to get to that locker. He opened the car door and saw Annie out of the corner of his eye as she raised the gun and pointed it at him.

"Hang on a second. You're not going anywhere without me."

He found himself smiling. She was one hell of a woman. "I thought I'd be a gentleman and open the door for you."

She stared at his blood-soaked chest. "I guess you're trying to look inconspicuous, huh?"

He checked out his shirt and sweat pants, then the rusty red sleeves of her sweater. Aw, hell. They looked like extras from a horror movie. "You didn't happen to notice a jacket or some spare clothes in the trunk when you retrieved your gun, did you?"

Or maybe a pack of cigarettes?

She jerked the Glock toward the back of the car, opened the door and walked to the trunk. He popped the lid, then slid from behind the wheel, noting the side street was deserted. Annie had the good sense to lower the gun and hug it to her side while he inspected the trunk and removed a medium-sized, soft-sided case. Unzipping the center section, he tossed her a grin. "We're in luck. Lou left his laptop." He closed up the case and set it on the sidewalk.

Her mouth thinned into a frown. "You can't take that. It's . . . it's stealing."

"I think that's a pretty stupid statement, considering we already stole a car, don't you?" He ignored her glare and pulled out a dilapidated leather jacket and bright yellow slicker. "Oh, goody. New costumes," he said wryly. "How about you be a biker chick and I'll be a flasher?"

Annie rolled her eyes. "I want it on record that this entire detour was your idea. If anyone asks, I was letting you take charge only because you had me so curious." She took the leather jacket and tugged it over her left arm, then switched the gun and shrugged up the other sleeve. Luckily it covered most of the bloody spots. Tucking the Glock into a pocket, she pushed until the barrel bulged discreetly. "Now you."

"Yes, ma'am." Tom did as he was told, noting that the slicker came to his knees and did a fair job of camouflaging his own ruined clothes. Bending down, he picked up the laptop. "You ready?"

Nodding, Annie took a step closer. "I'm your shadow, so no funny stuff. And once we get whatever is in that locker, we're going to Newark."

Sure we are, thought Tom. But he'd cross that little road-block after he found out what was hidden in locker C–101.

They strolled into the bus station arm in arm. Annie had figured out a way to jab the gun against his hip and make it look like she was a girlfriend all at the same time.

The bank of lockers sat against a wall that separated the public restrooms. C–101 was a third of the way down in the middle of the row. Tom stared at the combination lock.

Annie tapped her foot. "Get going. We don't have all day."

He raised his gaze to the ceiling.

"Hurry up." She poked her jacket against his ribs. "This place gives me the willies."

Wondering how in the hell he was supposed to get out of this one, he panned to the restroom. "I have to see a man about a horse," he muttered, shoving the computer into her chest. He strode through the door to the men's room with the sound of Annie's frustrated "hey!" ringing in her ears.

Well, crap. Annie turned on her heels and scanned the bus station. People walked past in their normal, East Coast whatever-you-do-don't-make-eye-contact manner. Sagging against the lockers, she had to admit that the jacket covered most of the mess, hiding anything out of the ordinary. Dominic would have to come out sooner or later. Come to think of it, she had to go, too. Another minor difficulty.

She let the Glock rest in her pocket and ran a hand through her hair. So far, she was in luck. No one had noticed the bloodstains. She walked to the water fountain, set down the case and rinsed her hands, then rubbed them on her cheeks, hoping that would take care of things. The running water reminded her she still needed to do her business and she started to pace. Where the heck was Dominic? How long did it take for a guy to pee?

He rounded the corner, whistling. She hurried to his side and gave him a shove. "Okay. Put a rush on it."

He smiled. "No problemo, doll face." Leaning forward, he blew on his fingers and rubbed his fingernails on his jacket front like a professional safecracker.

Irritating. He was the most singularly irritating man she had ever met, hands down. She grabbed at her gun and shoved it into his ribs through the leather. "You are driving me to pull this trigger."

"Okay. I was just having a little fun. Hang on a second." He moved the dial to the right, then the left, then right again. The lock snapped apart and he let out a breath. Opening the door, he reached inside . . . way inside.

Annie groaned. "Oh, for Pete's sake. Hurry up."

Drawing back his hand, he stared at the large padded envelope.

"Is that it?"

"I guess so."

"Okay, let's go outside and hail a cab. No, wait, there's a phone. Come on. I'm going to call my chief in Newark."

"Huh?" Dominic sounded as if he'd just awakened from a trance. "I don't think that's such a good idea."

"Of course it is." She tugged his arm and jerked him toward the phones. "Move it. Now."

Annie took a step just as a bullet whizzed between them and put a neat round hole in the locker next to her head.

Dominic stepped in front of her, grabbed her hand and started to run, whisking up the laptop as he went. Another bullet hit the wall above them and people in the bus station finally came alive. A mother screamed as she pulled a little boy back into the safety of the lavatory. Someone shouted as Dominic dragged Annie behind him like a sack of dirty laundry. They skidded into an older couple, spun in a semicircle and opened the door marked EMERGENCY EXIT, setting off a battery of ear-piercing alarms. Flying down the stairs, they raced from the building and out into the alley.

"Keep up, Deputy McAllister," he shouted, shoving her in front of him. They sprinted down the alley and around the corner to where she thought they'd parked the car. But the gray, four-door compact was gone. They'd been made.

"Aw, hell." Dominic stared at her. "Got any bright ideas?"

Annie whipped her head up the block and back again. Any second she imagined whoever had shot at them would come running around the corner out of the alley they'd just left. In a panic, she gazed across the street and nodded toward a rusty Ford pickup piled high with lawn and garden equipment.

"How are you at hot-wiring cars?"

He grinned. "Doll face, I thought you'd never ask."

CHAPTER SIX

"Give me the envelope."

"Sorry, doll, no can do. At least, not until we're somewhere safe."

That had been Annie's last conversation with Dominic Viglioni, more than two hours ago, just after he had hotwired the landscaper's truck. He'd stuffed the envelope under his slicker and into the waistband of his sweats, then shoved her and the computer case into the front seat, fiddled with the wires and driven from the side street at raceway speed. She was still amazed at how fast he'd managed to get the rusted white Ford running.

It was almost dark, and they were on the New Jersey Turnpike heading south. They'd passed every main highway that could have taken them into Newark, and Annie had no clue where they were headed. She still had her gun, but she had yet to use it as anything more than an empty threat—a point which had her silently fuming.

The way she'd been calmly going along for the ride while her prisoner called all the plays went against everything she'd been taught at WITSEC. Even more frustrating was the way he ignored her, as if he knew she'd never pull the trigger.

At first, she'd been fearful he'd take her to an abandoned warehouse, or maybe a deserted lot in the middle of nowhere, and toss her out of the truck—or worse. Then she figured that maybe he knew what he was doing. It made sense that the mob was after them, and who would know better how to fight the mob than a mobster?

Unfortunately, so far, all he'd done was drive, while his big muscular body took up more space in the front seat than she was comfortable with. If she stared at him for too long, her mind wandered back to their confrontation at the house, which made her cheeks burn and put her heart on stutter alert. Her head ached whenever she recalled how shamelessly she'd participated in that kiss, so she forced herself to concentrate on how poorly she'd done her job.

She'd tried to get him to talk, just to see if she could figure out his plan, but he'd been uncommunicative and sullen for the entire trip. And it was really spooky, the way he kept checking his face in the rearview mirror every few minutes, as if not quite sure he believed what he saw.

If, no, *when* they got to her superiors, she would probably be brought up on a raft of charges: allowing a prisoner to escape, aiding and abetting a fugitive, abandoning her post, failure to adhere to her oath as a federal marshal. . . . Oh, yeah, and let's not forget illegal fraternization with the enemy.

The list was going to be endless.

She sighed. She was in a real bind. She'd sworn to protect Dominic Viglioni, not shoot him. He'd thrown his body over hers when the bullets were flying; he could have gotten rid of her by simply leaving her on that side street in Morristown. If there was any hope of salvaging her career, Annie decided, she had to stay with her charge and see this thing through to the end.

Finally, as if reading her mind, he glanced at her and cleared his throat. "Did you read the last sign? The one that said how many miles until the next rest stop?"

"I don't remember. But exit four is coming up. We'll be in Cherry Hill. Plenty of opportunities to find a gas station there." *And pay phones,* she reminded herself. Plus, she still had to go to the bathroom.

"So we'll stop and fill the tank, maybe get a little dinner. What do you say?"

Annie longed to say *fine, great, yippee,* but a basic fact of their road trip forced her to ask, "Do you have any money?"

The exit loomed up ahead. He swiped a hand across his beard-shadowed jaw. "Crap. Okay, hurry up and check the glove box, take a look under the floor mats and seats. If we're lucky, the owner stashed some change away for a rainy day."

She opened the glove box and dug out a few coins. Lifting her floor mat, she scrounged further. Next, she scrunched down and worked her fingers under the seats, felt something crinkle and pulled out a five-dollar bill. All in all, she'd collected six dollars and seven cents.

They took the off ramp to the toll booth. After paying the toll, Annie figured they barely had enough money left to buy two gallons of gas, never mind a decent dinner. Too bad neither of them had thought to tuck cash or a credit card inside the pocket of their sweats before they'd played ball. They didn't even have a valid driver's license to show the authorities in case they were stopped. No wonder Dominic was being so careful following the rules of the road.

He pulled into a combination convenience store/gas station and drove into a parking space near the front. Before Annie could ask, he brought out the envelope. He'd yet to tell her what was inside, and now she realized why. From the way he stared at the package, he didn't have a clue.

"Well, open it." Keeping her gun in her lap, she turned

in her seat and rose up on her knees. "The suspense is killing me."

Tom swallowed. The envelope was heavy and stuffed to bulging. He'd wracked his brain on the ride, trying to get a handle on how he was supposed to react to their situation—and to Annie. He had no idea why he'd said and done some of the things he had. He'd never hot-wired a car, yet his hands had known exactly which wires to connect. And he'd certainly never had to dodge bullets or run for his life, yet he'd done that expertly as well.

From the moment he'd awakened in Viglioni's body, he'd been experiencing weird, unexplainable urges. The suggestions hadn't been too outrageous, so he'd gone along with them. He just hated when doing so made him look like a fool in front of her, as he was positive he did right now. She'd asked him about the contents of the envelope a half dozen times, and he still didn't have an answer for her.

He ripped at the flap and tore the envelope open. Staring inside, the first thing he saw was a wad of cash bound by a rubber band. *One thousand dollars,* the voice lurking in his brain instructed. That rubber band was wrapped around a thousand dollars in twenty-dollar bills.

"Jeez," muttered Annie. "Why didn't you open it *before* I ruined my manicure digging for all that loose change?"

Since he had no response to her wry comment, he set the money on the dashboard and retrieved a smallish, black leather wallet. The badge mounted on the flap read DEPUTY U.S. MARSHAL. In a compartment behind the badge was a card with Dominic Viglioni's picture—*his picture*—and the vital statistics of one Andrew Falcone.

Holy shit! He was a marshal.

He slapped the flap closed and sucked in air. If he ever saw Milton again, he was going to knock the little doughboy to hell and back for doing this to him. Once again, he hadn't been given all the rules before he'd been forced to make a decision. None of the three choices he'd been given in heaven for a body had been stellar. He thought he'd picked the best of the lot. Obviously, he hadn't. Then he remembered Warren Beavers.

"Is that a badge?" Annie's voice rose an octave. "A U.S. Marshal's badge?"

Tom closed his eyes, thinking hard. He was Andrew Falcone, not Dominic Viglioni. He was six feet tall, had dark brown hair and eyes, and weighed one hundred ninety-five pounds. He wasn't a mobster. He was a federal marshal. Jeez, could his life—make that his *new* life—get any more complicated?

Before he realized it, Annie snatched the wallet from his hands and opened it. He would have hooted out loud at her confused expression if he didn't think his own face mirrored her shock.

"Andrew Falcone? You're a U.S. Marshal, and your name is Andrew Falcone?" She punched his shoulder hard. "You creep. You rotten, low-down snake. What the hell did you think you were doing, dragging me along on this joyride to nowhere—letting me think I'd been kidnapped?" She tucked the Glock in her pocket and furrowed her fingers through her hair. "If I thought I could get away with it, I *would* shoot you. Hell, I should shoot you, just because you put me through so much misery."

"Annie, I—"

"Don't you Annie me." She grabbed at the cash and peeled off a couple of twenties. Opening the door, she glared as she zipped the leather jacket to her throat. "I'm going to the bathroom; then I'm getting a Reese's Peanut Butter Cup—make that two peanut butter cups—then I'm calling my boss. And frankly, I don't care whether you're here or gone when I get back."

Tom sighed. Now what was he supposed to do? He'd just managed to accept the fact he was going to have to live his life as an ex-mobster and a participant of the witness security program; now he had another name—and a different profession. How many surprises could one man handle in a day?

Glancing inside the envelope, he pulled out the remainder of its contents: a couple of ammunition clips, a gun identical to Annie's and a small piece of paper. He unfolded the lined page slowly, scared spitless of the next revelation. But the only thing written on it was a name, Martin Phillips, and a phone number and address in Arlington, Virginia.

Oo-kay. The paper was good. At least he had the name of someone who might be able to shed some light on his predicament.

He raised his gaze and spotted Annie standing in line at the pay phone. Her face a mottled red, she had a soft drink in one hand and a fistful of candy in the other. He was off to a good start at helping her find happiness, all right. After this, she probably wouldn't even get in the truck with him, never mind trust him to help find her soul mate.

He stuffed the bundle of twenties into a pocket of the slicker, picked up the gun and hefted it in his hand, wincing at the way it felt so *right*. He detested violence. It was one of the reasons he'd never agreed to let Annie go to the police academy. People got seriously hurt when they carried a gun. Not that his objections had done much good. The minute he'd gotten himself killed, she'd gone and joined one of the most violent professions on the planet. And thanks to Milton, so had he.

Tucking the gun, extra ammo, badge and paper into the other pocket, he climbed from the truck. He had enough money to fill the tank and buy a pack of smokes. Then he'd work at convincing Annie they had to stay together.

A nondescript black van turned into the parking lot, and his crazy gut instinct kicked in. Snatching up the laptop case, he made a dash for the store and threw a twenty on the counter. Then he rushed to Annie's side and grabbed her elbow just as she said "hello." The receiver dropped to the wall and he pushed her in front of him. He managed to get them to the rear entrance before she screamed.

"Hey! Let go of me, you . . . you fraud."

"Later, doll," he growled, wincing at the word. "Right now it's important we keep moving. They're here."

Annie sat wedged against the passenger side door. She didn't plan on getting any closer to this madman than she had to. Ever since Dominic—make that Deputy U.S. Marshal Andrew Falcone—had hot-wired the bright blue Corvette parked behind the convenience store and careened out of the parking lot, his personality had returned to sullen and self-absorbed.

They'd been followed, or at least that's what he'd told her when they jumped into the sports car. She figured an angel was watching over them, because it could only be an act of God that caused the expensive car to be unlocked and partially hidden by a Dumpster. No one had come running when Dominic—when Andrew Falcone gunned the engine and took off like the 'vette was entered in the Indy 500.

They must have made it out of the lot just as their tail walked in the store, because as far as she could tell, no one was following them now.

They'd crossed into Pennsylvania a few miles back and Annie wondered where they were headed. Tired of being ignored, she decided to demand some answers, but when she turned to confront him, her breath caught in her throat. Even with his rumpled hair, dirty hands and dorky yellow slicker, the man was eye candy. And the two peanut butter cups she'd just sucked down only made her hungry for more.

"So where are we going?" She sat upright in the seat and concentrated on the highway.

"Hm? Oh . . . uh . . . There's a little motel about twenty minutes down the road. I used to go there when . . ." *I sold ad space for the radio?* Nope, that would never do, thought

Tom. He had to start talking and thinking more like this Andrew Falcone guy if he wanted to make a success of his new life. Once he got a handle on why the marshal had been masquerading as a mobster, it would be a whole lot easier living in Falcone's body. Besides, that frustrating voice inside his head told him the motel was the next stop on his trip to Virginia.

Virginia! He heaved a breath and set another piece of the exasperating puzzle that was his life in place. He was heading to Arlington, Virginia, to find the guy whose name was on the slip of paper. Martin Phillips.

"I just know it's there, okay? And it's cheap and quiet. We have to get some rest and regroup. I think we'll be safe for a while."

They rode a little farther, until Annie shouted out, "Stop! Pull over! There's a Wal–Mart."

Tom had never in his life been in a Wal–Mart, but he remembered how Annie had enjoyed shopping at the giant discount chain whenever he was too busy to accompany her. She loved bargains, even though their combined salaries had been enough to buy whatever they needed from the higher priced mall stores.

What would a man like Andrew Falcone, a man who'd been living a cultured and wealthy existence for who knew how long, have to say about shopping in a Wal–Mart?

"Not tonight, doll. Tomorrow we'll go to a real mall and find a more upscale store."

Annie huffed out a sigh. "You sound just like my . . . like someone I used to know. Look, you may be a snob, but I'm not. And I refuse to spend another minute in these bloody clothes when you have a ton of money at your disposal. At least let me get a few essentials, some new sweats and a jacket. This outfit is disgusting."

He had to agree their clothes were rank And it wouldn't kill him to slum a little. He didn't know how much money marshals made, but he was pretty sure that after this fiasco, he'd be back to the daily law enforcement grind. A totally distasteful idea.

"Okay, but just for the essentials. I guess I could use a couple of things myself."

He turned into the lot and they got out of the Corvette.

"Aren't you afraid someone might steal the car?" Annie asked after he'd slammed the door.

Tom shrugged. "It doesn't matter because we're ditching it. The motel's about a half mile away. We can walk." Or maybe they'd steal another car. He was already guilty of grand theft auto times three. Milton had told him he had to lead an exemplary life, but they were in some big-time trouble, so he figured he had a little leeway.

Arching a tawny brow, Annie gazed at him as if he were something she'd just scraped off her shoe, then marched toward the store.

Her uplifted eyebrow was a look he remembered well, one she had used during their marriage to show disapproval without saying a word. He hadn't realized until this second how much he'd missed that raised brow.

Grinning, he snagged the computer and raced to catch up with her. Annie stopped in the store entryway and nodded. "The men's department is over there. I'll meet you back at the registers in about thirty minutes."

Tom grabbed a cart and tried to think like a man on the run—an officer of the law on the run, he corrected. They needed a duffel bag to hold their stuff, something light weight but roomy. He could use a change of clothes and a new pair of sneakers, a high-powered flashlight, batteries, maybe a pocket knife and a couple bottles of water. What else would they need if they were stranded and had to move on foot?

Half an hour later, he rolled his cart to the checkout, inordinately proud of his finds. Annie met him with her own cart, and he waited while the clerk rang her up. She'd bought a mountain of stuff—white cotton underpants, two flimsy-looking bras, an emerald green sleep shirt, navy blue sweatpants and a matching top, a fleece-lined sweat jacket, a trio of plastic-wrapped packages, socks, hairbrush, toothbrush and toothpaste, and enough girly stuff to fill a bucket.

When compared with hers, his purchases looked completely out of sync. The clerk rang up a set of gray sweats, two pairs of heavy duty gloves, two camouflage jackets, one in medium and one in extra large, a flashlight, batteries, pocket knife, nylon rope, first aid kit, canteen, backpack, matches and the best and biggest pair of hiking boots the store sold.

"And a pack of cigarettes." He pointed to a familiar brand.

"Plan on trekking the Swiss Alps?" Annie snapped, eyeing the smokes as the girl loaded their items into plastic bags.

"You never know, doll. You just never know." How could he tell her he'd been guided by the memory of another man's life?

"Hey, Drew. Long time, no see." The buxom woman behind the desk gave him the once-over from blue-shadowed eyes.

Andrew Falcone, or Drew as Annie assumed he was called by those who knew him better, gave the desk clerk an appraising look, and she fought the urge to slap the flirtatious grin off his bad-boy lips.

"Marie. How's business?"

"Oh, 'bout the same, I guess." She passed a registration card over the counter and gave Annie a brittle nod. "One room or two?" she asked, flipping her long, straight black hair off her deeply tanned face.

"One," he responded without glancing Annie's way

Oh, hell. Why hadn't she realized it sooner? Of course they had to share a room. If anyone came gunning for him, she had to be there. Even though Andrew Falcone carried the proper credentials, she couldn't let him out of her sight until she knew for certain he was a fellow deputy.

"I kept an eye on the stuff you left here after your last visit, just like you asked me to," Marie said, taking the three twenty-dollar bills he laid on the counter.

"You did? Oh, well, that's great. Thanks." He set down another twenty. "Uh, where is it?"

"Right where you left it. Here are the keys." She reached deep under the counter and retrieved a set of car keys, then took a room key from a desk drawer and passed both to him. "You know where everything is, so I'll say good night. And if there's anything you want, just call."

They walked out the door, and Annie gazed longingly at the diner in the adjacent parking lot, a typical rectangular, sheet-metal-sided icon of the East Coast highways. Then she noticed the blinking neon sign. Thanks to a string of broken letters, FAMOUS ART'S DINER read F ART'S DI E, which probably described the quality of food served there perfectly. The lack of cars in the parking lot only reinforced her suspicions.

"Let's pick up some sandwiches first," Falcone ordered, heading up the walkway.

Decorated in early seventies boring, Famous Art's booths had red, vinyl-covered seats and stools that ran along a counter, as well as the traditional glass-encased, rotating pastry tower in the entryway. A big-haired waitress with the word *Mimi* embroidered on her impressive chest, and who should have been drawing a pension instead of waiting tables, waved two menus their way, and they followed.

Annie took in the spotless floor and inviting smells, then scanned the plastic-covered tome that passed for a menu. She always wondered how these smallish roadside restaurants managed to make chicken liver omelets, eggplant parmesan, prime rib and every kind of sandwich known to man at all hours of the day and night, but they did. Some of the best diners in the world dotted the highways of Pennsylvania, New Jersey and New York. Maybe she'd judged Famous Art's too soon.

"Hey, Drew. The usual?" Mimi asked, smiling at Falcone.

"Ah . . . sure . . . fine, but no coffee. Just ice water with lemon."

Annie blinked back her surprise. At the safe house, Viglioni—Falcone—had swilled coffee like an addict, and he'd smoked the same way. Why hadn't he lit up on their walk over here? And how often did he come here, with the waitress and night clerk talking to him as though he was a regular?

"For you, miss?"

"Um . . . I'll have the same." She imagined it would be something Italian, which was fine. She was starving.

"You got it." Mimi tucked her pencil in her beehive and sauntered away.

"So." Annie fiddled with her napkin. "Are you going to tell me what this is all about?"

Falcone looked out the window and narrowed his eyes. Then he reached into his slicker pocket and pulled out the pack of cigarettes.

"You're not going to smoke those, are you?" she asked, ignoring the ashtray tucked next to the napkin dispenser.

"No, I'm gonna stick 'em in my ear." Shaking his head, he thrust the cigarettes back in his pocket. "Jeez, what a nudge."

"Thank you. Now, how about telling me what's going on?"

"In good time, doll. All in good time."

Annie huffed out a breath. "You *are* a federal marshal, aren't you? I mean, that much is correct, right?"

He quirked up a corner of his mouth. "This is a fine time to be having second thoughts, Deputy McAllister."

"Where did you go for training?"

"Brunswick, Georgia. Same as you."

"That was too easy. Everyone knows FLETC is where most of the U.S. law agencies train in this country."

"So ask me something harder."

His dare kicked her brain into fourth gear. "How many sit-ups do men have to do to pass the physical?"

"Forty-seven in a minute. The women have to do thirty-eight." He leaned back in the seat and folded his arms, drawing the slicker closer around his massive chest. "You did fifty."

"How do you—? Never mind, I don't want to know." Annie dragged her fingers through her hair. It would be easy to mock up a marshal's badge and ID, but a lot harder to access private records secured at Glynco and Arlington. Either Andrew Falcone was telling the truth or there was a big-time leak in security at the most basic government level.

Mimi brought their waters, his with two lemon wedges perched on the rim, and two plates piled high with pastrami, sauerkraut, Swiss cheese and thousand island dressing on thick slices of rye bread. Annie groaned. "A reuben. I haven't had a reuben in ages."

The waitress set a dish of dill pickles and two containers of coleslaw on the table. Annie picked up her fork and hunkered down, prepared to eat every bite. She hoisted half of the overladen sandwich and made eye contact across the booth in time to see Falcone cutting his reuben into four precise triangles.

"Something wrong?" he asked when he met her stare.

"Um . . . This looks yummy."

"It does, doesn't it?" He picked up a triangle and took a bite with laser white teeth, then threw her a blissful smile.

She shook off the eerie jolt of familiarity. When he didn't drink alcohol, Tom had always ordered water with lemon. And he'd *always* cut his sandwiches into four neat triangles, no matter how messy the middles.

They ate in silence while Annie digested this latest bit of information. Until now, Dominic Viglioni hadn't resembled her dead husband one iota. Andrew Falcone, on the other hand, shared similarities with Tom that made her head spin. Too confused to reason it all out, she chalked it up to fatigue and finished her meal.

Ten minutes later, he pushed his empty plate aside and leaned back in the booth. "You want some dessert?"

No similarity to her dead husband there, Annie told herself. Tom had never let her order dessert of any kind. "No thanks." She dabbed at her lips with the napkin and felt his gaze follow her hands. Refusing to blush, she said, "I'm stuffed."

"Then let's get to our room and that car Marie says she's been guarding."

He tossed a twenty on the table and slid from the booth with their packages and the computer. That was another thing Tom would never have done, Annie thought. He'd always made her carry her own bags. She sighed and told herself it was simply exhaustion that had her thinking of Tom. Nothing more.

"You're cheating."

"I most certainly am not."

Milton sat on the rooftop of Famous Art's Diner with Eloise at his side. He waited until Annie and Tom/Drew disappeared around the corner of the shabby motel before finishing his argument. "You can do whatever you like to make your point, as well you know."

Eloise sniffed. "I cannot. He's not mine anymore. And Andrew Falcone isn't yours."

Milton raised a brow, refusing to comment on her unusual outfit, a pink ballerina's tutu, matching tights and toe shoes. The vain angel loved playing at being human, she'd told him a time or two, mostly because she enjoyed *slumming*. "You could take Tom's soul back. It's in your power to ask Him. I'm sure He'd comply."

Eloise fluffed up her head of golden curls. "But the body would still belong to your human. Andrew Falcone was a favorite of yours, if I remember correctly."

Milton shook his bald head. As angels went, Eloise was one of the most beautiful, and she knew it. Sometimes that was part of the problem in dealing with her. "They belong together, El. They always have. And if Annie had graduated and gone to the police academy, as intended, neither of them would be in this pickle right now."

"But she didn't."

"Because you failed to guide Tom to *his* soul mate."

Eloise concentrated on her fingernails. "Oh, pooh. I've never bought into that claptrap about soul mates, and you know it. Annie said yes to Tom because she was too insecure to stand her ground and refuse him. Your little human was the one who decided the course of her life, Milton. Now it's up to her to recognize she's being given a second chance at happiness and get her life back on track—without our assistance."

Milton's *tsk* reverberated like a gunshot in the quiet evening air. "You are the most unromantic angel God ever created. Can't you see what I'm trying to do here? Andrew Falcone would never have accepted this risky an assignment if he'd met and married Annie Sanders after they graduated from FLETC. Tom stepped in before she was able to get there, and yes, Annie exercised her human right of free will. But Tom was in your charge at the time. You could have guided him toward another woman. Instead, you let him set his mind on Annie, then you gave up on him before he had the chance to do right by her."

He puffed out his chest just to show her it was a matter of pride. "My success ratio is unsurpassed, and I'd like to keep it that way. Annie is mine, and one of *yours* is intricately woven into her life; therefore, you are involved, as well. Besides, you owe it to Tom."

Eloise arched one golden brow.

"Please, El. Work with me here. Let's make a deal."

"You sound like a game show host. And do you really think manipulating the rules is fair?" She drifted skyward, boosted by her anger. "Besides, you no longer owe Andrew Falcone anything. He's with us now." She dropped to the roof with a plop, as if punctuating her statement.

Milton sighed. "I let him down. I should have helped him find another soul mate after Annie accepted her second choice. Getting him together with her now, even if it's only in body, is the least I can do. By using Tom, I'm giving all three of them a second chance and granting Annie her wish at the same time."

"How noble of you." Eloise tossed her head of blond ringlets, then tapped a finger on her chin. "You've certainly gone about it in the strangest way."

"It was all I could think of at the moment. I could use a lighter workload, and you'll get to realign yourself with a soul you gave up on. Thanks to me, you're going to up your own success ratio."

Eloise still looked skeptical, but Milton could tell she was weakening. "Do we have a deal? If Annie and the new Andrew fall in love, will you take on Andrew's soul, which will really be Tom's soul?"

She puckered her lower lip. "I'll go along with the scheme. For the moment. I just wish you'd tell me how you plan to get Tom's spirit and Andrew's body in harmony. From the look of it, the man is completely at a loss."

Milton winked a brilliant blue eye. "Eloise, you are *so* unimaginative. Haven't you ever heard of dreams?"

CHAPTER SEVEN

Located in the wing farthest from the highway, their motel room was isolated from the traffic of passing guests. Annie stood on the walkway and peered through the darkness into the deserted lot that curved toward the roadway on one side and met the parking area on the other. She scanned the strange mixture of discarded tires, scrub trees and abandoned appliances, then watched while Falcone inspected the classic, black Ford Mustang convertible parked in front of their door.

As per training, he slid under the car on his back, obviously on the hunt for an explosive device, then slid back out. Standing, he unlocked the driver's door and got behind the wheel. The motor purred to life and he let it idle while he checked under the front and back seats, then the glove box. After he turned off the engine, he walked to the trunk and opened it. Several seconds passed before she heard his hushed comment.

"Holy shit."

Annie ran to the rear of the Mustang and took a gander

at the inside of the trunk. "That about sums it up. There's enough fire power in there to take down a small country."

Hands on his hips, he continued to stare at the handguns, assault rifles, ammo clips and various stockpiled weapons, including grenades and a launcher. From the confused look on his face, she'd have thought the contents were as much a shock to him as they were to her, which was impossible, seeing as this was his car.

Blowing out a breath, he ran a hand through his disheveled hair, then began to dig. Finally, he pulled out a hard-sided notebook, squinted and thumbed through the pages. Annie wasn't surprised when he closed the book and tucked it inside the pocket of the slicker. The meager light coming from a lone, bug yellow bulb mounted over their door was barely enough to read the room number, never mind a book.

He slammed the trunk, picked up their bags and motioned her ahead of him. She unlocked the door, and he followed her inside.

The motel's standard colors of dull brown, muted red and garish yellow clashed with the faded green plaid bedspread draped over a sagging queen-sized mattress. A round table and two chairs sat under the front window; a credenza holding a small television backed against the wall opposite the bed. The rear of the room consisted of an open closet with a single shelf and rod situated across from a tiny bathroom.

He set their packages next to the bed and turned on the television. "Why don't you use the bathroom first? I'll catch up on the news and take the second shift."

Nodding mutely, Annie tugged off her oversized leather jacket and edged past him, annoyed that he always seemed to take up so much space. The idea he might not be here when she came out crossed her mind, but she pushed it aside. She had a pretty strong suspicion Andrew Falcone really was a marshal, so she didn't think he'd bail. Besides, until they contacted Lou or Bob, she was his only witness to what had happened back in New Jersey. He'd dragged her this far—why would he leave her now?

Picking up the bags holding her new things, she stepped into the bathroom and locked the door. After setting her parcels on the counter, she stared in the mirror. Grimacing at the dried blood matting her hair and streaking down one side of her neck, she peeled off her sweater and thermal undershirt. The blood had soaked all the way through her bra and panties, right down to her skin. Yuck!

From the condition of her clothing, Annie figured Falcone had to be made of iron to have survived. Any other man would have passed out, gone into shock or died from the blood loss, but he'd been operating like the Energizer Bunny for hours. She'd seen a first aid kit in his basket at the checkout stand and made a note to take a look at his wound. While doing so, she had to ask what kind of vitamins he took.

She emptied the bags and arranged her purchases next to the sink. After stuffing her ruined clothes, and that was every stitch she wore, into the largest bag, she set it next to the wastebasket, then turned the shower on hot, gathered her newly purchased bath gel and shampoo and a paper-thin washcloth and stepped into the tub. Steam swirled around her in a cleansing mist. Luxuriating in the warmth, she lathered and rinsed her hair twice, squirted the floral-scented gel onto the cloth and scrubbed until her skin burned.

Annie stepped onto the frayed mat and toweled dry, then set aside the extras she'd bought for her traveling companion: a brand of men's deodorant she was familiar with because it had been what Tom used, a toothbrush and a package of heavy-duty disposable razors. If she remembered correctly, the stuff Drew Falcone had purchased had little to do with personal hygiene and everything to do with trekking through the mountains or holing up in a cabin in the woods. He probably hadn't bothered to buy new underwear, either. At FLETC, she'd heard men joke about *going commando*, but until this moment, she'd never thought any of them actually did. Falcone would either have to rinse out his jockeys and hang them up to dry or go without.

Inspecting her clean self in the mirror, she frowned at the way the risqué thought had caused her to color from hairline to collarbone. That damned kiss on the driveway crept into her brain and she kicked it back out. A vision of Andrew Falcone in nothing but his underwear slowed her to a crawl as she slipped into a long-sleeved sleep shirt that stopped at her knees. She had no right to think about the man in or out of his skivvies. Hell, he could wear the bloody shorts on his head if he wanted. It was no skin off her nose. He just better not try any funny stuff.

Lucky for her she'd thought to buy an item tailor-made for the situation. Digging through her pile, she found the package of insulated thermal underwear, pulled out the leggings and stretched the heavy tights over her feet and up to her waist. Next to a chastity belt or pantyhose, this body armor was probably the best deterrent to unwanted sexual advances ever invented.

If he planned to get *frisky*, he'd have to wrestle her out of skintight long johns to do it.

She dried her hair with one of the room's few amenities, a low wattage blow-dryer, smoothed a dollop of moisturizer on her face, then gathered the mascara, lipstick and other cosmetics into a small zippered bag. Setting the men's toiletries in the middle of the counter, she recalled the last time she'd shared a bed with another human being. Her three-year-old niece had tossed and turned all night.

Tom, on the other hand, had been a cuddler. One of his few endearing habits had been the way he locked his hand with hers and entwined their fingers while they slept. After his death it had taken her quite a while to get used to sleeping without one of her hands held tightly by a warm body, but she'd managed.

The lip lock she and Falcone had engaged in did another

guilty tango back into her brain. The memory of his hard-muscled body and persuasive mouth set her upper lip to sweating and she took a gulp of air. Not only was it unprofessional, it was just plain stupid to be thinking about fraternizing with the man.

Besides, she was still trying to figure him out. One minute he was as annoying as a blister on her heel, the next he acted like a lost little boy struggling to cope with life's more frightening ups and downs. The last thing she needed was a man who bossed her around. Living with Tom had been bad enough. When Falcone played the little-boy-lost role . . . Well, he really tugged at her heart.

Annie drummed her fingers on the counter. She'd used every stall tactic she could think of. It was time to go out there and convince him to talk about the last twelve hours—his mobster act, the shooting and the reason they were on the run—everything. If he tried to get up close and personal again, she could take him down with a fast knee jerk to the groin and a stomp on his instep. It would be the last time he'd try to get fresh.

She opened the door and panned the room, but all she could see was the dim reflection of the television spotlighting a pair of huge male feet. Tiptoeing closer, she gave a thin-lipped sigh. Drew Falcone had taken off his socks and sneakers and fallen asleep fully dressed on top of the spread.

Tom knew he was dreaming, but the Technicolor visions were so satisfying, so informative and insightful, he didn't want to wake up. It was almost as good as watching a home movie of his new life—before he'd been there to experience it.

Standing in a fence-enclosed backyard and dressed in an oversized T-shirt and ratty jeans, he could actually feel the breeze ruffle his hair, smell the scent of wood smoke wafting through the air. The yard was fully equipped for kids with a tree house, swing set and a pair of white, free-standing goal posts he imagined could be used for a half dozen different sports. A flower-lined walkway led to a slate-covered patio crowded with a barbecue grill, picnic table and a raft of bicycles lying on their sides on the cement.

"Andrew! Hey, Drew!" a man shouted. "Heads up."

He looked skyward in time to see a football streaking toward him from the heavens. As Tom McAllister, his parents had never allowed him to play the game, but he knew in a heartbeat Andrew Falcone would be a natural. Jumping straight up, he caught the ball and began to run—directly toward a string of laughing boys, all a lot bigger and older than he seemed to be, shouting encouragement as if he were a puppy retrieving a stick.

"Come'n get me, squirt."

"Hey, short-stuff, try and pass me."

"That's the way, little brother. Give it your best shot."

Instinctively, he faded right, then left, dodging Joey's playful slap on his behind, then Sal's quasitackle, Anthony's waggling fingers and, finally, Rob's shuffle and slide. His lungs bursting, Tom ran joyfully into his father's arms. Only this wasn't his stern-faced banker father, but a big, smiling man with arms the size of tree trunks and a chest as broad as a front door.

"There's my boy," Vincent Falcone said with a booming laugh, swinging Tom in a circle.

His brothers gathered round and started roughhousing, pushing and shoving until all six men fell to the ground in a tangle of arms and legs. Tom—no, he was Drew now—thought he would smother at the bottom of the pile, until his dad stood and settled the boys down.

"That's enough for today, fellas. I have to get to the precinct. Joey, you have an exam to study for. You, too, Sal. Tony, the front yard needs mowing; Robbie, it's your turn to do the back."

"What about me, Pop?" Drew asked, following his father inside the white frame house.

"You?" Vincent turned and hung his jacket on a hook in the mudroom. "Well, let's see. The towels need to come out of the dryer, then you could load the dishwasher."

"But-but that's girl stuff," Drew answered, rubbing a grimy knuckle under his nose. The last thing he wanted was to appear childish in front of this larger-than-life man.

Reaching down, Vincent Falcone tugged at his youngest son's hair. "It's things your mom, may she rest with the angels, would have done if she were still with us, Drew. And remember, everything Sophia did was important. You're only eight. Next summer you can start mowing the lawn, I promise."

His father walked away, taking with him the comforting aroma of leather and cigars. Tom glanced around the cluttered room, so different from the massive, sterile kitchen he'd grown up in when he'd had his other life. No sign of a cook here, no cleaning woman, either. This kitchen smelled like spaghetti sauce and chocolate chip cookies. It was the kind of kitchen he'd always wished for, and the type of family he'd once dreamed of having for his own.

He sat at the table and closed his eyes. He had brothers—lots of older brothers. And a father who thought he was a great kid. Okay, so his new mom had died before he'd had the chance to know her, but she sounded like the kind of mother who would have tucked him in bed at night and made his school lunch every morning. She sounded like a mom who would have loved him.

He heard a noise at the back door and raised his head. "Hey, short-stuff." It was Anthony, five years older and a freshman in high school. "Want to help with the front lawn? Maybe I'll let you steer the mower. Would you like that?"

Drew shot to his feet. "Oh, boy. Yeah! Just give me a minute. I promised Dad I'd empty the dryer." Racing to do the simple chore, his heart lightened in his chest. He had a real family now, and people who cared.

Annie inhaled. Her nostrils filled with the scent of warm, musky male along with something foreign and unpleasant. Though the bed was lumpy, she didn't mind, because she was cradled from behind by a body that made her feel safe and secure. Wiggling her bottom into the heat, she was content to lie quietly for a few more minutes. If only the nasty smell would go away.

Blinking, she opened her eyes and gazed down at a big masculine hand resting just under her breasts with its long blunt-tipped fingers entwined in her own. It took her a few seconds to remember who she was with before she decided the scenario was too spooky for words—and certainly not something her superiors would tolerate.

Last night, after she'd found Falcone fast asleep on top of the covers, she hadn't bothered to wake him. His back had been to her side of the bed, so, exhausted, she'd crawled underneath the blankets and closed her eyes. She didn't remember a thing until a minute ago.

His deep, even breathing tickled the nape of her neck, zapping the pit of her stomach with a sizzle of desire. Something hard and hot prodded the back of her thighs, and the shock of it reminded her she'd felt the rigid body part before. She was in trouble again, and the day had barely started.

One by one, Annie tugged her fingers free of his grip. Trying to extricate herself from his arms, she inched to the edge of the bed, but it didn't work. Instead of moving away, she found herself held tighter, with his hand covering the mound of her breast. Her nipples peaked and throbbed under his searching fingers. Before she knew it, she was pinned on her back while he stared intently into her face.

"Going somewhere, Deputy McAllister?" he asked, his voice a rough, sleep-sexy growl.

Annie shoved at his shoulders. "Yes. Away from you."

His gaze slid to her lips, drifted toward the palm cupping her breast, then moved on to their lower extremities, still nestled together close as spoons in a drawer. One corner of his mouth twitched as he completed his assessment. "Sorry, guess I got a little territorial."

"Just like a man," she shot back. Struggling in his arms, she refused to meet his eyes. "If you don't mind—"

His expression sharpened as his breath hitched. Without a word, he rolled to his back, and Annie heaved a sigh. The intimate contact had been too close, too . . . dangerous for her to keep a level head. After swinging her legs over the side of the mattress, she stumbled to her feet and went into the bathroom to take care of business. She brushed her teeth, washed her face, puttered with her cosmetics, anything to get her mind off of the idea that he had the same sappy habit as her dead husband. But those strong fingers entwined with hers, that hovering mouth and his impressive, prodding erection, were hard to ignore.

Dressed in her new sweats and sneakers, she finally felt composed enough to face him. Walking back into the bedroom, she found him digging through his bag of goodies. Settling her gaze on the floor, she sidled to the table and chairs under the window and took a seat.

"Guess I'd better toss these clothes and take a shower," he said, still searching the bags. "When I come out, we can go to the diner for breakfast . . . or you can go without me and get a table. There might be something in the newspaper about us . . . um . . . being on the run. See if you can find a *Star Ledger* or New York paper."

Annie stood. "Us? On the run?"

"Yeah. Guess I fell asleep last night before I got the chance to tell you." Juggling his shoes, a Wal-Mart bag and whatever else he needed, he straightened and made his way to the bathroom. "We were on the news. It seems Dominic Viglioni escaped protective custody yesterday.

According to an *unidentified government source,* one of the marshals assigned to guard him helped him get away.''

Tom sauntered into the bathroom to the sound of Annie's howl. He heard her stomping footsteps, the creaking of bed springs and the slamming of the door interspersed with a few interesting and unladylike comments on his character. When the heck had she developed that temper? And where had she learned to curse like a sailor on shore leave?

He upended his bag, rested his palms on the edge of the sink and took the opportunity to fully check himself out in the mirror. He wasn't upset that his face resembled one of the better looking characters from *The Godfather,* but it did unnerve him. If what he'd heard was true, that most women had the hots for tall, dark and handsome, he'd have babes flocking to his side like squirrels to peanuts. But unless he could get used to the five-o'clock shadow, he would need to shave twice a day to stay well groomed.

Heaving a breath, he took off his ruined sweats and shorts. But when he tried to remove his undershirt, the fabric stuck to him as if it had been painted on. Worried about what he might find, he peeled the shirt down slowly. Under the dusting of dark chest hair, about five inches below his collarbone and slightly to the left of center, he spied a small, pink-colored slit surrounded by dried blood. The realization that the bullet had probably been a direct hit to his heart made his stomach churn.

Tearing his gaze from the wound, he inspected his broad shoulders covered in a formidable layer of muscle, which tapered over his ribs and trailed down to washboard abs, a trim waist and a . . .

Tom stepped back from the counter and gave a soft whistle of appreciation. Holy God and thank you, Milton. He'd been too preoccupied to notice yesterday, and too darned tired

last night to bother inspecting his new *equipment*. It was
... he was ... Well, to put it crudely, he was *hung*.

He stared in awe, then turned sideways and back again.
Finally, he put his back to the mirror and screwed his head
over his shoulder to check out the view from the rear. Damn,
if it wasn't just as good. Impressed with the new, better-
than-average body, he decided this crazy job might actually
be worth it if it kept him in such stellar shape.

And call him crazy, but, if the heat he'd felt burning off
of her a few minutes ago had been real, he was fairly certain
Annie had shown serious interest in this body. Maybe, when
this little project was over, they could take a long vacation
together or—

He shook his head, dismissing the dumb idea. There was
no longer any more *they,* and there never would be. Even
if the move he'd made on her earlier was something they'd
both wanted, he shouldn't have done it. Milton had told him
his job was to find her the perfect man, and he was fairly
certain the angel hadn't meant Andrew Falcone. He sighed.
He'd already failed with Annie once in a lifetime; he didn't
need to make the same mistake twice. His me-Tarzan-you-
Jane act was simply that of a healthy, normal male who'd
found himself in the same bed with a beautiful woman.

Ignoring the sudden craving for a cigarette, he closed his
eyes and tried to envision the Annie he'd been married to,
thinner with straight, champagne blond hair and a quirky-
yet-joyful attitude. He'd been attracted to her in college
mostly because she'd been so different from his stick-
figured, poker-faced mom. So why had he tried to make her
fit that mold after they'd married?

His hands itched at the way she looked now, with softly
curling, spun gold hair, fuller breasts and flaring hips. Damn,
if he couldn't still hear the way her breath came out in little
gasps when he touched her soft-as-sin skin, couldn't still
feel her nipple burning a hole in his palm.

Unfortunately, the new Annie also had the demeanor of

a N.O.W. member on steroids. If he didn't know better, he'd think she'd undergone a personality transplant. As a young widow, she'd been forced to redesign her life. He couldn't help but wonder if she'd mourned after he died. More than likely, she'd done the happy dance because she'd been lucky enough to lose her egotistical, controlling jerk of a husband.

But hadn't she missed him, just a little?

He concentrated on the array of personal care articles lined soldierlike next to the sink. His favorite deodorant stared up at him, and the idea that Annie had remembered something so insignificant yet so personal ate at his insides.

With his brain on overload, he could barely focus, never mind try and figure out his reaction to a woman who was no longer his wife and would soon, thanks to him, belong to another man. He had to get a grip, shave, shower and brush his teeth. No wonder she'd looked so grim when she'd found herself butted up against him first thing this morning. He smelled like the chimpanzee house at the Bronx Zoo.

Thoughts coiled in his mind like a snake about to strike. He was still a law enforcement agent on the lam from an unknown killer or killers. Why had Andrew Falcone been impersonating a mobster? Who had shot him? Someone in the marshals' office had given out a bogus press release. Why had the TV reporter made it sound as if he and Annie were in cahoots with each other? Who was Martin Phillips?

He hopped into the shower and let the hot water sluice over his aching muscles. Working up a lather with the soap, he shaved as he pondered. Yesterday, he'd followed a driving urge to open the trunk and find a notebook, which at first glance looked to be some kind of diary of the first steps Falcone had taken as a mobster. Right now, it was all he had to go on. He needed to read the notebook and memorize everything he could about the man. Then pray that muscle memory thing lasted long enough for him to get them out of this mess so he could start helping Milton fulfill his promise to Annie.

He toweled off and sifted through his new wardrobe looking for more than sweats, hiking boots and socks. Well, hell. He didn't have any underwear. Now what was he supposed to do? Wrapping the towel around his waist, he headed out to do another search of his bags. He couldn't have forgotten something so important. Tom McAllister *always* wore briefs and a pristine white T-shirt under his clothes.

He opened the door to find Annie engrossed in a newspaper, eating her breakfast at the table. She gave him a sideways glance, then went back to reading, but he didn't miss the bright red blush that raced across her cheeks.

"So, you found a paper?" *Duh, Tom, why don't you say something really stupid for a change.*

"I walked to the Wal–Mart for a *Star Ledger*. On the way back I picked up breakfast from Art's. Mimi had the kitchen fix your usual, whatever that means, and make it to go."

"Uh . . . thanks." Tom suddenly realized he was practically bare-assed naked and grinned. Common sense told him he should go into the bathroom and, jockeys or no jockeys, slip on those sweats, but his body was telling him something entirely different, almost as if he had an angel on one shoulder and a devil on the other. He was supposed to be Andrew Falcone, a tough-talking, street-smart Federal Marshal with an overabundance of guts and a treasure trove of secrets, so maybe it was time he started acting that way.

He hitched up the towel and took a seat. Opening the Styrofoam container, he took a long look at the cholesterol overload—crispy hash browns, fried eggs and bacon, all cooked in grease, with a side of toast slathered in butter. Picking up the plastic fork, he attacked the food. "What are you having?"

Annie eyed him from over the rim of the paper. "A poached egg, dry whole wheat toast and herbal tea."

"Sounds tasty," he said, remembering that was what he'd insisted they eat on weekend mornings when they were together. He scooped up another forkful of eggs and hash browns. He'd been such a putz.

"Listen to this," she muttered, and began to read out loud. "In a daring and what authorities expect was a well-thought-out plan, government witness Dominic Viglioni and his accomplice, Deputy U.S. Marshal Anne McAllister, escaped yesterday from the hideaway provided by the Witness Security Program, formally known as WITSEC. A gray Ford Taurus used in the escape was found abandoned on a side street in Morristown, where it is believed they stole a second vehicle. Authorities now suspect they are headed south in a late model, metallic blue Corvette with New Jersey license plate *blah-blah-blah*.

"Viglioni is six feet tall and weighs one hundred ninety-five pounds, with dark brown hair and eyes. His accomplice and suspected lov—" Annie cleared her throat. "Deputy McAllister has dark blond hair, hazel eyes and weighs one hundred and—"

She glared over the top of the paper. "Never mind that part. Listen to this. The U.S. Marshals' Service asks that the public call the number listed below if they have reason to believe they have seen the suspects and advise they do not try to apprehend. Both Viglioni and McAllister are assumed to be armed and dangerous."

Tom finished his eggs, then took a sip of his coffee.

"Well?" Annie crushed the paper to her chest.

"Well what?" he asked, trying to give the impression he knew what he was doing.

"Didn't you hear what I just read? There's a manhunt in progress for Dominic Viglioni and his moll. That's me, in case you didn't get the gist of the article. What the hell have you gotten me into?"

CHAPTER EIGHT

Annie waited while Drew took his time to answer. Picking up a slice of crispy bacon, he bit off half and offered her the rest, as if he hadn't heard her question. "Put a little fat in your system, McAllister. It'll grease the wheels and help get your brain in gear."

She blew out an angry breath. "Right along with turning my hips into cottage cheese and clogging my arteries? No, thanks, I think I'll pass. Besides, I want to live long enough to have children. Now, about this article—"

He closed the Styrofoam container and pushed it aside. "It'll be old news by tomorrow. Don't worry about it." Before she could manage a reply, he said, "So, you and your husband were planning to have kids?"

"I don't believe that's any of your business, Mr. Falcone."

His expression turned smug. "It's Drew, remember? And it looks like we're going be together for a while. If we don't find a variety of topics to talk about, we're going to have to figure out something else to do with our time. Something that won't require a lot of words.''

A flutter of warmth spiraled to her cheeks. The irritating bozo was referring to their kiss on the basketball court and the way they'd awakened earlier, but she wasn't about to travel that dangerous road. They had plenty of things to discuss. The *Star Ledger* story and television news update were only the beginning.

Leaning back, she folded the paper and smacked it down in front of her. ''Get your mind out of the gutter and pay attention. I want some answers to what's been going on, and I want them now.''

''Or . . . ?'' He rested his elbows on the table and gave her a look that screamed *I dare you.*

''Or I call my supervisor.'' Never one to back down from a bluff, she rose to her feet and headed for the phone sitting on the nightstand.

Quick as lightning, he grabbed her upper arms from behind. Pulling her hard against his chest, he breathed into her ear. ''Not a good idea, Annie.''

''Let go of me.''

He snaked his arms around her middle and clasped his hands under her breasts, lifting her off the floor. ''It's too soon to tell your supervisor anything.''

A jolt of electricity sizzled from her stomach to her toes and back again. She struggled, then remembered his superior strength and went limp in his arms. There was no way she could outmaneuver him in this position, even with her training.

''What's that supposed to mean?''

He loosened his hold, and she slid down his body. When her feet hit the carpet, he turned her in his arms. ''It means that right now I don't know who to trust. Everyone is a suspect.''

Not willing to meet his penetrating gaze, Annie closed her eyes. ''Stop trying to confuse me. Suspected of what?''

"Of what happened at the house. The ambush."

She gave a laugh of disbelief. "Get real. Marshals don't shoot other marshals. Besides, Deputy Fielding is a highly regarded professional. From what I could tell, so is Lou."

"And Butterworth—or Donovan? How about them? This is your first WITSEC assignment. How well do you really know your fellow deputies?"

She worked her hands up between them and pushed at his chest. "I don't have to know them personally to know they're on the up and up."

"Ow! Hey! Go easy on the merchandise, would you?"

"Easy on the—" Annie inched back and stared at his chest. "Oh, my God!" Tentatively, she placed a finger just below his breastbone. "That's—Does it—Oh, my God."

Shaking his head, he tugged her hand away and raised it high. "It's fine. I'm fine."

"But-but it's almost healed." She couldn't take her eyes off the near-death wound, now a small gash that looked days old and well on the mend. "I don't understand."

His chin turned to granite. "What's to understand? I'm a quick healer, that's all."

Annie covered her lips with the tips of her fingers. He'd been acting and moving so normally, she'd completely forgotten about his wound. "No, that's not *all*. You were shot less than twenty-four hours ago." She couldn't resist reaching out and touching him again. "I knew you'd lost a lot of blood; I mean, there was so much of it. Now that I have a better view, I can see the bullet went—I mean it looks like it went straight into your—"

"Use your head, McAllister. That would be impossible, now, wouldn't it?" After releasing his hold on her wrist, he turned and started rummaging through the bags. "I should get dressed, then I have some reading to catch up on."

Annie opened and closed her mouth at the sight of an identical pink slit marring his muscular back. How could the bullet have passed straight through him . . . through his heart ... and not done a lick of damage? Impossible was right.

Unwilling to believe her eyes, she stepped to the bed and whipped open a different bag, pulling out the first aid kit. "Sit down and let me have a look."

Drew ignored her and continued to search his own bag, until she jerked it away and tossed it on the floor.

"For cryin' out loud, McAllister, give it a rest." He made a grab at the first aid kit, and she shoved him hard with her free hand. Landing on the mattress with a thump, he glared up at her. "I said it was nothing."

Annie tossed the kit onto the bed, snapped open the plastic lid and pulled out a tube of ointment, a bottle of antiseptic and a variety of sterile bandages sealed in packets. "Sit still. Even though it's healing, it needs to be protected. If it rubs against your sweatshirt, it might get infected. Turn around."

He did as she asked and waited, wincing when she touched his back with something cold and wet. That task accomplished, she automatically moved to stand between his spread knees. After pouring a small amount of antiseptic onto a fresh pad, she dabbed at the one-inch gash.

"Ouch! That stings."

"Don't be such a baby."

He drew his eyebrows together until they met at the bridge of his nose. "You're a sadist."

"In your dreams." She tossed the pad on the night table, then opened the tube of ointment and ran a white line of cream over the wound. "This stuff should feel pretty good. It's cool and it contains a topical pain reliever."

He grunted.

Resisting the urge to smile, she began to hum a tuneless and purposefully annoying ditty as she did the same to the slit on his back.

"You're enjoying this, aren't you?"

"Sure. I like pulling the legs off grasshoppers, too. Now hold still while I anchor the dressing in place."

Annie opened another sterile packet, set a cotton pad over the wound and began to methodically wrap a gauze strip around his chest and up over one shoulder. Suddenly aware of their intimate position, she started to tremble. His skin, like satin-covered steel, felt burning hot under her fingers. His breath fluttered at her breast, his lips so close all he had to do was move forward and set his mouth on—

Her stomach dropped like it did whenever she rode a roller coaster at the amusement park. Until now, she'd been doing a pretty good job of ignoring his nearly naked body. Despite the bullet wound, the sight of his hard-muscled chest brought to mind a dozen *Playgirl* expressions, *hubba-hubba*, *yowza* and *holy moly* being the most repeatable, along with *cut*, *ripped* and *built*. No doubt about it, the man was trouble with a capital T.

Resting her hands on his shoulders, she gazed down and got a good view of his towel, now raised to the size of a pup tent by his arousal. This would be the perfect time for the floor to open up and swallow her whole.

Tom kept his hands fisted on his knees and reminded himself of all the reasons he shouldn't touch her, never mind let Annie touch him. But there was only so much torture a man could endure. Her fingers shook as they touched his skin, cool and soft as the wings of a butterfly. Memories of the way they'd made love in his other lifetime came rushing into his brain, as fresh and alive as if they'd occurred yesterday. The way she had tasted on his tongue, the heat of her desire all left him weak.

Annie may have been less than thrilled with him as a husband, but he'd bet his last nickel she'd never been unhappy with his performance in bed. And he'd been more than satisfied with hers. Remembering how she had writhed against him in passion and called out his name when she climaxed in his arms vibrated deep in his soul.

Slowly, he raised his hands and placed them around her waist.

Her voice was a breathy sigh. "What are you doing?"

"Touching you."

"Don't. Please."

He moved his fingers upward, until they rested under her breasts, then he cupped her, holding their firm weight in his palms. She felt womanly and so perfect he ached inside. Why had he ever wanted her thin and sticklike, when he could have enjoyed all this bountiful female flesh?

"This isn't a good idea," she said on a groan.

She stood statue still with her hands on his shoulders, but it wasn't enough. He wanted them skin to skin, muscle to muscle, bone to bone.

Carefully, he slid his palms down and under her sweatshirt, felt the silky smoothness of her stomach and the slight tremor of her body under his hands. She wanted him as much as he wanted her.

He raised her shirt and leaned forward, nuzzling at her breast through the flimsy fabric of her bra. She sighed and melted against him, her hands clutching at his neck, moving into his hair.

"Drew . . ."

The simple word hit Tom like a slap, freezing him in place. Annie wanted Andrew Falcone. He was the guy she was trembling for, the man who made her go soft as a marshmallow—not Tom McAllister, her jerk of a dead husband.

Deliberately, he tugged her sweatshirt back in place, then took her hands and set them at her sides. "You're right. This isn't a good idea."

With bright color shading her cheeks, she took a step back and crossed her arms over her chest. "I . . . um . . . You said you had to do some reading? Are you talking about that notebook you found in the trunk of the Mustang?"

"Yeah. But first I have to finish getting dressed." He walked to the bathroom without a backward glance.

* * *

Alone in the motel room, Tom worried the unlit cigarette clamped between his lips as he stretched out on the bed. With his head propped against two pillows, he studied the notebook he'd found under the cache of weapons. Surprisingly, it read even better than he thought it might—neither a ledger nor a list, but a diary Falcone had begun when he'd first gone under cover almost four years earlier.

By reading it, he could piece together the steps that had led him to this point. Talk about tracking a mouse through a maze. But Falcone had documented his movements so well, even a first-year deputy could follow them. There was only one problem. Instead of names, he'd developed a code for the cast of characters involved. Without the key to the code, Tom was afraid he wouldn't be able to put all the pieces together.

At first, Drew referred to someone named Papa Bear; then he talked about the Big Bad Wolf. There was no Mama Bear, but there was a Baby Bear; and every once in a while a reference to Goldilocks. He'd even seen the name Peter Pan come up once or twice. Either the guy had a misplaced crush on the Brothers Grimm, or he was a little kid at heart.

He thought back to the discussion he'd had with Annie, at breakfast and later, when she'd nursed what was left of his bullet wound. More and more, he found himself lost in the words and actions of Drew Falcone. More and more, *he* was becoming the marshal, not the other way around. Tom knew it made sense, seeing as he was the one who had to meld with his new body and its life, but it was still weird, doing and saying things that were so foreign.

From her reaction to Falcone's come-ons, he was pretty sure Annie liked the guy—probably a whole lot more than she should. If only he could find some way to talk with Milton and find out how he was expected to handle this attraction they had for each other.

He sighed. It was a living hell being the only one who knew the whole story without having anyone to confide in. Other than Annie, the only family he had left on the planet were his parents, who'd retired to Florida the year before he died. Not only wouldn't they believe he was back, they'd never claim a son with such a plebian career as a law enforcement officer.

Nope, he was alone in his misery. He had to adjust to his new body and stay focused. He had to figure a way to get them out of this mess, then set to work at finding the perfect man for Annie. Whether he liked the idea or not.

Immersed in his thoughts, the realization that someone was outside his door barely had time to register. Then he heard it, one knock, a second of hesitation, and two more raps. He jumped from the bed and slid the dead bolt, grabbed Annie by the wrist and dragged her inside. She fell into the room, and he caught her in his arms.

"Smooth move, Falcone," she muttered, righting herself.

"Sorry. What the heck took you so long?"

Annie held up an overstuffed paper sack with a popular fast food logo on the side and placed it on the table, then set down a second bag holding drinks. "After watching you eat breakfast, I figured you needed regular feedings, kind of like the gorillas at the zoo, so I stopped to pick up lunch."

The twinkle in her eyes caught him off guard. If he didn't know better, he'd think she was flirting. He frowned. "Where's the stuff I asked you to buy?"

She walked back to the door, opened it and dragged another large Wal–Mart bag into the room.

"Is that everything?"

Annie smiled. "I got what I thought we'd need. Of course, the choices were limited. If I'd been able to get to a Target or K–Mart, I could have done some comparison shopping."

"It wasn't supposed to be a shopping spree, doll. And you know you can't take the car. If the mob or someone in the Marshals' Service is on to me, the Mustang is a dead giveaway.''

"Maybe so,'' said Annie. She sat at the table and began to distribute the food. ''But sooner or later, we're going to have to leave this place. Then what?''

Good question. Tom crossed to the chair opposite her and sat down. He took the cigarette from his mouth and gave it a long look, then broke it in half and tossed it into one of the empty sacks. ''I'm not sure yet.''

Annie watched him say goodbye to the smoke, her eyes bright. Without a word, she handed him a double burger with cheese, then pushed a bag of fries across the table. "So, after lunch you're going to tell me everything, right? That was the deal.''

He had promised her before she left that if she ran a few errands, he would tell her why he'd been under cover. In the two hours she'd been gone, he'd had just enough time to piece together a plausible story. ''Yeah. I guess I can trust you.''

Annie opened her mouth, then snapped it shut. Her hazel eyes turned as wary as a treed cat's. ''Trust me? How do I know I can trust you? Other than that badge you had stashed in the bus locker, there's no proof you're a marshal. Even the newspapers say you're Dominic Viglioni. And it makes perfect sense that the guys chasing us work for that mafia boss you ratted out. Not the government.''

He had to agree she made a valid point. ''Look, what if I told you something personal about yourself, something only someone from the marshals' department would know? Would that make you believe I am who I say I am?''

She swallowed a mouthful of grilled chicken sandwich, then took a sip of diet soda. ''Were you spying on me— before I took this assignment?''

It only made sense that Andrew Falcone had known in advance Annie would be at the safe house. Otherwise, how else had he been able to repeat the stats she'd racked up at Glynco so easily? But why?

"You graduated third in your class of fifty-two, and you ran the mile and a half at close to the men's qualifying rate, fastest woman on the track."

Tapping the tabletop for emphasis, she sneered. "It's in the records, fella. Anyone who had a spy in the department could have obtained that fact."

Oo-kay. Tom hated cheating, but he had to get her to believe in him for the success of the mission and their safety. If Annie had been chosen specifically for this assignment, as he suspected, Falcone had to have known everything about her from the get-go.

"You have a sister named Julie. You took care of her from the time you were twenty and your parents died in a boating accident."

As if deflated, Annie's shoulders sagged and her eyes grew dim. "That's confidential information. It's supposed to be locked away in my personal file in Arlington, nowhere else."

"I made it my business to investigate each of the deputies assigned to this case thoroughly, *before* I agreed to go to that safe house."

"But—but it was my first WITSEC assignment. You didn't think I was one of the people you were after . . . one of the traitors? Did you?"

"Of course not," Tom said without thinking. There went that muscle memory thing again, weaving its way from his brain to his mouth before he could think. He took another bite of his burger.

"Maybe you should start from the beginning," Annie suggested dryly, picking at her fries. "And take your time. We've got all afternoon."

Uh-huh, sure, thought Tom. *If I knew where the beginning began.*

* * *

"Would you please hold still," Annie ordered. Her glove-covered fingers worked the water through Drew's hair, rinsing until it flowed crystal clear into the sink. For the past hour, she'd been working off her frustration by dying the big jerk's head of rich brown hair. Until she'd met him, she'd never known anyone so adept at dancing around, under and behind a topic without actually taking a step. "Okay, have a seat. It's time for the final process."

Drew had promised her answers, but she still only managed to wheedle bits and pieces of his story. He'd been so vague, all she knew for certain was that he planned on leading whoever was after them on a wild goose chase of a ride so that he could lure the bad guys into revealing themselves. Once he had a good idea of who he was dealing with, he was going to find a way to get them to Arlington, where someone he was working with in the marshals' office would help arrange a confrontation.

Drew sat on the commode and she gave him a towel, which he used to dry his hair. "That stuff stinks to high heaven. Why the hell do you females put up with all this crap? And how come you had to put that glop on my head so many times?"

"It takes a lot of bleaching to get hair as dark as yours ready to accept the dye." Annie took the towel and tossed it onto the counter. "And we put up with it because some of the more deluded members of the female gender think they have to go to any length to attract the male of the species. Stupid, huh?"

He shrugged. "I take it you don't subscribe to that theory?"

"Not any more." Moving to the second step, she removed the packet of color from the box, opened it and squeezed the contents onto his head, then used her hands to distribute the creamy concoction. Finally, she combed the dye evenly through his hair.

He winced when she hit a snag, and she *tsk*ed. "Like I said earlier, you are such a baby. First you complain about a little sting; now you're whining about a smell. How did you make it through training?"

Drew stared up at her, his expression mutinous, and she pursed her lips to halt her smile. She'd bleached out his hair to white and was almost finished applying the color, a soft, buttery blond, the exact shade Tom had always insisted she wear. With Drew's tan complexion and ebony eyes, the effect was going to be striking.

She removed the plastic bag from the box, wrapped it over his hair and clipped it in place, warning herself not to laugh. "This has to sit and process. While we're waiting, go out and try on the clothes I bought."

He slung the towel around his neck, then rose from the commode. The bathroom suddenly became as crowded as a coffin and Annie stepped back to give him room. Frowning at himself in the mirror, he stalked past her and she breathed a sigh of relief. This situation was becoming dangerous, for more than the obvious reason.

While she'd worked on his hair, Falcone had filled her in on the case. He'd gone under cover several years ago, not specifically to infiltrate the mob, but to smoke out a traitor in the Federal Marshals' Department. He'd done his job so convincingly, he'd been given a position of authority by a mob boss in training. When the man rose to a position of power, he'd taken Drew along for the ride. In the meantime, Drew had narrowed down the search for the traitor to one of four men: Fielding, Smithers, Butterworth and Donovan. The only way he could spring a trap on all four at once was to get arrested, rat out his boss and have the deputies assigned to the same safe house. They'd needed one more marshal to complete the team, and Falcone had chosen her.

She still wasn't sure why she'd gotten the assignment, because Drew skirted the question every chance he could, but she had her suspicions. She was new to WITSEC and hadn't had time to do anything subversive. She was low on the totem pole and unfamiliar with any information sensitive enough to warrant attention from the mob. And she was a woman. He'd probably figured he could wrap her around his little finger.

The idea that she might have been used set her anger to simmering. Had he studied all three of the deputies and decided she was the easy mark, the one marshal he could manipulate and turn into a willing accomplice? Yes, he'd been the one to suggest the basketball game, but the leg irons were her idea.

Then again, if the mob guys had the house under surveillance, it was merely a matter of him coming out in the open. But why would he make himself such an easy target?

She plopped onto the commode cover and sighed. The idea was impossible. Still, it could have been Butterworth or Donovan who did the shooting . . . even Lou. She and Falcone had been a little too *involved* just before the sniper had attacked to know exactly when Lou had left the porch. And what if Bob Fielding had only *said* he was going to bed?

Lost in thought, Annie raised her gaze and found Drew standing in the doorway, wearing tight-fitting, stone-washed jeans and a green-and-gold-plaid flannel shirt stretched tight over his broad shoulders. Like an obedient little boy, he still had the plastic bag wrapped turban-style on his head. She suppressed a giggle.

''What's so funny?''

She inhaled, ruminating on the idea that he might have intentionally used her to his advantage. She'd been known to follow her instincts a time or two, and enlist the aid of a few of her own unsuspecting coworkers, but this scenario smacked of a setup. She didn't usually jump to conclusions, but he was giving her no choice.

"Oh, nothing," she said brightly, knowing what she had in store for him. "Come on, kneel down and stick your head over the sink. It's time to check the masterpiece."

Grumbling to himself, Drew did as he was told. Annie rinsed, shampooed and rinsed again, after which she slapped another towel on his head and maneuvered him back to the commode. Then she took the scissors from the counter.

"What the heck are those for?" he asked, one brow raised warily.

The glimmer of terror she saw in his eyes almost made the confusion of the past thirty-six hours worth it. "You were the one who decided we needed disguises, and this is yours. Your hair is too long, so I'm going to trim it."

He didn't protest when she rubbed his head with the towel, then picked up the comb and positioned herself between his thighs. Now was probably not the best time to tell him the last thing she'd trimmed had been the hedges in the backyard of the house she'd shared with Tom.

"Do you know what you're doing?"

Oops!

"Just sit still. If you keep wiggling around, I refuse to be responsible." The heat from his body started to steam up the tiny room, and Annie realized that once again, she'd managed to get too close to him. His potent masculine scent mingled with the smell of the shampoo; his shoulders rippled whenever he moved on the seat.

Flustered by her wayward thoughts, she clipped and snipped as if she were on speed. Before she knew it, she was seeing a bit too much scalp. She stifled another giggle, fearful the next one would come shooting out of her like Old Faithful.

"I don't like the sound of your breathing, McAllister. What's going on up there?"

"Oh, nothing." She pressed down on a burly shoulder.

"Just hang on a minute. I don't want you to look without the full effect." She set down the scissors and reached for the jar of extra-strength hair gel she'd bought on sale. He shifted in place and she bit her lower lip. "Stay still. I'm almost through."

After working the gel into his hair, she grabbed the blow-dryer and began to hum.

"I know that song," he shouted over the buzz of the dryer.

Okay, so he recognized "I Feel Pretty" from *West Side Story*. He was into show tunes. Perfect. Before he could move, she turned off the dryer, picked up a pair of silver hoop earrings, the kind with a magnetic backing, and slapped one onto his right earlobe.

"That's it." Drew jumped up and shoved her aside. Whirling to the mirror, he gasped. "Holy hell, McAllister! I look like a flamin'—This was supposed to be a disguise, not an ad for Gay Pride Week."

Annie bent over and began to laugh. She stumbled out of the bathroom and rolled onto the bed, finally giving in to the hysteria that had been building all afternoon.

Falcone stood at the foot of the bed, his champagn blond hair standing up in uneven spikes like sprouts of that expensive white asparagus sold in gourmet grocery stores. The earring added a particularly nice touch, she thought as she giggled up at him.

"I'm gonna get you for this."

She wiped at the tears trickling down her cheeks, then rolled her eyes. "Ooh, I'm scared. The big tough marshal with the fancy earring and Ice Cube is out to get me."

Annie swallowed when he growled, his eyes narrowing to slits. Maybe she'd gone too far, but darn it all, he deserved it. He'd been treating her like a brainless idiot. It had taken him way too long to tell her what was going on, and even now she guessed she didn't know the half of it.

"Hey, you're the one who decided we had to look completely different, remember?"

He fisted his hands on his hips. "Yeah, but I never agreed to a gender change."

She shrugged. "I think you look kind of—"

"Gay?"

She shook her head. Never in a million years would anyone mistake a man like Andrew Falcone for gay. But he did look like a cross between an angry punk rocker and a lumberjack. Maybe she should have stuck a safety pin in his ear, instead of the magnetized earring.

"Of course not," she said, still grinning. "But how about a hairdresser on the prowl for a campsite?"

"That's it," he muttered, his eyes blazing.

He dove on top of her and pinned her beneath him. Trapping her between his thighs, he caught her hands and held them at her shoulders. Annie sucked in a breath when she felt the familiar prodding against her pubic bone. Her heart hammered in her chest and she bit at her lower lip.

He turned up a corner of his sexy mouth. "That's more like it, McAllister. Now I have you exactly where I want you."

CHAPTER NINE

A slow burn of desire flared from Annie's breasts to her belly. Drew's devilish expression quickly changed to one of concentration as he captured her gaze with his and nestled against the juncture of her thighs. If she was keeping score of dumb ideas, this one would be number three on the hit parade, right behind the kiss on the basketball court and this joyride to nowhere.

"I'm sorry." She was going straight to hell for the lie. "It was the look on your face that was funny, not the . . . um . . . transformation. I didn't mean to laugh—honest."

"Yeah, just like you didn't mean to buy this fruity-colored hair dye or the earrings."

She rolled her eyes and tried to pull her hands away, but he wouldn't let go. "It was a shade I recognized, that's all. I once used the same color. I saw the box and picked it up without thinking."

He took in her tangle of curls. "Your hair is nice—reminds me of honey. What made you dye it punk rocker white?"

Annie squirmed backward on the mattress. It was the first time in recent memory anyone other than Julie had complimented her dirty blond mop. "My husband liked it that color."

His gaze hardened, his eyes turning a deep espresso brown. "And you always did what he asked you to do?" He shook his head. "Somehow I find that hard to believe."

"I liked it until I realized how much I had to do to keep it looking good. It was one of the items on a long list I'd decided to talk to Tom about the night he—" She thinned her lips and struggled again. "You really need to get off me."

"Tell me something." He shifted a little, but still kept her pinned beneath him. "Why is it so hard for you to talk about your husband? He's been dead what, five or six years?"

"Six, this January first. And I don't see how our being thrown together this way gives you the right to the details of my personal life. You haven't given me any about yours."

Realizing the position they were in, stacked against each other like cookies in a box, she groaned inside. Short of actually *doing the deed*, this was about as personal as they could get.

Judging by the grin on Drew's face, he knew it, too. His gaze roamed from her mouth to her throat and down to her breasts pressed intimately against the wall of his chest. The hunger simmering in his eyes set her insides to fluttering.

"There's a lot going on here, McAllister, and it doesn't all involve what happened yesterday."

She frowned, and he matched it with one of his own.

"Was it your husband or your marriage that was so bad you can't bring yourself to talk about it?"

Annie had mulled over the very same question plenty of times in the past, both before and after Tom's death. The grief counselor she'd seen for the six months following his funeral had posed the same query as well. On the rare occasions she felt despondent or lonely, she searched her psyche for an answer. So far, she'd had no luck finding one she could accept. Heck, if she, Julie and Dr. Bennet couldn't figure it out, what could it hurt to let this guy try?

"Husband or marriage? Isn't that one and the same?"

"No." Drew rested his forehead on her chin for a second, then rolled to his side. Propping his cheek on his palm, he gazed at her intently. "Sometimes guys are stupid. They don't mean to be, but they are. Maybe if I—he'd been pointed in the right direction—"

"He refused to go to counseling," Annie snapped, then thought better of it. Why was Andrew Falcone making it sound as if he was to blame because Tom had been so controlling? The error had been hers for allowing it to happen. Turning toward him, she mimicked his casual pose and focused on the drab paint-by-number landscape mounted on the wall next to the bed. "And it was my fault for letting him get away with it."

Drew's shuttered gaze said he wasn't buying her excuse. "Besides the hair, what else did he make you do?"

Annie sighed. Once, as a therapy exercise, Dr. Bennet had asked her to write down everything she'd wished she could have changed about Tom. The list had covered two sheets of notebook paper, and she'd only touched the tip of the iceberg. "Little things. Because of him, I was always on a diet . . . and he liked to tell me what to wear."

"Maybe he just wanted you to look your best?"

Annie could sense Drew's thought process, could almost hear the wheels turning. From where he sat, she probably sounded just like a host of other women, the ones who wanted to turn their husbands into someone else the second they said "I do."

"He ordered for me when we ate in restaurants."

"I thought women liked it when a man made the decisions?"

"Not when they order meals so tasteless a starving rott-weiler wouldn't eat them."

One corner of his mouth lifted. "That bad, huh?"

"The worst, though I have to admit Tom seemed to enjoy that kind of food. For all their money, Sunday dinner with his parents was like dining at a POW camp. His mother and father were wealthy and controlling. Dr. Bennet thought his stringent upbringing was the reason Tom tried to make me over, and I was vulnerable enough to let him."

His jaw clenched when he asked, "Was there anything else?"

Annie figured she'd blabbed this much, she might as well reveal the most serious of Tom's faults. "My dad was a judge, nothing important, just family court. I always wanted to do something positive with my life, only not so boring or formal, so I decided to get a criminal justice degree and figure out later what I wanted to do with it. I met Tom at Rutgers, then my parents died. It was easier to let him take charge so I could concentrate on my younger sister. I took a year off to pull myself together and saw to it Julie got into a good college. When I told Tom I was ready to go back to school, he convinced me to stay home, be a good wife and keep house, entertain his clients and accompany him to business functions. I acted like a wimp. I didn't go back to school until after he—"

"A career in law enforcement can be dangerous. Maybe he was worried you'd get hurt. A cop's life is no picnic, and being a federal marshal is a big commitment. Why them, by the way?"

"Simple. The FBI had a freeze on hiring, and the marshals were recruiting on campus that last year. It sounded exciting and interesting, a total change from my old life."

"Do you enjoy the work?" Drew's brows rose with the question, as if he couldn't believe she was doing what she truly wanted.

"The only career I thought I might enjoy more was opening my own restaurant. But the idea of using the insurance money left to me by Tom and my parents to go to cooking school, combined with the hassle of owning my own business, was a deterrent. The marshals were accepting applications, so . . . *voila,''* she said, trying to sound cheerful. ''Here I am.''

Tom felt lower than a snake's belly. She'd brought up the hair thing and the diet thing *and* his refusal to go to counseling, then thrown the knockout punch with his derailment of her career. It had been bad enough listening to Milton recite his transgressions. Hearing Annie voice them out loud made the sins sound worse . . . much worse. All the time he thought he'd been taking care of their future—taking care of her—he'd been keeping her from her dream.

''My turn,'' she said, bringing him back to the present. ''May I ask you a question?''

''Sure.'' *Let's just hope it's one I can answer.*

''How come all the people who work at the diner and the motel seem to know you? Are you related to Art or something?''

The vague memory of a scuffle, punches being thrown and everyone's profound gratitude lurked in the back of Tom's mind. He opted for a scenario that sounded good and gave silent thanks when the words tumbled freely from his mouth.

''I've been using this room as a home away from home since I went under cover on this assignment, and I did them a favor once. Besides, I'm probably their only regular customer.''

''What kind of favor?''

''About two years ago, I stopped in the diner for a snack. Some gun-toting perp came in and tried to rob the place. I took care of it.'' This body had taken care of it, Tom amended silently. If the identical incident had posed itself last night, he wondered, would he have had the courage to do the same?

"Took care of it how? Do they know you're a marshal?"

"Not from me, they don't. I left the guy handcuffed to a counter stool and took off. Since then, everybody's just assumed I'm on the up and up."

"Kind of like Batman or one of those X-Men characters, disappearing before they received their just reward, huh?"

It was tough enough for Tom to imagine himself as a marshal, never mind a super hero. But viewing things through Annie's eyes made him think it was possible. More and more, he was beginning to admire the guy who'd owned this impressive body. Maybe he *could* be the kind of man willing to put his life on the line for the safety of others— like Andrew Falcone.

Unfortunately, what she'd said about his mother and father had been on the money. As a boy, he hadn't been allowed to climb a tree or get dirty, never mind roughhouse with the guys. According to his parents, the only respectable physical activity for a young man of quality was golf or tennis, maybe racquet ball. He'd never told them he ran track or shot a bow and arrow. They'd have had a conniption fit.

Annie's smile bathed him in liquid sunshine. Reaching out, he gently traced the line of her jaw. With her hair in tousled curls and her body relaxed and womanly, she was downright beautiful. The air pulsed between them, and he leaned forward, so close he could see flecks of amber in her eyes.

"I figured I'd get my super hero reward for helping them out sooner or later. Maybe this is it."

They jerked apart at the sound of one solid thump on the door, a second of hesitation, and two more fast raps.

Tom cursed as he raced around the bed. Who the hell else knew the signal he'd given to Annie? Peeking between the drapes, he spied a gnarled, pint-sized man standing outside the door. The old-timer caught him staring and smiled through a mouthful of missing teeth.

Great. They were being visited by a friendly troll.

"Who's there?" Annie whispered, rising from the bed.

"Someone from the cast of *Lord of the Rings,*" he muttered, sliding the chain off the door.

The man slipped inside, stared up at Tom's albino porcupine hairdo and began to cackle. Tom folded his arms and glared. If this was the reaction he could expect from the outside world—

"Art." Annie walked over, her lips twitching in what could only be described as a mischievous grin. "What are you doing here?"

So this was Art. No wonder Drew Falcone had been forced to overcome a thief and save the restaurant. This guy didn't look strong enough to wrestle a bird for a worm. Annie must have met him when she picked up breakfast.

Art wheezed out another chuckle, then wiped the tears from his eyes. After casting Tom one final leering grin, he trained his gaze on Annie. Or rather, Annie's bountiful chest. "Time to get movin', you two. There's trouble a brewin'."

"What's up?" asked Tom. *Besides your testosterone level.*

"There's a suspicious-lookin' fella at the diner askin' if anybody's seen a man and woman matchin' your descriptions. Mimi and I said no, then I snuck back here to warn ya. He's at the motel right now, talkin' to the desk clerk."

"Did he show you a badge or identification?"

"Not a thing, but he's carryin' a piece. I saw the bulge under his jacket."

"That's not good," said Annie, worrying her lower lip.

Tom ran a hand through his gelled hair. Following Art out the door, he called over his shoulder, "It's very bad, doll. Pack up our gear while Art and I see what we can figure out."

Wind whistled past Annie's ears from between the gaps in her helmet. Squeezing Drew tight around his corded middle, she turned her head and pressed her cheek against his back. They hit a dip in the road, and her teeth rattled as her stomach lurched with the rise and fall of the pavement. The one and only other time she'd ridden a motorcycle, she'd hurled all over the back of the guy's leather jacket. Lucky for Drew, his clothes were wash-and-wear.

She took a deep breath and tamped back the rising nausea, concentrating on what had happened at the motel. By the time she'd packed their toiletries and clothes, Drew had locked the Mustang in an old shed at the rear of the parking lot, and Art had offered them his *hog* for as long as they needed it.

After stuffing their bag in a side compartment, Drew had slapped a helmet on her head and dragged her up and behind him on the bike. Then they'd tossed Art a quick wave and zoomed out of the lot and onto the highway. It had taken the better part of ten minutes for her heart rate and her eardrums to return to normal.

She opened her mouth to shout a question and swallowed something small and hard and . . . crunchy? Yuck!

Gathering her courage, she finally managed a peek at the passing road signs and noted they were heading south into Maryland. Drew had eased up on the gas until they were riding in the slow lane at a sedate and steady speed. Breathing through her nose, just in case any more winged appetizers flew by, Annie loosened her hold and settled her backside against the bike's shiny chrome backrest. They had to pass through Maryland to get to Virginia, but that didn't mean they were going to Arlington. The least Falcone could have done was given her a clue.

She wished he trusted her a little more. Though he'd told her the basics of the past four years, he hadn't offered to let her read the notebook or answered many of her questions. Then again, she sometimes got the impression he didn't really have any answers to give. Weirder still, she sometimes thought she knew what he was going to say or do before he did it, as if she'd known him for a long time. Which was, of course, totally impossible.

She definitely would have remembered if she'd met Andrew Falcone before.

The bike hit a bump and Drew slid backward, nudging the cradle of her open legs. She smiled at his mumbled curse. Her gaze rested on his mile-wide shoulders. Most of the time, he was capable and in control, which annoyed her to no end. Other times, like when she'd been dying his hair or they'd been together on the bed, he acted sweet and funny and vulnerable.

She didn't have trouble handling either of those personas. What had her stumped were the times he took advantage of the budding attraction she knew was growing between them. She'd only ever made love with one man. Since Tom's death, she hadn't thought about getting close to another. But when Drew held her in his strong yet gentle hands and savored her lips as if she were a slice of strawberry shortcake he wanted to devour whole . . .

After Tom's death, it had taken her a while to crawl out of her depression and get her life on track. She was proud of the woman she'd become—tough, decisive and smart— and a damned good marshal. She'd been promoted in rapid steps, accepted for WITSEC and given a plum assignment all in a short amount of time. Life was finally swinging her way, and she wasn't about to let Drew Falcone's mission frighten her or ruin what she'd accomplished.

Annie still didn't know if she'd simply fallen into the assignment at the safe house or if he had requested her, but she was going to find out. If he thought she could be easily swayed or manipulated, she would prove him wrong. Now that they were linked, she was going to do her part to help get them out of this mess. Her career depended on it.

* * *

Tom had careened out of the lot as if his tail were on fire. Right now, Annie's hands clutched his stomach in a death grip, and he didn't blame her. He was hanging on to the handlebars of the bike the exact same way. Good thing she was so busy saving herself she couldn't see his white-knuckled panic hold.

He'd never ridden a motorcycle before, but the way Art acted, Tom figured Falcone had. When he'd hopped on the bike and headed onto the highway, he'd just hung tight, secure in the knowledge they were going in the right direction. If there was one thing he'd learned to do with this new body and mind, it was to *go with the flow*. At least Milton's advice on that score had been correct.

Annie relaxed her hold, which prompted him to loosen his own fingers. Her thighs still gripped his hips, but she was definitely more at ease with the ride—and with him. Back on the motel bed, they'd had a real conversation. He'd found out more about her observations on their marriage in those fifteen minutes than he had in the five years they'd lived together.

And every word of what she'd said had been true.

Too bad he couldn't tell her he was back, and he was going to make up for all the misery he'd caused her. Too bad he—

But he could. It was, after all, the reason he'd been allowed to return to earth. He was here to find her a man, and not just any man. The perfect man.

He sighed and automatically leaned into a turn, grinning when Annie leaned along with him. They were cruising as if they were one being, the machine vibrating under their bodies. She was beginning to trust him. A few more talks like the one they'd shared back at the motel and he'd know exactly what kind of guy he had to find to make her happy.

An eighteen wheeler pulled up alongside the bike, its

bright lights cutting a path through the darkness, and Tom realized it was late. They'd made slow but steady progress through Delaware and Maryland and were now in Virginia. But they weren't headed toward Arlington. They were going to the one place they could regroup and be safe. After he took care of his marshal business, he'd set to work at finding her a prince of a guy, because that's what she deserved.

He needed time to finish reading the journal and get his head straight. Their haven was nearby, but it was dark, and he didn't trust his bike-handling skills enough to maneuver in the dark. Tomorrow, after a good night's rest, he'd be able to relax and let that muscle memory thing guide him. He had to remove Annie from the line of fire before she got hurt.

He spied an exit up ahead and took the off ramp to a side road which led to a string of fast food joints, gas stations and motels. Steeling himself, he pulled to a pump, hopped off the hog and almost crumpled to the ground. His legs folded like rubber bands, forcing him to bounce in place until he found his land legs.

Watching him wobble, Annie tugged off her helmet and grinned. "I know I'm going to have to get off this thing eventually, but I'd rather not fall flat on my face."

He held out both hands, and she swung a leg over the seat. Tom caught her, and she sank against him. A few seconds later, she pulled away with a muttered "thanks" and scanned the station.

"Where the heck are we headed?"

"To my family's cabin in the mountains, but we won't make it there before dark."

"I take it you have some idea of where we're spending the night?"

He walked to the pump and busied himself reading the directions. Maybe if he acted as though he knew what he was doing, she would believe him. "I have a couple of ideas."

"Good, because right now I need some dinner, a bathroom and a bed, and not necessarily in that order. I'll be back in a few minutes."

He nodded. "Go ahead. I'll fill the tank, then you can guard the bike while I go inside. I'll find us a place to take care of everything. How does that sound?"

"It sounds great." She hung the helmet over the backrest and, fluffing up her curls with both hands, took off for the ladies' room.

He watched her stride away, her hips and long legs moving with determined grace toward the store entrance. Even in baggy sweats and an oversized jacket, she looked shapely and fine. The guy pumping gas at the next bay followed her with his eyes until she disappeared through the door, then gave a low whistle. Before Tom knew it, his hands were balled into fists, and he was growling low in his throat.

Holy Christ! He was acting like a Neanderthal!

The man, tall and tough looking, glanced his way and gave him the once-over. The guy had to have heard him, because he looked ready to bolt as he climbed into his pickup and pulled away. Impressed by the easy way the macho display had come to him, Tom smiled behind the face mask of his helmet. Seconds later, Annie returned and propped herself against one of the pumps.

"I asked the checkout clerk about motels in the area and she said the nicest one was the Sleepy-Bye. It's down the road about a half mile, and there's a decent restaurant attached. What do you think?"

Tom ran his gaze over her wind-kissed cheeks and spar-kling eyes, annoyed at the way his gut tightened. If he said what he was thinking out loud, Annie would probably slap him . . . or pull out her gun. It was going to be one hell of a long night.

"Yeah, sure. I'll pay for the gas and be right back."

* * *

"I don't know if your leaving is such a good idea. That place looked kind of seedy to me." Annie gazed up at Drew from the doorway of their motel room. "Maybe it would be better if you stayed here. I'll even be magnanimous and let you laugh at me while I undergo my transformation."

Drew rested a forearm on the doorframe and ran his other hand through his spiky hair. "I just want a little time alone while you do all that girly stuff. The desk clerk said the Two-Step on Wheels was a respectable bar, pool tables and all, so I don't think you need to worry."

"You sure you're going to be okay?"

"In case you haven't noticed, I'm a big boy. I've been taking care of myself for a long time now, McAllister."

She folded her arms and arched a brow. Was this his polite way of dumping her, or did he really just want some time alone? "Just remember who took care of who at the safe house, ace."

He frowned, as if he didn't want any reminders of how she had saved his life. "Look, to tell you the truth, this familiarity stuff is making me itchy. I'm used to being alone. I could use a little space, and you probably could, too. I'll have a beer while you do whatever it is you do and be back before you know it."

He pulled a wad of bills from his jacket pocket and passed them to her. "Here, you keep this. The last thing I need is to get robbed." Patting himself down, he pulled the gun and badge from his jeans pocket and set them down on the floor behind the door. "I probably ought to leave this stuff here, too. I don't want anyone to suspect I'm the law."

Annie bit at her lower lip. Still not sure he was doing the smart thing, she made a joke of his decision. "Okay, but watch yourself. Oh, and maybe you should take a pen and paper, just in case some teeny bopper mistakes you for Eminem and asks for your autograph.''

''Har-har-har.'' He backed up a step. ''Keep the chain on until you go to bed. Then slide it off so I can get in.''

''Okay, fine. Just remember, this wasn't my idea.'' She slammed the door in his face, then peeked through the curtain to make sure he didn't hop on the Harley and leave her stranded. True to his word, he walked through the parking lot and headed across the road to the bar.

Maybe being separated for a while was for the best, she told herself. She needed breathing room, too. Pressed up against his back for the better part of the day was about all she could take of their forced togetherness. He'd said all the time they'd been spending together was making him itchy—well, she'd been itchy, too. But the last thing she needed was for Drew Falcone to find out how badly she wanted him to be the one to do the scratching.

Resting her backside against the door, she surveyed the room. It didn't look much different from the one at Art's, just a little bigger, with the same round table and chairs under the window, the same thin, puke green carpet covering the floor and almost identical dirty beige wallpaper closing in on all sides. Even the cheesy landscape on the wall next to the bed looked familiar. If she didn't know better, she'd think someone had figured out a way to design a kit—Build-Your-Own-Sleazy-Motel-Room—and was marketing it over the Internet.

The room even had the same sad-looking plaid quilt over a saggy queen-sized—

Oh, great. Peachy-keen. They'd asked for two double beds, and the clerk had given them a single. Annie sighed out her frustration, hauled back her leg to kick the gun Drew had propped next to the door, then thought better of it. The way her luck was running, she'd probably break a toe or shoot herself in the foot.

She'd really been looking forward to a bed she could call

her own and a stress-free morning. One where she didn't wake up with a long-fingered male hand entwined intimately with her own, or strong muscular arms wrapped around her from behind. Or the throb of an erection—

Annie dismissed the disturbing thought by fanning a hand in front of her face. No, no, no. She would not think of Drew that way. Whether he admitted it or not, they were professionals working together on a case. She was going to come through this assignment with her virtue and her dignity intact.

And speaking of her assignment, she still had a really bad feeling about turning him lose at that bar, even for a couple of hours. Not only didn't they know *where* the bad guys were—they didn't know *who*. Leave it to Drew to get the urge to visit a honky-tonk hog palace at a time like this. Men!

They hadn't discussed phone calls since that morning at Art's. Maybe now was a good time to leave a message on her boss's answering machine. She sat at the side of the bed, picked up the phone and read the instructions. Then she spotted the neatly printed card propped against the bed-side lamp. The phone wouldn't work unless they'd produced a credit card at check-in. Which wouldn't have flown because she didn't have a credit card, and they'd paid for the room in cash.

Nope, she was just going to have to put the call to her superiors on hold a while longer.

She went to the door, hoisted the duffel and carried it to the bed. Searching inside, she dragged out the box of hair dye, her bag of toiletries and her sleeping gear. The first thing she had to do was color her hair, then she'd soak in a nice hot tub, after which she would pull on her nightly armor, crawl under the sheets and curl up in a corner of the bed.

She checked the bag and felt something flat and hard at the bottom. A smile curved her lips. Too bad Drew had been in such a hurry to leave her alone that he'd forgotten his notebook. She loved reading in the tub, and this little gem of a book looked like it would fit the bill nicely.

Carting everything into the bathroom, which was only about two inches bigger than the one at Art's, she dumped her bounty on the counter and set to work. Fifteen minutes later, she'd applied the hair color, filled the tub and added a splash of shower gel for bubbles. After carefully setting her watch on the commode seat so she could check the time, she held the book high, slid into the warm scented water and began to read.

She skipped through the part where he told about the day-to-day routine of setting the sting up, but read more carefully through the cast of characters. The odd barrage of names, Papa Bear, Baby Bear, Peter Pan, the Grinch and Goldilocks all swam before her eyes, and she tamped back a laugh. She only hoped she'd be in on the take-down so she could match the names with the faces of the different crooks and good guys.

Drew had folded down the corner of a page, and Annie assumed it was where he'd left off in his reading. She was still puzzled. If he wrote the book, why did he have to read it? Did he have a memory problem, or had it been a while since he'd taken a look and he needed to organize his thoughts?

She came across an entire paragraph dedicated to Goldilocks and blinked. Now Drew used the words *she* and *her*, which could only refer to a woman. Since she was the singular woman involved in the safe house, the paragraph had to be about her.

> *Goldilocks was the perfect choice. Good thing Papa Bear took my suggestion and gave her the assignment. The records indicate she's got above average skills for a woman, and she's bright enough to do the job. It's to my benefit that she's also naïve, and will proba-*

bly follow my cues. According to her history, she doesn't date much, so she should eat up the attention and be eager to please. If the targets don't take the bait, I'll have to figure out another way to get her cooperation.

Annie turned to stone, every nerve ending in her body on alert. *Goldilocks! Eager to please? Eat up the attention!*

That egotistical, self-centered jerk. She'd been such a dope. His sensitive concern about her marriage—the pathetic plea for exercise—was nothing more than a great big ploy to manipulate her into doing what he wanted. No wonder he'd been so short-tempered with her. She'd thrown a major monkey wrench into his plans when she'd thought up the chain and shackle scenario.

She closed the book with a thump, blew a froth of bubbles from her face and checked her watch. It was time to rinse out the hair dye and unveil her new do. But her plans had changed. The naïve and apparently desperate widow was going to transform herself from Goldilocks into Spiderwoman, then spin her own little web of deceit.

"I'll show him *eager to please.*"

CHAPTER TEN

Tom approached the parking lot of the Two-Step on Wheels, thinking this side trip was probably one of the dumbest moves he'd ever made. But he had to get a break from Annie and their in-your-face togetherness. They'd been so close to each other for the past two days, all he could think of was jumping her bones—not a smart idea.

Spending a couple of hours in this unusual-looking establishment would give him a little breathing room, plus the time to sort out the next few days. But since they were in the mountains of Virginia, somewhere past the back of beyond, he figured it best to exercise caution, just in case the place was less civilized than he was used to.

The good-sized, gray frame building with its wide-boarded porch and weathered exterior could have doubled for the home used in *Little House on the Prairie,* while the packed parking lot looked like something from a combination Harley/monster truck rally. Adding to the ambience were two ten-foot-high, motorcycle-riding, neon pink pigs done up in full western regalia and perched atop the black-shingled roof. Honky-tonk music blared from speakers mounted on either side of the pigs, as if the proprietor expected the overflow of customers to dance in the gravel-covered lot or on the roomy porch. A colorfully painted, three-foot-tall sign mounted next to the double doors proudly proclaimed:

> Wednesday is Ladies' Night
> Dollar a Rack Pool
> No Spitting or Swearing Allowed

Three men wearing boots, faded denim and cowboy hats nudged past him, and Tom caught the echo of their snickers. Dressed in sneakers, jeans and flannel couldn't be the problem, so it had to be his hedgehog hairdo and fruity earring that had them so amused. Damn Annie anyway for getting cute with his disguise when they were supposed to be incognito.

Ignoring the trio's laughter, Tom followed them into the bar, confident he could lose himself in the crowd. Inside the dimly lit interior smoke billowed, a nagging reminder of the last time he, or rather his lungs, had enjoyed a cigarette. If he took deep breaths, maybe he could suck up enough second-hand smoke to quiet the craving.

He walked to the bar and ordered a beer, then found a seat at a table against the wall. From there, he had a clear view of the crowded dance floor to his left and to his right, an open area holding a half dozen pool tables and the paraphernalia that went with them.

He'd thought he would enjoy the space, but sitting here inhaling the foul air and tossing back a watery draft didn't seem to be working. Tom McAllister had been a people person, quick with a joke and eager to buy a round of drinks for clients and strangers alike. Some inner sense warned him that Drew Falcone wouldn't be comfortable doing the same.

He drummed the tabletop with his fingers. Pulling out a pen and small spiral notebook from his shirt pocket, he started to think. He'd already made up his mind to cross Bob Fielding off the suspect list for several reasons, the most obvious being he'd seen the marshal in action. Annie had to beg to get his approval for the basketball game. If Bob had wanted Dominic Viglioni or Andrew Falcone dead, he wouldn't have been so hard-nosed about something that would have made the mobster such an easy target.

His first choice for skunk of the year was Lou Smithers. Too bad they'd left Lou's computer back at Art's. With a little luck, Tom was certain he could have cracked the guy's password and been able to delve into his e-mail messages and reports. Now it would have to wait until they returned to the other motel.

Either Butterworth or Donovan had to be involved. Lou had been sitting on the porch right up until he and Annie had made their final charge to the net. There hadn't been enough time for the deputy to slip off the porch, find cover and fire those shots. Tom had yet to discuss it with Annie, but he was certain Lou had gone inside and put Fielding out of commission while Butterworth or Donovan ran the sniper attack.

He thought a bit more, realized what he was doing and tamped back a grin of satisfaction. He was the one in control right now—not Andrew Falcone. It was *his* brain thinking about the problem and working on the solution. He was doing the job of an undercover marshal.

He was a smart guy. He just needed to study the notebook and piece together the rest of the puzzle. Then he could wrap up the case and move on to the reason he'd been sent back here in the first place. Annie.

After their intimate conversation on the bed this afternoon, he had a pretty good idea of the qualities she'd want in a man. First off, he had to be someone who wouldn't tell her what to eat or how to dress or wear her hair. Someone who would love her for her honey blond curls and her lush, womanly hips and soft, ripe—

Running a hand over his jaw, Tom blew out a breath. He had to stop thinking about his wife—who wasn't his wife any longer—in *that* way, or he was going to give his own sexually explicit impression of Mount St. Helens right here in the bar. He had to accept the fact that Annie be allowed to make her own decisions in her career and her personal life, as did the man he found for her. The guy also had to be willing to talk out their problems, something Tom McAllister hadn't wanted to do.

"You want another beer?"

Tom raised his head and met the gaze of a petite-yet-curvy, dark-haired young woman dressed in a low-cut sweater, high-heeled boots and a denim skirt the width of a Band–Aid.

"Um ... yeah, sure," he said, returning her friendly smile.

The girl looked him over through black-fringed lashes. "This your first time at the Two-Step?"

"Yep," he answered. *And last.*

"Nice hair cut. I really like Blink 182. You know them?"

Who in the hell was Blink 182, and why was this high school chippy making small talk with him? Pocketing the notebook and pen, Tom glanced past her shoulder to the group of men who seemed to be watching their discussion with interest.

"Not really."

"How about Limp Bizkit?"

It finally dawned on him she was referring to music groups. "I'm more into Z Z Top or Bob Seeger."

Her crimson lips drooped into a pout. "Who?"

"Never mind," Tom muttered. "Just the beer, and maybe some pretzels?"

"Coming right up." She sashayed away with a swish of her hips, and he wondered what would happen if she bent

over. It might be worth dropping a twenty on the floor just
to find out.

He shook his head. Six years ago, that kind of crude
observation never would have entered his mind. He might
have been a jerk, but he'd been a faithful jerk. In the few
years he and Annie had been married, he'd never strayed
or even thought about another woman. Tom McAllister's
hormones had run on plain ordinary regular. The way he
was feeling right now, Andrew Falcone needed high test.
And Tom was beginning to enjoy it.

He watched while the waitress stood at the bar and chatted
with the men, then picked up his order. On the way back,
she dodged two pair of roaming hands and one beefy guy
with a Fu Manchu mustache who tried to get her to set her
tray down and dance. After a few seconds of fending off
the unwanted attention, she made it to the table.

"Here you go. That'll be two-fifty."

Tom placed a five-dollar bill on the tray.

"Thanks." She stayed put and stared longingly at the
couples whooping it up on the dance floor. Tapping her foot,
she turned to him. "Do you dance?"

"Not so's you'd notice," he mumbled, embarrassed to
admit the few times he'd tried to strut his stuff he'd resembled a chicken that had just swallowed a grasshopper.

"Oh, come on. You look like a guy with natural rhythm."

He did? Then he remembered she was sizing up a different
man's body. "Don't you have to take care of the customers?"

She smiled coyly. "Those good ol' boys can get their
own beer while I take a break. My name's Natalie. What's
yours?"

"I'm . . . um . . . Drew." Still unable to believe she was
asking him to dance, he kept his butt planted in the chair.

Natalie took a step backward and held out her hands. As
if on cue, the music slowed to an easy number that wouldn't
require too much gyration. Tom stood and followed her to

the dance floor. Maybe if he shuffled his feet from side to side or—

Natalie settled comfortably into his arms, rested her cheek on his chest and followed his lead. She felt small and fine-boned, just as he'd expected, not the tempting, full-figured armful that was Annie.

What the hell, he thought, swaying with the soulful refrain. He'd already told Annie he needed his space. Sooner or later he was going to have to get used to living the single life. He might as well start getting used to it.

Annie found the jeans she'd left in the bottom of the Wal–Mart bag and crossed her fingers. She never bought clothes without trying them on, but there hadn't been time. These pants looked a little smaller than usual, even though they were her regular size. She tugged them up, hopped in place and did a few squats to get them over her fanny, but she still had to lie on the bed in order to get the zipper closed. She could only pray she'd be able to breathe, never mind walk, once she stood up.

The final item in the bag was the top that matched the tights she'd been wearing as body armor. With a pink bow at the neckline and tiny pearl buttons marching halfway down the front, she'd dismissed the thin, skin-tight shirt as too scanty to keep her warm. Now, as she unbuttoned the clingy knit to the top of her bra and rearranged herself for more cleavage, she knew it would be perfect for tonight.

Inspecting her cosmetic bag, she pulled out a blush, plumy pink lipstick, beige-colored eye shadow and brown-black mascara, pretty much what she wore every day. But the bargain lipstick also had a free lip liner, and the eye shadow had come in a dual-color compact with a contrasting shade and a thin brush that could be used on the brows or the lids.

For the next fifteen minutes she primped, puckered and lined, until satisfied she'd done the best she could with what she had on hand. The wide-eyed dramatic look was over the top as far as she was concerned, but just what she needed to spin the web she'd conjured earlier.

It took a full five minutes and a lot of tummy sucking to bend over and tie her sneakers. Then she slipped on her leather jacket, ignored the biting cold wind and crossed the highway to the colorful bar.

Two men held the door to let her in ahead of them, and she smiled her thanks. Once inside, the smoke stung her eyes even as the music set her feet to tapping. She stepped into the center room, slipped out of the jacket and hung it on a row of pegs lining the wall. Waiting for her eyes to adjust to the hazy light, she perused the crowd. There were more men than women, which she thought was a bit odd, but it didn't worry her. The fact would work to her advantage.

Sidling up to the bar, she purposely edged between a pair of men she knew had been watching her from the second she'd walked through the door.

"Diet Coke with lemon," Annie ordered, pleased at the way the fit of her jeans made her voice sound breathy, kind of like Marilyn Monroe when she'd sung "Happy Birthday" to Jack Kennedy.

The guy on her left grinned. "Sure you don't want a little something stronger in that glass, sweet cheeks? Maybe some vodka or a shot of gin?"

"No, thanks." She took a sip of the cool fizzy liquid, letting it soothe her smoke-dry throat. "I don't need alcohol to have a good time."

Besides, nobody here needed to know that a few swallows of anything more potent than fizzy water made her say and do the strangest things. For her plan to work, it was imperative she keep a level head. Before she'd met Drew Falcone, she'd been a thoughtful planner, yet she'd left the hotel tonight with little more than a germ of an idea on how best to prove her point. Now that she was here, she needed to think her next move through carefully before she did something dumb.

She made her way to the end of the bar, where she had a good view of the room. With Drew's neon white spikes, she expected him to stand out like Billy Idol at a Buddhists' convention. Maybe she hadn't done the smartest thing in making him up to look so *out there,* but whatever happened to hiding in plain sight? No one in their right mind would ever associate a man who resembled a punk rocker with Dominic Viglione.

The customer standing next to her, a bear of a guy with a black Snidely Whiplash mustache and an engaging grin, nodded toward her glass. "Can I buy you another drink?"

"I'm fine." She tried to hoist herself onto a bar stool, but her pants refused to bend at the hip, which caused her to slip back to her feet.

Fingering a tip of his mustache like a prized possession, he watched her graceful slide. "Care to dance?"

The music faded to a halt and she worked up a disappointed frown. "Gee, I'd love to, but it sounds like the band is taking a break."

"No problem," Snidely countered, setting his beer on the bar. "They play a tape in between."

Sure enough, a throbbing country beat began to reverberate through the speakers. So much for trying to be polite, Annie thought, realizing she'd been scammed. She scanned the room. Maybe Falcone was playing pool. Either way, she had to circulate to find him, or she would never make her point.

The rhythmic tempo vibrated the scarred wood under Annie's feet as she followed Snidely onto the floor. It had been a long time since she'd danced with a man. Tom hadn't been very good at anything but the slow steps, and even then he'd just moved his feet from side to side. This guy was acting so eager, she hoped she could keep up.

Bouncing in time to the music, she stepped into his arms

as she checked out the room. Most of the couples had taken a break with the band, but there were still a few diehards . . . .

She did a double take when she spotted a couple executing some fancy footwork on the far side of the floor—Drew Falcone, gyrating like a pro as he twirled a tiny bit of a girl who looked to be fresh out of high school. Not only did he have Tom beat to hell in the sweet feet department, but several other dancers had stopped to watch the show.

Snidely swung her around and glanced over her shoulder, then leaned in close. "Don't know about you, darlin', but I sure as hell hate to be showed up on the dance floor. You game?"

Annie saw more people clearing a space, forming a circle around Falcone and Ms. High School. Biting her lower lip, she shrugged. "If you don't do anything too crazy, I guess I can keep up."

He nodded, spun her like a roulette wheel and jogged them to the middle of the floor. Annie knew the moment Drew spotted her because his expression raced from curious to shocked to cocky in a matter of seconds. Shuttling past him in a whirl, she ignored the jolt of heat arcing from her feet to her face when their gazes met. Her partner twirled them faster, moving his feet in double time to the beat, and she stumbled. Trying to regain her footing, she saw Drew rocket by, his teeny bopper partner staring adoringly into his face as if he were Michael Flatly.

Snidely eyed the other couple and decided it was his cue to set the dance floor on fire. "Hang on, honey," he muttered. "We're movin' in for the kill." Jostling her upright, he propelled them across the worn boards at warp speed.

Unable to do more than he suggested, Annie heaved a breath. Her partner's determined gaze settled on the exposed flesh between her pearl buttons and he licked his lips. "Darlin', when this is over, you and me are gonna get better acquainted. I can feel it in my bones."

Don't you mean one big boner? Annie wanted to ask,

kicking into his next dip and spin. Still, his macho reaction was exactly what she'd hoped for. After tonight, Drew Falcone would never again think of her as desperate.

Egged on by the applauding crowd, she and Snidely joined Drew and Ms. High School in a second number. When shouts and whistles numbed her eardrums, Annie decided to sit back and enjoy the ride, putting her all into the aerobic workout. If she could exercise like this a few times a week, she'd never need another morning jog to get her heart rate going.

The two couples continued their dancing duel. Annie lost the ability to keep an eye on Drew when she realized she had to concentrate if she wanted to match Snidely's intricate footwork. Finally, the music skidded to a halt. After the dancers accepted the praise of the crowd and a few pats on the back, she wheezed a murmur of thanks in her partner's direction and headed for the bar. She didn't get more than three steps before he grabbed her hand and corralled her into the next tune, a slow, bluesy song about a love done gone wrong.

"That was mighty fine dancin', little lady." Snidely tightened his grip. "I just might claim you for the rest of the night."

"Claim me?" Annie tossed him her best maybe-next-time frown. "I didn't know this was a horse race." She gazed around the room hoping to spot her target. "If you don't mind, I'd really like to go back and finish my drink."

"Aw, come on. Right now, there's 'bout a half dozen women here wishin' they were in your shoes. You should be honored I'm choosin' you."

She disengaged her hands and tried to make nice. "Far be it from me to deprive them of the joy of partnering with such a fine dancer. Spread yourself around. Now, if you'll excuse me, I really need a drink."

Undaunted, he dogged her steps back to the bar. "It'd be my pleasure to buy you one, darlin'."

Annie stopped mid stride to face him. "Alone."

His wounded expression almost made her laugh out loud. "Look, I just need to catch my breath. Maybe we can do it again later." *Like in another century or two.*

She finally spied Drew sitting on a stool next to her soda. By the time she arrived at his side, she was mad as a wet cat. Rounding on Snidely, who apparently didn't understand plain English, she enunciated each syllable like a pistol shot.

"Please. Find. Some. One. Else. To. Dance. With."

"But, darlin'—" Snidely whined.

Drew raised a brow and took in her five-alarm hair, then her makeup and finally her clothes. "Let me guess," he quipped. "Instead of getting some rest, you decided to go to a Hooker Hoe Down and the trailer exploded."

"At least I didn't rob the cradle while I was there." She grabbed her drink and took a huge swallow. Grimacing at the bitter taste, she leaned into the bar. "Bartender? This Coke is flat. Can I have another?"

"Do you two know each other?" asked Snidely.

"Yes," said Drew.

"No," said Annie at the same time.

The bartender set a fresh Coke in front of her, and Drew reached into his pocket, as did the whiner. Annie beat them to it and slapped her money onto the bar.

"What happened to staying in the room and giving me a little down time?" Drew asked, stuffing his money back in his pocket.

"Nothing. I simply decided I needed some of the same." She picked up the drink and sauntered away. Things were moving along rather well, she thought, mentally patting herself on the back.

Miffed, Tom sipped his beer and watched Annie head for the pool room. What the hell just happened here? His slow dance with Natalie had started out fine enough, but the second his body heard the raucous music, it had jump-started like a competitor at a Boot Scoot competition. He'd almost

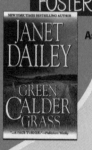

To start your membership, simply complete and return the Free Book Certificate. You'll receive your Introductory Shipment of 3 FREE Zebra Contemporary Romances, you only pay $1.99 for shipping and handling. Then, each month you will receive the 3 newest Zebra Contemporary Romances. Each shipment will be yours to examine FREE for 10 days. If you decide to keep the books, you'll pay the preferred subscriber price (a savings of up to 20% off the cover price), plus shipping and handling. If you want us to stop sending books, just say the word… it's that simple.

Be sure to visit our website at www.kensingtonbooks.com.

FREE BOOK CERTIFICATE

Yes! Please send me 3 FREE Zebra Contemporary romance novels. I only pay $1.99 for shipping and handling. I understand that each month thereafter I will be able to preview 3 brand-new Contemporary Romances FREE for 10 days. Then, if I should decide to keep them, I will pay the money-saving preferred subscriber's price (that's a savings of up to 20% off the retail price), plus shipping and handling. I understand I am under no obligation to purchase any books, as explained on this card.

Name _____

Address _____ Apt._____

City _____ State _____ Zip _____

Telephone (___) _____

Signature _____

(If under 18, parent or guardian must sign)

Offer limited to one per household and not to current subscribers. Terms, offer and prices subject to change. Orders subject to acceptance by Zebra Contemporary Book Club. Offer Valid in the U.S. only.

Thank You!

CN053A

THE BENEFITS
OF BOOK CLUB
MEMBERSHIP

- You'll get your books hot off the press, usually before they appear in bookstores.

- You'll ALWAYS save up to 20% off the cover price.

- You'll get our FREE monthly newsletter filled with author interviews, book previews, special offers and MORE!

- There's no obligation — you can cancel at any time and you have no minimum number of books to buy.

- And—if you decide you don't like the books you receive, you can return them. (You always have ten days to decide.)

lll..l..lll....lll.l.l.l...ll.l.l.l.....ll.l.l.l.l.l.....lll.l.lll..l

Zebra Contemporary Romance Book Club

Zebra Home Subscription Service, Inc.

P.O. Box 5214

Clifton , NJ 07015-5214

swallowed his tongue when Annie had high-stepped onto the dance floor in the arms of Fu Manchu. And if her bright red mop of curls and sultry makeup hadn't shocked him enough, her painted-on jeans and figure-hugging top had hit him dead center and points south of his midsection.

He remembered how Annie had loved to dance. Maybe the music booming from those roof-mounted speakers had been too much for her to ignore. Or maybe she'd come here hoping to spend some time with him—

Well, hell, if that were the case, she was doing a damn poor job of showing it.

"Woo-eee," said the guy with the mustache. "That is one fine woman. Big and sassy, just the way I like 'em."

A compatriot at the bar nodded, then muttered something Tom couldn't hear. Yucking it up, they grabbed their drinks and followed after Annie, with Tom in hot pursuit.

Annie threw a dollar into the box and walked to the only free pool table. By the time she chose a cue stick and racked up the first round of balls, three men stood around the table, cues in hand and expectant grins on their eager faces.

"You lookin' for a partner?" the man next to her asked.

She gazed into his craggy face, her smile as seductive as she knew how to make it. "Sure. Loser buys the second round. Winner plays the next man."

"Name's Buck," he said, raking her with his cool gray gaze. "And that's fine with us. You can have first break."

"Nice to meet you, Buck. I'm Annie." She shook his hand, fluttering her eyelashes when he played tug-of-war with her fingers.

"This here's Frank and Bobby Ray."

Nodding politely to the other men, both tall and rugged looking in identical blue chambray shirts and worn jeans, she chalked up her cue stick and silently crossed her fingers. It had been a while since she'd last racked up a game, but she'd been able to beat half the men at FLETC. Of course, many of them had enjoyed taking her down a peg, just because she'd bested their times on the track and firing range. She was betting on these friendly cowboys to be gentlemen.

Concentrating, she leaned into the table and made her first shot. So far so good. She peeked up at her opponent. Buck grinned encouragement, but his gaze was stuck on her cleavage.

"That's the way, darlin'. You're doin' fine."

Fine my fanny, she thought, biting back a smart retort. If she were back in Georgia, she'd have smacked him with her cue stick by now.

After sinking the first three balls, she scratched. No big deal. She was just getting warmed up. It looked as if Buck was going to clear the table and win the round until Bobby Ray, or was it Frank, *accidentally* bumped his arm.

"I'm mighty sorry about that, Buck," the other man said, a cocky glint in his eyes. "Looks like it's your turn, Miz Annie."

She tossed him a flirtatious smile, then neatly pocketed the two ball. Obviously, she'd have to try harder at playing the inept, helpless female if she wanted things to go her way.

"Pony up a dollar, Buck. I'm next," said Bobby Ray.

"No problem," answered Buck, conceding defeat. "It'll be a pleasure watchin' the little lady whup your sorry ass."

Listening to their banter, Annie picked up the drink she'd left sitting on a shelf next to the cue sticks and downed the entire glass. Darned if this Coke hadn't gone as flat and bitter tasting as the first. A flash of heat raced from her stomach to her chest to the top of her head as she finished the drink. The room slanted left, and she clutched the table, waving a hand in front of her overly warm face. Without thinking, she undid two more buttons on her shirt, then plucked an ice cube from her glass and ran it over her throat and collarbone.

Sighing at the slippery coolness, she sucked in a lungful of air. When had the room gotten so hot?

Bobby Ray racked up the balls, raised his head and gave her an openmouthed stare. Buck and Frank kept watch at the opposite side of the table, their drooling gazes locked on her chest.

"We decided you could break again," said Bobby Ray, his voice ragged. "You being the winner and all."

Annie nodded her thanks and took aim, but the cue ball shot off on its own and did a squiggly little slide on the felt. She blinked the ball back into focus just as her opponent set a hand on the table.

"What say we make this a little more interestin'?" Bobby Ray suggested, glancing at his buddies. Frank and Buck nodded in agreement.

"You want to play for funny—I mean money?" Annie asked, wondering why she'd just tripped over her tongue.

"I had something a bit more personal in mind."

"Yeah," echoed Frank. "Like a kiss a ball. You know, for every ball you beat us by, you owe us a kiss. It's only fair, since we're the losers."

Listening to their convoluted logic made Annie's head spin, which didn't help any because the room was already swaying in a Tilt-a-whirl rhythm of its own. "What if I say no?" she reasoned, fanning her face with her hand. "I mean, if you're the losers, shouldn't I be the one to win something?"

Frank tossed his friends a hangdog look. "She's right, boys. It's us ought to be owin' her the kisses, Annie bein' the better player and all."

Sagely, the trio nodded. She grinned her relief. Put that way, the idea made a lot more sense.

Propped in a corner of the pool room, Tom watched Annie bend over the table to make the break. With her shapely rear just begging for the touch of his hands, it was all he could do to stop himself from stomping over there and dragging her away. She seemed to be having the time of her life, but she was doing a bad job of keeping them inconspicuous.

She'd played the first game in a fairly demure fashion, but that trick with the buttons and the ice cube had caught the attention of every man within twenty feet of the table. The way she was wiggling her fanny and leaning into the shot had those three goobers salivating like starving dogs.

And how could she have fallen for their stupid *kiss-a-ball* bet? Sidling over to the next table, he strained to hear the rest of the conversation.

"Oops!" said Annie after she scratched the shot. "Looks like I'm losing my tush . . . I mean touch." She heaved a sigh and undid another button. The men threw each other wolfish grins.

"That was my fault, honey," said the guy she had yet to play. "I bumped the table. Sorry."

"You should be," the man she'd just beaten scolded. "That means Annie can have two shots to get it right." He walked next to her and set his hand low on her back. "Go ahead, darlin'. I'm here to help."

Instead of taking a poke at the guy, she turned her head and blew the goober a kiss. A kiss! What the hell was that all about?

Seething inside, Tom moved closer. This woman wasn't acting like the Annie he'd been traveling with for the past two days, and she definitely wasn't the same Annie he'd been married to. He accepted the fact that she'd changed since his death, but he found it impossible to believe she would sink to the depths of flirting with these . . . these . . . roughnecks.

Roaming to the next table, he tried to stay out of the way, which was easy, because Annie's antics had drawn a crowd of men who refused to let him join their inner circle. And every one of them had his eyeballs glued to her chest or her ass.

Holy Shit, they were ogling his wife!

Annie scratched again, and the gaggle of goobers moaned a collective gasp of sympathy. "That's all right, little lady," one rube shouted. "It's only gonna cost you a kiss."

She moved back and leaned into her cue stick, a puzzled frown marring her face. The man she was playing finished off the table, then swaggered over with a sly grin on his face. Annie shook her head. "Let's see. I got one, two, four balls in the little holes and you got—?"

"All the rest." Showing dimples and a flashy gold front tooth, he took her stick and set it on the table. She stumbled into his chest, and he caught her in an embrace. "Guess it's time to pay my debt."

Bending down, he planted his lips on hers, and the crowd went wild. Annie wrapped her arms around his neck, and the men climbed over one another like ants on a cracker crumb, all fighting for the chance to play a game with her.

Tom saw red. Shoving his way through the mob, he made it to her side just as the they broke apart. Staring through glassy eyes, she gave him a wide-eyed smile. "Why, hello, Mr. Falcone. Fancy feeting you here."

Tom set his hand on her arm, and the guy holding her pushed it away. "Get in line behind the rest of the pack, punk face. I'm still payin' up."

"Punk face. That's cute." Annie giggled. "You heard the man, funk face. Line up like a good boy. Frank here—"

"I'm Bobby."

"You're Bucky?"

"Whatever." The guy moved to kiss her again.

A growl spewed up from somewhere deep inside of Tom as he grabbed Annie's arm and pulled.

"Hey! Let her go."

After that, everything seemed to move at light speed. Tom ducked Bobby's meaty hand, and Bobby shot forward, plowing his fist into the nose of the guy standing behind Tom.

Gathering Annie close, Tom led her around the pool table, hoping they could make it to the door before someone else—namely him—got hurt.

"Isn't this great?" chirped Annie. She turned and started heading back to the action. "L'emme go. I wanna kick some butt."

"Yeah. Friggin' wonderful." Tom held her tight and steered her in front of him. Someone tapped him hard on the shoulder and he spun on his heel. Another fist headed his way and he darted right, dragging Annie with him. Unfortunately, she wasn't quick enough to get out of the line of fire.

The shot connected with her face and she whirled in place, then fell backward into his arms. Together they stumbled toward a chair along the wall, where he propped her like an oversized rag doll, legs stuck straight out in front of her.

Tom hadn't even caught his breath when a beefy hand clamped his shoulder and jerked him around. Just before the burly guy's fist made contact with his gut, Tom blocked the punch and aimed a right cross dead center in the man's jaw.

The guy staggered back against two of Annie's pool buddies who were charging to her rescue. While the trio disentangled themselves, Tom hoisted her over his shoulder in a fireman's carry and snaked his way toward the door.

Behind him, all hell broke loose.

CHAPTER ELEVEN

Annie groaned. The hammering inside her head rose to a dull-but-steady clanging, reminiscent of steel on steel. She furrowed her brow and the pounding switched to sharp jabs, tiny pitchforks stabbing behind her eyes and face.

The idea that she'd been hit by a bus briefly crossed her mind. Then she remembered who she'd been with for the past few days. The way her luck was running, she'd probably been thrown from the Harley and Drew Falcone had backed over her. She wouldn't put it past him to do something despicable, just to get even for that haircut.

She opened her right eye, then her left and found the room barely light. She took a deep breath and her skin came awake inch by agonizing inch with an aching tingle that started in her hair and moved over her face to her neck and shoulders, shooting prickles of pain along the way.

The tingle drilled her arms and hands and she peered down at her fingers, entwined with the same strong-looking, blunt-tipped digits that had held her so possessively the other morning. The manly hand flexed against hers and she stifled another groan as the rest of her muscles came to life.

The memory of all the times she'd awakened nestled against Tom rushed back in a disconcerting wave of longing. Her husband might have been an insensitive clod, but he'd been a wonderful lover. He'd always known just where to touch her, exactly how to kiss her to make her feel complete. And he'd had a special way of using his tongue on her nipples that could bring her to climax even before he'd stroked her G-spot.

Something told her Drew Falcone had the ability to do all of the above . . . maybe better.

Annie knew the smart thing would be to jump out of bed and run from the room, even though it felt as if the entire tympani section of the New York Philharmonic had taken up residence inside her head. But she was frozen in place. Drew settled his big, hard body closer against her back and she shuddered at the familiar prodding of his erection. The urge to turn and lose herself in his embrace was so compelling it almost obliterated the tingling jabs still pummeling her from the inside out. It had been such a long time since she'd been held by a man or found pleasure in the touch of another human being that the foreign sensation made her physically weak.

Besides, she ached so badly it hurt too much to resist. Dare she let nature take its course and . . .

Inhaling a breath, she inched to the edge of the mattress. No matter what had happened to her last night, this morning she needed to wise up and listen with her head, not her hormones. So what if her personal life wasn't all that fulfilling? She had the respect of her coworkers and a career she enjoyed. She'd worked too hard and too long to throw it all away on a loose cannon like Drew Falcone.

Still, she couldn't help but wonder what she'd be doing right now if this were another time, another place.

Another man.

His hands wandered to her breasts, and she stifled a moan. Drew's thighs cupped her from behind and the proof of his masculinity nudged against her bottom. When his searching fingers plucked at her nipples, it was as if she'd been touched by a live wire.

Flying off the mattress, she fell onto the twelve inches of floor between the bed and wall. The room spun as she fumbled to her knees. Holding her head in her hands, she raised her gaze to meet his too-cheery grin.

"Feeling a little under the weather, are we?"

Annie wished she had the strength to reach out and slap him. "What the heck happened to me?"

"You don't remember?"

She thrust out her jaw and cupped her cheek in her palm. Hissing at the pain, she poked tentatively at the tender spot. "Jeez, what did I do? Run face first into a brick wall?"

Drew's expression turned as innocent as a choir boy's. "You got in the way of a fist last night."

"I did? When? Where?"

"You really don't remember, do you?"

Annie gritted her teeth, but that only made her face feel as if it were caught in a vise. "Give me a clue, would you?"

"Hmmm. Maybe it had something to do with the fact that you'd dolled yourself up, poured yourself into a pair of jeans and stopped in that bar down the road. You looked kind of like a—a—" He snapped his fingers, searching for the words. "Cat on the prowl."

Insulted, she knelt upright and set her palms on the bed. "Me? On the prowl? You've got to be—" She stared down at her shirt, skimpy and unbuttoned far enough to expose her bra. Struggling to stand, she ran her hands over her thighs and tugged at the skin-tight denim. "Oh, crap."

"That about sums it up," he said through smug lips. "I couldn't believe it when I saw you drinking."

I was drinking?

Closing her eyes, she rested her backside against the wall

and clutched at the open expanse of shirt. The night was coming back to her in a haze of broken images. Drew had left her alone, pleading that he needed peace and quiet, which had ticked her off royally. Then she'd read that notebook and gotten really angry. She'd dyed her hair a radical shade of red, squeezed into a new pair of jeans and troweled on enough makeup to put Tammy Faye to shame. After that . . .

She inhaled the stale after burn of cigarettes clinging to her hair and clothes. The sickening smell brought the night into sharper focus. A dim noisy bar with a band and country dancing. She'd two-stepped with a man she didn't know, downed a diet soda, played pool with a couple of good ol' boys, and guzzled more Diet Coke.

I kissed a total stranger.

"You heard me order a soda. Someone must have doctored my drink."

"Knowing your tolerance for alcohol, I guessed as much." He propped his head in his hand. "You were shit-faced."

"Shit-faced! My tolerance for—What do you know about me and alcohol? I'm a grown-up. I'm entitled to drink if I want to. And who the heck hit me?"

Drew's mouth thinned to a frown. "What I meant to say was it's obvious you can't handle booze. My guess is one of those guys you were flirting with slipped a shot of gin or vodka into your drink, just to see what would happen. Probably did it to your second glass, too."

The choir boy innocence returned. "Then there was the fight. Thanks to your precision with a pool cue—or maybe it was your quest for attention—things got a little . . . wild."

Flirting? A fight!

The flat, bitter-tasting soda, the overly warm room and the rolling floor, as steady as a rowboat in a hurricane, crept into Annie's memory. The only reason she'd gone to that bar in the first place was to show Drew Falcone she wasn't as desperate or eager to find a man as he'd written in that damned notebook. She'd never meant to make a fool of herself or cause a brawl. They were supposed to be in hiding, and she'd been reckless enough to let her anger override her common sense. Whatever happened had been all her fault.

"And my face?"

"You were in the wrong place at the right time. I came to your rescue."

"This is what you call a rescue?" She pointed to her cheekbone. "I'd hate to see what would happen if you led the attack."

He frowned again and glanced over his shoulder. Annie followed his gaze to Art's Harley, which took up all the spare space in the front of the room. "What is that doing in here?"

Drew stood and stretched, pulling his plaid shirt taut over his wall-sized chest. His porcupine hairdo had flattened against his head, he needed a shave and his clothes were disheveled, but he still looked like a man who could set female hearts from eight to eighty on fire.

She stared at the rumpled bed linens, the two pillows so close they overlapped. It was then Annie realized they'd shared the bed *under* the covers, side by side but fully clothed. Thank the Lord for small favors.

"I'm not criticizing, but you didn't exactly do your part to keep us low-key last night." He scratched at his head, ruffling the spikes to attention. "After the fight, we left some pretty angry men at that bar. I was afraid one of them might wander over here, put two and two together and disable our transportation. Believe me, this is the last place we want to be stranded."

Her stomach heaved. Drew was telling her in the nicest way possible that she'd gotten them into trouble and he'd been the one clear-headed enough to keep them safe. The room did a three-sixty and tilted to the right. She swallowed a breath. "I have to . . . um . . ."

Annie turned three shades of green and rushed around the wall into the bathroom. Poor kid, thought Tom. That shiner was going to last a good long time. Too bad he hadn't rounded up some ice last night and figured out a way to keep it on her cheek.

He heard the toilet flush. Just wait until she caught a look at her—

"Oh, my God."

He shook his head. The sound of the shower running warned him he'd been given a reprieve. Annie had rarely imbibed when they'd been in college and never after they'd married. If he was lucky, she'd be so embarrassed over what happened she'd forget to grill him on the stupid comment he'd made about her not being able to hold her liquor. He had to remember to keep his guard up. Milton had stated quite specifically that he wasn't supposed to let Annie know who he was. This time around, he intended to follow the rules.

Tom figured it was his turn to go out and get breakfast. He could use the men's room in the motel lobby, find a fast food joint and be back by the time Annie washed and rinsed. After last night, she deserved a real breakfast. No more prisoner of war food and nothing that hinted at a diet. Fu Manchu had been dead on. Big and sassy was looking damned good, even with a nasty hangover, firecracker-colored hair and a wicked black eye.

Annie towel dried her hair, wincing when the hot air shooting from the blow-dryer caused her pain. She leaned into the mirror and checked out her throbbing eye and cheek for the tenth time. The entire area from her eyebrow to the corner of her lip and from her nose across to her hairline was swollen and dark purple. She shook her head. The entire cosmetics section of Wal–Mart wouldn't be enough to cover up this bruising.

Sighing, she tugged on a clean bra and panties, then her sweats and heavy socks. Fluffing up her curls, she sat on the commode seat and listened for activity in the other room. From the quiet, it was apparent her traveling companion had gone out, probably to scrounge up breakfast.

Breakfast. The very word made her stomach churn. The few times she'd tried to drink in college, the only thing that helped had been hot tea, wheat toast and aspirin. She'd tried alcohol again one final time after graduation from FLETC, with the same results. She'd been such a dope not to have realized what had happened the second she woke up.

Then again, it was no wonder she'd been confused. Drew Falcone was a menace, the way he made her forget things— her job, her morals, her common sense. Okay, so maybe she hadn't done the most prudent thing when she'd marched to that bar in anger, but darn it, he'd forced her hand. Sort of.

Satisfied she'd rationalized it all, she stood and gave herself a final inspection in the mirror. Aside from a layer of fast-setting concrete, nothing man-made could cover up her shiner, but a towel full of ice might reduce the swelling and help with the pain. If only she looked decent enough to crawl to the ice machine and make herself an ice pack.

She strode into the main room to find the sun streaming through wide-open curtains and the Harley gone. Picking up the notebook off the credenza, she flipped through the pages, then stuffed it back in the bottom of the duffel bag. Reading the cursed thing was only getting her in trouble. At least Drew hadn't noticed she'd left it out in plain sight. The last thing she wanted was to be given the third degree on why she'd snooped. When the time was right, she'd give him a chance to explain the rude remarks he'd written about her. Until a week ago at the safe house, they'd never met.

After last night, he had to know she wasn't desperate—just stupid.

One knock, a hesitation and two more raps had her stumbling toward the door. She opened it and Drew walked jauntily inside. He set a couple of paper bags on the table, then turned and gave her a quick once-over.

"You look better. How do you feel?"

"Like road kill. What is that smell?"

He opened the first bag and began unloading the contents. "Bacon, egg and cheese croissants, breakfast fries—"

"Barf." Annie clutched at her queasy stomach.

"Hot tea for you, coffee for me. And these." He tossed a small plastic container on the table. "They're for headaches, body aches, all kinds of aches."

Annie rolled her eyes. Good thing he hadn't brought her wheat toast, or she'd be forced to think he was clairvoyant.

"Oh, yeah, I almost forgot." He opened the second bag and took out a foil-wrapped packet. "I bought a loaf of wheat bread at the convenience store and had them toast a few slices, just in case none of this stuff appealed to you."

She staggered into the nearest chair.

"Hey, you okay?" Drew opened the tea and set the Styrofoam cup in front of her, then uncapped the bottle of ibuprofen and handed her two. "Swallow a couple of these while I get some ice for your face."

He grabbed the ice bucket and was out the door before she could speak. Annie sat forward and hunched over, inhaling the steam rising off the tea. He'd even been thoughtful enough to find the spicy orange kind she liked best. Could things get any weirder?

She dunked the tea bag a few times, then blew across the top of the cup. She downed the pain pills he'd given her, then took two more, letting the warm, tangy liquid soothe her rolling stomach. She stared at the foil-wrapped toast and shrugged. What the heck, she might as well take a bite, just to see if it helped. She'd worry about his E.S.P. later.

* * *

Tom filled the ice bucket and took his time wandering back to the room. It was a beautiful morning, one of those crisp fall days when the sunshine was so bright it cut like a laser through the clouds and polished the sky to a brilliant azure blue.

Glancing toward the mountains, he felt a powerful rush of awareness. Last night, he'd had another dream, this one more vivid than the first. It had again been like watching a home video, only things had moved at a faster pace. He'd been on a vacation with his brothers, the last one they'd taken together before Drew left for college. They'd driven up to the family cabin in Sal's battered Jeep, nose to nose with food, outdoor gear and a couple of two gallon cans of gasoline for the generator. He'd relived that entire two weeks in just a few hours of sleep, found out the basics of his brothers' lives and gained insight into many of the things he'd need to fit in with his new family.

Somewhere in those mountains was a picture perfect lake where the fish practically jumped into the boat he knew sat tucked under a little pier that ran out into the water. And next to the lake was a cabin with four rooms of rickety-but-serviceable furniture, a gas-powered generator and total peace and quiet. He wasn't sure of the exact road he and Annie needed to take to get there, but he knew he could depend on that muscle memory thing to guide him.

They'd stock up on groceries at a rundown bait-and-tackle shop they would pass on the way to the lake. The store sold everything from worms and candy bars to gasoline and roast beef. The cabin even had a cell phone they could use, once the generator was up and running. He could call Martin Phillips, and Annie could call her superiors. He could even phone his dad.

His dad. The simple words conjured a gut full of jitters. He wasn't going to call Florida. He didn't even know if

Marion and Forest McAllister were still alive. But he did know the number for Drew Falcone's father . . . his father now. The same gut jitters that prodded him to call, told him the man was supposed to help. Eventually, Tom was going to have to interact with Vincent Falcone.

He ran a hand through his hedgehog hair and sighed. When he'd awakened this morning with Annie in his arms, it had taken him a while to absorb all that he'd learned from the dream. He prayed to God he wouldn't blow it.

At the motel room door, he gave the secret knock, but no one answered. Frowning, he used his keycard to open the door. Annie had closed the curtains, and the room was dim; but he could still make out her shapely form lying on the bed.

"Hey, you awake?" He stepped inside and carefully slid the dead bolt and chain in place.

Receiving no answer, he tiptoed to the bathroom, took ice from the bucket and used the plastic liner to put together a makeshift ice pack. He walked to the bed where Annie was sound asleep, curled into a protective ball facing the wall. Tom sat next to her on the mattress and tried to figure out a way to use the pack without waking her or causing her pain. Finally, he moved her pillow and gently adjusted her head so that her left cheek rested on the ice-filled wash-cloth.

He smiled at her crazy red curls. Little Orphan Annie immediately came to mind, but she'd be furious if he said it out loud. After her parents had died, someone at school had made the tasteless remark, and Annie had wiped him off her list of friends forever.

Tentatively, he brushed at a burnished corkscrew, soft and glistening under his hand. He'd been an idiot when he'd demanded she dye her hair that weird shade of blond. If she knew his present hair color was giving him a taste of his own medicine, they'd have a good laugh over it. But she couldn't know, mustn't ever find out who he was or why he'd returned.

He had a long list of regrets rolling around inside his brain and so many challenging scenarios he was having a hard time keeping them all straight. Milton had warned him it wouldn't be easy, but he hadn't listened. Instead, he'd smart talked his way into this situation just like he'd smart talked his way through his old life. He didn't even want to think about how he'd hurt Annie. Or what he was feeling for her now. All he knew for certain was that his world had changed. He had a father and brothers, a completely different career . . . a completely different life.

He rose from the bed and ran a hand over his jaw. First things first. Annie needed sleep, and he needed to finish reading that notebook. It was up to him to get them out of this mess so he could do the job he'd been sent here to do.

Find the perfect man for his wife.

Annie woke snuggled under a blanket. The room was dim, and there was something wet and cold pressing against her cheek, but she was toasty warm and comfortable. Even the ache in her head had faded to a dull throbbing.

Rolling over, she scanned the room and spotted Drew sitting at the table reading a newspaper. It was apparent he'd showered and shaved, but he had on the same plaid shirt and jeans he'd worn last night. His forehead rested in his hands as he read, and the concentrated pose triggered a distant memory. Who else that she knew read the paper that way? Her father? Her sister or Phil? The image slipped from view and she sighed.

Stretching under the covers, she thought about what had transpired in the bar last night. She finally remembered the fight and getting socked in the face. After that, everything blurred into the single fact that Drew had taken care of her.

He'd brought her back here, tucked her in bed, tended to her needs and stood guard while she slept.

Maybe he wasn't such a jerk after all.

"Hey, sleepy head. You awake?"

"Hmph." Annie peered from under the edge of the blanket. "What time is it?"

He folded the paper and stood. "Almost time for dinner. You hungry?"

"Dinner? Why didn't you wake me? We need to be on the road." She swallowed a wave of nausea at the thought of climbing onto the back of the motorcycle. "Don't we?"

Drew walked around the bed and sat next to her. "I made an executive decision while you were sawing wood. We're going to stay here until tomorrow morning. There's no way you can travel, unless I strap you to the Harley, and that didn't sound like a good idea."

Annie struggled to sit up and the room did another spin and tilt. Placing his hands on her shoulders, he pressed her back into the mattress and laid a hand on her forehead.

"What are you doing?" she said, trying not to groan.

"Checking to see if you have a fever. Lie still." His fingers feathered over her eyebrow and around her eye to her cheek. "Does this hurt?"

She nodded yes, unwilling to admit the touch of his hand felt soothing and tender as a baby's breath against her skin.

"This?" He ran his fingers to the bridge of her nose and down to the tip.

"Nuh-uh."

His thumb traced the shape of her lips, stopping at the edge of her mouth. "How about here?"

She sucked in a breath and pushed his hand away. "I'm fine. You should—"

"Kiss it and make it better?" Before Annie could stop him, he leaned forward and placed his mouth lightly against hers. A tingle started in her toes and worked its way up to her belly and breasts. Her nipples puckered as he moved his lips as though savoring the taste of her. Nibbling gently, he feasted, running the tip of his tongue along the seam of her mouth.

She parted her lips as if it were the most natural thing in the world, and he took full advantage, using his tongue to melt her insides. When he cupped the pain-free side of her face and deepened the kiss, she grew dizzy with desire.

Don't stop. Please, don't ever stop.

The urge to lose herself in his arms was overwhelming. Fisting her hands, she clenched at his shirt front and tugged him closer. He settled against her and snaked a hand between them. Fondling her breast, he squeezed a throbbing nipple in his fingers, and she moaned at the exquisite sensation.

He pulled away with a jerk and stared into her eyes. "Sorry, I didn't mean to hurt you."

"You didn't. I'm . . . fine. Perfectly fine."

"Sure you are." He shook his head and sat upright, his gaze on her lips. Finally, he sighed. "I think it's time I found us something to eat. What sounds good?"

You? Shocked by the instantaneous thought, a wave of heat flooded her chest. She sat up and the soggy ice pack slid from somewhere around her shoulder to her lap. "Umm, something warm. Soup maybe, or . . . soup."

He picked up the sodden towel and stood. "Soup it is. But it might take me a while. I could probably buy a can at that convenience store and heat it in the microwave. How does chicken noodle sound?"

Annie worried her lower lip. Aside from the fact he wanted to get in her pants, why was he being so nice? Pivoting on her fanny, she sat on the side of the bed and found the headache she thought she'd lost lurking just behind her eyelids.

"First, I want to ask you a question."

He grinned and propped himself against the wall. "Are you alive? I'd say barely. How bad is the shiner? On a scale of one to ten, I'd give it an eight. Can you go out in public?

Only if you don't mind people staring while their kids flee in terror.''

"Very funny," she mumbled, testing her jaw. She rose to her feet, and he reached out to steady her. "I want to know how I got here after the brawl."

"Simple. I carried you." Backing out of the narrow space, he guided her to the bathroom door.

Another rush of heat raced to her cheeks. She was no light weight under the best of circumstances. All she could have been last night was ballast. "You shouldn't have done that. I mean, you could have hurt yourself. I'm . . . um . . . heavy."

He let go of her arm and ran both of his hands through his hair. His dark-eyed gaze raked her from head to toe and back again as he exhaled a breath. "You're just right. Now, I'm leaving to get dinner. I'll be back in about a half hour."

CHAPTER TWELVE

Inhaling the brisk autumn air, Annie rested her right cheek against Drew's back, held on tight to his waist and clutched his hips with her thighs. Common sense told her this was the only way they could ride the Harley, but she wasn't happy about the way it made her feel all warm and tingly inside, not to mention just a little bit naughty . . . and decadent . . . and alive.

The powerful bike climbed like a champion racer, taking the twists, turns and steep grades of the mountain in stride. Wind whistled past in a bracing rush, blurring the blazing fall colors of orange, umber, red and gold as leaves swirled off the trees and flew up from the pavement in their wake.

Letting the past few hours play in her mind, she realized the time had passed in a crazy quilt of experiences. The bar, the dancing, the alcohol and the fight were still a fuzzy memory. She'd overdosed on ibuprofen, slept like a brick, ate what her stomach could handle and slept some more. Last night, after her dinner of chicken noodle soup and whole wheat bread, she and Drew had watched the news.

Though their escape was a sidebar to other more important stories, their pictures were still plastered on the screen for the world to see.

Not only was she annoyed she hadn't been able to call her superior to set the record straight, she was ticked that some public relations idiot had chosen an old photo from one of her training sessions at FLETC to air on nationwide TV. Wearing baggy sweats, a Kevlar vest, ratty sneakers and a baseball cap, Annie thought she looked like a female bank robber in search of a lineup. Drew's shot, on the other hand, was flattering to the point of a movie star press release. He looked like a smooth, cultured man of the world. It was hard to believe Dominic Viglioni would want the woman in that picture for his *maid,* never mind his *moll.*

Better still, after viewing those photos, Drew had agreed that traveling via the Harley and radically changing their looks had probably been the right way to go.

The ritual of eating dinner and watching TV had wiped her out, and she'd fallen asleep on top of the covers. This morning, she'd awakened to find him gone while she was bundled toasty warm under the blankets with another soggy ice bag against her cheek. The idea that tough guy Drew Falcone was taking care of her and she was starting to enjoy it unnerved her, so she pushed it to the back of her mind. By the time he'd returned with their breakfast, she had showered, dressed and begun the task of packing up and moving them out.

They'd been on the road for hours, and over the last thirty minutes, Annie had spied several stretches of sparkling blue water peeking from the foliage. Relieved they were nearing the cabin, she ordered her empty stomach to stop grumbling and be patient. As if reading her mind, Drew slowed the bike and steered toward a rundown little store fronted by two ancient globe-topped gas pumps. After stopping at one of the pumps, he held the motorcycle steady, dropped the kickstand and swung off the seat. Removing his helmet, he gazed at the doors of the Lake Mary Bait, Tackle and Grocery.

"This is the place I told you about. Earl's the owner. Go inside and start shopping. We'll need to stock up for a few days."

Hauling herself off the bike, Annie's knees buckled, and he caught her in his arms. While he'd adapted quickly to riding the Harley, she was still trying to find her "biker legs." She took off the helmet and grimaced at the way the sudden release of pressure jarred her cheekbone. Time for another dose of pain killers and hot tea, she thought, scanning the store and, in the distance, a boat dock that led to the lake. She needed to use the restroom, but had a sneaking suspicion she'd find it about thirty yards away, hidden behind a door branded with a star and moon.

"You hurt much?" Drew asked, taking in her swollen face.

"I wouldn't call it much, but I bet I look a fright. Black and purple were never one of my best color combos."

He grinned. "Earl wears coke bottle lenses. I doubt he'll notice. Besides"—he reached out and touched the tip of her nose—"you look kind of cute, all lopsided and puffy."

She raised the right side of her mouth. "Gee thanks. I'll try to remember that when Earl's jaw drops and he starts screaming."

She headed into the store, grabbed a plastic basket from a stack next to the door and began to tour the aisles. After ten minutes she had to admit the selection wasn't half bad. The store carried a decent variety of baked goods, canned food, lunch meat and condiments. She even found fresh fruit and a pile of string beans that looked just picked. She'd filled one basket, set it on the worn counter and started on the second by the time Drew walked inside.

He stepped to the counter and rang the silver bell next to the register. "Hello! Anybody here?"

Seconds later a stoop-shouldered fellow with a limping

gait and a tuft of gray hair on his head ambled through a door carved into the back wall of the store. Annie ducked, hoping she wouldn't fall prey to his scrutiny, while Drew stayed put and concentrated on counting his money.

"Sorry 'bout that. I was out on the dock seein' to the boats." Squinting through thick glasses, the man paused, then gave a toothy grin. "Well, I'll be damned. Haven't seen one a'you Falcone boys in a coon's age. How's ol' Vince doin'?"

Drew stopped flipping through the stack of twenties and looked toward Annie, then the man she assumed was Earl. Hoping the old guy would get so caught up in the reunion he wouldn't have time to examine her face, she pretended to shop while she eavesdropped.

"Um . . . fine. Vincent—my dad—Vince, um, he's fine." Tom's gut fluttered. It was weird, talking to some guy who knew him and his brothers and father, when he didn't know the men at all.

"Which one are you, anyway?" Earl scratched at his jaw. "No, no, don't tell me." He ran his watery gray gaze over Tom as if he were inspecting a five-year-old kid. "Sal's taller, so you can't be him. Hmm." The old codger snapped his fingers. "Hold up yer hand," he ordered.

Tom did as he was told.

"Not the right one, ya id'jet. The left one."

He jumped when Earl grabbed his hand and brought it to the tip of his nose. "Yep, you're Drew, just like I thought. Still got the scar where that fish hook punctured yer palm the summer you was ten." He let go of Tom's hand and laughed. "Near bled to death right there on my floor, you did. Lucky for you and Vince I'd had medical trainin' in Korea. That sucker took six stitches to close."

Spotting the blotchy brown spot about twelve inches in diameter staining the weathered floorboards in the area where Earl was pointing, Tom swallowed hard. It was a miracle his new body hadn't contracted tetanus, getting sewn up in a place this filthy. He stared at his hand and the small, thin scar. Then again, the white line looked almost as neat as the one he'd had on his former body, where he'd gashed his leg after falling off his bike when he was seven.

"So, how's your old man? Haven't seen him in oh, 'bout a month. He stocked up real good when he left here. Thought maybe he'd brought company up to the cabin, he bought so much food and gasoline."

"Dad is fine, like I said," Tom muttered. "I filled a motorcycle tank. I was wondering if you'd sell me a couple of cans of gas so I could power up the generator."

Earl raised one gray eyebrow. "Shoot, I'm still loanin' the cans to my old customers. Grab what you need from behind the front door and fill 'em up—bring 'em back when you leave, is all." He rang up the amount Tom told him was on the pump and added enough to cover the extra gas, then pointed to the basket. "I imagine this here's yours, too."

Annie strolled to the counter with her right side toward Earl and set down a second round of groceries. Earl's eyebrows did a bob and roll as he squinted toward Annie then Tom.

"Well, well, well." He let the simple-yet-profound words speak for themselves.

With Tom carrying the gasoline cans and Annie the groceries, they walked to the Harley. In silence, he unloaded and rearranged the dual side compartments on the bike. Finally, he slung the duffel over the chrome backrest, balanced it across the rear fender and used a bungee cord to anchor it in place. Stepping back, he nodded that Annie should mount the bike.

"This thing is packed to the gills. Are you sure we're going to make it?"

Tom crossed his mental fingers. "This bike has plenty of horsepower. We just have to drive at a more sedate pace.

We should make the cabin in a half hour, then you can fix us something to eat while I get the generator going.''

Annie tugged on her helmet and winced.

''The water in the lake should be near frigid. We won't have ice, but I'll figure a way to get something cold on your cheek. How does that sound?''

Shrugging her shoulders, she sat back to make room for him. He climbed aboard and waited until he felt her arms wrap around him before he took off up the mountain toward the lake.

Annie stood on the front porch of the rustic cabin and gazed onto the tranquil water. A silvery moon hung low over the trees, surrounded by a sprinkling of stars that reminded her of crushed diamonds on black velvet. The mournful trill of night birds blended melodically with the sing-song chatter of insects and the croaking of frogs to form a tuneful symphony of nature. Every once in a while she heard the splat of water and imagined it was a fish jumping up to feed on a bug darting across the mirrorlike lake.

Drew had spent the remainder of the afternoon fiddling with the generator, hauling wood for the fireplace and hooking up the phone, while she'd taken care of putting away the groceries and familiarizing herself with the small-but-tidy house. Besides a kitchen with a large eating area and living room with fireplace, there was a small foyer that lead to a miniscule bath and two bedrooms, both equipped with double dressers and bunk beds. The fact that Drew's father had spent time here less than a month ago was evident from the pantry shelves lined with canned goods, fresh linens and two full containers of gasoline he'd left beside the generator, almost as if he expected to return at any moment.

She'd done a gourmet job with their dinner of bow-tie pasta, alfredo sauce, canned artichokes and tomatoes. Then, as if they had some unwritten agreement, Drew had told her to go out on the porch and relax while he cleaned up the serviceable kitchen.

She heard the rattle of stoneware and metallic clink of forks and spoons, a drawer closing, then the sound of the shower. An image of Drew standing wet and naked not twenty feet away set Annie's insides to churning, and she wrapped her arms tight around her middle. After sitting so close to him on the Harley, her body missed the feel of his powerful thighs and muscular back. He'd been difficult to ignore at the motel, when he filled the room with his presence. Alone here in the wilderness, without another living soul to interrupt them, the cozy cabin would be just like a real home.

And with their new-found domestic tranquility would come all the reminders of married life. Though she and Tom hadn't always seen eye to eye, she'd enjoyed their special dinners and chatty evenings almost as much as she'd enjoyed the cuddling. It wasn't that she didn't look forward to another man-woman relationship; she simply didn't want to make a second mistake with her life.

The crazy idea that she might find a better match in Drew Falcone had blindsided her, and she'd worked hard to shove it into a mental compartment labeled *don't even think about it.* From their conversations about FLETC, she knew they would have met there if she'd graduated from Rutgers and enlisted on schedule. How different things might have been if instead of marrying Tom, she'd followed her dream.

The door opened and Drew stepped onto the porch. Standing next to her in the darkness, he set his hands on the railing and sucked up a lungful of crisp mountain air. His hair was damp and tousled, and he had on his sweats and a clean white T-shirt. "It's beautiful out here, isn't it?"

"Like a little bit of heaven." Annie raised her gaze to the diamond-filled sky, hoping he wouldn't notice her frustration. "The stars are so close I bet if I climbed up on the roof I could touch them."

"I know what you mean. I used to love stargazing when I was a kid." A heartbeat passed before he asked, "Did you ever wish on a star, you know, like in that song from *Pinocchio?*"

Tom had loved watching the stars, too. That fact, coupled with what she'd done on the night he died, rushed up to claim her. "Once, a long time ago."

"When you were a kid or a grown-up? And what did you wish for?"

She shook her head. "I did it when I was all grown up, and it doesn't matter. My wish never came true."

"Never?"

"Well, actually there wasn't time for it to come true."

"You're talking in riddles. Come on, what was it? A new car? Winning the lottery?"

"Nothing that simple." But it could have been, she reminded herself, if Tom had lived.

"I'll tell you a wish I made once if you'll tell me yours."

Don't share your wishes with me, she wanted to say. *Don't tell me anything that might draw us closer or make me care.*

"I wanted a dog."

She held back a smile. Surely she could handle the typical little boy wish without losing her common sense. Besides, it would be rude to rebuff his attempt at pleasant conversation. "What kind of a dog?"

"Big or small, the breed didn't matter, just so long as it slept with me at night and played ball with me after school. I was a lonely little kid."

She gave a laugh of disbelief. "With four older brothers?"

"Oh . . . um . . . yeah. I was the baby, see. My brothers never seemed to have time for me. I got a fish instead."

Annie's stomach did a drop and slide. Except for the part about being the youngest brother, Tom had told her the same story once, almost word for word. She'd always felt sorry that he'd had to substitute a goldfish for siblings. Maybe if he—

"Now it's your turn. Tell me about your wish."

She sighed. What could it hurt? He already thought she was a nutcase, and from the sound of it, he'd believed in wishes once upon a time. "Okay, but no laughing. It wasn't nearly as concrete or sensible as the one you made."

He sidled closer and turned to rest his hip on the railing, which enabled him to gaze directly into her eyes. "This ought to be good," he said with a grin.

"I wished for my husband . . . our marriage . . . to be better. I wanted more from the relationship, and he hadn't been willing to compromise, so I thought that maybe God would help me find a way to make it happen."

Drew's teasing expression changed to one of sadness.

"Sorry, I told you it was different."

"No problem," he muttered, staring at his bare feet. "I just find it hard to believe."

Hoping to put some distance between them without making it obvious, Annie leaned sideways and propped her shoulder against the post. "Believe what? That I thought wishing on a star could help save my marriage, or get my husband to love me more?"

Drew's jaw clenched. "Don't say that."

"Say what?"

"That stuff about your husband. It isn't true that he didn't love you."

She rolled her eyes, trying to lighten the mood. Why was she arguing with a man who had no idea what she was talking about? He'd never met Tom. He hadn't even met her until a week ago. She had to be crazy, telling him all this personal stuff to begin with.

"Never mind. Forget I said anything. I told you it was—" She sighed. "Just never mind."

"I can't believe your husband didn't love you," he continued with almost stubborn determination.

"I didn't say he didn't love me. I said he didn't love me *enough*. There's a difference."

She focused on the lake, but he grabbed her elbows and turned her around to face him. "Don't pull away from me, Annie. I want to hear your side of it. Why do you think he didn't love you enough?"

She tugged from his grip and ran shaking fingers through her hair. "Why are you making such a big deal out of this? Tom is gone and I'm doing things my way now." Tossing her head, she frowned. "Besides, it doesn't matter anymore."

Drew cupped her chin and guided her head back around. "It will always matter. The guy was an idiot and he hurt you. I can't believe anyone would do that intentionally."

"He didn't," she said gruffly. "No one can hurt me but me. Dr. Bennet said so."

Hard as polished onyx, his dark eyes glittered in the moonlight. "Who's Dr. Bennet?"

She raised her shoulders up and down. "A psychologist I saw for a few months after Tom's death. He's a grief counselor."

Drew ran a hand through his hair. "Christ."

"And on that cheery note—" She turned toward the door. "I'd say it's bedtime."

With Tom following behind her, she walked into the cabin and straight to one of the bedrooms. She'd made up a set of bunk beds with sheets and blankets, but she wasn't looking forward to sleeping on the thin, musty mattress.

He stared at the uncomfortable-looking bunks and shook his head. "There is no way I'm letting you sleep on one of those rock beds. They're lumpy and damp, and it's cold in here. Come on."

He stomped to what she guessed was the newest piece of furniture in the cabin, a brightly colored plaid sofa angled directly across from the huge stone fireplace. After taking off the cushions, he unfolded the queen-sized hide-a-bed, revealing a plush mattress, a set of sheets and a quilt. "You can sleep here. I'll take one of the bunks."

Overtaken by a sudden rush of loneliness, Annie worried her lower lip. It had only been three nights, but she'd grown used to the feel of Drew's big, hard body pressed against hers in the night. The warmth of his breath tickling her ear and the comfort of his hands as they held her close had made her feel secure and, dare she say it, happier than she'd been in years. Yes, she was a deputy marshal, but she was a woman first—a lonely woman with a powerful attraction to a man she barely knew, but trusted with her life.

The idea came to her like a bubble of clarity floating on the evening breeze. Happiness, at least for a short while, was hers for the taking, if she was brave enough to grasp it.

"There's no heat in those rooms. You're going to freeze."

Drew stood across from her, his arms folded over his impressive chest. "I can use two blankets."

"There might be bugs or . . . or . . . mice."

He gave her a teasing half smile. "I'd say that's a pretty good possibility."

Darn it, but the conversation wasn't coming out the way she'd planned. "I'm . . . um . . . going to use the bathroom to take care of . . . things."

Tom watched her walk slowly into the back hall. Jeez, she was killing him. She'd all but issued him an engraved invitation to share her bed and he'd acted like a fool. He'd also let slip that business about the star, the dog and the goldfish. If she ever remembered he'd confided that story to her when they'd been married, he was dead meat.

He thought back to everything he'd been told by Milton. His main job was to find Annie the perfect man, but the angel hadn't said whether or not she'd have the right to accept or reject his choices. He'd also ordered Tom to go with the flow, take advantage of that muscle memory thing and follow his instincts.

Right now every instinct, hell, every muscle in his body, told him that tonight was the night he was supposed to sleep with Annie in this bed.

He heard the toilet flush and the sound of running water. He hefted a log from the woodpile and heaved it on the fire, still at a loss. He needed a sign, something concrete from a higher authority, telling him he wasn't out of line, that it was all right to give each other what they wanted. Resting his arms on the fireplace mantel, he set his forehead on his fists and did something he hadn't done in a very long while.

"Please, God, if you're out there and you're listening, send me a clue. Tell me what I'm supposed to do."

A gust of wind rattled the shutters, and Tom sighed. He'd really hoped the sign would be more substantial, maybe a voice booming down from heaven, or a bolt of lightning up the ass. Even the sound of Milton's voice whispering in his ear.

"The bathroom's all yours."

Definitely not something he would hear from Milton.

A hand, tentative and trembling, touched his shoulder. He turned and his mouth went dry. Annie stood a foot away, her voluptuous body backlighted by the blazing hearth. She wasn't wearing her heavy tights or much of anything else underneath her sleep shirt, which resembled a film of emerald green plastic wrap.

"I don't want to be alone tonight," she whispered, her golden eyes telling the rest of the story.

"Are you sure you know what you're asking for?"

Nodding, she stepped into his chest and wrapped her arms around his neck. "I know and I trust you. Make love to me, Drew I promise not to blame you in the morning."

Tom sighed as he gathered her up against him. She'd called him Drew again, but this time he was going to Ignore the hole it ate in his gut. It was his name now, and would be for the rest of his time on earth, with or without Annie.

"Yeah, but is it really what you want? Will it make you happy?"

She snuggled closer, then raised her head and gazed into his eyes. "I'm counting on you to make it perfect."

"I certainly hope you know what you're doing." Her elbows resting on her knees, Eloise sat Indian-style on the peak of the cabin roof. Dressed in a red flannel shirt, faded jeans and hiking boots, with her golden curls tucked under an Elmer Fudd hunting cap, she looked like heaven's version of a cartoon lumberjack.

Milton's *tsk* echoed in the night. "Of course I do. This is exactly what I hoped would happen. You're going to owe me an apology, once you see that I was right."

"Oh, really?" Eloise sniffed. "Tom still has to get them out of the mess they're in and convince Annie they belong together forever—without telling her the truth. In case you haven't noticed, he's had some pretty close calls."

"I've noticed." Milton gazed into the heavens. "But he's caught himself each time and recapped the rules admirably. I just hope He's otherwise occupied while my plan has time to unfold."

"Ah-hah!" the angelic Elmer said with a snap of her fingers. "So you admit your plan is unconventional and unapproved. I knew you were cheating."

"Not cheating—helping. And it was approved, in a round-about way." Feeling put upon, Milton decided to go on the attack. "May I remind you that you're the reason both of them—no, all three of them—are in this mess in the first place. If you hadn't—"

"Abandoned Tom and blah-blah-blah. All right already. I get your point. But even He agreed I had just cause, Tom being such a lousy husband and all." One delicate brow disappeared under the brim of her hat. "You do realize you can't cross any more lines here? Whatever feelings Tom and Annie have for each other must evolve naturally and from the heart, without any further *help* from you."

Milton adjusted the lapels of his snowy white tuxedo. "Of course I understand. But I still have the right to aid Tom in his quest . . . unless you'd like to take him back?"

Eloise's ocean blue eyes grew round as dessert plates. "Now? While the two of them are down there doing who knows what with each other." She wrinkled her upturned nose. "Ee-uuu. No thank you."

"Oh, honestly. Sometimes you are such a prude. Sexual intercourse is a perfectly natural human act when practiced between two people who genuinely care for each other and are hoping to find meaning in their relationship. Besides, it leads to babies. Lots and lots of glorious little babies." The idea of a plethora of tiny, sweet-smelling humans who might need him in the future tickled at Milton's heart. There was nothing he enjoyed more than getting a new soul to care for, a new—

"Hold it right there!" Eloise snapped, drifting upward from the roof. "Getting Annie with child would be cheating. A baby would force them to marry, which is not what this bet was about. She and Tom or Andrew or whatever you're calling him these days must fall in love with each other because they want to, not because they have to. If she gets pregnant, all bets are off."

"I know, I know. That's why I'm hoping Tom has the good sense to check the medicine chest. They'll have plenty of time for babies once they get their lives back on track."

Eloise nodded curtly. "Then I suggest you make sure it doesn't happen."

Milton watched the pale golden glitter of angel dust rise like a mini geyser as the too-beautiful being disappeared. Good riddance, he thought. Eloise was nothing but a bucket of cold water on the fires of romance. As far as he was concerned, things had been going swimmingly between Tom and Annie. Knowing that she and Drew had been perfect for each other, and that she and Tom had been husband and wife in a prior life, made their foray into intimacy totally acceptable in his book. Too bad Eloise had called him on the baby business. He'd hoped she wouldn't notice. And lucky for everyone he'd prepared for that very possibility.

CHAPTER THIRTEEN

From the second Drew Falcone knocked Annie flat on her basketball-playing fanny, he'd scrambled her hormones and thrown her entire life into turmoil. It had taken time, but he'd finally wormed his way into her system. She didn't doubt he could still be a jerk, but her heart had elevated him to a sexy, funny, caring jerk, which changed everything.

Until this moment she'd been positive he wanted to take her to bed. So why was he staring at the floor instead of making a move or giving her a word of encouragement? Pressing closer, she felt the rasping of his breath, almost as if he were in pain, while his erection prodded against her thigh. Obviously, he wasn't immune to her presence, so what was the problem? Could it be that he still thought her desperate or sex-starved—or that she was joking? The man had shown her he was willing in a dozen different ways, practically from the moment they'd met. If he didn't react in the next three seconds, she was going to haul on her sweats, hop on the Harley and make a run for it.

When he hesitantly enfolded her in his arms, she exhaled

a huge sigh. "Say something, please, or I'm going to die of embarrassment right here on the spot."

His chest shook, and she realized he was trying not to laugh. Great. Instead of being irresistible, she was doing a stand-up comedy act. She had humbled herself to the point of begging, and he thought it was funny.

Dropping her arms to her sides, Annie took a step back and concentrated on the crackling fire. "Okay, I get it. You don't want to go to bed—have sex—er—You don't want to do what I want to do. Fine. Great. Just go to sleep on that bottom bunk in the other room. If you're lucky, the mice won't make a midnight snack out of any of your important parts."

Drew took her chin in his hand and raised her head. He smiled, but not in the usual go-to-hell way he did when he was egging her on. "You've got it all wrong, Annie. The laugh was one of relief. I wanted you the second I laid eyes on you. Hell, I pulled back so many times I'd prepared myself for a week's worth of cold showers while we were up here. Your offer is an answer to my prayers."

His candid confession had her heart skipping into overdrive. At least she wasn't wrong about the signals he'd been sending. "Then what's so funny? I know I look like a prize fighter with this big ugly bruise and all—"

"You look adorable. And sexy as sin. But you're also very vulnerable right now. I kidnapped you, dragged you into my assignment without your permission and turned your entire life sideways." He traced a gentle finger along her aching cheekbone. "Not to mention being partly responsible for this."

She jabbed a no-nonsense finger in his chest. "It was my decision to go to that bar, not yours."

He caught her hand and pulled her close. "Maybe so, but I should have protected you better. If there was any way I could go back and take that punch instead of you—"

She pressed shaking fingers to his lips. "Okay, so you

have a hero complex. Next time, I'll be sure to stay behind you instead of at your side. Now can we forget about the past and work on what's happening right this second?''

One by one, Drew kissed her knuckles, then moved his lips to her wrist, up her forearm to the sensitive skin inside her elbow. The tingling sensation rose to an electrical jolt as he followed the path of her arm to her shoulder and throat. When she felt his teeth nibble at her pulse point, she did a whole body tremble in his arms.

"We have all night to work on it." The suggestive whisper tickled her ear, sending shivers of anticipation dancing through every nerve in her body.

Then he kissed her for real, long and slow and deep, letting his tongue seduce her in a heady tango of desire. With their lips locked tight, he cupped her bottom with his hands and lifted her against his chest. Annie clutched his neck and wrapped her legs around his hips, intent on making them one being.

The kiss stretched to an eternity, until she thought he would suck all coherent thought from her mind. Inhaling a ragged breath, she pulled back and saw herself reflected in his eyes. Before she could speak, he let her slide down his body and she felt every impressive inch of him. Then he stepped back, dragged his T-shirt over his head and shucked off his jeans.

And this time she was the one smiling. He *had* been going commando, the devil.

Standing before her in the firelight with his rippling shoulders and perfectly sculpted chest, he called to mind the fairy tales she'd read of heroes prepared to brave all for the honor of their quest. She inspected the only visible evidence that he'd been shot, a small pink ridge next to his left nipple. Her gaze wandered down his washboard abs to his pulsing shaft rising from a nest of thick black hair. All controlled power and finely honed muscle, he was everything she'd ever imagined and so much more.

His grin grew cocky and Annie's cheeks burned. Between the heat from the fire and the inferno blazing inside of her, she thought she might incinerate before he held her.

"One of us is wearing way too many clothes." His statement hung in the air, fluttering against her senses like the wings of a trapped bird. "Unless you're having second thoughts."

Tom caught the shadow of doubt in her eyes. He could almost hear her heart, hesitant and thumping against her ribs, and he fought the urge to sweep her up and carry her to the bed. In the past, he'd been the one in charge. Tonight was for Annie. The next move was hers. He couldn't do a thing but wait.

Slowly, she raised the hem of her sleep shirt, inching the satiny fabric up her thighs, over the gentle swell of her belly to her magnificent breasts. His mouth watered at the memory of her nipples, tight, sweet-tasting buds of desire he'd suckled in his other life. The shirt rose higher, until she tugged it over her head and placed it on the foot of the bed. She was so sexy, so feminine, so beautiful, he thought his heart would stop beating if he touched her.

Her golden eyes darkened to molten copper. "I'm not exactly a fashion model."

He shook his head. "You're incredible."

Giving a small upturn to her lips, she flushed to her collarbone. Relieved he'd said the right thing, he gathered her up to his chest and kissed the top of her head. "I need to make a side trip. Climb into bed. I'll be right back."

Careful not to stumble over his feet in the dark, Tom hurried to the bathroom, searched the medicine chest and removed the box he'd seen there earlier. Ol' Vince had thought of everything the last time he'd stocked the cabin, right down to the condoms. He tore open the packet, grabbed a few extras for good luck and returned to the sofa in record time.

While he'd been gone, Annie had made the bed and turned

back the linens. Sitting up straight with the sheet pulled to her chin, she looked as if she were awaiting her execution. After setting the packets on the side table, he crawled beside her under the covers. She took one look at the rolled-up bit of latex and put a hand over her eyes.

"I forgot about birth control."

"No problem. The Falcone men are always prepared."

"I see."

But he knew she didn't, not really. "With five sons, I guess my dad thought it better to be safe than sorry. I've never brought a woman to the cabin, Annie, and I'm not into casual sex. Believe that."

She didn't answer, just stared at her fingers knotted with the sheets.

"We don't have to do this," he said, though the words scraped his throat raw.

She rose to her knees, tugged down the sheet and took the condom from his hand. Seconds later, he was breathing like a marathon runner, his hands on her shoulders as he leaned forward and began to torture them both with long drawn out kisses and butterfly touches of desire. Annie relaxed under his careful attention and became a willing participant. The tantalizing places on her body that he'd enjoyed so long ago were still there, only magnified a hundred fold. Her breasts were fuller, her nipples more sensitive, her hips more womanly, her cries a deeper, more complete surrender.

Cupping a breast, Tom suckled the throbbing peak and felt her shudder beneath him. Flicking her nipple with his tongue, he ran a hand between her thighs where he found her woman's core and the sensitive spot hidden inside. Circling the swollen bud, he led her to the brink of fulfillment time and again, until he thought they both might burst. The intimate gesture had her arching off the bed, her scream a joyous song to his soul. Her shattering climax brought a contentment he hadn't thought possible creeping into his heart, reminding him of all he'd missed.

Why hadn't he realized what he'd had years ago? Why had he been such a fool?

Kneeling back, he caught her in his arms and held her quivering body close, basking in her afterglow. She shuddered, and he pushed a tangle of damp curls from her forehead. Gazing up at him through amber-colored eyes, her face registered wonder—and surprise.

"That was—"

"Amazing?" The mind-blowing feeling set him on top of the world. "Thanks."

Her fingers feathered over his mouth to his cheek and sifted through his hair. "You're welcome."

"The night is young," he added, sitting back to cradle her in his lap. The soft burn of satisfaction shining from her eyes was almost enough to distract him from his aching erection. "I'm yours to command."

Annie had no idea how to respond. Though Tom had satisfied her in every way, he'd always been the one in control, the one who'd taken the lead in their loving. The thought that she could do whatever she wanted to Drew left her intrigued . . . and speechless.

"Hello. Anybody home?" He kissed her just above her bruise. "I didn't hurt you, did I?"

She hadn't a clue how to answer him. She ached, all right, but only for more of Drew Falcone. The desire to have him hot and pulsing inside of her became a sudden desperate need eating at a secret place deep in the hidden part of her heart.

Moving her hand down his corded stomach, she grasped his rock-hard shaft and teased him with her fingers. "You could never hurt me."

He groaned through clenched teeth. "Then how about you stop torturing me? Let me love you for real, Annie. Let me do it for both of us."

Never had she been more fully aware of her power as a woman. Catching his face between her palms, she saw a glimmer of something she'd long forgotten shining in his eyes and pushed it to the back of her mind. Taking what she'd longed for over the past several days, she kissed him as if he were the only man she'd ever kissed, held him as if he were her first love.

Together they leaned back down onto the mattress. Looming over him, she tasted every inch of sleekly honed muscle and salty-sweet skin. Sliding against his rigid body with her breasts and hips, she used her mouth to tease and adore until she had him writhing in her hands.

Scant seconds passed before Tom could stand no more of her tender ministrations. Gently, he guided her beneath him and settled into the cradle of her heat. Locking their hands above her head, he entered her in one sharp thrust that cut to his very soul. Annie moaned a cry of surrender, and he moved in rhythm to her searching hips, taking both of them to the place they were meant to go.

Her screams of passion echoed his own pangs of desire. Their heartbeats became a single sound drumming between them in a steady tattoo of passion, until finally they reached their climax in one endless explosion.

Time passed, filled only with the sounds of ragged breathing and the whisper of bed covers. Reluctantly, Tom rolled to his back. Pulling Annie over his chest like a luxurious blanket of warm cashmere, he tucked her head under his chin and absorbed the trembling of her pliant sated body.

Complete satisfaction overwhelmed him as she drifted to sleep in his arms, but it was a long while before he found his own rest.

Annie woke to the pleasant echoes of forest chatter. Birds chirped loudly from somewhere overhead while autumn wind played a cheery tune as it blew through the cracks in the cabin's old-style window frames. She smiled at the sound of squirrels engaged in verbal combat on the porch, probably arguing over the acorns she'd seen yesterday dropping like hailstones from the mighty oaks that surrounded the house.

Turning on her back, she peered down the bed, past her toes and into the fireplace. The warming blaze, now a pile of embers, still glowed in the morning light. She had no idea of the time and really didn't care. Last night, after the best session of sex in her life, she'd slept like a baby. It had been the most restful sleep she'd had since she'd reported to the safe house.

A niggle of guilt inched its way into her brain and she huffed out a breath. *Go away!* she commanded, slamming a pillow over her head. *I will not let you spoil it for me.*

But the budding bubble of doubt ignored her direct order and continued to bounce around in her brain, forcing her to delve past the passion and into the heart of what she'd done.

Making love with Drew had been a dichotomy of the senses. So many sensations had been new and wonderful, yet others had been eerily familiar. His generous lips and the way he'd used them belonged to him alone, but the placement of his mouth where he'd touched and tasted had been an exact replica of her dead husband's.

Drew's callused hands, so different from Tom's smooth ones, had stroked every inch of her body, but the journey they'd taken was a route she remembered well. He made love so much like Tom, it was a wonder she hadn't stopped him in his tracks.

Yet, even those disturbing thoughts hadn't a chance against her raging desire. She had totally surrendered to the feelings, taking comfort in the sameness as she gave herself up to the differences. After all, wasn't sex mostly a state of mind? And how many ways were there to do it anyway? Aside from size and shape, body parts were pretty much identical on everyone. The *Kama Sutra* might show hundreds of positions, but when you got right down to it, the basics were always the same.

Having sex with Drew Falcone had been like having sex with any ordinary Joe. If it resembled what she'd done with Tom, it was because Tom was her only comparison. The fact that the physical sensations had been miles above that which she'd experienced with her husband was only because she'd gone too long without the touch of male hands. Once the novelty wore off, things would be pretty much the same.

Snippets of the things they'd done with and to each another tapped inside the bubble, bursting to be free. Even without the warmth of the fire, she felt the heat singe her cheeks as she remembered the way Drew had taken her, first for her pleasure, then to satisfy them both. Instead of walking on the earth, they'd been waltzing on the clouds.

Oh, God! How sappy could she get? The syrupy analogy was not only over the top, it was overblown, overly romantic and ridiculous. She had to keep everything in perspective and remember that the basics were the same in order to keep the entire affair exactly where it belonged—out of the clouds and on good old terra firma.

Crawling out from under the pillow, she concentrated on the noises of the cabin, the generator churning out power, water running in the bathroom, Drew talking to himself—

Talking to himself? She stifled a giggle and tried to decipher the murmur of his voice. What in the heck was he doing in there?

Tom stared into the mirror and gave himself a hearty mental pat on the back. Last night had been incredible. Annie had always been eager and uncomplicated in bed, but damn he'd done a fantastic job of pleasing her. Of course, his new *equipment* was probably a big part of it, as was the long dry spell.

Once it had come to him that she'd grown into her own

person since his death, he'd been compelled to let her take the lead. Giving her pleasure before he'd taken care of himself had been a natural reaction to her surrender and, looking back on it, a fine move on his part. So what if she thought he was Drew Falcone? Inside, where it counted, Tom knew he was the same man. The moves had been his, and Annie had loved them.

"Feeling pretty good about yourself, are you?"

Tom jumped a foot. "Holy jee—I mean chri—I mean—Hell!" Breathing hard, he glared into the mirror, then spun around and trained his gaze upward toward Milton, perched on the shower rod, a Pillsbury Doughboy in miniature.

"You scared the shit out of me." Turning, he dabbed at the cut the razor made when it had sliced into his face. "What do you want?"

"Me?" The angel floated to the ground, magically returning to his full height. "I thought I'd stop by to see how you were doing, that's all."

Tom stared warily from the mirror as he finished shaving. "I didn't expect . . . I mean, I didn't think I'd see you until . . . later."

"Later?" Milton took two steps to the toilet, sat down on the lid and crossed his legs. After rubbing his fingernails on his lapel, he studied his manicure. "Oh. You mean when you pass over again?"

Tom drained the water from the sink, then blotted his face with a hand towel. "Yeah, I guess. You never said there'd be any surprise visits before then."

"I didn't?"

Perturbed and just a little embarrassed, Tom turned and propped a hip against the sink, grateful he'd remembered to wrap a bath towel around his waist. "No, you didn't."

"Hmm. I must have forgotten to mention it." Milton raised a snowy white eyebrow. "So, are you making any progress?"

"Progress?" Tom crossed his arms over his chest. He

had so many questions for the slippery little stinker, he didn't know where to begin. "On which front? I've kind of got my hands full, in case you hadn't noticed."

"They look pretty empty to me." The angel grinned. "Nice haircut. Love the color."

"Don't get cute. You know what I mean." Realizing he'd raised his voice, Tom hunkered down into a squat and dropped his tone. "For starters, why didn't you tell me Dominic Viglioni was Andrew Falcone, an undercover U.S. Deputy Marshal? I could have gotten myself killed before I'd found out, and then where would I be?"

"You didn't ask," came the simple yet infuriating reply.

Tom saw the twinkle in Milton's eyes and snapped back to his feet. "You lousy—you set me up! You knew I wouldn't have picked this body if I'd known I had to be a marshal, didn't you?"

"Let me put it to you this way," Milton responded, still grinning. "If you had known, would you have chosen Esther or, heaven forbid, Warren Beavers?"

"Of course not." Itching to throttle the pompous weasel, Tom made a noise in the back of his throat. Damn, there he was again, acting out on that muscle memory thing.

"How very *Drew* of you," Milton said at the sound of his growl. "You're beginning to act just like him."

"So what if I am?"

"It suits you. The tough guy attitude, the snazzy hair— even the motorcycle. Annie's doing an admirable job."

"Annie? What's she got to do with the way I'm handling things? I thought this was my gig?"

"It is. It is. But she's involved up to her curly brown— I mean red—hair. She's quite a woman, isn't she?"

Praying for patience, Tom swiped a hand over his face. "Yes, she is. Now, about my problem?"

"Your problem? Oh, you mean this mobster-marshal thing and the fact that someone is trying to kill you. What about it?"

"What about it!" Tom clenched his fingers into fists. "What the heck am I supposed to do to make it go away?"

"Why, exactly what you've been doing." Milton scratched at his head, his owllike expression one of innocence. "You've been doing an admirable job of protecting Annie, by the way."

"Thanks. I guess." The compliment bolstered his courage. "So, Annie and I are going to come out of this okay? Neither of us is going to die or anything?"

Milton tugged at an earlobe, as if thinking hard. "Mercy me, I hope not. It's important to remember that your real goal is to find the perfect man for her. You won't achieve it if you manage to get yourself killed again, now will you?"

"I have no intentions of letting that happen to either of us. I just want to . . . um . . . take care of . . . er . . . keep us both alive while I'm doing it. Got any suggestions?"

Milton rolled his eyes. "Honestly, I've laid out so many clues a blind man could follow them. How much help do you think I can give you? And please bear in mind, you're not mine to watch over; therefore I can only do so much."

"Clues?" said Tom, feeling like a parrot at a ping pong match. He narrowed his gaze as the angel's words hit home. "The money? The gun and badge? The notebook?" He was so furious he wanted to shout. Instead, he hissed out, *"The dreams?"*

"And a few other things." Milton's gaze strayed to the medicine chest.

"The condoms!"

"I have to go. By the way, Annie's up and she can hear you. It's a fairly good bet she's thinking you're as nutty as one of those oak trees."

"Hold on a second. Are you trying to tell me you've been spying on us? You know what I . . . we . . . did? Last night?"

"Goodbye, Tom, or have you started thinking of yourself as Drew yet?"

"Wait." Tom reached out a hand and grabbed at a puff

of air. "Just tell me if what we did was okay. I mean, is Drew Falcone the right man for her?" *Am I?*

"That's for Annie to decide," came Milton's voice from far away. "Now, use the good sense locked up inside that head of yours and figure it out for yourself."

Once Annie realized the one-sided conversation coming from the bathroom had ground to a halt, she tugged Drew's flannel shirt over her nightgown, donned a ratty-but-clean apron and got busy making breakfast. Even though the idea of listening to a man like Drew talk to himself tickled her funny bone, she didn't think it wise to eavesdrop. A few seconds later, the bathroom door banged open, and she wondered if she should mention she'd heard him mumbling. His surly expression advised her to play dumb.

"Good morning," she warbled cheerfully, holding her curiosity in check.

"Hmmph." He sniffed the air. "Bacon and eggs?"

"And toast. The coffee's ready, and there's butter in the cooler. That setup is interesting."

He followed her glance to a corner of the kitchen where a power line from the outside generator fed into a mini-refrigerator. "My dad rigged it up a couple of summers ago. No freezer capability, but it does a good job of storing the perishables."

At least he was talking to her, Annie thought, heaving a sigh. Golly but this morning-after stuff was complicated. How did women who slept around handle themselves after a night of mind-blowing sex with a virtual stranger? Standing at the stove, she set the bacon to drain on a paper towel and cracked four eggs into the grease, vowing to go back to her normal breakfast of fruit, toast and tea the next day. Right now, her stomach was growling, and she had more important matters to ponder. She had to call her superiors.

Without warning, Drew came up behind her and whisked

the spatula out of her hand. After lowering the heat under the cast-iron skillet, he turned her in his arms. "You didn't have to go to all this trouble, Annie. I expected you to sleep late, so I could be the one fixing you breakfast. In bed."

The sweet suggestion hit her heart like Cupid's arrow. "Too bad I was starving. I've never had a man—anyone— do that for me before."

"Then let me be the first. Tomorrow?" The look in his eyes told her he was expecting another experience like the one they'd shared last night.

She concentrated on the dark hair peeking over the collar of his sweatshirt. "Um . . . if you want."

"Annie, look at me." He cupped her jaw and angled her head up. "Are you okay . . . about what happened between us?"

Was she? Hard telling with a flock of butterflies dancing a mambo in her stomach and her face as hot as the skillet. "I . . . guess so. What about you?"

He ran a thumb over her lower lip, then gently kissed the corner of her mouth, just below her bruise. "I'm very okay."

He dropped another kiss on the tip of her nose. "If you need to use the john, I can finish up out here."

"You don't mind?"

"Not at all. You've already done all the hard stuff."

Annie found her sweats and walked to the bathroom. Ten minutes later, they were at the table eating breakfast. Drew still seemed uneasy, but things had settled down to a companionable silence. He even cleared the table and put the dishes in the sink. She dawdled over the last of her tea, giving him an opportunity to tell her about his plan.

Finally, Annie cleared her throat. "I want to check in with the Newark office. Is the phone charged yet?"

"You aren't going to let this die, are you?"

She set a hand on her hip. "We have to check in with someone . . . now. You promised that once we were at the cabin—"

"Okay, okay. Hang on a second."

She waited while he retrieved the phone from a wall unit, listened for a dial tone, then handed it to her. "Look, I know you want to explain what happened at the safe house, but it's important you don't blow my cover to just anybody. Try to wheedle a little information first, before you tell them where you are or who I really am?"

"I don't want to lie."

Snorting, he ran a hand through his hair. "Look, McAllister, this is important. Anyone can be the enemy here, even someone you report to."

McAllister? So much for romance and all that lovey-dovey, morning-after stuff. They were back to the difficult situation of being adversaries playing on the same team.

"I'll try. But while I'm talking to my boss, maybe you ought to concentrate on doing what you promised—getting us out of this mess." She didn't mean to sound nasty, but he was being rude and insensitive and . . . and . . . impossible.

He shot her a glare and walked out the back door.

CHAPTER FOURTEEN

"Hi, Ruby, it's Anne McAllister. Can I talk to Charles Brinkman, please?"

Instead of the usual friendly chatter, Annie heard the receptionist's sharp intake of breath. When she'd called Brinkman in the past, she and Ruby had always exchanged pleasantries or shared the latest gossip running through the department. Today, the woman's tension almost jumped through the phone line, telling Annie *she* was the newest topic on the rumor loop.

"Please wait while I connect you, Deputy McAllister," Ruby said, her tone just shy of a command.

I'm not a traitor, Annie wanted to shout, but knew the words would be wasted. Only one opinion mattered, that of Senior Marshal Charles Brinkman, the man who'd assigned her to this case and was in charge of WITSEC for the tri-state area.

She sat patiently on hold, mentally preparing a speech that would convince him she'd done what she had to do to protect her charge from certain death. Lost in thought, she didn't notice Drew had returned until he came up from behind and whispered in her ear.

"What's the matter? Why aren't you talking to anyone?"

Annie almost shot out of her chair. How could a big guy move so quietly, she wondered, willing her heart to stop pounding. "Have you been eavesdropping on my call?"

"I couldn't help but overhear that you *weren't* speaking. What's happening?"

She frowned. "I've been on hold for a while now."

He snatched the phone from her hand and pressed the disconnect button.

"Hey! Give me that!"

"Shit, McAllister. Don't you know anything? They were probably tracing the call." Running fingers through his hair, he paced to the counter and back to her chair. "Best guess. How long do you think you were on hold?"

Annie dropped into her seat and set her forehead on the table. She was an idiot. The receptionist's voice had sounded cold and aloof, and she didn't remember ever having to wait that long to speak to Brinkman.

"Maybe a minute, ninety seconds at the outside. But there weren't any strange sounds on the line," she reasoned, trying to talk herself into believing he might be mistaken. "Besides, I didn't think you could trace calls made from a cell phone."

"You wouldn't hear a thing. And since September 11, they found a way to work magic with the satellites. I'm willing to trust your supervisor, but I have no idea who else could have access to the line. If our position falls into the wrong hands, we run the risk of marshals roaming these hills like a swarm of angry bees. I'll have to come out of hiding, and that will flush this whole operation down the toilet."

Duh! How could she forget the technological advances made since the World Trade Center tragedy? Damn if the man hadn't scrambled her brain cells until she lost all common sense.

"But I have to talk to my superior. He needs to know where I am, and I'd like to explain how I happened to run off with you. He can't be thinking I was Dominic Viglioni's moll or sidekick, or whatever they're calling me in the papers, and you aren't a mobster on the lam."

"Trust me, everyone who needs to know about us does. The rest of the department can't learn who I really am until this case is over. In the meantime, who do you suppose is feeding the press that bogus information?"

Annie thought a half second before she pieced it together. It made sense, but she still didn't appreciate that she'd been thrown into the mix without her knowledge. "You mean Brinkman and Phillips are in on this together? Brinkman already knows why I'm with you, and they've decided to purposely release false data to the media in order to keep us under cover?"

Drew ran a hand through his hair. "I've been thinking about it and I've decided this might be a good time to let you in on a few things."

"Gee, thanks," she deadpanned.

Ignoring her sarcasm, he stuffed his hands in his pockets and paced to the cabinets. "All WITSEC assignments are approved through Brinkman, Annie. Your assignment to the safe house had to be a joint decision between him and Phillips. The way the papers have painted your part of this was necessary if we wanted the story about Dominic Viglioni and his escape to jive. If it doesn't stay that way until this is over, my cover will be blown before I can finger the bad guys."

Still confused, she pursed her lips. "They still need to know you've been shot, and what about me? Isn't it important they know why I'm with you?"

"If my boss is on the ball, your boss knows everything, and I'm sure he's not questioning my reason for taking you along. Unless the shooter bothered to stop and mop up the blood, it's also safe to assume they know one of us was hit." He quirked a brow. "Besides, Phillips and I had a deal. No communication from me until I'm positive which marshals are guilty. Then I make the call."

"And if you'd been killed?" she tossed out. "Then what?"

His expression unreadable, he took his arms from his pockets and folded them across his chest. "It wasn't something we dwelled on. And trust me, they'd know."

"Didn't you have a plan? A . . . a direction you wanted the investigation to take?"

"Yes, we had a plan, but it was up to me to decide how to carry it out. I just needed a little cooperation from—" Making like a clam, he closed his mouth and stared out the window.

"Cooperation from who?" Annie demanded. Just because he seemed to know what he was doing, didn't mean she was about to let him keep any more secrets.

"Nothing. Never mind."

"What is it you're not telling me?"

He shrugged. "It's not important."

"The hell it isn't." Annie sprang to her feet and took her own turn at pacing. Finally, she gazed at the ceiling and smacked a palm against her forehead. Charging to where he stood, she raised her chin in challenge. "You did set me up. It's just like I thought when I read the notebook. You needed help on the inside and thought you'd found a female marshal gullible enough to fall for your line. You knew I coached basketball, so you dangled the possibility of a game in front of me, positive I'd convince Fielding to let us play."

"That notebook was private," he said through clenched teeth.

Not a bit frightened by his scowl, she skipped over the part about her reading the notebook to find out more about *him*, and pressed her case. "I was alone and bored and . . . curious about the assignment. You hadn't shared enough information to fill a thimble. What else was I supposed to do? Besides, it's too late now. You're just going to have to deal with it.''

"It contained data you shouldn't have seen. Confidential facts that could get you . . . us killed."

She set her hands on her hips and gazed around the room, her eyes wide, her expression exaggerated. "Hel-oo-oo! What the heck do you call my getting shot at outside the safe house? Or racing around with you on that Harley? I was in danger *before* I ever read the damned thing."

Tom hated that she was right. Worse, he hated the way he had to lie to her about everything. He had finished the notebook when she'd slept the day away after the bar brawl, and had to admit Annie knew what she was talking about. From the way he'd interpreted the entries, she *had* been specifically chosen. Hell, they could have picked any one of a dozen women, but she'd been the one he, or rather Falcone, had told Phillips to request.

He took a deep breath and made up his mind to tell her what he *thought* she could handle. "You're jumping to conclusions. No one said let's use Deputy Anne McAllister because we can play her for a fool. I had a raft of women to choose from. I needed a newer deputy with a clean record, and you just happened to be fresh out of WITSEC and salivating for an assignment."

The fact that she was a young, attractive widow was icing on the cake. But Tom knew better than to admit to that part of it. From what he'd witnessed the morning of the shooting, Falcone had been completely taken with her. Hell, he'd probably been halfway in love with Annie from the minute he'd laid eyes on her.

"And eager. Let's not forget eager. Or desperate? Maybe that's a better word." Propped against the counter, her arms wrapped protectively around her middle, she stared at the worn linoleum.

Her voice wavered, and Tom guessed she was on the

verge of tears. "I didn't mean it to sound like that. You're making way too much of this."

She raised her too-bright eyes. "Then answer me this. If I hadn't jumped at your suggestion to play basketball, would you have tried to make me do something else that would have gotten you out in the open? Something that would have made me break my oath as a marshal?"

Would he have? How was he supposed to know? He hadn't been in Drew Falcone's head at the time, and he didn't want to be there now. Annie was making him sound like a creep, a womanizer and a user all at the same time, and he was completely innocent.

He thought fast, a feat at which he'd been getting better and better. "Of course not. If you hadn't cooperated, I would have found another way to lure them into action. But time was growing short. Viglioni's trial is set for after the new year. I needed to force a break."

She huffed out a breath. "Do you think they tried to kill you because they knew you were an undercover marshal, or because they believed you were Dominic Viglioni and that mob boss asked them to take care of it?"

"I'm still trying to figure that out."

"So where do we go from here?"

"From here?"

Annie stood up straight, her arms at her sides. "What's the next step in this so-called plan? I don't imagine we're staying here much longer."

"We're not. But I can't tell you any more. It's against regulations." *And I don't have a clue,* he admitted to himself. That part of it wasn't coming to him like the rest of it had, so he'd thought to wait and see.

"If you trust me, you'll tell me."

Her strident words cut like a razor. "I do trust you. But I can't tell you what you want to know."

Annie stared at him as if he was just one step up the food chain from pond scum, then left the kitchen. Returning with her socks and sneakers, she slumped into a chair, finished dressing and rose to her feet, her eyes still damp. "Just answer one more question, and please make it the truth."

"Anything," Tom said, mentally preparing himself to tell another lie.

She stood behind the chair with her hands wrapped tight around the backrest. "What happened between us last night—was that part of the plan?"

"Annie, I—"

"Just tell me."

He searched for an answer. When nothing plausible popped into his brain, he did the only thing he could think of—he spoke from his heart. "No, it wasn't."

Her face a wash of pink, she nodded, then turned and walked out of the cabin.

Afternoon sun warmed Annie's bruised face, while a cool November breeze raced across the lake and skittered up her skin. She'd been sitting on the dock for hours, alternately dozing and thinking. And she definitely enjoyed the dozing part better. Thinking hurt her cheek and tweaked her anger thermostat from hot to cold to frigid and back up to blast furnace level with every new idea. Just when she was certain she had things figured out, another doubt would wriggle its way into her mind, and she'd have to start the process all over again.

Was Drew telling the truth about why she'd been chosen for the safe house? Had someone tried to trace the call she'd made to her boss? Did last night's intimacy mean anything to him, or was it simply another part of his secret plan? Had he made love to her because she'd begged, or because he truly wanted her? Or was it a little of both?

She'd been dangling her legs off the edge of the dock so long her toes were numb. She was hungry, and the cold had started to seep into her bones, even with the long underwear she wore beneath her sweats and the blanket *someone* had tossed over her during one of her naps.

Damn, but why did Falcone have to be so considerate and caring one second and so cocksure and contrary the next? The man was driving her crazy.

She heard a door slam but refused to turn around. Things at the cabin had been fairly quiet all afternoon. Maybe he was making a trip for firewood or taking a ride to Earl's store. It didn't matter as she wasn't about to speak to him.

The rickety pier quaked with the force of footsteps, and Annie pulled the quilt tighter around her shoulders. A shadow fell across the worn wood. Even though he didn't say a word, she felt the heat of his stare laser straight to her heart, but she wouldn't turn around. Long seconds ticked by as he sat beside her and imitated her casual pose.

"You okay?"

She set her lips in a thin line and gave her impression of a block of wood. Of course she was okay. Couldn't the big lug see she was okay?

"All right, don't answer me. I just thought you might like to know I did what you wanted. I called Martin Phillips."

Annie swung her feet back and forth, the need to know itching like a week-old scab.

"Want to hear what we talked about?"

Gazing out over the peaceful water, she gave a disdainful sniff for emphasis.

He sighed. "Annie, come on. It's interesting news."

In the distance, a huge bird, probably a hawk or an eagle, swooped low, then bounced off the water with a small silver fish dangling from its beak. She shrugged. "I thought I couldn't be trusted with anything related to your assignment."

He barked out a laugh. "Jeez, McAllister, you are one tough nut. I'm doing my damnedest to get back in your good graces, and you're freezing me out. Can't you cut me a break?"

"I'm merely being frank. You wouldn't want me to lie, would you?"

Ignoring her sarcasm, Tom hitched himself around until he sat facing her and leaned back against a piling. He was prepared to stay out here all night if that's what it would take to get Annie to forgive him. "I haven't exactly lied to you. There are just certain things I'm not at liberty to share. Now, do you want to know what I know, or not?"

"Are you in trouble for calling him?"

They still hadn't made eye contact, but the fact that she was asking questions gave him hope. "I don't think so," he answered, fairly certain it was mostly because he'd done a darned fine job of sounding as if he knew what he was talking about when he'd explained their situation to Phillips.

"Bob Fielding is in the hospital, and Smithers, Butterworth and Donovan have disappeared."

That got her attention. Whipping her head around, she clutched at the quilt. "The hospital? Then, Bob's alive?"

"He was shot, just like I figured. We think the creep didn't have time to finish the job or thought he would bleed out. Fortunately, Fielding managed to make a call on his cell phone. By the time help arrived, he was unconscious, and everybody else was gone."

Shading her eyes with one hand, she stared accusingly. "I told you Bob was innocent. So what do you think happened to the other deputies?"

"Good question." And Tom was pretty sure he had the answer. He'd even run his theory by Phillips who was, from the tenor of his words, a fair and reasonable man. They had a date to talk again tomorrow, just to fill in a few holes. "My gut feeling is Smithers took out Fielding, while Butterworth or Donovan shot me. If the plan had worked, Smithers would have had his sidekick kill you, too. Then they would have arranged for Smithers to be wounded in order to protect their cover. Smithers would have blamed the whole thing on mob hit men and kept on playing the dirty game. My

guess is either Donovan or Butterworth is dead. They probably ditched the odd man somewhere in that state park, or
maybe locked the body in the trunk of a car.''

''So you think two men are involved? And it's not the
mob, but our guys?''

''Right now I'm thinking our guys and the mob are one
and the same, they just dress differently. Since our contacts
say they don't have any concrete information that points to
a mob hit, and there are three marshals unaccounted for—''

''That's the only logical conclusion.''

''Correct.'' He decided not to tell her Fielding was hooked
up to life support and hanging on by a thread, or that Phillips
had been in touch with Brinkman, and they'd had a talk
about her. All of that could be sorted out when this mess
was over.

''So what do we do now?''

Tom rose to his feet and reached down to help her up.
''Cook supper? I don't know about you, but I'm starving.''

Wrinkling her nose, Annie inspected his hand, then took
it and let him haul her up. Her gaze as warm as an iceberg,
she rested her bottom against a piling, folded the quilt and
draped it over her arm.

''Not so fast. There has to be more you're not telling
me.'' Raising a hand, she began to tick off questions. ''Do
you think Smithers and his accomplice will find us here?
Are we going to get backup, or are we supposed to lead
these guys into an ambush? Did you tell your boss where
we are? How long before—''

Tom grabbed her fingers and pulled her close. ''Maybe,
yes, yes, and I don't know. How does that sound?''

She started to argue again, but he stopped her sassy mouth
with a body slam of a kiss. Dropping the quilt, she melted
against him and went buttery soft in his arms. The kiss
exploded into an avalanche of sensation, enveloping him in
a cocoon of lust. Lost in the taste of her lips and tongue,

all Tom could think of was Annie, a woman he knew so well, yet was a total surprise in every way.

She curled into him and threaded her fingers through his hair. Cupping her bottom, he hoisted her up, and she wrapped her legs around his hips, pushing against his straining erection. Her ragged moan fueled his desire, and he devoured her mouth, her tongue, her very essence.

Desperate to get them skin to skin, he wrestled with her clothes while he walked them toward the cabin. Staggering up the porch steps, he paused at the door to catch his breath. Annie's sweatshirt was caught around her head, but he could still hear her muffled giggle.

Panting, he set her on her feet. "What's so funny?"

When she finally pulled the shirt off, her lips were twitching with mischief. "I told you I wasn't a lightweight."

"Don't be a smart-ass. I just need to get off this case and back in the gym."

"Hah! A fat lot of good that'll do if you're dead."

He raised a brow in challenge. "If I wanted, I could carry you around this lake on my back without breaking a sweat."

"You and whose pack mule? You're breathing like a bellows." She thumped his chest one time hard, to punctuate her point.

"Wanna bet?" Tom rubbed at the spot she'd nailed with her finger, inordinately pleased he was getting good at this macho-man stuff. "Or are you chicken?"

"Me? Not on your life. I can handle anything you have to offer. Go ahead, give it your best shot."

He stuffed his hands in his pockets and stared up at the porch overhang. "Hmm. Okay, how about this? Tomorrow morning before breakfast we do push-ups. Last person to fall flat wins."

Just to irritate her, he added, "I'll even let you do the girly kind."

"The girly kind!" Annie snorted her disgust. "For you

maybe, but not for this woman.'' She opened the cabin door and flounced inside. ''And it's your turn to do the cooking.''

He sighed, all hope of a romantic interlude before dinner fading from sight.

Several hours later, Tom faced Annie across the pulled-out sofa bed. They'd already straightened the sheets and blanket, and he was now helping her to arrange a quilt on top of that. She'd changed into her sleep shirt, but he was still dressed in sweats. The roaring fire warmed the room, so why was she acting as if she were frozen? Could it be nerves that had her running her hands over her arms and shivering?

After a dinner of tinned beef sandwiches and condensed soup, he'd reread the notebook. There was no doubt in Tom's mind that Goldilocks was Annie and Papa Bear was Phillips. The other names were still a mystery, but he had a suspicion Peter Pan was Smithers, the guy who lived in never-neverland thinking he could get away with his larcenous actions forever. So who was dirtier—Donovan or Butterworth? And who was Captain Hook?

In going over his observations out loud, he'd hoped Annie would help him reason out a few clues to the mystery. Each time she asked a direct question about some of the stuff Falcone had written, he made up what he thought was a plausible answer. But every lie punched another hole in his gut, until he was positive his stomach lining looked like a slice of Swiss cheese.

He left her standing in front of the fire while he secured the kitchen door and turned out the lights. With luck, they'd be safe here for one more night, possibly two. Unless something surprising happened, it was logical that they start the trek to Arlington. If Smithers knew he was an undercover marshal, it would be easy enough to trace Falcone's background and learn of the cabin. Tom didn't want to put Annie in danger, but he had no choice. Where could he leave her that she would be safe?

Standing at the back of the sofa, he took in her feminine form, her halo of fiery curls, her voluptuous body a muted silhouette framed by firelight. What were they doing out here together in the back of beyond? If he hadn't been such a fool, they'd still be living in New Jersey, in a quaint old colonial ringed by a white picket fence, with maybe two or three kids playing out back in a sandbox or on a swing set. Instead of running for their lives, they'd be happily married and—

Tom shook his head. Yeah, right. Who was he kidding? If they'd continued the way they'd been, with him taking and Annie giving at every turn, they'd be divorced. And he would be living alone.

Annie turned, and he caught a glimmer of longing shining from her golden eyes. Only her desire wasn't for him, not really. It was for a man so completely opposite the real Tom McAllister he wondered how she had ever loved him. Hell, right about now he didn't even like himself. What Milton said was true. She deserved better. She deserved a man who would let her fly free and follow her heart, a guy who was brave. A hero. She deserved someone like Drew Falcone.

"Are you coming to bed?" she asked. Biting at her lower lip, she knotted her hands in front of her.

His gaze intent, he countered, "Are you sure you want me there?"

Annie's ragged sigh tore at his heart. If she had any sense at all, she'd order him to go sleep with the mice. *Please, God,* he prayed, *let her be foolish for one more night.*

"I've never been more sure of anything in my life."

Tom's blood was already thick and pumping below his waist. By the time he walked around the sofa and took her in his arms, he was fully aroused and about to go off like a bottle rocket. Annie rested her hands on his chest and he quivered at her touch. Leaning forward, he kissed her lips and she opened for him, offering herself so completely he thought he might burst.

In seconds they were naked and on the bed. He grabbed a condom and ripped open the packet with his teeth. She took it from his trembling hand and rolled it over and down his shaft, while her teasing fingers fondled and explored.

Memories of their past and the present melded into one glorious moment. If he was breaking Milton's rules, so be it. Annie needed him tonight, and he was hers.

Enjoying her newfound power, Annie grew bold. She refused to believe their coupling could be wrong, when it felt so right. Kneeling on the mattress face-to-face with him, she stroked Drew's thighs, his pelvis, his corded stomach and up his broad chest. His body shuddered under her palm, chained energy held in check by the touch of her hand.

Running her fingers through his hair, she pulled him to her breast to show him what she wanted. He caught an aching nipple between his teeth and she thought she would fly off the bed. With his mouth fused to her breast, he raised her up and leaned back, easing her onto his erection until she straddled his thighs. Then he gripped her around the waist and lifted her up and down, showing her what she needed to do.

Setting her hands on his shoulders, she rested her forehead against his and began to move, slowly at first, then faster as she found her rhythm. He caressed her breasts and thumbed her nipples, driving her on as she rose and fell with the thrusting of his hips.

Colors swirled behind Annie's eyelids. The heat from his body stoked her passion, taking her higher and higher until she thought she would soar out of the cabin and across the lake. He took her breast into his mouth and suckled, his tongue stroking her to a frenzy. Sobbing out her release, she fell against him in a blaze of fulfillment.

Tom felt her shudder and gave a shout of triumph. Holding her face with his palms, he gazed into her eyes, hoping she would recognize some small bit of who he really was. Instead, she smiled and continued her erotic ride, taking him to the edge a second time.

At that moment, he didn't care who Annie thought he was. Every nerve in his body, every cell in his gray matter, told him nothing counted but the woman in his arms. She belonged to him now, just as she'd been his years ago. Damn the consequences. He knew in his heart this was right, and he would prove it to Milton, to God Himself if need be.

Shouting her name, he clutched her to his chest and surged up and into her in one last thrust.

CHAPTER FIFTEEN

"One-twenty-seven. Twenty-eight. Twenty-nine." With his arms board straight, Tom held himself up from the floor and blotted his forehead against the sleeve of his sweatshirt. "Ready to give up yet, McAllister?"

Annie's eyes flashed sparks from under her mop of damp red curls. "Not on your life, buster. Get cranking."

He huffed out a breath. So much for waking up after a night of mind-blowing sex and having a second helping. Instead of wanting to cuddle, Annie hadn't wasted a minute hustling his butt out of a warm, cozy bed so they could begin their ridiculous contest. In a way, this dopey test of strength was fascinating. He'd accepted the fact that Falcone's body was bigger and more powerful than his old one from the get-go, but aside from the punches he'd thrown in the bar and carrying Annie a couple of times, he'd yet to put his new physique to a real test. In his former life he would have been lucky to manage fifty push-ups, not even close to the number he'd accomplished so far.

What else could this souped-up, super-charged body do?

How fast could he run? How many tough guys could he wipe out with a single blow?

Feeling invincible, Tom grinned through gritted teeth and sneaked another peek at Annie. Good thing he hadn't bet ten bucks on her wimping out, because he would have lost.

"You ready to cry uncle, ace?" she commented, blowing a wisp of hair from her eyes.

"Not a chance," he muttered. "But don't say I didn't warn you."

Annie called out the next number and lowered slowly, touching her nose to the linoleum. He matched her pump for pump until they hit one-fifty; then he stole another glance her way. Jeez, she was hardheaded. What little of her face he could see was flushed, and her arms were shaking. But she still refused to give up.

When they hit the two hundred mark, Tom silently admitted he was getting tired. Raising his gaze, he saw Annie shift her shoulders and take a deep breath. Great, not only was she dripping sweat, but her arms were quivering like overextended rubber bands. If she kept this up much longer, she was going to get hurt. It was only a stupid bet they'd made on a whim . . . wasn't it? He glanced at her again, and the set of her jaw gave him pause. She looked so determined, almost as if she had something to prove.

Assuring himself this next lie didn't count, he crumpled to the floor in a heap. Making a big production out of catching his breath, he wheezed out, "Jeez, McAllister, what are you made of—iron?"

Annie stayed in the push-up position, staring suspiciously through her good eye. "You're joking, right?"

Damn. When had she gotten so stubborn . . . and so strong? "What do you mean—joking?" He inhaled another gulp of air just to make it look good. "I'm beat."

She licked at her bottom lip, then hung her head and pumped out ten more push-ups. Tom wiped his mouth with his hand just to keep from laughing out loud. What the hell was he supposed to do now—pounce on her back and pin her to the mat?

Her expression grim, she propped herself against a cabinet and sucked air like a Hoover while she continued to glare as if she thought he was an escaped mental patient.

"You are such a liar," she accused with a snort of disgust. "You let me win."

Wincing for dramatic effect, he gave her his best wounded frown. "Now, why in the heck would I do something that stupid?"

"Who knows?" She pushed a cluster of curls from her forehead. "It's not as if you've ever lied to me before."

"Those are harsh words, doll," he said with a shake of his head. He rose to his feet and folded his arms across his chest. Damn if it wasn't getting harder and harder to cover his tracks with her. Either he needed to get more creative with his stories, or he was going to have to stop talking to Annie altogether. And no way was he going to offer her a helping hand. She'd probably bite it off and fry it up for breakfast.

She puckered her mouth and lurched to a stand. Grabbing a paper towel from the roll on the counter, she dabbed at her face, still eyeing him warily. "By the way, what did I win?"

Win? Uh-oh. He'd been so busy trying to figure out a way to let her down easy, he hadn't given a thought to that part of the bet. With his luck, she'd want to pierce his nose, or dye his hair purple or tattoo his . . .

He shuddered at the possibilities. "Um, I don't know. What were you hoping for?"

With her expression just short of devious, she set her hands on her hips. "I'll let you know. Right now, I'm taking a shower." Wrinkling her nose, she held her sweatshirt away from her body. "Then we have to find somewhere to do a load of laundry. This stuff is rank."

Tom sniffed his armpit and grunted in agreement. Funny,

but the *old* Tom wouldn't have dared wear his clothes a second day, never mind wearing them through a week of motor biking and strenuous exercise. "If I remember correctly, Earl has a dryer and a pair of washers hidden away in a backroom. This time of year they should be pretty much free."

Annie headed for the rear hall, calling over her shoulder as she walked, "Yeah, but everything we own smells like week-old gym socks. I need to wear something clean to go to the store."

She closed the bathroom door, and Tom heaved a sigh, still amazed at how much she'd changed. Throughout their marriage, Annie had been a reasonable, malleable woman. Since his death, she'd become more confusing than a Chinese jigsaw puzzle. An intoxicating mix of college cheerleader, *Playboy* centerfold and Amazon warrior, she'd matured into a fully grown Goldilocks—with an Uzi and an attitude.

Just like Milton had warned, it would take a special guy to earn her trust and respect.

It was obvious she enjoyed Drew Falcone, at least in the sack. But it didn't sound as if she trusted him or held him in very high regard. And no matter how fantastic it felt when they were together in bed, he still wasn't sure if what they'd been doing for the past two nights fell within the angel's stringent guidelines.

Mulling over what he could remember of Milton's frustrating rules, Tom wandered into one of the bedrooms and started to scrounge for spare clothes. Maybe his, er, Falcone's brothers had left a change on their last visit. Pulling out a dresser drawer, he sorted through a promising array of flannel shirts, athletic gear and jeans. Finally, he set aside a frayed George Washington University sweatshirt and pair of smaller sweats for Annie and a T-shirt, jeans and flannel shirt for himself, along with two pairs of heavy socks.

Toting his selection to the bathroom, he knocked and opened the door a crack. "I found some old clothes in one of the bedrooms. If you don't mind dressing down, you can wear them to do the laundry.''

The sound of running water drowned out her reply, and Tom poked his head around the door frame. ''I said I found some—''

He gulped and found he had a hard time swallowing with his tongue stuck to the roof of his mouth. Even though the room was enveloped in a steamy haze, Annie's lushly curved body was outlined clearly behind the pale pink shower curtain. The vision he conjured, her dripping wet with warm, silky rivulets of water cascading over her generous breasts and taut rosy nipples, gave him an instantaneous erection.

Hesitantly, he took another step into the room. What would she do if he stripped and joined her under the pounding spray?

''What did you say?''

''Um . . . clothes.'' He ran a hand across the back of his neck. ''I found clothes,'' he managed to grind out.

''Set them on the toilet seat. I'll give them a try,'' she answered, as if his presence didn't matter. ''When I get out I'll make breakfast, and we can leave for Earl's store.''

''Sure. Fine.'' Tom did as she suggested and backed out of the room, but not before he took a long look at the thin plastic curtain separating them.

Scowling, he thought about their morning meal. They'd gotten up early, but no one had cooked because Annie seemed so intent on their contest. The least he could do was start coffee and toast or—

Turning the corner, he plowed smack into what felt like a brick wall made of muscle. His hand went automatically to his waist before he remembered he wasn't wearing a gun. The beefy wall grabbed him by the shoulders, and Tom raised a fist, prepared to take the guy out. Instead, he was pulled against a massive chest and squeezed until the breath escaped his lungs in one long whoosh.

Even with his gut clenched in fear, Tom was overwhelmed

with the innate sense that he was safe. Curious to see his assailant, he pulled away and found an older man with a good twenty pounds of added girth appraising him with amusement. Salt-and-pepper hair just a tad on the long side framed an oddly familiar, olive-skinned face wreathed in a smile.

"Interesting haircut," the man commented, giving Tom a second thorough inspection. His chocolate brown eyes crinkled at the corners, as if he'd had a lot of practice at laughing. "Who talked you into the fruity dye job?"

When Tom didn't answer immediately, the man quirked a coal black brow. "Don't scare me like this, Drew. Please tell me it's part of your disguise."

Tom felt his face form a smile, but his gut was still tied in knots. This was it. Time for that muscle memory thing to kick in big time. He'd been made or, as he'd often heard said in old crime movies, the jig was up.

He swallowed hard as an unfamiliar word slipped from his dumbly grinning lips. "Dad?"

The bathroom door closed, and Annie's breath hitched in her throat. She'd been about to step out of the shower when she heard Drew's deep voice, and the sound of it made her knees weak. For a second she'd been tempted to invite him to join her in the stall. Then she remembered all the reasons it would be a dumb move and pretended she didn't care.

Resting her hands against the slippery tiles, she let the steamy water pummel her aching shoulders into submission, groaning as she accepted every painful twinge. It was exactly what she deserved for being such a hard-ass, but she had to be practical. If she'd followed her hormones and taken Drew up on his amorous offer of spending the morning in bed, he might be with her right now, sharing the shower and a whole lot more. . . .

They'd already stepped over the line by a yard. Neither of them needed any more intimacy or entanglements.

Cursing to herself, she turned off the faucet. When would she get a brain? She was a U.S. Deputy Marshal who'd been unknowingly dragged into a case and, in turn, had allowed herself to become involved with her partner. It was time she stopped romanticizing the affair and learned to accept it for what it was: a woman who'd been without a man for a long while, alone with a guy who was used to getting every female he wanted. Couple that with the danger of being on the run, throw in a healthy dollop of animal attraction and there it was, plain and simple as the nose on your face. Sex.

Tough-yet-tender, bone-melting, fly-me-to-the-moon *sex.*

She'd tried to be prudent this morning and ease up on their togetherness, but even that had gotten her in trouble. She should have figured Falcone would perform like a machine when it came to tests of strength. Her first hundred push-ups had been a piece of cake, but after the second hundred, she thought she'd never be able to use her arms again. Those last ten had wiped her out.

To complicate matters even further, Drew had let her win. The big jerk. Who did he think he was, pretending to be a nice guy and cutting her some slack over a couple of lousy push-ups? Why had he been so gallant? Only a week earlier, he'd had no qualms about almost getting her killed. If he thought to take it easy on her simply because they'd had a few nights of fantastic sex . . . Well, she'd just have to clue him in.

Somehow she would find a way to make him sorry he'd chosen her as his unwitting accomplice, and for labeling her a desperate woman. The last thing she needed—or wanted— was to be beholden to Drew Falcone.

Stepping from the shower, she grabbed a towel and dried off, then wrapped it around her wet hair. After wiping down the mirror over the sink, she inspected her face, as she had done for the past several mornings. Probing with her fingertips, she pursed her lips. The eggplant-colored bruise had been disgusting. Thank God it had faded to an interesting palette of blue, green and yellow. She turned her head from side to side, noting that the swelling had lessened and the pain was almost gone.

A murmur of voices in the distance had her biting back a smile. Either Drew was talking to himself again or he'd turned on the radio. He'd probably found an all-news station so he could check up on the press reports and learn more about their supposed escape.

She'd come to accept the fact that she'd been dropped into the middle of this assignment without fair warning. She even understood that she was a newbie to WITSEC, unproven and completely ignorant of the protocol of going under cover. But the idea she'd been chosen because she was a woman, and therefore considered susceptible to a man like Dominic Viglioni's dubious charms, was embarrassing, even though it had worked. She had succumbed. Lucky for her he was only pretending to be a bad guy.

But it was humiliating to admit that everyone involved in the case had been right about her. All the mobster'd had to mention was exercise and basketball in the same sentence, and she'd jumped at the chance to convince Fielding into setting up that game.

Talk about being caught between a rock and a hard place. If she hadn't tried to bend the rules, Drew wouldn't have been shot, and they wouldn't be on the run. But if she'd ignored his suggestion, he might have found a more personal way to enlist her aid. That incredible kiss on the cement could have just as well happened in the kitchen or on the back porch—maybe even in one of their bedrooms.

And if he'd persisted, and she'd let it get to her, their simple game of one-on-one might have escalated into a lot more than a couple of slam dunks and a lip lock.

Annie removed the towel from her head and finger-combed her hair. Then again, if she hadn't helped Drew in his quest to lure the bad guys into action, he still might be sitting in that safe house, no closer to wrapping up the assignment than when he'd started. Surely that counted for something.

What was going to happen to her career? Did helping Viglioni escape—which was actually part of their plan—constitute a breach of ethics on her part, even though she was simply following orders and protecting the man to the best of her ability? Sure, the mobster had flirted with her, but until that morning on the court, there had been no impropriety, not one iota of a reason to think she was a twittering, weak-willed female.

Were they going to condemn her or praise her for doing her job?

Inspecting the clothing Drew left on the commode, she gave a hesitant grin. The sweatshirt and pants looked and smelled clean enough, and she did want to wash *everything*. What would he say if he knew she was going commando herself in order to do all her laundry?

Annie put on the socks and stepped into the sweatpants. Braless, she eased the sweatshirt over her head, then fluffed up her curls. The rest of her clothes were in the duffel or strewn around the living room. She'd have to go on a hunt for their dirty laundry, then repack the duffel so they could tote it to the bait shop.

She opened the door to the aroma of coffee and food. The scent and sound of bacon sizzling mingled with the undercurrent of serious male voices deep in conversation, and she realized Drew hadn't been talking to himself, nor was it the radio.

They had company.

Still reeling from shock, Tom busied himself by making a pot of coffee, then starting a pan of bacon to fry. Great, just what he needed—another surprise Milton had neglected to prepare him for. He'd hoped for a little reprieve before he had to meet his new family. The dreams had helped, but they hadn't done justice to Vincent Falcone and his commanding presence.

Chair legs scraped across the linoleum, and Tom figured the guy was making himself at home. Now what was he supposed to do?

"Mind telling me why I'm here, son?"

Not at all, thought Tom, *once I figure it out myself.* Deep in thought, he opened a drawer and searched for utensils. Maybe if he pretended he hadn't heard the question—

"Andrew? Are you listening to me or are you going to play chef for the rest of the morning?"

Sighing, Tom took mugs from the cabinet, filled them with coffee and handed one to his fath—his guest. "It's good to see you . . . Dad."

Vincent smiled, then sipped at the steaming liquid. "Good to see you, too. I was getting worried when you hadn't surfaced. You warned me this assignment was dangerous, but when I saw your picture on the evening news, I about swallowed my tonsils. You should have called again to let us know you were okay."

Us? And when had Falcone found time to make a phone call for the first time?

"Your brothers are upset. My phone rang off the hook after that news flash hit the screen."

Tom's mind went on information overload. Jeez, how could he have forgotten his brothers? Four of the toughest, most demanding siblings a guy could want. Joseph, the oldest, was a district attorney in Baltimore. Salvatore was a fireman in Washington, D.C. Anthony and Robert, both black belts in karate, had degrees in business and computer programming and had joined forces in opening an Internet security firm. His father, now retired, had been a homicide detective in Alexandria, Virginia, for over thirty years.

"I didn't know they would run the picture," Tom hedged,

turning to rest his backside against the stove. "Did anyone besides family recognize me?"

Vincent snorted out a laugh. "The next day when I was out raking leaves, old lady Foster made a half-assed comment about the resemblance, but I managed to convince her she was mistaken. She walked away mumbling something about how all Falcone men looked like thugs, so I figured you were safe. Besides, your hair was slicked back, and you had on fancy clothes. You've been out of touch for so long, I don't think anyone will make the connection."

From the way the notebook read, Tom figured Falcone had been under cover for close to three years, so what the older man said made sense. And it gave him another piece of the puzzle that was his new life. His family did care about him, er, Drew. The fact that his father was here now, with affection and concern radiating from his eyes, was proof they loved him.

"Um . . . yeah, time flies . . . I can't remember when we talked last," he added, hoping something would jog that muscle memory thing.

"A couple of days before you arrived at the safe house. You asked me to meet you here sometime this week, remember? I was supposed to wait a few days, and if you didn't show, I was to go back home. I would have come sooner, but that old truck you left at my place decided to give me trouble. I parked it behind the tool shed, like you told me to."

"Right . . . right," said Tom, choking out another lie.

"So, here I am," Vince said jovially, "as ordered." He set down his coffee mug and folded his arms across his chest. "Mind if I ask you a few questions?"

Why not? They can't be any more difficult than the ones I've already asked myself. He transferred the bacon to a couple of paper towels, then cracked four eggs into the hot grease. "Fire away."

"That female deputy they say helped you to escape? Anne

McAllister? You never mentioned that you were working with another marshal. What's that all about?''

''She was necessary to the success of the operation.'' Tom answered, as if on autopilot. ''If I told you the reason why I had to bring her along, you wouldn't believe me.''

''Okay, I guess I don't need to know right now. But the news reports made it sound as if you two were . . . involved.''

He removed plates from the cupboard and set them on the counter, then flipped the eggs. ''You know how the press likes to exaggerate everything. Besides, I couldn't very well leave her there after she saved my life.''

''Saved your life!'' Before Tom could explain, Vincent crossed the kitchen, grabbed him by the shoulder and spun him around. ''What the hell happened to you?''

Annie stood in the hallway, listening with interest to the conversation Drew was having with his father. When she'd first realized they were no longer alone, she had tiptoed to a bedroom, found her Glock and checked the clip, then tucked Drew's gun into her waistband and headed toward the kitchen. Once she heard the familial banter, she'd stopped short of the doorway to eavesdrop.

And she'd found out more about Drew Falcone in the last two minutes than she'd learned in the past two weeks.

He had a loving family. His father was aware of his undercover assignment, and Drew trusted the man enough to ask him for help. From the sound of it, he wasn't the rough, tough macho man he liked to portray, but a caring son who took the time to let his relatives know he was all right.

Resting her forehead against the wall, Annie wished she hadn't been privy to the touching scene. It was a lot safer to think of Drew Falcone as a smart-assed loner and ladies' man than a warm and dutiful son.

When his father said her name, she perked up and paid closer attention. Drew's explanation of her being *necessary to the operation* didn't bother her, but she wondered what he meant by the rest of it. She breathed a little easier when he didn't bring up their personal involvement. It was nice to know he credited her with saving his life.

She peered around the corner and smiled. The sight of two linebacker-sized men embracing was comical, especially when the one with punk-rocker white hair was sporting a day's growth of beard and a thoroughly perplexed expression. Before she could control her laughter, a giggle escaped her lips.

She and Drew locked gazes, and he struggled from his father's embrace. Throwing her a glare of warning, his face flushed red. "Deputy McAllister." He ran a hand through his hair, sending the blond spikes straight to the ceiling. "We have a visitor."

The man turned, and Annie held back a gasp. Except for a smattering of silver threaded through his thick dark hair and a few extra pounds and wrinkles, Drew's father could be his double. If all the men in the Falcone family looked like the two of them, the female population was in big trouble.

Holding out his hand, their guest gave a nod and took a step toward her. "I'm Vince Falcone, Drew's father. It's a pleasure to meet you."

Annie liked the way he shook her hand as if he meant it, but she wasn't too sure about the almost professional way he assessed her with his deep-set brown eyes. Then it hit her—the man was a cop or in some form of law enforcement. Surely Drew would have told her if his father was a marshal?

"It seems we owe you a debt. Drew says you saved his life."

"I . . . um . . . It was nothing, really, Mr. Falcone." She grew warm under his appraising stare. When his gaze drifted to her cheek, she felt herself blush and prayed the attractive rainbow covering half her face would cover it up.

"So, McAllister, are you ready for breakfast?" Drew asked a bit too loudly. "There's bacon and eggs, toast, coffee

. . . or tea. How about tea?'' He came up beside her and hustled her to a chair. ''Sit and I'll get it.''

Weird, she thought, totally weird the way he was fussing and fumbling like a little kid. She took a seat at the table, and Vincent sat across from her, a half smile lighting his handsome face as he watched his son scramble with their meal.

Finally, he turned to her and said, ''That's some shiner you got there. Does it feel as bad as it looks?''

Annie touched her cheek and shook her head. ''Not anymore. Drew took care . . . I mean, I took care of it.''

He raised his voice to speak over the whistling kettle. ''Mind if I ask how you got it?''

Drew rushed over and set a cup of steaming water on the table. ''Tea's ready.''

Raising a brow, Annie stared at the mug. ''A tea bag would be nice, don't you think?''

''A t-tea bag?'' he stammered. ''Oh, yeah.'' He raced back to the counter. ''Just a second.''

Vincent shrugged his massive shoulders. ''About that shiner, Deputy McAllister.''

''It's Annie, please,'' she said, watching Drew jitterbug around the kitchen like Emeril on speed. What in the world was wrong with the man?

''And I'm Vince.''

Drew made a production out of delivering her tea bag and setting a fully loaded plate of bacon and eggs in front of his father. ''Eat up, Dad. Annie and I have to get to Earl's to do some laundry.''

She dunked her tea bag, then picked up a piece of buttered toast. ''Don't be silly. Your father just got here, and it's obvious the two of you have a lot to talk about. Maybe I could borrow his car and drive to Earl's by myself. That way, you could have your discussion without any interference.''

Vincent flashed her an approving smile. ''What do you say, son? Care to take the boat on the lake and go fishing with your old man?'' He raised a brow in question. ''We do have time before things start happening around here, don't we?''

Drew brought his own breakfast to the table and began to shovel in the food.

''Drew?''

''Hm?'' He stared at his father, then Annie. ''Oh . . . um . . . sure. I don't expect fireworks for another day or so.''

Still confused by his frantic actions and uncomfortable-looking expression, Annie sipped at her tea. What the heck was going on inside Drew's head?

Why was he acting like a completely different man?

CHAPTER SIXTEEN

Lulled by the gently lapping waves, Tom dozed in the family rowboat, his back cradled by the bow, his legs hooked over a plank bench in front of him. Annie had left several hours ago, and since then he and Vince had spent what Vince kept referring to as *quality time* together. Every once in a while, the older man would make an observation on the local wildlife or comment on what he'd been doing back home to pass the time, and Tom would let that eerie muscle memory part of his brain take over, answering with the first words that came to mind.

Lucky for him, they'd been the right words, because after the shock of meeting Vincent Falcone face-to-face had worn off, it became obvious from the friendly banter that Drew and his dad were a lot closer than Tom had ever been with his own father. The man was going to be an integral part of the rest of his new life. If he didn't start better playing the role of a devoted son, he could blow his second chance at finding happiness, not only with Annie, but his new family as well.

After he'd digested that fact and accepted it, the uncomfortable feeling of not belonging had been replaced by one of affection. It scared the spit out of him to know he had brothers, sisters-in-law, friends and neighbors he'd never met, but at the same time, it made him feel warm and fuzzy all over.

"You awake?"

Tom felt a tap against the sole of his foot. "Just thinking," he muttered, sitting upright.

"Last time we were together up here, you couldn't wait to get the two of us out on the lake so you could best me in a contest of fishing skill. Since you haven't so much as held a rod in your hand the entire afternoon, I'm thinking what's going on here is serious. So when are we going to talk about it?"

Tom hoisted himself onto the seat and rubbed his face with his hands. Thank God the older man hadn't forced the pole and bait bucket on him. The one time he'd gone fishing with Annie when they were married, he hadn't been able to muster the guts to thread the slimy worm onto a hook, never mind reel in and gut a bass. It figured Falcone would be a champ at the disgusting hobby.

Right now, the only thing that interested him was getting a better handle on this assignment and figuring out how to see it through. How much did Vince actually know about his son's undercover work, and how far was he willing to go to help?

Trying to make it sound as if they had talked over the case a dozen times in the past, he said, "I think the trauma of getting shot paralyzed a couple of brain cells. If you don't mind, I'd like to run a few things by you, just to see if I have my head on straight."

Vince reeled in his line and set his rod in the boat, then checked his string of fish. "If the case is what you want to talk about, I'll be happy to give you some advice. But I'd rather be a parent. I'm not asking about the assignment. I'm asking about Deputy McAllister.''

"D-deputy McAllister?" Damn, but he hated sounding like a tongue-tied parrot. He'd already braced himself for a hefty bout of questioning over his involvement with Annie, but he didn't think it would rate higher on Vince's list than his son's current job. "What do you want to know?" he asked, swallowing down a none-of-your-business response.

"I've got eyes," Vince said in return. "I might be retired, but I'm still a man with a healthy libido. Last I heard, it was against regulations for marshals to have sex—er, a personal involvement with other marshals, even ones as attractive as Anne McAllister. If you're breaking a rule, it has to be serious.''

Tom furrowed his brow. It was serious, all right. And dangerous. And stupid. And forbidden, unless Milton told him otherwise. But it was also impossible to stay away from her. Annie had gotten under his skin all over again, exactly as she had years ago, and this time he had no intention of letting her get away. He just had to figure out how to work around the problem while he satisfied the angel at the same time.

Still struggling with the close relationship Drew had with his dad, Tom decided to keep up the teasing banter. "And you're making this observation because . . . ?''

Vince leaned forward and chuckled. "I'm claiming my right as a buttinsky father. I haven't known you to do more than love 'em and leave 'em since you were a sophomore in high school. Besides the condition of the living room and that stack of condoms on the end table, I saw the way you looked at the woman.'' He swung the string of fish in front of Tom's face. "Kind of like these here fellas—all goggle-eyed and strung up for life. In fact, this big one at the bottom sort of reminds me of you.''

Tom's mouth slipped into a nervous grin. "Don't be ridiculous.'' He reached for the oars and began to row for the dock. "When this assignment is over, so is the affai—so is my association with Deputy McAllister. I'm not supposed to—I mean—we can't stay involved. She has her career to think of, and so do I."

"I've heard that song before." Vince shook his head. "You sound exactly like your big brother, right before he went down for the count. Joseph almost lost his job when he fell for Mary Lou, but it worked out fine when she quit her position as a prosecutor and went into private practice. There are ways, son. If it's meant to be, you and Deputy McAllister will find yours."

If you only knew, thought Tom as he continued to row in long, smooth strokes. He wanted to believe what his fath—what Vince was saying, but he knew better than to think about the future. Before he could plan any kind of life with Annie, he had to get them out of this mess.

It was high time he picked Vince's brain and soaked up a little *official* information. Mentally crossing his fingers, he stopped rowing and rested his elbows on his knees. "So, I guess we should get down to it." He cleared his throat. "Do you think the scenario I concocted is doable?"

Vince thumbed up the brim of his battered fishing hat. "Luring the traitors out in the open by forcing them to hunt you down? It's dangerous as hell, but yes, it's doable. By the way, someday you're going to have to tell me what possessed you to let Deputy McAllister tag along."

Unbidden, the image of Annie chained to his, er, Falcone's leg while she slam dunked the basketball like a pro came to mind. Wait until she played on his team against his brothers. The sides would be even now, with the six of them. His dad could referee, just to make sure everything was on the up and—

Damn! Where the hell was his head? Somewhere up his ass, because it sure wasn't on the here and now

"At the time, there wasn't a choice," he answered, striving to keep his voice even. "Now, how about you remind me again what we'd decided to do?"

Vince assembled his features into the same suspicious mental-patient-on-the-loose expression Annie wore when she thought he was acting strange. "If you weren't here, I was supposed to hang around the cabin a couple of days. If you didn't show, my orders were to go home and wait for your next call. Now that we're both here, I assume the rest of the plan is the same."

"It is. I just thought we could go over it one final time . . . to be sure it will still work . . . because of Ann—Deputy McAllister and all."

Unfortunately, Vince was too smart to fall for his son's innocent act. "Have you been in the sun too long? I don't see how her presence changes anything."

"Humor me," Tom said, running a hand through his porcupine hairdo. "It's been a rough week."

"I can see that." Vince's gaze shot to Tom's furrowing fingers. "McAllister's idea, I imagine?"

This time, Tom's grin was genuine.

Vince hooked the string of fish over the side of the boat. "Tell me, is that hot-as-a-pistol hair color of hers for real?"

"Only in temperament," he answered wryly. "Normally it's darkish blond, with streaks of honey and gold running through the curls. It's—"

"Oh, boy." Vince wiped his hands on his thighs and let out a long whistle. "You have it bad."

"And that ain't good," Tom answered automatically, staring at the bottom of the boat. Great. Now he sounded like a teenager on testosterone overload. "So . . . um . . . What did you think of the rest of the plan?"

Vince huffed out an impatient-sounding breath. "The part where we trade vehicles and you head to Arlington, while I lead whoever is after you on a merry chase around the lake? Shoot, I don't know. If they catch on and go after the truck, you and Martin might not have enough time to set a trap. We can only hope twenty-four hours is long enough to divert their attention until I draw them in.''

"Isn't that kind of dangerous for you?'' Tom asked. Inside he was wondering how a son could let his father take that kind of risk. And had he just called Drew's superior Martin?

His mouth set in a thin line, Vince suddenly looked angry enough to toss the nearest live body overboard. "Don't start nagging me with that *it's too dangerous* crap again. We both know how important it is for me to be a part of this case. Especially if your original suspicion was correct.''

Oo-kay, one more tiny detail he didn't know a thing about. Darn Milton for not warning him about his fath—er—Vincent Falcone's involvement.

The older man folded his arms across his chest, but it was clear his anger still simmered below the surface. "How about you answer me this. Are you sure it's rogue marshals?''

"After talking to Phillips, I'm fairly certain of at least one of them.''

"And how much of this does Deputy McAllister know?''

"Just enough to get her royally cheezed off at me,'' Tom admitted. He picked up the oars and started to row again. "She gets touchy when I say it's not her duty to catch these guys. Says I dragged her into this case and put her job on the line, so she has as much right as I do to be a part of it. Says she wants to be recognized as a marshal first, then a woman, as if I could ignore that fact. She has me so tied up in—''

He felt his face heat up for the second time and cursed under his breath. "You know what I mean.''

"Damn that Gloria Steinem for convincing women they were equal to men,'' Vince sympathized, coughing politely behind his palm. "And God protect me from all the bra burners, militant or otherwise. They'll drive you crazy—if you let them.''

Tom shook his head when he saw Vince's lips turn up at

the corners. Was the older man a mind reader or were Drew Falcone's feelings for Annie so obvious they were written in red across his forehead?

And did it really matter? Either way, he was in deep trouble.

With the telephone receiver to her ear, Annie rested her shoulder against a wall in the cramped backroom Earl had optimistically designated his "customer lounge." Scanning the space, little bigger than a walk-in closet, she decided the older man either possessed the most imaginative sense of humor on the planet or he needed a new pair of glasses.

Besides two ancient washers, a lone dryer and a shelf cluttered with open boxes of caked laundry soap, the only things in the room that might pass for amenities were three cracked plastic chairs and a wooden rack holding yellowed magazines clustered under a wall-mounted pay phone.

After listening to Vincent talk about the family's shock at seeing Drew's face plastered on the evening news, it dawned on Annie that her sister probably had viewed the same reports and experienced an even more horrified reaction. With the washer and dryer rattling the floorboards, it was high time she gave Julie a call and put her mind at ease.

A minute later, the answering machine picked up and warbled its cheery we're-not-at-home message. "Jules, it's me," Annie began, hesitant to leave her name in case someone had bugged her sister's line. "I just wanted to let you know I'm fine. I'll be calling soon to give you the details."

Satisfied her message had been informative enough to give her sister some peace of mind, yet short enough to not be traced, Annie replaced the receiver on its tarnished hook. She would tell Julie the rest of it in person, when this mess was cleared up and she took some time off for a nice long vacation.

After a moment's hesitation, she dropped another quarter

in the slot and dialed the number of her superior, Charles Brinkman. Drew had never said she couldn't give the man a second call, and with his father here to help with whatever he had planned, she didn't think it mattered whether or not Brinkman knew where they were.

After leaving a message on his private voice mail, telling him where she was and letting him know she would contact him again in a day or so, she walked three steps to the spinning washer and propped her bottom against its rusted front. Heaving a sigh, she reviewed the morning's activities. From the sporadic bits of conversation she'd had with Drew's father, she'd learned he was a retired homicide detective who kept busy doing private investigative work for various law enforcement agencies in and around Washington D.C. He even took on an occasional gig in Baltimore, where his oldest son was a prosecutor.

As per Drew's earlier request, he'd arrived at the family's lakeside cabin in a truck he'd been storing specifically for situations like this one. "I might be retired, but I'm not dead," Vincent had informed her proudly over his third cup of coffee. "If one of my boys needs me, I'm there."

Aside from the fact that Drew seemed as surprised as she was to have the man turn up on their doorstep, the strangest part of the visit was his reaction. Annie didn't think he had once looked either her or his father in the eye or grown comfortable in their presence.

Even though Vincent hadn't done any more than quirk a brow when he'd taken a gander at the living area, the fact that she'd been embarrassed in front of the man still annoyed her. With the open sleeper sofa and their clothes strewn across the room, anyone with half a brain could tell she and Drew were sharing the bed and all the perks that went with it. Since they were consenting adults, it shouldn't have bothered either of them that Vince knew what they'd been doing. But Drew had skulked around like a sinner hunting for a confessional all morning.

Still pondering his childish actions, she folded towels, jeans and sweats, then put a load of delicates in the dryer and slid another trio of quarters home. After this batch finished, she'd pack everything in their duffel and return to the cabin. With a little luck, father and son would still be on the lake trawling for dinner and putting the final touches on their plan. She'd have time to straighten the cabin; then she could meditate on this latest bump in the road and try to make sense of it all.

In the meantime, she needed a diet soda. Digging a crumpled bill from the pocket of her borrowed sweats, she headed for the front of the store. It didn't matter where Earl was. When she'd first arrived, he'd given her a fistful of change and showed her how to open the register to exchange her paper money for more quarters. Apparently, any friend of the Falcones' was a friend of his, and therefore trustworthy as an Eagle Scout.

On the way, she stopped at the freezer case lining the back wall of the store, thinking it might be a nice touch if she picked up dessert. She didn't want to make a big production out of Vincent's visit, but she kind of liked the guy. In between watching his son act like an about-to-be-caught felon and enjoying his breakfast, he'd confided to her that he was a widower who'd almost single-handedly raised five wonderful boys. The idea that he'd managed so daunting a task had Annie wishing she could find a nice single woman who would jump at the chance to date such an admirable man.

Stifling a moan of disgust, she gave herself a healthy mental slap upside the head. The last thing she needed was personal involvement with another Falcone male. Dealing with one of them was bad enough—sticking her nose into a second one's private life would send her back to therapy faster than a nervous breakdown.

Concentrating on the items in the cold case, she didn't turn around when the bell hanging over the bait shop door tinkled. A muffled hum of male voices rumbled through the air, and she felt a prickle of unease scrape the base of her spine. Glancing toward the front of the store, she spied a pair of men with their backs to her talking to Earl. Dressed in expensive-looking leather jackets and new jeans, they seemed out of place in an area where bib overalls, hiking boots and flannel shirts were the dress code *du jour*.

Earl never looked her way, but the odd expression on his wizened face made Annie wary. Sneaking past the paper products, she tiptoed to the end of the aisle and peered around a display of canned vegetables. Swallowing a wave of panic, she crouched and willed herself invisible. From this angle, she could see and hear everything . . . and clearly recognize Deputies Smithers and Butterworth.

"We're trying to find the Falcone cabin," said Smithers, his voice a polite drawl. "Vince told us if we got lost, someone at the bait shop would give us directions."

Looking dumb as the proverbial stump, Earl raised his bushy eyebrows toward the ceiling and scratched his balding head. "Falcone, ya say? Hm, don't think I know that name."

"Older guy, nice dresser with dark hair and an attitude. He has a bunch of sons. We're good friends of the youngest—Andrew," Smithers added.

Annie fisted her hands against her chest and willed her wildly thumping heart to slow down. *Friends my fanny!* Taking a deep breath, she ducked lower and paid attention.

Butterworth pulled his wallet from his back pocket, and she caught a glimpse of the gun tucked out of the way over the rear of his hip. Removing a bill, he placed it on the counter. "Drew told us they've had a cabin on this lake for years. Invited us to stop in any time. He's supposed to be fishing with his father this week, and we thought to join them."

To his credit, Earl smoothly pocketed the money and assembled his features into a pleasant road map of wrinkles. "You could try heading west out of the drive and takin' the first right. The road's a little bumpy, but you keep to followin' it until you see a mailbox without a name. Take that road about a mile and go up to the door and knock, and you just might find what yer lookin' for.''

Smithers repeated the directions, then said, ''Much obliged. Oh, and could you do us another favor? If Vince or Andrew stop by, don't mention we're on our way. This visit is a surprise.''

Annie exhaled slowly as she stood, but waited until she heard their car pull away before double-timing it to the counter to face Earl.

He set his hands on his scrawny hips. ''You and Drew know them fellas?''

''Yes, unfortunately.'' Unclenching her fists, she placed her palms on the counter. ''Where exactly did you send them?''

A flicker of devilish amusement was magnified a hundred fold behind Earl's inch-thick lenses. ''Fella name of Nathan Baxter's got a place at the far end of the lake. He and his three king-sized German Shepherds don't take much to strangers.''

Annie threw him a grin of approval. ''Drew and Vincent will be glad to hear that.''

Earl took off his glasses and stared through narrowed lids. ''I'm aware of the kind of business Drew is in, as well as Vincent and a few of his other sons. Know better'n to send them a pistol-toting stranger who don't know the way to their cabin. Besides, I didn't like the looks of that tall one. Somethin' around the eyes made me think he was out to do more than pay a surprise visit.''

Fairly certain Earl didn't need to know any of the details, Annie asked, ''How long do you think it will take them to find their way to Baxter's cabin?''

''Oh, they'll be there right quick.'' The older man reseated his glasses over his jug-sized nose and thrust out his grizzled jaw. ''It's how long they'll be stayin' that's the question.

If Nathan's in a good mood, he might only keep 'em for a couple of hours. If he's feelin' cantankerous, they could be there until morning. Then again, I once heard tell those dogs treed a trespasser for two whole days before Nathan found the good manners to let 'im go." Grinning, he shook his head. "You just never know."

Overloaded by the wealth of information, Annie said, "Then I guess I'd better get back to the cabin and give Drew and his dad the news."

Waggling her fingers, she trotted to the laundry room. After setting the duffel on the floor, she pulled the rest of their clothes from the dryer and stuffed them in the bag, then stood and slung the duffel over her shoulder. She had to warn Drew and Vincent. They had to come up with a plan to apprehend the rogue deputies before the men had a chance to set up an ambush and shoot Drew again.

Suddenly overcome by a flash of brilliance, she stopped in her tracks. Smithers and Butterworth had just left. That meant she'd only be a few minutes behind them on the road. She knew where they were going, so she had the upper hand. If she could catch them before they got to Baxter's cabin, Drew's life would no longer be in danger.

And apprehending them would prove to Drew that he'd been wrong about her. He would have to admit she could be trusted to do her job as a marshal. He'd have to eat those words he wrote about her in his journal.

Instead of thinking her desperate, he would be forced to call her a hero.

Tom raced back through the front door of the cottage and did a second thorough check of the bedrooms and bath, then returned to the kitchen, a tremor of fear niggling at his gut.

Vince's sharp-eyed gaze took in the empty cabin, which looked exactly as it had when they'd left to go fishing hours earlier. "I don't like the looks of this. Deputy McAllister should have been back by now, even if one of the washers was out of commission.''

Pacing from the front door to the kitchen sink, Tom asked, ''Any chance the truck could have had a breakdown or a flat?''

''I doubt it,'' said Vince. ''Once I got that engine running, I gave it a good tune-up, and the tires are brand-new top of the line. Besides, from what you told me of the woman, she'd have fixed a flat herself before going for help.''

Thinking out loud, Tom ran a shaking hand over his hair. ''The truck isn't behind the tool shed, and there are no signs of a struggle, so I don't think anything happened here. That means she's still at the bait shop. Question is, do we go there to look for her or wait?''

''We could call,'' Vince suggested, nodding toward the phone. ''Of course, that doesn't mean Earl will answer. You know how the old fool hates talking to people unless he thinks there's some kind of emergency.''

''Tell you what,'' Tom said, heading for the door. ''You call and let the phone ring while I rev up the Harley and take a ride down the road. If I don't find her, I'll keep on going until I hit the store. If Earl answers before I get there, tell Annie I said she should put her fanny in gear because it's time for her to come home and start dinner. That ought to make her mad enough to fly here under her own power.''

''Gotch'a,'' Vince said, punching out the numbers. ''And, Drew, be careful out there.''

Tom jumped on the motorbike and zoomed toward the bait shop, alternately cursing Annie for being such a hardheaded, stubborn woman and praying she was safe. On the way, he peered into the foliage on either side of the road. With the trees almost barren, he could see straight to the lake on his left and across to the mountains on his right. As far as he could tell, no one had pulled over or driven into the woods at any point along the narrow highway.

She had to be at Earl's, probably gabbing with the old

guy. It would really get her goat when he caught her red-handed gossiping like a local. Or maybe one of the washers was broken, and Earl had sent her to the nearest town or . . .

Aw, hell, who was he kidding? Either way, he was going to strangle her for giving him cardiac arrest.

The second he spotted the parking lot with one dilapidated truck parked at the pumps, a full-blown bubble of fear burst in his chest. He jumped off the bike and took the porch stairs two at a time, then charged into the store and plowed straight to the counter.

"Earl. Has Annie been here to use the washers?"

"Yep." Oblivious to the dull ringing of a phone coming from the rear of the store, he handed the man standing at the counter his change. "You take care now, Morris. Tell Ada I hope she's feelin' better."

Tom hot-footed it to the pay phone while the customer said his goodbyes. The dryer door stood open, but he peered inside anyway and found a lacy, foam green bra sitting at the bottom. *Annie's bra.*

Shoving the underwear in his pocket, he reached for the still-ringing phone. "Dad? Nope, not yet . . . I haven't had time to ask any questions, but she was here. As soon as I get a few answers from Earl, I'll be home."

Tom slammed the receiver in the cradle and stalked to the front of the shop. "When did she leave? Was she alone?"

The older man scratched at his jaw. "Been gone 'bout an hour now. Right after those two fellas left. Said she was going home to warn you and Vince about 'em."

Tom's heart stuttered in his chest. "Two men? What two men? Did they give you names?"

"Nope." Earl's eyes grew bright behind his pop bottle lenses. "One of 'em was tall, thin and shifty lookin', t'other was just too smooth. I could tell they was up to no good 'cause they was carryin' guns."

Great. He'd just described Smithers and Butterworth to a T. "Did Annie see them? Did they see her?"

"She saw 'em, all right, even said she knew who they were, but she was real careful to stay out of their sight. Course, I realized they were trouble the second I laid eyes on 'em, askin' for directions to your cabin the way they did. Vince always warns me ahead a time when there's someone comin' to use the place."

Tom set his hands on the counter. "This is important, Earl. Do you know where they went, and did you tell Annie?"

"I sent 'em on a wild goose chase, then told her what I'd done. After that, I went outside to drag in some cartons. When I came back, she was gone."

It was all Tom could do to keep from leaning across the counter, grabbing the geezer by his overalls and shaking out the entire story. "Where did you send them?"

Looking pleased as a paper-trained puppy, Earl shot him a satisfied grin. "Not to worry. I took care of 'em, all right. Sent 'em to Nathan Baxter's place over t'other side of the lake. Nathan don't cotton to strangers. If I know him, he and them dogs a his will handle things just fine."

Tom didn't have a clue to what the man was babbling about, but he knew Vince would. Shouting out a "thanks," he ran to the Harley and booted up the engine. He had to get to his dad.

CHAPTER SEVENTEEN

Just past sundown, the rising moon cast an eerie glow over barren trees, throwing pale sticklike shadows across the ground at Annie's feet. She'd parked behind a cluster of rocks situated beyond the rusted mailbox she assumed belonged to Nathan Baxter, but didn't see a sign of Butterworth or Smithers. The deputies must have driven like the wind to get here, because she hadn't caught a glimmer of tail lights while she'd followed Earl's sketchy directions to the cabin.

Comforted by the weight of the Glock resting in her sweats, she walked to the rear of the truck and climbed into the bed, where she hoped to find something of use: another weapon, more ammo, or maybe a flashlight. The bed itself was clean, but she hit pay dirt when she opened a side-mounted storage bin and found a black knitted hat and matching gloves sitting atop a pile of jumper cables and other automotive paraphernalia.

After pulling on the gloves and tucking her hair under the cap, she jumped from the truck. The added clothes wouldn't do much to help her plan, but they would keep her warm and enable her to blend into the shadows. If things worked out the way she hoped, she could find the rogue deputies and hand them over to Drew Falcone before the night was over.

A brisk autumn wind rustled the branches, causing Annie to shiver, and not just from the cold. Random sounds of the forest and an owl hooting its mournful call sent a chill tripping up her spine. On second thought, maybe it wasn't such a brilliant idea to traipse through unfamiliar terrain on a damp November night wearing nothing but old sweats and a borrowed hat and gloves. She clasped her arms around her middle and willed a bit of warmth into her bones as the idea she might be making a mistake tiptoed fleetingly through her thoughts.

Out here in the chilly twilight, things didn't look as simple as they had back at the store. There was still time to return to the cabin, collect Drew and his dad and bring them here to set up an ambush. Or maybe she could just wait for Smithers and Butterworth to drive back down the road and follow them until they took their next step.

Her mind ping-ponged with possibilities. By now, Drew and Vincent had to have realized something was up. They might already have gone to the bait shop and talked to Earl. But the way the Harley announced its presence a half mile in advance, they wouldn't be so foolish as to ride it here. They would make the trek on foot.

No, it was too late to rethink her idea. She just had to keep a level head and do what she'd originally planned before the Falcone men arrived.

She stepped gingerly onto the rutted road and walked about a quarter mile before she detected the outline of a shape looming ahead of her. Moonlight illuminated a nondescript, older model Jeep, its rear end partially tucked into the trees, its front bumper aimed for a quick getaway, exactly like she'd parked her own truck. Back at the store, she hadn't caught a glimpse of what the marshals were driving, but common sense told her this vehicle belonged to them.

Crouching low, she paced out a wide half circle and approached the Jeep from behind. After making certain it was empty, she placed her hand on the hood. The warmth she found confirmed her suspicions. Smithers and Butterworth had to have arrived just a few minutes ago.

She climbed into the back and groped around until she found a flashlight. Pointing it toward the floor, she turned it on and gave the interior a thorough inspection. She had no qualms about helping herself to the lone ammo clip and worn jacket she spied sitting on the rear seat. She shrugged into the jacket, then stuffed the flashlight and clip into one pocket, slid her gun into the other and hopped onto the leaf-strewn ground.

In moments the fleece-lined coat had her toasty warm. At least she wouldn't freeze before she got to the cabin, and she had extra ammo in case of an emergency. Too bad she hadn't found an object sharp enough to puncture the Jeep's heavy-duty tires—and double too bad the marshals hadn't been dumb enough to leave the keys in the ignition.

The sound of dogs barking in the distance stopped Annie in her tracks. What was it Earl had said about Baxter's dogs and trespassers? Not that it mattered. She got along just fine with most four-footed creatures, and they got along with her; dealing with them shouldn't be a problem.

Wrapping her courage around her like a blanket, she took a deep breath, sidled to the edge of the forest and began walking toward a faint light shining ahead of her. She wished she could remember how far down the drive Earl said Baxter had his cabin, but she'd been so shocked to see the deputies in the bait shop, she'd absorbed only part of the older man's rambling. It was growing darker by the second, and this trail looked to be the only way in or out. Smithers and Butterworth were probably being just as cautious as she was, inching up the road and watching their backs at the same time.

Threading her way through the trees nearest the drive, she stepped carefully over fallen logs and around boulders, wincing whenever her feet caused a twig to snap or leaves to crackle. After a few minutes, the distant light grew brighter, but she still sensed an aura of foreboding, along with the disconcerting feeling of being watched.

Something rustled the ground to her right, and she ducked behind a tree. With her heart hammering in double time, she leaned against the rough bark and stood still. The rustling sound was closer now, accompanied by a low rumble she couldn't quite place.

She drew her gun and waited.

Movement, this time from the left, had her scanning in that direction. The rumbling intensified until it seemed to surround her. She'd never asked Drew, but could there be wildcats in these woods?

Or worse?

Suddenly the rustling noise stopped, as did the rumbling, and Annie peeked around the tree. Shining directly at her from the darkness were six pinpoints of light—red glowing light that reminded her of the eyes of demons she'd seen depicted on the television and in movies. For a second, she couldn't think of anything but a three-headed monster. Then she recalled Earl's comment about Nathan Baxter owning *three* dogs.

"Hey, fellas," she said in her most jovial whisper. "Good boys. I'm not here to hurt you, so let's be friends, all right?"

Grrrr.

Deep and menacing, the chorus of growls echoed in the night.

Annie stuck the gun in her pocket and slowly held out a trembling hand. "I'm friendly, honest."

The scattering of eyes moved out of the shadows, close enough for her to see that they did, indeed, belong to dogs.

Huge, ominous-looking dogs with gaping mouths full of very large teeth.

She swallowed down the billow of fear bubbling up like a geyser from somewhere in the vicinity of her stomach and pasted a smile on her lips. *Yeah, like these three brutes are going to recognize a happy face.*

"Easy, fellas. Just take it easy." Sucking in a breath, she kept her hand steady, her voice even, as she let the first, second and finally the third dog sniff her fingers. After a moment, the canine trio moved as one, sat back on their haunches and stared at her expectantly.

The air escaped her lungs in one long sigh of relief as her body relaxed. Everything would be fine, providing none of these king-sized canines decided she was the perfect candidate for an evening snack. "Nice boys. See, I'm not the enemy. I won't hurt you."

Annie felt the cold press of steel behind her right ear and cursed silently.

"We'll just have to see about that, now won't we?"

Feeling like a character from an action adventure movie, Tom rowed steadily, cutting a swath through the murky water with his oars. Back at the cabin, he'd squeezed himself into the smaller of the two camouflage jackets he'd bought at the Wal–Mart with Annie, while Vince took the larger one. Then the older man had pulled a can of what looked to be shoe polish from his oversized duffel and ordered Tom to blacken his face.

While Tom did as he was told, Vince had worked the canvas bag like a magician's top hat, producing a pair of night-vision binoculars, two dark-colored knit caps and a host of gear that looked suspiciously army issue.

"When was the last time you saw this Nathan Baxter?" Tom asked in a whisper, flexing his arms in the constricting jacket. He wanted to ask why Vince hadn't been surprised when he'd learned where Earl had sent the marshals, but thought it might be a dumb question.

Vince turned from his position in the bow. From the set of his burly shoulders and narrow-eyed stare, it was obvious to Tom that he'd made another mistake.

"I ran into him at the bait shop this past summer, and he invited me to stop by and take a look at the new place he was building. Don't worry. Nathan will remember the kind of work you do. If you don't recall meeting him a few years ago when he and his family first came to the lake, then your memory must still be messed up from the shooting, huh?"

"Guess so," Tom muttered, ignoring the subtle dig. "Earl made the guy sound like some kind of hundred-year-old hermit. Said he had no tolerance for strangers."

"Leave it to Earl to exaggerate the details." Vince went back to riding point. "Baxter's no hermit. He just likes to keep to himself is all. I can't blame him after what he's gone through the past few years."

Tom heaved a sigh. Okay, one more tidbit of information he didn't have access to. Milton was really going to get an earful the next time, if there was a next time, they met.

"What about the dogs?" Tom had always loved the idea of owning a dog, but that goldfish story he'd told Annie had been a true one. In reality, he had never been allowed near them as a child, and he'd had no reason to interact with them as an adult.

"Don't worry, I've got it covered." Vincent patted at a side pocket in his jacket, then raised the hi-tech binoculars to his eyes. "Row to the right. I think I see the house lights."

"How do you know they belong to Baxter?"

Vince shrugged. "I've respected the guy's privacy, but I couldn't resist drifting over here a couple of times this summer to check on his progress. Besides, Nathan's one of a handful of folks who live at this end of the lake on and off during the year. It stands to reason the lights are his." A blustery wind took that moment to whistle across the water. "In case you don't recall, not many people come up here after Labor Day."

"Oh, yeah. Right." Tom cleared his throat as he maneuvered the oars. He did remember, but vaguely, as if his muscle memory was idling in neutral. "You worried?"

Vince's whole body shook, and it took a few seconds for Tom to figure out he was laughing.

"What's so funny?"

"You are." The older man studied him in the moonlight. "If I didn't know better, I'd think my real son had been snatched by aliens and replaced by a different model."

"Too much soft living," muttered Tom, groping for a sensible answer. "I haven't been in the field for a while."

"Don't get me wrong. You don't look any worse for it. Except for the hair, of course."

"I plan to dye it back as soon as this mess is over."

"And the cigarettes. You haven't had a smoke since I've been here. What's up with that?"

Tom stopped rowing and set his hands on his thighs. Vince was right. Somehow, when he hadn't been looking, his craving for nicotine had been replaced by a more potent addiction. An all-consuming desire for Annie had seeped into his bloodstream, dulling his senses and blinding him to everything else.

"Annie ... Deputy McAllister didn't approve. It was easier to go cold turkey than listen to her lecture me twenty-four-seven," he lied. In truth, she hadn't nagged him that much, but it was the best explanation he could give at the moment.

"Then I owe her one, seeing as she managed to accomplish what the entire family couldn't, God bless her."

"Yeah, well—"

"Okay, there's the dock. Can you see it?"

Tom peered in the direction Vince was pointing and spied the barest outline of pilings, pier and boat. As he rowed closer, a large modern cruiser moored at the end of an impressive-looking dock came more clearly into view.

"Pretty fancy boat—expensive, too. I got the impression

from Earl this guy existed one step up from the Unabomber, living in a tarpaper shack and threatening harm to all who dared approach.''

Vince gave another chuckle. ''That's just what Nathan wants everybody to think. The boat is new, so he must be getting his life back on track. Good for him.''

Tom decided to let the strange comment rest and steered their smaller craft to the edge of the dock, then guided it to rest in shallow water. Vince climbed from the bow, tied the boat off and began hauling out gear.

''Are we really going to need all that?'' asked Tom.

Vince stuffed a coil of rope in his pocket, then handed him a thick leather sheath. Tom grimaced as he pulled out a knife with a blade that had to be eight inches long. Another thing he'd missed while growing up was campouts and joining the scouts. From the look of it, his trekking through the woods with Vincent Falcone would be like sending Truman Capote on a nature hike with Daniel Boone.

''You never know what you might need out here in the wild. What happened to all that outdoor training I drilled into your head when you were growing up?''

Wincing at his error, one of about a dozen he'd made so far tonight, Tom said wryly, ''Must have gone the way of my memory.''

Vince raised a brow, as if to say *uh-huh, sure.* ''Got your gun and extra ammo?''

He felt the weight of the Glock in his outside pocket and nodded. At least that was the truth. Two weeks ago he would have been appalled to admit he even knew how to shoot a gun. Tonight it was a comfort.

A sharp wind kicked up, and he pulled the jacket tighter around his middle, then gave up trying to stay warm. Right now, he was worried about Annie. When she'd left the cabin, she'd been wearing little more than sneakers and borrowed sweats. If she was out here, she was probably freezing. What the hell had happened to her? Why hadn't she come back to the cabin after she'd spotted Smithers and Butterworth?

When he found her, he was going to kiss her cross-eyed, then lock her up somewhere safe and throw away the key. Or maybe he'd just chain her to a bed and . . .

The air echoed with a chorus of frantic barks, and he straightened.

"Sounds like the boys found something," said Vince, but he didn't seem worried. "Time for us to have a look-see."

Tom assumed they were headed toward the pale shimmer of light beckoning through the trees. Vince had stuffed a flashlight in one of his pockets, but Tom knew better than to suggest they turn it on. This was a covert operation, one he was *supposed* to know all the proper procedures for. Inhaling a breath, he dredged up everything he could remember about those shoot-'em-up flicks Annie used to drag him to—the ones that starred Schwarzenegger and Stallone. If he'd known what kind of predicament he would be in, he would have paid closer attention.

Following Vince's lead, Tom crouched low and walked up the slope and into the trees. The white gravel path leading from the dock to the house was clear, but taking it would have made them perfect targets for anyone watching. And it stood to reason that Smithers and Butterworth would be watching.

Unless Baxter had already captured them.

A dozen different scenarios raced through his mind. The deputies could have gotten the drop on Baxter and coerced him into telling them where to find the Falcone cabin. Or Baxter and his dogs could have turned the tables and hogtied them. Or Smithers and Butterworth might still be waiting to approach the cabin.

Then there was Annie. He had no doubt she'd taken it upon herself to come out here and find the men. But what had she hoped to accomplish by pulling this kind of stupid stunt? And where the hell was she?

Baxter's home came into view, and Tom's mouth dropped open in surprise. Even in the dark he could tell that the house was magnificent. Two stories tall and nestled in the hillside, its second level had a wall of windows and a sweeping balcony that overlooked the forest and the lake.

In front of him, Vince dropped low and began to walk in a zigzag pattern, signaling Tom to do the same. Concentrating on his task, Tom followed as they slowly snaked an uphill course to the side of the house. Without warning, a bank of floodlights illuminated the area, washing everything within a fifty-foot radius with light.

"Jeez," Tom muttered, blinking at the blinding brightness.

"You can say that again," agreed Vince. "No way anybody could sneak up on him with this fancy setup."

Without another word, they faded back into the trees and waited. From this vantage point Tom could see that the house was still under construction, but it was going to be a beauty when finished.

After a minute, the lights went out, and the property was again enveloped in darkness. "Where is everyone?" Tom asked in a whisper.

"Damned if I know," said Vince just as quietly. "But I think we'd better lay low and find out, don't you?"

"I'd rather look for Annie," Tom responded. "She's the one who's out here alone."

"You are positively, absolutely cruising for trouble." Eloise sat on top of one of two chimneys flanking the house. Dressed in a sleek black wet suit with Day-Glo yellow flippers on her dainty feet and a snorkel strapped to her forehead, she looked ready to dive from the roof straight into a coral reef. With a thoroughly disgruntled expression on her lovely face, she huffed out a breath. "And I still don't understand why you had to get *him* involved, when you could just as easily have kept this entire business on the other side of the lake.''

Milton perched on the roof and scanned the area. From this spot, he could see Tom and Vincent, Annie and her new canine friends and the rogue marshals. He'd taken the liberty of freezing them in place, so that they resembled pieces in a game of virtual chess, while he pondered how to proceed— and half listened to Eloise complain.

''Don't blame me for the direction this situation has taken. Earl was the one who sent the bad guys here. And I'm glad he did. Things are starting to heat up, as they say in cop-speak. What sane woman could resist a man who would brave the frigid darkness in unknown terrain to rescue her from the clutches of evil?''

''Annie?'' Eloise suggested with a sniff. ''Whom I'm beginning to admire, by the way. She was doing just fine until that hulking Neanderthal found her. Given the chance, I'm sure she would have been able to get out of this situation all by herself.''

Milton turned his head and raised a brow. Never in all his past dealings with the quixotic angel had he heard her refer to an individual human in such a negative manner, unless, of course, they were her own charges. Yes, she'd made disparaging remarks in the course of conversation, but always about the predicaments in which humans managed to mire themselves or their frailties in general, not the humans themselves.

''What is it, exactly, that bothers you about Nathan Baxter?''

Folding her arms, Eloise gazed at her flippers. If Milton wasn't so sure it was impossible, he'd swear his companion was blushing.

''He's a . . . I find him . . . he never . . .''

''He's had a difficult life, El. And he isn't one of yours, so why do you care?''

She gazed up at him, a true glimmer of sadness shining

from her china blue eyes. "Why is it your memory always seizes up when it's most convenient for you? You know how I detest handling assignments where—They make me—" Placing her hands on her hips, she threw him a suspicious glare. "Say, are you trying to pull a fast one, dragging me into another one of your less than legitimate schemes?"

Milton gave her his best who-little-old-me look. "Of course not. Our being here is merely a coincidence. Now, tell me what it is about Nathan that makes you so uncomfortable."

She waved a delicate hand in dismissal. "Just move on with this current business, if you please. I really don't feel like dwelling on old news."

Still skeptical, Milton tapped a finger to his chin. She was correct. He needed to move along. "Hm, let's see. Who should rescue who? Or is it whom? I never can remember those pesky grammar rules about—"

"Will you get on with it! I have other needy souls to see to, you know. And so do you."

"Yes, yes. It's just that things are hanging in a very delicate balance. My goal, of course, is to set Tom up as Annie's hero, but Tom has yet to see that she can take care of herself. That she's grown into an incredibly strong and resilient woman who can make her own decisions and run her own life. He needs to appreciate her so much that all he can think of is how he failed her. And how much he wants her back."

"Not asking for much, are you?" Eloise stretched out a flippered foot and inspected the length of her shapely leg. "He's already telling himself he wants her, can't live without her, and all that other blah-blah-blah humans wax poetic over when they think they're in love. Isn't that enough?"

"For a normal woman, maybe. But not for Annie. I made a promise to myself to give her a perfect love, and I'm not certain Tom is ready to help me keep my word. I want him to apologize."

With her eyes never leaving his, Eloise popped off the roof like a jack-in-the-box and plopped back down with a thump. "Now you're being ridiculous. Male humans hate to apologize, especially to the female ones."

"Are you ready to take Tom back?"

"No!"

"Will you, if he apologizes?"

Hunching over, Eloise rested her chin on her fist. Looking for all the world like an eccentric version of Rodin's famous statue, she pondered for a full minute before saying, "All right. If Tom apologizes to Annie, I'll take him back as Drew Falcone. But you're making a sucker bet, Milton, and I'm not ashamed to admit I'm taking full advantage."

Before he could respond, the heavenly being disappeared. Bathed in a shower of glittering angel dust, Milton shook his head. The time for Eloise was drawing near, he could feel it in his deepest core. All angels, at one point or another, were given *the choice*. He'd had his millennia ago, and hers would be coming soon. Problem was, angels only learned of *the choice* after being told they had to make it. If he knew Eloise, she was going to be furious, right up to the very end. It would be interesting to find out her decision.

A gentle-yet-commanding breeze blew up around him, ruffling the few hairs on his head. Flustered, Milton raised his gaze to the stars. "Sorry, sorry, just doing a bit of thinking," he muttered. Returning to the scene below, he snapped his fingers. He'd been so distracted by Eloise and her future, he'd almost forgotten a main player in the mix.

Captain Hook, as Drew had named him, needed to be present, along with Papa Bear and a few of the others, in order for everything to fall into place.

Milton heaved a sigh. No doubt about it, he'd definitely made the correct choice all those years ago. Poor Eloise. He had a feeling she wasn't going to have the same easy time.

It had been ages since he'd had to work this hard at setting things right, but each past endeavor had been worth the risk. Andrew Falcone had been special. Doomed to a life of loneliness because he'd missed out on meeting the woman meant to share his life hadn't stopped him from becoming an exemplary human being and an honorable man. One who had never asked for a single thing in his short time on earth, who cared for his family and did his best to get the job done.

Annie had made a valiant effort to do the same, only she'd been saddled with a vain, insecure man who had refused to recognize her true worth. She had voiced only one wish in her lifetime, and Milton had already decided, before her husband had died, that she deserved to have it granted.

On top of all that, Eloise had been wrong about Tom. He was redeemable, even if it took hitting him in the head with a brick to make him see the way of things.

Two lives, more importantly, two souls, were at stake here. He only hoped he didn't ruin his record and screw it all up.

CHAPTER EIGHTEEN

Taking her cue from the intimidating German shepherds, Annie stood rigid. Gut instinct told her the man wielding the gun wasn't Butterworth or Smithers, but Nathan Baxter, the hermit Earl had implied was a loose cannon. Great. Her choices were getting worse by the second.

"Who are you? What do you think you're doing?" she asked, playing for time.

"I'll ask the questions if you don't mind. Hands flat on the tree on either side of your head, and tell me where I can find some identification."

She heaved a disappointed sigh. His deep, well-modulated voice tripped over her skin, sending a flock of goose bumps dancing up her arms—and not in a good way. He didn't sound menacing or nasty, just very savvy and a tiny bit . . . amused? *Definitely not a loose cannon.*

Mentally calling up all the do's and don'ts of capture etiquette, Annie did as she was told.

His hands stilled for a moment before initiating a brisk, impersonal and thoroughly professional search, which sur-

prised her. In her line of work, she'd run across plenty of
men who would, given half the chance, try to take advantage
of a woman alone in the woods in the middle of the night.
Then he found her Glock.

"Well, well, well, what have we here?"

"I have a perfectly logical reason for carrying that gun."

"Go ahead. I'm always willing to hear a good joke."

"I don't suppose you'd believe me if I told you I'm a
U.S. Deputy Marshal?"

A derisive snort ruffled the hair on the nape of her neck.

"That's a new one. You reporters never know when to
quit, do you?"

"I'm not a reporter. I'm a—"

"U.S. Marshal, I know. And I'm Sister Mary Holywater,
abbess of the local nunnery. Put your hands behind your
back."

"Wait a second. We have to talk first."

He jerked one arm, then the other behind her and tied her
wrists together, then removed her ammo clip and flashlight.
"What were you planning to do? Hold me at gunpoint for
an interview?"

"I am not a reporter, Mr. Baxter."

Spinning her around, he glared. There was just enough
moonlight for Annie to make out the hard-chiseled planes
of a rough-hewn face shaded with several days' growth of
dark beard. Surprisingly, he was young, maybe in his early
thirties, and tall; she had to tip her head to see into his eyes.
From the look of him, he was no hermit, but she'd bet her
last bullet Nathan Baxter was some kind of law enforcement
agent. Darn Earl for giving her the totally wrong impression.

"Then how come you know my name?"

"Earl . . . at the bait shop . . . mentioned it."

"Too bad I can't call him to confirm." Studying her, he
ran the hand that wasn't carrying a gun through his unruly
hair. "Look, I don't usually have to roust women from my
property, but it's a little late for a social visit. You sure as

hell aren't dressed like the Avon lady, so what am I supposed to think?''

"How about thinking that I might be telling the truth?'' she said wryly. "My name is Anne McAllister. I'm a deputy marshal out of Newark, New Jersey. I'm on a case with another marshal, and we have reason to believe the two men we're in the process of tracking down are somewhere around here.''

One corner of his mouth quirked up.

"I know it sounds unbelievable but—''

"You're telling me that besides the far-fetched federal marshal story, I'm also supposed to believe you're hunting two men from New Jersey and you've ended up all the way down here in Virginia—on *my* land.'' He shook his head. "Talk about going to the wall to get a story.''

"I'm not making it up . . . and I'm not interested in your *story,* whatever it is,'' she insisted.

"Who are these men?''

Annie swallowed. Hadn't she been told in training that sticking to the truth, no matter how crazy it sounded, was always best in a gnarly situation? "Umm . . . They're marshals, too.''

Baxter raised one dark brow. "Marshals tracking marshals?''

"Actually, they started it. I'm here to apprehend them before they get the drop on us.''

Exhaling loudly, he grabbed her upper arm. "As jokes go, that one is really lame. Let's move.''

"Wait a second.'' Annie shifted her brain into overdrive. "How many reporters do you know who carry a Glock nine millimeter?''

A flicker of awareness sparked in his eyes, as if he'd just realized what type of weapon he'd pulled from her pocket. Glancing right, then left, he said, "So where's your partner?''

Annie bit at her lower lip. Now came the tricky part.

"He's checking out the rest of the grounds. We're supposed to link up . . . soon."

At least she hoped that would happen, once Drew and Vince figured out where she was.

He waved his gun toward the rutted driveway. "Uh-huh. Okay, that way. Get moving."

With her body set on stubborn, Annie leaned back against the tree and stuck out her chin. "Okay, okay. I'm here without him, but once he talks to Earl, he'll know where I am. Then he'll come find me, honest."

Straightening, Baxter folded his arms across the front of his jacket. "That's the second time you've mentioned Earl. Mind telling me how you know him?"

She almost laughed out loud. Just her luck it took the old storekeeper's name to get some positive attention. "Earl is a friend of the Falcones'. They have a cabin on the south shore of the lake and—"

"Most folks around here are well aware of the Falcone family. How about telling me something you can't find out by listening to the locals gossip at the bait shop or reading a mailbox?"

"My partner is Andrew Falcone. You might know his father—Vincent," Annie said quickly, relieved she could pass his test. "He's a retired homicide detective from Arlington."

"Is that so?"

She nodded.

"How many sons does Vincent have?"

"Umm . . . four."

"Sorry, wrong answer, sweetheart." Unfolding his arms, he waved the gun toward the light she'd noticed earlier. "This way. Let's go."

"Wait, I meant four *plus* Drew. There are five altogether."

His eyebrows rose to meet the rumpled hair resting on his forehead. "Name them."

"Oh, for Pete's sake," she snapped. "I've never met

them. I just know Drew and his dad. Drew is the youngest, and he's a marshal, just like me."

"So you say." Baxter's steely gaze raked her face. "Care to explain why you're not carrying your ID?"

Sighing, Annie shrugged. "It's a long story. Drew and I were protecting someone in the WITSEC program—" That part was close enough to the truth to count. "And we had to make a quick getaway. We were lucky to escape with our guns."

"Why are these other deputies hunting you?"

His relaxed stance gave her courage. "Two of the marshals went bad, and Falcone was put in place to prove it. They found out and tried to kill both of us. We ran, and they followed us to the cabin. Vince is here, too."

Baxter bit out an unintelligible reply, then stuck his gun into the waistband of his jeans and snapped his fingers. The three monster dogs, who'd been sitting like statues the entire time, trotted docilely to his side while he wrapped a large hand around her forearm.

Annie planted her feet and stood her ground. "Where are you taking me?"

"Somewhere a little warmer. I still don't know if I should believe you, but you've definitely got my attention. What did you say your name was?"

"McAllister. Deputy Anne McAllister."

"Okay, Ms. McAllister. Let's go. And be quiet. If you're telling the truth, those renegade marshals could be anywhere."

Tom followed close on Vince's heels as the older man stalked through the edge of the woods surrounding the house. Not used to tiptoeing through a forest in the moonlight, he felt as clumsy as a bull moose in a pottery shop, while Vince seemed to have all the right moves. For a big man, he practically floated like a ghost through the trees, his steps barely registering on the leafy ground.

Worried about Annie and concerned his stomping might give away their position, Tom kept his gaze lowered and in front of him. He didn't realize Vince had stopped short until it was too late. Tom bounced off Vince's broad back and dropped to one knee. Vince stumbled forward and fell against a tree. The racket they made would have alerted a hearing-impaired squirrel at twenty paces.

"Sorry," muttered Tom, rising to his feet. "Are you okay?"

Vince pushed from the tree, his gaze fixed on the ground. "Damn, I lost my gun." Dropping to his hands and knees, he searched for his weapon, mumbling a few colorful expletives in the process.

Tom realized he'd done the same and returned to the forest floor. Now what was he supposed to say? *Sorry I'm such a klutz, Dad, but I still don't have a handle on how to live in your dead son's body?*

He found his gun and stood, then reached down and helped the man up. "Sorry," he repeated. "It's been a while since I've done night duty or any kind of um . . . outdoor work."

Vince opened his mouth to speak, then snapped it closed. Cocking his head, he waited a half second before grabbing Tom by the shoulder and pulling him behind a tree.

Narrowing his gaze, Tom peered into the darkness, but all he saw were forbidding shadows and unfamiliar shapes. Other than the sound of trees creaking in the wind, the woods were eerily silent, as if every creature in the forest was on high alert.

Vince tapped a finger to his upper lip and tipped his head. "I'm gonna take care of a little business. Find some cover and sit tight."

Crouching low, he moved toward the rear of the house. Tom stepped behind a cluster of bushes and ducked down to wait. Well, hell. Now what?

Go with the flow, Milton had told him. *Let your body lead until you get the hang of it.*

So far, he'd done a pretty good job of faking this tough guy marshal thing. Something told him tonight was going to be his moment of truth. No more relying on muscle memory for every smooth move or clever idea. And no more half-assed attempts at being in charge.

Unless she'd already been caught, Annie was out here somewhere, and he wasn't going to let anything happen to her. If Smithers or Butterworth harmed one hair on her beautiful golden head, he was going to come at them swinging . . . with both barrels blazing . . . and all that other macho stuff.

He took the safety off his Glock and hefted it in his hand, testing the weight, forming his fingers to the butt and trigger. Falcone's hand-to-eye coordination was probably perfect, just like every other hotshot self-defense move he'd mastered. Tom told himself he was big and he was strong, yet agile and light on his feet. He could do this.

He could be Drew Falcone.

But how close could Vince get to the house before those pesky lights blasted the perimeter into high noon again? What was up with Nathan Baxter that he'd wired the place to go off like a football stadium?

Suddenly the lights blazed, giving a clear view of the unfinished structure. Cursing silently, he scanned the open walls and jumble of lumber and supplies. In less than a minute, the floodlights flickered and winked out.

Tom sucked in a breath. He heard a faint rustle and hunched down lower. Not much cover, but at least he was out of sight. Where the heck was Vince?

Aiming the Glock toward the ground, Tom waited. When Vince emerged from the shadows, he stood.

As he waved a pair of wire cutters in one hand, the older man's smile was almost as bright as the lights had been. "That takes care of one problem," he said in a whisper.

Tom shook his head. "Baxter's going to be pissed."

"Nah. He'll understand, if he doesn't already. Any sign of Deputy McAllister or our targets?"

"Nothing. It's too quiet," was all Tom could manage.

"Yeah. I know." Vince kept his voice low as he glanced around the woods. "Nathan has to be here somewhere, or Earl would never have sent those men in this direction. Besides, we heard the dogs. They wouldn't be on the property without him. Maybe we should check his cabin."

"Cabin?"

"Baxter's living in his original cabin until the big house is finished. It's down toward the lake and off to the left, but it's fairly hidden by the trees. Our targets might be holed up there. Or Annie."

Or the three of them together. Frowning, Tom pushed the frightening thought away.

"Could Smithers and Butterworth have gotten the drop on Baxter? Taken him prisoner, and now they're putting the screws to him?"

With a nonchalance that made Tom shudder, Vince scratched at his temple with the gun. "Don't think so. We didn't hear any shots, and there aren't too many other ways to distract Huey, Dewy and Louie. Besides, Nathan's too smart to—"

"Distract who?"

Vince's teeth gleamed in the darkness. "Oh, yeah. You've never met them, have you? The dogs, I mean."

Huey, Dewy and Louie?

Tom didn't know whether to laugh out loud or just throw down his gun and call it quits. Maybe they were on a wild goose chase. Maybe Earl had been all wrong about Butterworth and Smithers, and Annie was back at the cabin, warming her feet in front of the fire. Because it sure didn't sound like tangling with a pack of dogs named after Donald Duck's freakin' nephews was anything to worry about.

''Someone's coming.'' Vince set his hand on Tom's shoulder and made a broad gesture with his gun.

Tom nodded, figuring he would follow the man's lead, until he realized what the sweeping movement meant. He was supposed to circle one way while Vince went the other, trapping whoever was out there between them. Before he could comment, Vince disappeared into the darkness.

Tom's heart rate kicked up a notch. Ducking down, he stepped lightly and began to circle the house. Raising his gun, he inched around a corner and stepped directly into the path of three shapes he'd swear were the size of Shetland ponies. Deep, menacing growls filled the air around him, and he froze in place. In the distance, three soft whistles echoed. Hackles raised, the huge canines stood their ground while Tom considered what it would feel like to have his face torn off one piece at a time.

He waited, unmoving, until he spied Vince walking from the opposite side of the house. Voices carried in hushed whispers as two figures emerged from the trees. Worried about Vince, Tom stepped forward, but the dogs' guttural warnings kept him in check.

The shadowy figures joined Vince, and Tom heard a single short whistle. As if one being, the German shepherds sat at attention, eyeing him sagely through the pale light of the three-quarter moon.

Annie deeply resented being trussed up and shoved through the forest like an overstuffed bag of rocks. By the time she and Baxter arrived at a clearing in the trees, she was ready to clobber not only him, but anyone else foolish enough to dare lay a hand on her.

She'd kept her mouth shut on their trek, because she was fairly certain Smithers and Butterworth were somewhere on the property, but once she saw Vince, all bets were off.

"Vince," she whispered through thinned lips. "I thought you'd never get here."

Vince stuck his gun in his coat pocket. "You did?"

"Vince. Good to see you again." Nathan lifted an arm in greeting, and the two men shook hands.

"Same here." Vince eyed Annie's awkward stance. "I see you two have met."

Annie showed him her back. "Please tell this bozo who I am. And get these ropes off me. Where's Drew?"

Baxter ran a hand through his hair. "She's telling the truth, then? She really is a federal marshal on assignment with your son?"

"That she is," said Vince, his voice just short of a chuckle.

After he untied her, Annie threw Baxter an in-your-face scowl. Baxter shrugged, and she itched to smack the pompous expression off his face. The jerk owed her an apology and he knew it.

Ignoring her, Baxter said to Vince, "Any sign of the men Deputy McAllister claims are chasing her and your son?"

"Not *claims*. Are. There *are* two men chasing me—and Deputy Falcone." She rubbed some feeling back into her aching wrists. "Where's Drew?"

Both men turned their heads, and she followed suit, smiling when she spotted an immobile figure standing some thirty yards away. She'd been held at bay by those same three dogs and knew how helpless he must feel.

"Guess it's time to ride to the rescue," said Baxter matter-of-factly. He took off toward Drew with Annie and Vince on his heels. Nearing the German shepherds, he snapped his fingers twice and the animals shifted their attention. "Better let them see that you're friendly," he advised when one of the dogs advanced on her.

She held out her hand and the brute gave it a cursory sniff.

"Wait a second. I've got something he might like." Vince

fiddled in a side pocket and pulled out a plastic bag. ''Try giving him some of this.''

She took out a slice of raw bacon and offered it to the dog, which immediately got the attention of the other two. Feeding them gave her time to study Drew's reaction at finding her with Baxter. The idea she'd been so green as to let herself get caught only reinforced the obvious. Her plan had been half-baked, half-assed, half-witted and half—okay, thoroughly unprofessional.

She had acted without thinking.

''Falcone. It's been a while.'' Baxter offered Drew his hand.

''Same here,'' Drew mumbled. His expression shifted from cordial to furious when he caught Annie in his gaze. ''I thought you were a smart girl, Deputy McAllister, but it's obvious you're determined to prove me wrong. What the hell did you think you were doing, coming here alone?''

Annie stuffed the empty bag in her pocket and took the gun Baxter held out to her. No way was she going to accept being dressed down when she'd been trying to help. ''Saving your ass. There wasn't time to go back to the—''

''Is she really your partner?'' Nathan interrupted, his voice tinged with amusement.

''Only until this is over,'' Drew answered tersely. ''After that, I'm going to lock her up and throw away the key.''

''You need me, Falcone. Don't try to deny it,'' Annie hissed in reply. How dare he intimate she was a hindrance. And why was he acting like such a puffed-up jerk?

''Can the bickering, you two.'' Vince scolded as if they were kids squabbling on a playground. ''We have more important things to discuss than who's right or wrong.''

Baxter nodded in agreement. ''Follow me.''

Vince took him up on the suggestion, but Annie hung back. The last thing she wanted was to be chastised further in front of Nathan Baxter. She had to make Drew realize it was her concern for him that had prompted her actions. ''I did what I thought was right at the moment,'' she said, hoping she sounded tough as nails. ''You should be grateful.''

''Grateful?'' he growled out. ''Hell, I was worried sick.'' He rammed the gun in his jacket pocket. ''You need a keeper. What made you think you could take down Smithers and Butterworth without backup?''

''It's what I'm trained for, just like you, remember?'' She realized he was wearing face camouflage to go along with a knitted cap and one of the coats he'd purchased at the Wal–Mart and threw him a taunting grin. ''Nice makeup, by the way. I didn't know Covergirl came in black face.''

Drew grabbed her upper arms and tugged her to his chest. Heat radiated from his body into hers, and she fought the primal longing to melt into his hard, protective embrace. His expression seemed cast in stone, until she saw the twitch of a grin tighten his squared jaw. He looked dark and danger-ous, and so knock-her-to-her-knees attractive it was all she could do to keep from jumping his bones.

He shook his head. ''I ought to take you over my—''

A sharp whistle pierced the night, just before the trio of German Shepherds appeared from out of nowhere, their eyes glittering with doggie determination.

''Save that thought,'' she said in her best go-to-hell voice. ''We're being summoned.'' Thank God she hadn't followed her instincts and acted on that stupid hormonal whim.

He dropped her arms and huffed out a breath. ''Come on. Baxter's right. We're sitting ducks out here.''

''No kidding.'' She turned and followed the dogs toward the house. Drew's muffled footsteps rustled the ground behind her as she went around the corner and walked to Baxter and Vince, who were huddled together talking softly.

Vince set a hand on Annie's shoulder. ''Did you see or hear anything on your way over here?''

She tucked her gun in the waistband of her sweats and gave a report. ''There's an old Jeep about a quarter mile up the drive. That's where I got this charming jacket and extra ammo clip. The Jeep's hood was warm, so they couldn't have gotten here much before I did.''

Baxter snapped his fingers twice, and the dogs sat guard duty, facing outward around them. "The boys and I were in the cabin. They started acting restless, then the floodlights went on up here." He flashed Vince a cocky grin. "You owe me a hand repairing the wiring, by the way. Anyhow, I let the dogs out and they took off, with me hightailing after them. Next thing I knew we were heading for the drive. That's where I met up with McAllister."

Vince nodded. "Drew and I came by boat, but we didn't spot anyone at the dock."

"How serious are these guys about killing you?" Baxter asked.

Drew locked gazes with Annie and gave her a half smile. "Let's just say I'd be dead if it weren't for the lady deputy." He straightened. "They must have gotten spooked by the lights. My guess is they're either waiting for us back at the dock, or they're hoping we'll head to the safety of your cabin."

Heartened by the fact he was giving her credit for saving his life, Annie said, "They don't know Vince is with us. It'll be four against two—even better if we can surprise them."

"I'd say the boys would be surprise enough," added Vince.

Baxter snorted softly. "I haven't met a man yet who had the guts to take on Donald's nephews."

"I say we pair up." Drew inclined his head toward Annie. "McAllister and I will circle around to the cabin—you, Vince and the dogs can go to the dock."

"I don't know if that's such a good idea, son," muttered Vince.

Drew ignored his father's questioning tone and concentrated on Baxter. "Is there anything we need to know? Any surprises waiting for us there?"

Baxter's face transformed to down-right handsome with his first true smile of the night. "Now that you mention it, there is something you need to be aware of."

"That's what I thought," Drew said, shaking his head. "I just hope it's not too complicated."

Caught off guard by his cocksure attitude, Annie couldn't help but wonder what they were in for.

"Nothing a smart man like you can't handle."

Did she imagine it, or was that a groan she heard from deep inside Drew's throat?

"Okay," he muttered. "Let's have it."

CHAPTER NINETEEN

Tom peered up at the tangle of naked branches, an eerie, sticklike canopy in the black night sky. Since they'd taken off for Baxter's small cabin, the clouds had assumed a life of their own, scuttling with the wind in billowing waves that reminded him of a herd of angry horses.

He and Annie had agreed to split up about twenty feet from the cabin's rear door. She would move to the front porch and wait while he disengaged the fancy automatic warning system Baxter had in place, then they would storm the cottage together through both entrances. At the time, it had sounded like a textbook take-down scenario.

Now, standing next to her in the light of the shadowed three-quarter moon, Tom had the chance to think again. Annie's eyes had grown huge with excitement, while her breath hitched in anticipation—a clear sign she was relishing the danger to come. He recognized the reckless emotions because the federal marshal part of him that he knew belonged to Andrew Falcone was warring with his saner inner core, warning him not to tackle this plan until he did something—anything—to show her how much he cared.

He put his hand on her arm and she turned, her gaze eager and expectant, as if she were having the adventure of her life.

"What?" she asked, her voice an impatient whisper.

"Annie, I—"

Her eyes locked with his and she smiled. Raising a hand, she laid comforting fingers against his cheek. "Stop worrying about me, ace. I know the drill. I'll be fine."

"Yeah," he said, trying to mask his concern. "I know you will."

"Then what are we waiting for?"

What were they waiting for? He shuddered at the very thought. Who had he been kidding? Annie was the one with the training, not him. The fact that they were on their own, practically face-to-face with the bad guys, seemed to only whet her appetite for more. Didn't she understand that anything could happen in the next five minutes that might tear them apart forever? Why couldn't she see he was a fraud, a bumbler masquerading as a poor man's James Bond? If he screwed up, there would be no help from a higher power, no do-overs or third chances.

If things went sour, they were toast.

The idea sat aching and raw, like a boil at his beltline. Whatever had made him think he could protect Annie and keep her safe? Milton had to be a few bricks shy of a load for putting him in this body and giving him this responsibility— trusting him with the life of another human being.

He stuffed his gun in his pocket and grasped her upper arms. Dragging her close, he searched her face. "I want to give you something to remember me by . . . in case I don't . . . in case, you know, something goes wrong."

Raising her brows, she tucked the Glock in her waistband and settled her arms around his neck. "Jeez, some tough guy you're turning out to be. After all we've been through together, this is a fine time to be getting sentimental.''

The thought that he might never hold her in his arms or make love to her again so filled Tom with terror he almost shouted to the heavens. *Please, God,* he begged in silent prayer, *if one of us has to die, let it be me. And if I do die a second time, let it be in Annie's arms. Just keep her alive and well.*

Smiling, he did his best to prolong the precious moment. ''Not a chance, McAllister. I just like to keep you guessing . . . and warm for my form. Don't forget, I still owe you for this fruity haircut.'' He eased his grip and slid his arms to her back. ''Consider this a down payment.''

Gathering her up, he fused his lips to hers in a hungry, burning kiss. Annie melted against his chest, her mouth anxious and demanding, her fingers tangling in his hair. They were joined from shoulders to hips, so close he felt her tremble in his embrace. Their tongues dueled in a primal dance of mating, while their bodies hummed an identical note of desire. Time seemed to stand still while they became a single heart beating out a lone rhythm of longing.

Her total surrender gave him the courage to hope. She would love him—Tom McAllister—again. Even if she didn't realize it right now, she was going to be his. And this time no one, not Milton or all God's angels, would keep them apart.

Finally, gasping for air, Annie tore her mouth away and rested her forehead against his chin. ''Holy moly, Falcone. Now's a fine time to be turning me into Silly Putty.''

Falcone. Funny how a week ago he'd been fuming inside whenever she'd called him by that unfamiliar name. Tonight, it was music to his ears. After all, Annie had the hots for this body, so how could he grouse? Even though he would never be able to repay Drew Falcone for loaning it out, he vowed then and there to do his damnedest to keep it safe.

"I just wanted to remind you of what you'll be missing if you do anything stupid," he warned with a quiet chuckle.

Still breathing hard, she nodded through a too bright smile. "You, too. Now let's take care of these punks. Okay?"

Tom stepped back and pulled out his gun in agreement. The cabin looked empty from the rear, but that didn't mean Smithers and Butterworth weren't inside. In fact, it was a ninety-nine percent certainty the two men were in there stewing on red alert. It was the reason he'd argued with Vince before they'd parted company back at the big house. It had taken a full fifteen minutes of fancy talking on both his and Annie's part to convince the older man that they had to go to the cottage on their own.

"Remember to follow the plan. Give me sixty seconds to find the box and cut the wires before you climb the stairs, then give me another thirty to get in position at the back door. My guess is they're ready for Baxter, so stand aside and let me surprise them from behind before you charge in head first. I'll be rolling to my left, so you do the same. Got it?"

"Sixty seconds, then the stairs. Thirty seconds before we take down the doors, then I roll to my left. Got it." Annie jutted her chin and gave him one final, blinding smile. "Good luck."

Ditto to you, Anna-banana, Tom thought, using the pet name he'd coined for her in college. Shortly after they'd gotten married, he'd dropped that tender endearment and all others, mostly because his mother told him it wasn't dignified for a married couple to call each other by such childish names. God, how he wished he was back in college with Annie now. He'd call her Anna-banana or any other crazy name she wanted, just as long as they were together.

He waited until she was safely around a corner of the cabin before he crouched down and searched for the small box Baxter had told him was anchored low to the ground near the base of the rear stairs. The box was set to trip an electric eye, which in turn triggered an invisible beam of light that sent a warning beep into the cabin, alerting whoever was inside that someone had breeched the first step of the porch.

After a few seconds, he found the fancy wiring. Counting slowly to himself, he willed his pace to match the one he'd practiced with Annie and lowered his flashlight to the box.

Snip! He cut the blue wire. *Snip!* The green wire split cleanly in two. A few more clips took care of the red and white wires.

He raised his gaze to the house and saw nothing, not a flicker of movement or sign of life. He hit sixty in his head and heaved a breath. Sidling up the first step, he ticked off the final moments like a crazed fan at a hockey match as he carefully climbed the stairs.

Five seconds to go.

Instinctively, he raised his leg to batter down the door.

Annie tiptoed to the front of the cabin, her heart beating somewhere in the back of her throat. Drew had just kissed her as if they might never get the chance to be intimate again, and darn if that hadn't neutralized every intelligent cell in her gray matter. She'd been high on the thought of taking out Butterworth and Smithers, until he'd given her that mind-blowing kiss. Now she was having a hard time getting her bearings. Instead of concentrating on her job, she was fantasizing all kinds of happily-ever-afters with Drew Falcone.

Sucking in a breath, she shook her head to clear the silly thoughts. She had to focus and stay alert. She was a trained professional, as was he. Even if he thought he was in charge, he was still under her protection. Her primary duty at the safe house had been to protect him, and she'd felt the burden of that duty every second of every day they'd been on the run.

Twenty . . . nineteen . . . eighteen . . .

She ducked down at the foot of the front stairs and inhaled a dose of courage. If she tilted her head just right, she swore she could see a faint glimmer of light seeping through a crack at the bottom of the window shade, almost as if there was a candle or lantern burning inside. Had Baxter said anything about leaving a light on?

Five . . . four . . . three . . . two . . .

She climbed the stairs one at a time, praying she and Drew were in sync and the steps wouldn't creak. Lucky for her the blustery wind was making a racket, blowing the barren tree branches and swirling the dry leaves.

Hugging the wall to the right of the front door, she grasped her gun in a two-fisted grip. Straining to hear against the noisy breeze, she thought she detected a murmur of male voices. Undeterred, she counted down the final thirty seconds as she went over the plan.

Drew would break in first and take them by surprise. All she had to do was keep the bad guys busy, while she covered him and made sure he didn't get shot. She had to keep him safe. . . .

Three . . . two . . . one . . .

The sound of the rear door crashing open rocketed her into action. Ramming her foot into the front door, she slammed it wide just as Drew gave the command.

"Federal marshals! Stand down and drop your weapons!"

Straightening her arms, Annie leveled the Glock and crouched in the doorway. Bullets splintered the door frame over her head. She dropped and rolled to her left, firing at what she hoped were her targets.

Gunfire echoed around her, brightening the room and pinging into the floor. She heard a muffled cry, then a thud. Another round of shots split the night, along with a barrage of vicious-sounding expletives.

It was all over in moments. A second of blessed silence passed before Drew shouted out, "Throw down your guns and put your hands in the air." The shadowed outline of his head moved in her direction. "You doing okay, McAllister?"

At the sound of his voice, she all but jumped in place. Rising to her feet, Annie aimed her Glock at one of the perps—Smithers?—standing in a corner of the room. She could barely make out Drew, bent over a second body that lay flat in the middle of the living room floor. He removed something from the body's back pocket, and she heard handcuffs snapping into place.

"McAllister? Talk to me."

She swallowed a cry of relief. "I'm fine. How about you?"

He moved across the room toward Smithers. She heard a scuffling sound, then the glow of an overhead fixture washed the room in blinding light. Blinking, she focused on Drew, who had Smithers jammed against the wall next to the switch.

"I'm good." He found Smithers's handcuffs and used them.

She glanced around slowly, taking in the destruction: an overturned kitchen table and two chairs, one of which was splintered into a couple of dozen pieces; a living room sofa dotted with holes and tufts of cottony stuffing; shards of shattered lamp scattered throughout the two rooms like bits of confetti-colored shrapnel.

"How about you gather their guns, then give me a hand applying a little first aid? Butterworth's been hit." Smithers made to turn around, but Drew shoved him hard against the wall. "Stand still, dirt bag. I'm getting to you."

Heaving a breath, she dropped her gun into her jacket pocket, collected the weapons from the floor and placed them on the kitchen counter. Then she walked to the fallen marshal. "Drew, he's bleeding. A lot."

"I know, but we're the only chance he's got. Even if we called the nearest EMTs, it would take them an hour to get here. Go into the bathroom and find some towels to plug up the holes, and I'll take a better look. I don't want to lose him after all this time and effort.''

As if frozen in place, she stared at the crumpled, motionless body oozing life onto the tile. Except for her terrifying experience with Drew at the safe house, this was the closest brush with death she'd had in six years with the agency. Butterworth might be a criminal, but he was also a human being. Had it been her bullet or Drew's that had taken him down?

''Towels, McAllister. On the double.''

Her legs shaking, Annie raced to the bathroom.

The next hour passed in a blur. Drew hadn't wasted a second before he had Smithers hog-tied and sitting on the sofa. By the time they'd gotten Butterworth's bleeding under control, Vince and Baxter had made their appearance. After a few minutes of discussion, Nathan left his dogs on guard duty and disappeared. Drew made an effort to get the prisoners to talk, but both captured marshals were sullen and uncooperative.

Vince, on the other hand, took the opportunity to crow. Listening to his cocky banter, it became apparent he'd had a past run-in with Smithers.

''So, Deputy Smithers. Nice to see you again.''

Perched on Baxter's sofa like a rat on a block of Swiss cheese, Smithers glared straight ahead.

''Oh, by the way, I'd like you to meet my son, Andrew Falcone.''

''I know who he is,'' Smithers bit back, staring glumly at the linoleum.

''What the heck are you doing,'' Drew asked, after his father tossed out another round of taunting remarks.

''Who me?''

Drew rolled his eyes. ''Yes, you. What do you know that you're not telling me?''

The look of innocence on Vince's face was so phony Annie almost burst out laughing.

''I told you months ago that Smithers and I go way back. As soon as you gave me the name of the guy you thought might be guilty, I knew he was your man.''

''Because—?''

Vince set a chair to rights and straddled it, then patted Huey's, or was it Dewey's, head. ''Remember that shake-down I had working two years ago? The one I'd put about two thousand man hours into? The one that was going to be the final star in my crown before retirement?''

''Um, yeah, sure,'' said Drew, glancing at Annie. He looked confused, which was exactly how she felt. ''The Gaither case, right?''

''Gunther. A mob guy out of Detroit who hit a goon on my beat.'' He cast a disgusted frown at Smithers. ''This was the creep who stole my thunder and screwed up all my hard work. Took the case right out from under my nose and claimed it as part of the federal marshals' jurisdiction. Next thing I knew, my airtight evidence was full of holes, and Gunther was let go on a technicality.'' He shook his head. ''I always figured there was something fishy about this guy. The second you mentioned his name in conjunction with your assignment, I knew I was right. Too bad it took so long for you and Deputy McAllister to catch him in the act.''

''Where was I while all this was going on?'' Drew asked, hands on his hips.

''Under cover in Manhattan, so you couldn't have helped. It wasn't the kind of case I normally handled; but it tied in with another homicide I was working, so some guy named Brinkman got me on special request. Still can't figure out why he didn't step in when this punk botched the job.''

Vince shrugged. "Not to worry. It's all over now. My son took care of him."

Brinkman? Goose bumps rose on Annie's back and slithered up her spine. Since when did Smithers know her boss? Hadn't Bob Fielding told her he was out of the Miami office? And why would the local police have been brought in on a federal case?

Just then, Baxter stormed through the front door.

"Okay, I've driven their Jeep to the big house, where it will stay until someone from the marshals' office arrives to impound it. Your truck is outside and running. Vince, you're going to hang out here and help me rewire the floodlights, correct?"

"You got it," said Vince, standing. "Drew? Are you two going to bring them in?"

"As soon as I pick up a few things from the cabin. I want to wash off this camouflage makeup, get a jacket that fits. Annie said she wants to put on some under—"

"Hey!" Annie jabbed him in the side with her elbow. "Let's get going, okay?"

Vince grinned at them both. "Enough said. Just call me when you get back to the office."

Drew walked his dad to the door while Annie waved a goodbye. Smithers wore a look of pure hatred as he watched Vince leave, then turned his gaze on her. "Want to know something, McAllister? That day back at the safe house, I told Butterworth to hit you first. With that perky attitude, I just knew you were going to be trouble. Too bad he didn't listen to me."

Before she could answer, Drew reached Smithers in one huge step, picked him up by the back of his jacket and shook the sneer from his face. "Touch one hair on her head and I'll personally rip your prick off and feed it to you for breakfast, you got that, wiseguy?"

Annie stood mute. The air around her still teemed with

the acrid scent of spent gunpowder laced with testosterone. She'd never seen him so harsh, or so determined.

"Drew, please. I can speak for myself." She took a step toward Smithers. "Well, he didn't shoot me. And because of it, Deputy Falcone and I are going to see that you're both put away for a long long time."

Drew let out a frustrated-sounding breath. "I'm going to run a couple of things by Nathan before we leave. Keep your distance, okay?"

Annie nodded, watching as he walked to the back porch. Turning, she locked gazes with Smithers, who was smiling shrewdly, an evil glint in his eyes.

"How touching. Pity it's going to look like shit at the hearing when I tell them about that lip lock you and Falcone were practicing out on the driveway back in North Jersey. Fraternizing with the prisoner is a big fat no-no, McAllister, just in case you've forgotten. And at the time, you didn't know any different."

A rush of warmth crept up Annie's neck, heating her cheeks to blast furnace level. Damned if that wasn't one of the things she'd been worried about. Of course, she could always deny they'd kissed, but not if she was under oath. If she lied, she'd be no better than the creep sitting in front of her. She glanced at Drew, who was deep in conversation with Baxter. Good thing he hadn't heard the threat, or Smithers might be eating his teeth right now.

"Go ahead and tell them what you *think* you saw. After Deputy Falcone and I get through with you, no one will listen to anything you have to say." She glanced at Butterworth, a moaning hulk cuffed and swathed in bath towels, propped in a wing chair near the rear door with one of the dogs at his feet.

Crossing her arms, she walked to the kitchen on the pretext of getting a glass of water, but it was mostly to calm her jangled nerves. Maybe, if she acted righteous, he'd let the threat rest . . . for the time being.

"You all right?" Drew reached her side and helped himself to her drink, finishing the water in one long swallow.

"Me? Sure. Why?"

"You look a little spooked, is all. I thought I heard Smithers toss you another wisecrack. What did he say?"

"He ... He was complaining that his cuffs were too tight."

Drew raised a brow. "That wasn't the way it sounded to me." Reaching out, he tucked a stray curl behind her ear.

Knowing Smithers was watching, she jerked back her head.

"Hey, what's wrong?"

"Nothing," she lied, her voice low. "I just think we need to keep things strictly professional until—you know."

"I know—?"

She frowned. "Until this case is over. We're already in trouble for taking off together the way we did. If they find out that you and I have been—" Annie felt her face heat up again. "We could both be put on probation, or worse."

"The hell with probation. Besides, there were extenuating circumstances." He ran a hand over the back of his neck. "Let's not worry about it unless we have to, okay?"

"Okay." Later, after they brought the prisoners to headquarters, would be time enough to tell him differently. Right now, something else was nagging at her. "I have to ask you about Vince. Did you know he was working for Brinkman, or that he and Smithers had been involved on a case?"

Drew fisted a hand on the counter and glanced back at Smithers, who was making cartoonlike shooting motions with his finger at a growling Huey.

"He says he told me, but I don't remember. I was on this case for three years. Sometimes we didn't talk for months. It's probably just a coincidence."

"Yeah. Probably."

"So, you ready?

Suddenly chilled from the inside out, Annie wrapped her coat tight around her middle. "Is Nathan coming with us?"

"Don't see that he has to," Drew answered, setting the glass on the counter. "Besides, he can't leave the dogs unattended. Says he'll be at the trial if we need him. I think we can take it from here, don't you?"

Faced with his cocksure attitude, she felt marginally better. All they had to do was drive to the cabin, call Martin Phillips and inform him they were bringing in the perps, then make the two-hour ride to Arlington.

"Sure," Annie answered. "Lead the way."

Tom drove with one hand on the wheel, his other holding a gun on Butterworth, who was folded up and moaning against the front passenger door. In between watching the road and his prisoner, he stole sidelong glances at Annie through the rearview mirror. Sitting in the narrow confines of the backseat with her gun trained on Smithers, she seemed somber, almost grim.

It was just past midnight, but it felt as if he'd been up for weeks. His insides were still tied in knots, and he was edgy and impatient, as if he were back up on that high dive in high school waiting to take his first plunge at thirty meters.

Funny thing was, he knew Annie felt the same. Since the take-down, it was as if they'd become totally in sync and were vibrating on one wave length. If he wasn't so worried about the spooky feelings, he'd be thrilled they were in tune with each other.

They rode in silence, until he pulled the truck in front of the cabin. Tom parked and turned to her, his voice calm. "Let me get Butterworth taken care of, then you can let Smithers out ahead of you. We'll escort them to the house together."

He slipped from the driver's seat and walked around to open the passenger door. Butterworth tumbled into his arms, and he propped the wounded deputy against the front fender. Flipping the seat forward, he motioned for Smithers to get out. When the marshal took his time, dawdling and pretending to stumble, it was all Tom could do not to give him a crack to the jaw.

"Move it," he muttered with a toss of his head. "The sooner we make that phone call, the sooner we can get rid of you two."

Smithers went up the stairs first, with Annie marching closely behind, her gun pressed into his back. Tom pushed Butterworth ahead of him and brought up the rear. When they reached the door, he grabbed the wounded man by his good arm and tapped Annie on the shoulder.

"Hold on a second. We'll go in first, then you."

Opening the door, he and Butterworth stepped inside. Tom turned on the lights and gave the room a careful going over, then motioned for Annie to escort her prisoner into the cabin. Once they were in the kitchen, he sat Butterworth in a chair and shoved Smithers into another.

"Hand me the phone," he ordered Annie, his gaze never leaving the rogue marshals.

She placed the phone in his outstretched hand. "I have to use the bathroom. Will you be okay out here alone?"

"Sure. No problem."

He thumbed the on button, frowning when he didn't get a dial tone. He couldn't remember whether or not they'd left the phone charging, but even so, there should have been enough juice to make the call.

Without warning, a muffled scream echoed from the bathroom.

Tom whirled, scanning the living room.

Suddenly, there was Annie, her expression one of wide-eyed terror as she hobbled stiff-legged from the foyer.

Her body twisted, and he caught the dull glint of steel, just before he saw the man holding her at gunpoint.

CHAPTER TWENTY

"Drew! Run!" Annie stumbled forward into the living room, one arm twisted behind her back, her face a grimace of agony.

"Shut up, Deputy McAllister, and get moving." Jerking her upright, the stranger kept Annie close to his chest and walked them both to the sofa.

Tom didn't recognize the interloper or his voice, but he understood the threat. Every instinct, every bit of muscle memory he possessed, vibrated from his inner core as he tried to set the final puzzle piece in place in his mind.

This was the one player from his notebook he hadn't been able to identify. The elusive Captain Hook.

"Set your gun on the floor and kick it over here, then uncuff Deputy Smithers." The man shook Annie for emphasis, and she winced.

When Tom hesitated, the stranger moved his weapon to her temple. "Do it now, and Butterworth, too, even though it looks as if you've rendered him worthless."

"Don't do it, Drew," Annie bit out, twisting to get away. "Once they're free, they're going to kill us."

Captain Hook's gaze hardened to tempered steel as he motioned to Smithers. The deputy tossed Tom a smarmy smile. "Do what Brinkman says, Falcone, and maybe we'll make it quick."

Brinkman! Annie's boss was the man responsible for all this? Tom raised his hands in the air, using the time to study the enemy. About two inches taller than Annie but with a stocky build, the senior marshal reminded him of a fireplug wearing a custom-made suit. If he could get close enough, Tom knew he could take the man down, but it would be risky. Then again, if he didn't do something, they were still sentenced to die.

The calm leer on Brinkman's florid face sent a frisson of error zinging up his spine. The man's words were too polite, his voice too controlled. With his lantern jaw clenched to the breaking point, he looked like a guitar string strung so tight it was ready to snap.

Tom read the pain in Annie's eyes and guessed her arm was close to breaking. Deliberately, he set his gun on the linoleum and kicked it into a corner of the living room.

"Smart man," Smithers said, holding out his wrists. "Now the cuffs."

Tom pulled the key from his jacket pocket and did as the deputy ordered.

Smithers dropped his handcuffs on the table and pulled two guns from Tom's other pocket, then set one of the weapons in front of Butterworth. "Now do my buddy."

Tom moved slowly. Walking around the table, he stood next to the wounded marshal. Butterworth's face was hidden, his body slumped over, his breathing labored.

"He needs to get to a hospital or we're going to lose him," Tom said, playing for time.

"I'd say it's his own misfortune that he got in the way of a bullet," said Brinkman. "Now do as you've been told."

"Drew, don't listen to him," Annie cried out. Jumping in place, she sucked in a yelp of pain.

"Shut up, Deputy McAllister, or I'll take care of you right now." Brinkman raised glittering eyes to Tom. "I'm waiting."

"Look," said Tom. "Don't hurt her. Just answer a few questions and I'll cooperate."

"I don't have to explain myself to either of you," Brinkman stated calmly.

"I know, I know." Tom ran a hand through his hair. "But you can't blame me for being curious. How did you manage to keep up this elaborate plan without anyone in the department getting wise? How long have you been working for the mob?"

"Long enough to know that you're a serious impediment to my—our income." Brinkman nodded at Smithers. "My men hate it when their livelihood is threatened."

"I understand that part," Tom said. "But how—when did you know who I was?"

Brinkman's face went blank. "Looking for kudos, are you? All right, I'll give you one. I didn't, at least not at first. Three years of giving an Academy Award-winning performance had everyone fooled, Deputy Falcone. Even the men I report to. The hit was their idea, by the way. They believed your main objective was to testify against them in a court of law, thus convincing a jury to send them to prison for life. They ordered me to make you disappear, and passed the word. I thought it was taken care of, until Smithers and Butterworth bungled the job and I learned of your dramatic escape.

"Anne McAllister was supposed to be an unfortunate sidebar to your murder. When Smithers told me about your touching scene on the basketball court, I grew suspicious. She wasn't known to be flighty or derelict in the performance of her duty. Even with your reputation as a ladies' man, it was inconceivable she would run away with a known felon.

If nothing else, she would have demanded you abandon her in that Morristown bus station when you had the chance. I figured there was something funny going on, so I waited for things to develop. Not long after that, Martin Phillips made the mistake of taking me into his confidence, which confirmed who you really were.''

Tom gave himself a healthy mental kick. If only he'd followed his instincts and put his foot down when Annie insisted she be allowed to call Brinkman, they might have found a way out of this mess.

''What are you going to do to us?''

Brinkman's lips curled upward. ''What I was ordered to do in the first place, of course.'' He pressed the gun to Annie's temple again. ''Now undo Butterworth's cuffs. Carefully.''

Tom surveyed the table and checked out the wounded deputy's gun, lying within easy reach. Was it possible that Milton had orchestrated Smithers's dumb move, or was the guy really that stupid? Raising his head, he locked gazes with Annie. Imperceptibly, he let his eyes dart to the left, hoping to remind her of the drop and roll technique they'd used at Baxter's cabin.

Stay with me, sweetheart. Just do what I do.

He mimicked unlocking the handcuffs, fiddling with the key just long enough for Brinkman to relax his hold and lower his gun. Shoving Butterworth with all his might, he let his muscle memory take over as he pushed the deputy off the chair and crashed him into Smithers.

Smithers went down with a shout as Tom grabbed the gun and rolled to his left, toppling the table and dragging it in front of him like a shield.

With the element of surprise on her side, Annie pulled from Brinkman's grip and did the same drop and roll, skidding toward the gun Tom had kicked into the corner.

Brinkman dived behind the sofa, aiming and firing at Tom, but the bullets went wide.

Crawling to an overstuffed chair in the corner of the room, Annie huddled for cover, then shot into the mass of arms and legs that were Smithers and Butterworth.

Smithers howled. Leaving Butterworth to fend for himself, he scrambled for his weapon. Clutching a bloodied shoulder, he scuttled out the front door.

Long seconds passed before Tom found his voice. "Annie, you okay?"

"I will be, as soon as you get us out of here," she answered, her tone quivering.

"It's just the three of us, Brinkman," he shouted into the silence. "Throw out your gun."

A round of shots hit the table, splintering the wood above his head. He heard gunfire from Annie's direction, and his gut clenched. What the hell was she doing, egging the guy on? He edged sideways, pulling the table along for cover. Brinkman fired again, and Tom flopped to his belly.

"Get down and stay down, McAllister!" Looping an arm from behind the table he fired toward the sofa, sending tufts of stuffing dancing into the air.

Annie cringed. She could see the soles of Brinkman's shoes peeking from a corner of the couch. Damn, but the bastard had nerve, admitting to her face that he'd wanted her dead. Taking aim, she fired at Brinkman's feet. A smile of satisfaction lit her face when his shoe heel went flying into the fireplace.

Brinkman did a mad scramble and twisted himself in her direction. She raised her gun to fire and pulled the trigger. Nothing happened, and she tried again, without success.

Her gun was jammed.

Sweat beaded her upper lip. Grinning ferally, Brinkman sidled toward her, shoving the sofa along with his shoulder, using it for cover the same way Drew was using the table.

She crawled around the back of the chair, but he lunged and grabbed her ankle, locking her in place. Kicking out, she felt her free foot hit home, but Brinkman wasn't deterred.

His fingers dug into her calf, gouged at her knee and up her thigh, reeling her in.

Rolling away from him, she jabbed with her other leg, catching him in the jaw. He grunted, but kept on tugging until he had an iron grip around her hips.

"Annie!"

"Drew! Get out of here!" She jammed an elbow into Brinkman's side, heard the breath whoosh from his lungs with the force of the jab.

"Think a second, McAllister," he growled in her ear. "Smithers is out there. He'll gun Falcone down the second he sets foot outside this cabin. If you keep him in here, you keep him alive . . . for the time being."

Annie struggled, but it was no use. He'd worked his way up her body and now held her in a hammer lock, his gun stabbing against the back of her head. Reluctantly, she nodded.

"Tell him you're all right and we're coming out."

She hesitated, and he pressed against her windpipe. Tensing her upper body, she tried to break free, but the breath constricted in her chest. Pinpoints of light danced on the back of her eyelids.

"Now. And make it convincing."

She struggled to speak, and he eased his chokehold.

"I'm fine, Drew. Don't shoot. We're coming out."

Brinkman eased her up from under and tucked his gun between them, pretending to be her prisoner. They rose to their feet side by side, just as Drew stood up from behind the table.

Drew held his gun in front of him. "You okay?"

She nodded as she and Brinkman began to walk toward him.

After that, everything happened at warp speed. They neared the table, and Brinkman loosened his grip. Annie felt him raise his weapon at the exact second Drew lowered his own. Drew stepped from behind the table, and she pushed

Brinkman away from her, then leapt toward Drew just as the senior marshal fired.

As if protecting her, Drew whirled the two of them around, exposing his back. The slam of the bullet tearing into him was so real Annie thought it had pierced her own heart.

He crumpled to the floor as Vince charged inside and blasted the gun from Brinkman's hand. Clutching his forearm, the marshal fell to the floor, and Vince raced to his side.

She dropped to her knees and rolled Drew over until he lay flat on his back. Staring, she took in the bloodstain spreading across his upper chest. *Not again! Not again!* The words beat from inside her brain, begging to be free.

"Annie! Talk to me!" Vince called. He knelt over the downed man, and she heard a mumbled curse and the snap of handcuffs.

She shook her head, her voice a pitiful-sounding mewl at the back of her throat. "Please, God, no," she whispered.

Stripping off her jacket, she turned it fleece side out and stuffed it up his sweatshirt, then pressed down on the wound.

Drew's eyes remained closed, his voice ragged, his breath a rasp. "Annie? I'm sorry ... so ... sorry ... for everything."

Weeping openly, she refused to believe this was happening a second time. Fate wouldn't be so cruel to take him from her, just when they'd found each other.

"Shh. Don't talk. Lie still."

"Annie. I have to-to tell you ..."

She touched his bloodless lips with her fingers, felt the warmth seep from his face. "Don't talk. Just lie still. You're going to be all right."

A shadow fell over them, and she raised her gaze to Vince. "Help me. I don't know what to do."

He dropped to one knee, his heart in his eyes, and raised up Drew's sweatshirt. After inspecting the wound, he said

"Hang on, son. Help's on the way." Then he laid a hand on Annie's shoulder and reassured her with a hesitant smile. "He's a tough one, Annie. And it's not as bad as it looks."

"I—how—what are you doing here?"

Vince took both her hands and put them back on Drew's jacket, showing her where to apply pressure. "I'll explain later. Right now, I just want you to lean on his shoulder, nice and easy. I caught Smithers stumbling around outside and tied him up, then used his cell phone to call the bait shop. Earl was a medic in Korea. He's on his way." He stood. "I'm going outside to check on things. Will you be okay for a couple of minutes?"

She nodded as Vince double-timed it out the door. Swiping her forehead against her shoulder, she kept her hands steady and inhaled a gulp of air. For the first time, she noticed the damage was centered over Drew's right shoulder, not his heart. The bleeding had already lessened. Thanks to Vince, Earl would be here soon.

With her eyes locked on his face, she hunched over and whispered a no-nonsense command. "Stay awake, Falcone, and pay attention. I have to tell you something important."

His eyes fluttered open, then closed. "I'm all ears, doll," he mumbled, a hint of amusement slipping in alongside the pain.

"This isn't funny," she huffed out, willing him to stay alive. "Don't you die on me. Don't you dare."

He grimaced and shifted under her hands, "Oh, and why is that?"

"Because I love you, you dope."

His eyelids lifted as he gave her a cocky smile. "Ditto to you, Anna-banana. Ditto to you."

Annie opened and closed her mouth, her heart pounding so loudly she almost didn't hear him. "Wha—what did you say?"

* * *

"Tom? Tom, can you hear me?"

Tom winced at the dull, throbbing pain in his shoulder, hell, his whole body. His eyelids felt weighted down with wet cotton, his head filled with fog.

"Drew? Andrew? Give me a moment, if you please, then I'll let you return to sleep."

Milton? Oh, crap, now what? Panic flared when Tom remembered why the guiding angel was in his life. "Are you here to take me back?" Tom asked from his heart. "Cause I won't go, dammit. I will not leave Annie."

Strangely, he felt Milton's smile. "Oh, really? Well, that's good to know."

Tom shifted, groaning at the pain. "Jeez, can't you do something about this? And what did you mean by that last remark? Are you here to tell me I can stay?"

"If you want to," Milton said softly. "I've even arranged to have Eloise take you back."

"Eloise?" Okay, so he was staying and he'd gotten his guiding angel back. Not a bad few weeks work. Still, there had to be a catch somewhere. It was the way the doughboy operated.

"Goodbye, son. Have a nice life."

"Wait! That's it? No more tests, no more rules? I'm on earth for good? With Annie?"

"Oh, there are rules, but I think you'll follow them fairly well. Do I have to spell them out for you?"

Tom shrugged, noting the ache in his shoulder had eased a bit. "Well, yeah, if it's not too much trouble. I don't want to screw up again."

Milton chuckled. "I can answer the question with one word, and that is *love*. It's all Annie ever wanted and I think you've given it to her. Now, I really must be going."

Love? Heck, he could do that. He could love Annie the way she deserved to be loved for the next hundred years or so. It would be his pleasure—his joy—his own personal gift from heaven. He just needed to know one more thing.

"But who the hell am I? I mean, am I Tom McAllister, or am I Andrew Falcone? Which one of me is the right man for Annie?"

"Hmm. Good question," said Milton, his voice amused. "Judging by recent developments, I'd say you're both definitely right for her. You can take your pick."

"But I don't know who I want to be," Tom muttered.

"Does it matter?" came Milton's sage reply. "Think about it. The answer is inside of you. It's been there all along."

Filled with relief, Tom breathed easier. Milton was right. Hearing that he had Annie back was the important thing. He could sort out who he was later, once he had her in his arms. Once he knew for certain she wanted him for as long as they both were on earth. And beyond.

Cool mist swirled in his brain, dragging him back to a place of peace and rest. Tom slept. And he dreamed of the woman he loved.

Annie sat in a padded vinyl chair next to the hospital bed, her gaze locked on Drew Falcone. Except for the time he'd spent in surgery, she hadn't let him out of her sight. Two hours had passed since he'd been brought to this neat, sterile room. The morning sun streamed through the blinds, cutting through the haze in her mind, but she still hadn't come to any logical conclusions about what Drew had said to her at the cabin.

During his surgery, while Vince and Earl paced, she'd perched on a molded plastic chair in the waiting room and calmly answered Martin Phillips's probing questions as best she could. It was only now sinking in that if Vince hadn't called Earl and Earl hadn't arrived when he did, she might be sitting in the local mortuary instead of waiting for Drew to wake.

She was pretty sure neither of them would be alive right now if Vince hadn't decided to row their boat back to the house after he and Nathan had come to the conclusion it was too late to work on the wiring. And lucky for her Vince had pull at this small-but-efficient walk-in clinic located in the town nearest to Lake Mary. He'd been able to convince the surgeon on call that she was family and arranged for her to stay.

She ran her free hand over her tired eyes. No matter how she reasoned it out, no matter how many times she pieced together the sequence of events that had taken place over the last few days, she knew there were some things that would never ring true.

She was head over heels in love with the man on the bed in front of her . . . and she had no clue who he really was.

She thought again about all the times over the past week when she'd wondered if he was crazy. His evasive answers and the goofy way he sometimes stared vacantly when she asked him a question had never made sense, but she'd always chalked up the bizarre behavior to his almost compulsive need for secrecy.

Now she wasn't so sure.

Automatically, she drifted back to their first few days on the run, after he'd been shot and they'd fled the safe house. The cavalier answer he'd given for the ease in which his wound had healed, the spooky way he'd cut that first sandwich into quarters, the familiar posture he'd taken when he'd read the morning paper, and the intimate way he'd held her when they slept—even the way he'd made love—became a jumble in her mind.

Tom had died six years ago. She'd mourned his loss as his body lay in the casket, had watched as the casket was lowered into the ground. She had a death certificate to prove he was gone. There was no way to bring him back. . . .

Ditto to you, Anna-banana.

No one had uttered those sweet-yet-silly words to her since she'd been in college, and even then it had been no one but Tom. Only Tom.

Every atom of common sense screamed out what she knew to be true, told her *she* was the one who was crazy— the one who needed help. She'd experienced a huge amount of stress over the past few days. It was normal that she wasn't thinking straight, that her mind was looking for a way to rationalize every weird moment and eerie occurrence. Perfectly normal.

Maybe it was time she paid another visit to Dr. Bennet for a second round of grief counseling. Because the only other truth was one she simply couldn't comprehend.

Somehow, Tom had found a way to return to her.

Drew stirred under the whiter-than-white sheet, and she shook herself back to reality. Shifting her focus, she watched as he opened his eyes and stared at the ceiling, his face as pale as the bed linens.

She squeezed his hand, the one she'd been holding in a death grip, and he turned to her. A second passed before he gave a feeble grin.

"Hey, doll, did you get the number of the truck that ran me down?"

She sniffled back a sob. "It's about time you woke up. How do you feel?"

He groaned and closed his eyes. "As a fellow marshal once said, *'like road kill'.*" Shifting his body, he hissed out a breath. "What happened to me?"

She pursed her lips, debating what to tell him. How much could a person fresh out of a drug-induced coma understand? "Brinkman shot at us, and you shoved me out of the way. You saved my life."

Still smiling faintly, he muttered a wry comment. "Guess that makes us even for the push-up contest, huh?"

She rolled her eyes. "Even my foot. What did you think

you were doing, putting yourself in the line of fire that way? If you ever do anything that stupid again, I swear, I'll—''

With surprising strength, he tugged her hand to his lips. When he kissed her knuckles, she melted inside.

''I said I was sorry, didn't I?''

Unable to find her voice, she choked back a sob. Lowering her forehead carefully against his chest, she let the tears flow while he patted the back of her head and crooned a litany of comforting words. Words that made her feel cherished and loved.

Before she realized what she was doing, she climbed onto the bed and snuggled into his good side. Torn between wanting to pound him to a pulp and crawling up inside of him forever, she sucked in a heaving breath.

''Promise you won't scare me like that again. Do you understand me, Tom?''

His body tensed as his breath hitched. Touching her cheek, he turned her face to his. ''What . . . who did you call me?''

Annie stiffened when she realized what she'd said. Mortified, she swiped at a tear. ''Nothing. It was a slip, that's all. I meant to say Drew, but I was thinking of Tom. I've been thinking of him a lot lately.''

He rubbed his thumb over her lower lip, his eyes so steady and solemn they seemed to penetrate to her very soul. ''I know what his name is, Annie.'' His voice dropped to a whisper. ''In fact, I know everything about him.''

She swallowed another round of tears, puzzled when his expression remained calm. Was that a hint of mischief she saw dancing across his face?

''But how? Why? I don't get it.''

''Does it matter?''

Annie closed her eyes and let his simple statement sink in. A light switched on inside her heart, brightening the darkest corners as the reality of what had happened settled over her. She loved this man with every fiber of her being.

It wasn't important who inhabited the body, because she was sure who owned the soul.

Tom was Drew, and he had changed. He'd become kind and loving, he'd trusted and protected her, and he'd let her do things her way—even if her way didn't always work out.

It was as if Tom had absorbed the very best qualities of Andrew Falcone and given them his own special imprint.

She didn't understand how it had happened, didn't even know if she wanted to. "I don't get it," she managed to utter. *I may never get it,* she thought in silence.

"Me neither." He shrugged a shoulder and winced. "But I figure life's too short to try and analyze everything that doesn't make perfect sense. My name is Andrew Falcone, and for what it's worth, I'm the guy who loves you. Forever and always, Anna-banana. And beyond that, if you'll let me."

Annie felt his heart beating solid and strong under her fingers. Second chances happened less than never, and were so precious she knew better than to waste one that was handed to her on a golden platter. If a miracle had occurred, it was hers—no—theirs alone to cherish.

"Oh, I'm going to let you, all right." She swallowed back her tears and dredged up a smile. "And I'll hold you to your words. This time, you're going to love me forever and always. Until the end of time and beyond."

Annie sighed when Drew tucked her tighter against him. His breathing deepened and she settled close to his heart. Content with the idea of falling asleep beside him every night for the next fifty years, she realized that sometimes, wishes really did come true.

EPILOGUE

Six months later

Church bells chimed, their musical toll pealing across the crystalline air in joyous waves of abandon. Milton smiled to himself. He loved the sound of caroling bells. Whether ringing loudly with grandeur or trilling gently from a breath of rushing wind, church bells were a clarion call to the angels, a way of honoring the Lord.

Pleased with his position on the roof of the simple white church, he glanced toward his companion dressed in a plain woolen gown of dove gray. He knew it was Eloise's own personal ensemble of mourning. With her lovely face puckered into a frown, she looked as if she'd just swallowed a slice of lemon, or maybe an entire humble pie.

"Cheer up, El," Milton said, doing his best not to gloat. "Annie and Drew are getting married. This is a happy day."

Resting her elbow on an upraised knee, she set her chin in her hand. "For you maybe. All this wedding does for me is make more work."

"Now, now. You should be ecstatic that you're recovering an old soul. Tom is back in the fold, so to speak, and Andrew Falcone has finally found the woman of his heart. All's right with the world."

Peering through the roof and down onto the ceremony, he watched as Vincent Falcone, Drew's best man, aligned himself on the altar next to his son. Both men looked handsome and dashing in matching black tuxedos adorned with boutonnieres composed of a single white rose surrounded by a spray of baby's breath.

The organist pumped the instrument to full volume, and Annie's niece and nephew began their side by side march up the aisle. Wearing a gown of pale apricot, Peanut dropped white rose petals from a wicker basket, while Rory carried a satin pillow upon which rested matching gold wedding bands. Close behind them and beaming walked Julie, Annie's matron of honor, dressed in a simple gown in a shade identical to her daughter's.

"Aren't they adorable?" Milton concentrated on the children, but he couldn't help notice Eloise's sullen glare. "I wish one of them was mine."

"I, for one, just cannot abide humans when they're that age, all giggly, grubby and goggle-eyed, not to mention constantly in trouble. They're simply too much work."

"Come now," he said, leaning forward to watch for Annie. "All humans start out that way. It's when they grow up I find them to be the most trouble."

"They're *all* trouble," Eloise said, exaggerating the words. "I have enough to do without taking on any more souls. By the way, I reached my quota last week," she said with a spark of happiness. "I'm full up for a while. No more souls for me."

"Really?" Milton stared, as if he didn't believe her. To the best of his knowledge, no angel was ever "full up" . . . unless they were going to be given *the choice* within a very short time. "Who gave you that interesting bit of news?"

She shot her bluer-than-blue eyes skyward.

"Ahh," he said, returning his attention to the ceremony. Annie, looking more heavenly than an angel in a snow white dress of classical lines, began her walk up the aisle. "Beautiful. Simply beautiful."

"I suppose they're going to have children?" Eloise said, gazing intently at her fingernails.

Milton's insides did a little flip-flop when Annie met Drew at the altar and took his hand. Their expressions were so filled with love and devotion he wanted to give a shout of triumph. With exquisite care, Drew raised Annie's veil to gaze into her eyes, and Milton sighed.

"Of course they're going to have children. Thomas Vincent Falcone is perched on a star at this very moment, just waiting to be sent to earth."

"Tonight?" Eloise sniffed her disgust. "They're going to make a baby tonight?"

"That's the plan. And it's perfect. He'll arrive right after Annie opens her restaurant. With Drew taking that desk job at WITSEC, he'll have plenty of time to baby sit and give her a hand with the marketing. Even Vince is planning to stop by and lend a hand."

"*Hmph.*" Eloise fluttered upward, sprinkling angel dust in her wake. "Well, I have to run. One of my charges is getting ready to make a decision about which college to attend. I have a dozen more agonizing over whether to accept or turn down marriage proposals, and another couple of hundred worried about their jobs. Honestly, it's as if they couldn't do a thing without me."

"Don't forget Tom . . . er . . . Drew. He's going to need lots of patience learning how to be a father while accepting the fact that it's best he retire from the field."

"You're sure he wants to retire?"

"Very," said Milton. "After all, he promised Annie, and he's never going to go back on his word again. You'd better see to it."

Eloise stuck out her tongue, a very unangel-like gesture, and disappeared from the roof.

Milton sighed as he focused on the scene below and gave himself a mental pat on the back. For the time being, his task here was done. He'd only need to pop in on Annie and Drew every few months or so to be sure things were progressing as they should.

How lucky for Tom, Drew, and Annie herself that she'd taken a leap of faith and made that heartfelt wish.

And how sensible of him to have granted it.

ABOUT THE AUTHOR

Judi McCoy is living her dream. She writes whimsical romance while living on the Chesapeake in Cape Charles, Virginia, with her loving husband and two spoiled dogs. Please visit her website at *www.Judimccoy.com*. Judi loves hearing from her fans.

Watch for the rest of Judi's Heavenly Trilogy

HEAVEN SENT
(Fall 2003)
and
A MATCH MADE IN HEAVEN
(Spring 2004)

Thrilling Romance from Lisa Jackson